FORGING THE
SWORD

THE FARSALA TRILOGY
BOOK 3

FORGING THE SWORD

HILARI BELL

Simon Pulse

New York   London   Toronto   Sydney

SIMON PULSE

An imprint of Simon & Schuster Children's Publishing Division

1230 Avenue of the Americas, New York, NY 10020

Copyright © 2006 by Hilari Bell

Maps on pages viii-ix drawn by Russ Charpentier

All rights reserved, including the right of reproduction in whole or in part in any form.

SIMON PULSE and colophon are registered trademarks of Simon & Schuster, Inc.

Also available in a Simon & Schuster Books for Young Readers hardcover edition.

Designed by Greg Stadnyk

The text of this book was set in Cochin.

Manufactured in the United States of America

First Simon Pulse edition December 2007

10 9 8 7 6 5 4 3 2

The Library of Congress has cataloged the hardcover edition as follows:

Bell, Hilari.

Forging the sword / Hilari Bell.

p. cm.

Summary: Farsalans, including Lady Soraya and her half-brother, Jiaan, Kavi, and others, work relentlessly and often secretly in their shared strategies regarding the ultimate defeat of the Hrum.

ISBN-13: 978-0-689-85416-3 (hc)

ISBN-10: 0-689-85416-1 (hc)

[1. Fantasy.]

PZ7.B38894   2006

2005017730

ISBN-13: 978-0-689-85418-7 (pbk)

ISBN-10: 0-689-85418-8 (pbk)

This book is dedicated to my A-team: my excellent agent, Irene Kraas, and my extraordinary editor, Julia Richardson. Without both these women, the book you're looking at would never have existed.

Acknowledgments

ALL OF MY BOOKS owe a huge debt to my writers' groups, the Denver Science Fiction Writers Guild, and the Wild Women Writers of the West. I would also like to offer my deep thanks to Simon Tasker of Simon & Schuster. If you're reading this book now, there's a good chance that it's because of him—whether you know it or not. And finally, thanks to my family for their support—always.

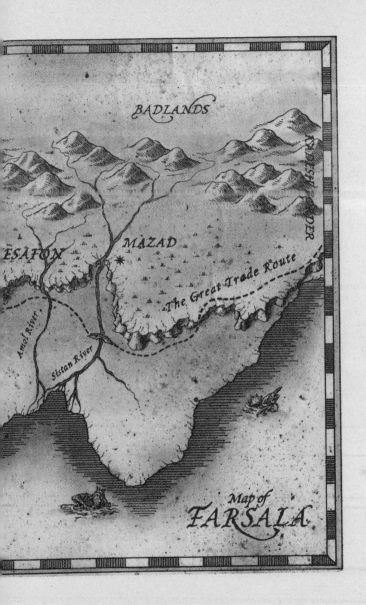

BADLANDS

KADESH BORDER

ESAFON

MAZAD

The Great Trade Route

Amol River

Sistan River

Map of
FARSALA

FORGING THE SWORD

WHEN THE HRUM INVADED FARSALA, destroying the deghan army that defended it, they rejoiced. They thought, as victors will, that the gods favored them, and that they always would. Perhaps it was that arrogant assumption that angered Azura. Perhaps it was something else about the Hrum that displeased him. Who can claim to know the mind of a god?

But displeased Azura must have been, for the spirit of the ancient champion Sorahb was reborn into the body of a deghan youth, who raised an army of peasants to resist their Hrum conquerors. Then Azura sent to Sorahb three tests—not tests of courage, which any brute may have, but tests of his divine farr, his worthiness to rule as well as to command.

Sorahb passed these tests, and learned from them too. He resolved to not only lead his peasant army, but to work with them, and with others, too, that he might find new ways to defeat the Hrum, since the deghans' ways had failed. Yes, Sorahb had passed Azura's tests and won the god's favor.

But the tests that the Hrum would set him were still to come.

CHAPTER ONE

KAVI

I T WON'T WORK," said Hama, looking down the road that ran through the rolling foothills. "It's too complicated."

"No, it's not." Kavi spoke absently, for most of his attention was fixed on the empty road as well—or, more exactly, on the bend in the road where the Hrum soldiers should be appearing before long. "As soon as the siege towers are in front of us, Commander Jiaan and his luna . . . his troops will ride in for a brief raid and draw off most of the Hrum guards. Then our archers will pepper the towers with fire arrows and they'll all go up in smoke. Dead simple."

"And if it's not," said the lady Soraya's icy voice

behind him, "then you will be. Dead, that is."

Kavi grimaced, but he didn't bother to look back at her, though Hama cast her an uneasy glance. What Flame-begotten whim had possessed him to agree to work with Soraya and Jiaan, who had plainly stated their intention of killing him if anything went wrong—and, once the Hrum were gone, of killing him even if everything went right! He must have been mad. Not to agree, for that was the only way they'd have let him live past the moment, but it was truly crazy for him to be seriously intending to help them.

He peered through the screen of gold and brown leaves that protected the archers from sight and stifled a sigh. He knew why he'd agreed—and it wasn't just because that was the only way they'd let him live. He needed their help to defeat the Hrum as badly as they needed his. He couldn't even blame them for their desire to kill him, since he had, even if indirectly, contributed to the loss of the battle that had resulted in their father's death.

Their relationship was a strange one, to Kavi's way of thinking. Both of them knew they were brother and sister, but Kavi had never heard either of them acknowledge it aloud. Jiaan called his half sister "Lady," as if he were still a page in his father's household, and the lady referred to her bastard half brother as if he were a servant. Yet they were perfectly united in their determination to free Farsala from the Hrum, and in their desire to kill him. Kavi understood that desire, though that didn't mean he intended to lie down and let them cut his throat when the time came—and it made dealing with them on a day-to-day basis a major pain in the ass!

"He had to go and arrange for the paint," Hama told the lady Soraya indignantly. "You sent him!"

They'd had no choice but to send him, and Kavi had taken a grim pleasure in how much it had galled the suspicious pair to let him out of their sight—not just for a few marks, either. It had taken him several weeks to arrange for an accelerant to be mixed in with the three barrels of imperial scarlet paint a Hrum officer had ordered, in the town nearest to the hidden camp where the siege towers were being built.

It was Hama who had brought word to Kavi that the peasants who supported the resistance had finally located the Hrum's construction site.

Brought word to *Kavi*, for though Jiaan commanded the army, it was Kavi who had formed the peasant resistance. Kavi the peddler, who had visited their small villages for years, selling them knives and ironmongery, was the one they trusted.

So it had to be Kavi who went to convince the lads who were mixing the paint that they should change their formula a bit. And to arrange a faked burglary of the Hrum supply depot where the paint was stored, so that when the siege towers went up like tinder, the blame would fall on the anonymous burglars and not the paint mixer. He'd also arranged for the peasants who farmed the fields along the shortest road to Mazad to send him warning when the Hrum brought their towers along, which was how they all came to be sitting here on this sunny autumn morning.

He'd understood Soraya and Jiaan's reluctance to let him go off on his own. He'd scoffed at their vague threat to use Hama as a hostage; no matter how much they hated him, neither of them would harm a sixteen-year-old girl just to get him back. He'd even felt a bit smug over their astonishment when he'd turned up again of his own free

6

will, mission accomplished, and the plan—his plan!—ready to run.

It hadn't occurred to him that they would respond by placing the lady Soraya and two loyal men from Jiaan's army behind him, with orders to kill him instantly if anything should even start to go wrong.

And no plan was that good.

He wished Hama hadn't insisted on staying to see how it worked out, even after she'd heard how he had worked with the Hrum to destroy the deghan army. She hadn't entirely forgiven him herself—or she'd have been arguing a lot more with the lady-bitch behind him—but at least she understood why he'd done it. He only hoped her mother would feel the—

"They're coming!" Hama hissed.

Kavi had already seen the first rank of Hrum soldiers marching around the bend in the road. They were only five abreast on this narrow track, but their scarlet cloaks were almost as bright as their helmets and breastplates in the sunshine. A mounted soldier passed the troop, cantering up the road, his head turning back and forth as he looked for signs of ambush.

The archers, under the lady Soraya's direction,

had chosen their clothing to match the colors of the autumn leaves and dying grass, and she'd made Kavi change his clothes twice before she'd been satisfied. At least his hair wasn't a problem, peasant-brown and curly, like Hama's and most of the archers', as well. The straight black hair—short, since Kavi had cut it—that showed Soraya's deghan blood was concealed by a rough cap that went with the rough boy's clothes she wore, so the lot of them blended nicely into the brush of the hillside. It must have been something the Suud tribesmen taught her, Kavi thought, for deghans hunted from horseback, in silks and jewels, with a great deal of noise.

Crouching motionless in the brush, he could almost feel her stillness behind him.

The scout rode past without so much as a twitch that would reveal he'd seen anything. Then he reached some invisible limit, turned his horse, and trotted back, paying even less attention on the return trip.

Kavi frowned. Why weren't the Hrum sending men out to check the sides of the road? One rider wasn't enough to trip an ambush, and though the Hrum's overconfidence sometimes led them into folly, he'd have thought they'd take more care with a cargo as valuable as the siege towers. Towers it had taken them almost two months to build, and which would probably give them victory over the city of Mazad. A victory their commander needed desperately.

The main unit of the towers' guards had marched around the bend by now, more than a hundred of them, and Kavi could see the four-ox hitch that pulled the long wagon that held the first length of the tower. The towers were being shipped in two sections, the peasants had told him: the long, upper halves on one set of wagons, and the thicker bases on another—four wagons in all. Only the framework had been assembled; the boards that would clad them were stacked in the wagons under the nest of beams. Yes, he could see the scarlet-painted lattice now, and beside it . . .

Kavi felt the blood drain from his face, leaving it numb and cold, even as the lady-bitch behind him hissed a curse.

On both sides of the tower's skeleton walked a line of slaves, each with one wrist shackled to a bolt driven deep into the hard wood—shackled with a very short chain. If the towers burned, the slaves would too. They couldn't—

"Arzhang and Gudarz take you, you treacherous beast!" The hissing whisper was softer than the sound of her knife being drawn from its sheath.

"You think *I'm* responsible for this?" Kavi glared at her, too insulted to be afraid—though judging by the fury in her face, he should be. "Only a deghan would be after guarding property with . . . with a wall of lives! No peasant would ever do such a thing."

Arzhang, the djinn of treacherous ambition, and Gudarz, the djinn of cruelty, were deghan inventions—and it seemed to Kavi as if they possessed every deghan who'd ever been born!

"Those are Hrum, not deghans," she whispered fiercely.

"Sometimes there's no difference," said Kavi, turning back to survey the column.

His neck prickled. But when you came down to it, a deghass was more likely to stab you face to face than in the back—more fool she. Several long seconds passed and nothing sliced into his flesh. Kavi relaxed slightly and returned his attention to the towers.

All four wagons had come around the bend by now, each one with its living shield tethered to its side and a line of Hrum soldiers marching beside it. Yet another troop brought up the rear.

Jiaan's attack would draw off the soldiers, perhaps even more soldiers than they'd expected, since the Hrum could leave the vulnerable slaves to guard their precious cargo. Could the Farsalans carry the towers off into the hills and free the slaves at leisure? No, the hills were too steep, too choked in brush, and the towers would be too heavy. They'd chosen this place because an unburdened man could make his escape more easily than an armored soldier marching in formation. Carrying the towers they wouldn't get ten yards. Drive the oxen down the road? Oxen couldn't run for long, not laden as these were. They wouldn't make it far enough. Which only left —

"We have to destroy these towers," said the lady softly. "If they get through, Mazad will fall. And Mazad is our only hope."

Kavi turned to face her, but his bitter words about deghan willingness to burn peasants alive were checked by the despairing misery in her

11

expression. Besides, many of the slaves chained to those towers likely were deghans, for more of the deghans had resisted outright than peasants had. They might even be poor fools from some other land entirely—but whoever they were, Kavi couldn't let them be roasted alive.

"Let me go," he said rapidly.

The towers were approaching their position. Jiaan would attack soon. Or would he abandon the plan? No, curse him, he would go ahead with it, sticking Kavi and Soraya with the task of freeing the slaves. Being chased by the Hrum was easy compared to that.

"Let me go. I was a smith once. I can pick locks. I'll set them free, then you can signal the archers to fire."

"No," said Soraya flatly. "I'm not letting you out of my sight. Not after this. I ought to kill you now. And besides, you could never free them in time."

"Then I'll go too," said Hama. "I can pick locks faster than he can."

Kavi opened his mouth to protest and then shut it. He had taught Hama to pick locks himself, training her to be a burglar. This was far more dangerous than anything he'd ever dreamed of getting her into, but she really was faster than he was with his scarred right hand.

"No," said the lady again. But there were tears in her eyes.

"Can you give the order to fire if they're not free?" Kavi demanded. Giving that order was her job.

Her gaze turned to the towers creaking down the road behind the oxen. "They're barbarians," she whispered. "Worse than barbarians! The Suud would never do this!"

"They're not barbarians," said Kavi slowly. "At least, not most of them. This is—"

The first section of siege tower was now in front of them, and, right on time, Kavi heard the snap of bowstrings. From the lower rise on the other side of the road came a flight of arrows—headed not for the helpless slaves, but for the Hrum troops who marched at the head of the column.

Kavi had heard tales of the speed with which the Hrum could raise their shields into formation, but he hadn't really believed them. Oh, in battle, when they were ready for the command, perhaps—but marching down the road with no reason to expect attack?

13

The moment the strings snapped, half the Hrum soldiers began lifting their large rectangular shields—some even got them up and angled in the right direction. But for all their training and discipline the Hrum were only human, and some of them didn't move swiftly enough.

The arrows pelted down, thudding into shields and rattling off armor, but a few of them found flesh, and Kavi bit his lip as several men screamed in pain. He'd spent time in the Hrum camps—first spying for them, later spying on them. They weren't bad men, for the most part; most were guilty of nothing but serving the empire into which they'd been born.

He was almost glad when, in the handful of seconds before the next flock of arrows swooped down, they rallied their ranks and got all their shields above their heads, positioned so precisely that no more arrows got through—though one man somewhere in the tightly packed formation was still screaming.

"They're not barbarians," Kavi repeated. "Except maybe a few. This is Governor Garren's work, trying to force us to be as barbaric as he is."

Commander Jiaan's mounted archers were

streaming down the road now, but instead of charging, they stopped just inside bow range and began firing arrows at the Hrum's front rank.

The lady Soraya had moved up beside Kavi, and now she snorted softly. He supposed their horsemanship was a bit ragged. Even as he watched, one man slipped in the saddle and nearly fell off—he would have fallen if he hadn't dropped his bow and clutched the saddle's cantle. But until the deghan army had been crushed at the Sendar Wall, these archers had been foot soldiers, most of whom had never sat on a saddle before, much less fired a bow from one in battle. And if their horsemanship left something to be desired, their aim was dead on target, their arrows pounding into the shields of the first line of Hrum troops.

But the thundering approach of the horses had given the Hrum the warning they needed—there were no chinks in that wall of shields. As Kavi watched, the men under the carefully constructed shell started down the road toward the horsemen, and the troop that had followed the column was already moving into the hills to drive off the first set of archers.

Arrow fire from the hillside ceased as the

archers proved themselves sensible men and fled. But as Kavi knew, their orders were to run, and on the swift horses that awaited them they'd soon catch up with their companions on the road. Young Commander Jiaan was surprisingly good at this kind of thing.

The mounted archers got off two more ragged volleys before Commander Jiaan's voice rang out, "Retreat! Retreat! Rally on Sorahb and flee!"

Kavi had to smile. Jiaan himself had been called Sorahb—who else could be leading the army, after all?—and Kavi had said, as he raised the countryside to resist the Hrum, that he worked for the legendary champion. As far as he could tell, every lad who stole a Hrum mule or broke the supports out from under a bridge before a Hrum troop marched over it was claiming the name Sorahb.

But Governor Garren, commander of the conquest of Farsala, had succumbed to the myth. "Sorahb" now had a price of three hundred gold centirus on his head—so that name was guaranteed to get the Hrum's attention.

The Hrum's mounted scouts took off at a gallop after the fleeing Farsalans—not to catch them,

Kavi knew, but to keep them in sight and signal the foot soldiers, who now broke into not a run but a ground-eating jog. No man could catch a galloping horse, but a fit and determined man could outlast a horse and run him down when he tired. Jiaan's order to rally on Sorahb had encouraged a lot of determination.

But they were still competent. The Hrum were almost always competent, curse them. The officer in charge of the troop that followed the column took two thirds of his men with him, racing to join the others in chasing a myth down the dusty road. But that left fifty armed soldiers guarding about sixty slaves, who were chained to piles of very flammable wood.

The score of Farsalan archers who remained, with most of their arrows wrapped in pitch-soaked rags, couldn't possibly defeat them. And those towers had to go.

"This is Garren," Kavi repeated, looking down at the black-haired deghass who could order his death. "Trying to force us to be as bloody as he is. Don't let him do it, girl. Lady. Don't let him bring us down to his level. Let us try, Hama and me. Trust me that far."

17

It maybe wasn't the most eloquent speech he'd ever made. As a peddler, Kavi took pride in his ability to talk people into buying whatever he happened to be selling. But his words came from the heart, and sometimes that would make folks loosen their purse strings when nothing else would.

The girl was looking at him, but her expression was distant and still, and for a moment her eyes didn't seem to see him at all. It was an expression Kavi had seen on Suud tribesmen's faces a time or two, and his shoulders shifted uneasily. Then she blinked, and the familiar sharpness returned.

"Yes," said the girl. "Go, both of you. And hurry. If they're too far from the towers, the soldiers might decide to keep chasing Sorahb, even when they see the smoke. I'll signal the archers to fire the moment everyone is clear."

Without waiting to hear another word — she could always change her mind — Kavi turned and crawled down the hill, keeping to the cover of the brush. He could hear Hama behind him, and without even looking back he knew she was doing a better job of keeping quiet and concealed than he was. It was supposed to be good to have a student surpass you, and Kavi was proud of her, but to be out-sneaked by a girl four years younger than he was still annoyed him.

In a sense it didn't matter how stealthy they were, for most of the remaining Hrum soldiers were staring down the road after their departing comrades and, from the sound of it, cursing their bad luck at being left behind—though one deci master had mustered enough wit to send his men to tend the wounded who had been left beside the road. The man who had screamed was moaning; Kavi hoped he'd be all right, but right now he had other matters on his mind.

Hama edged away, making for the wagons at the rear of the column. Kavi forced aside the thought of what her mother would say if she came to harm, and slithered through the bushes at the edge of the road. The only Hrum soldiers in sight were far ahead of him, with their backs turned to boot, but several of the slaves noticed him.

They had dropped to the road to rest when the wagons stopped. The wagons—specially designed to carry the siege towers, Kavi realized—were low enough that the slaves could sit on the ground with their wrists suspended at about the level of their shoulders. Now they stared at him, and one young man started to his feet in alarm.

"Shh!" Kavi whispered. "Stay down. No, stand up, and spread word for the others to do the same." His drab clothes weren't so different from their rough tunics and britches. "I'm going to pick the locks and free your wrists, but no one is to run until I give the signal. You got that? No one runs till all of you are free!"

Half a dozen heads nodded agreement, and a middle-aged woman set the example, climbing casually to her feet and stretching as well as she could.

"We'll be passing word down the lines," she murmured as Kavi slipped in behind her and pulled out his lock picks. He'd taken to carrying them on his person at all times, since he'd first started spying for the Hrum. As he'd taught Hama, if you engaged in a risky trade, it was best to be prepared for things to go wrong.

"Are you working for Sorahb?" the woman whispered.

KAVI TOLD HER YES, and replied similarly to other questions as he worked down the line, assuring folk that once they escaped the Hrum, Sorahb would see to their safety. Even the ones who weren't Farsalan had heard of the rebel leader and seemed willing to trust Kavi's statements in his name. In fact Kavi thought that most of the men would choose to join Commander Jiaan's army, and welcome he'd make them, for he needed all the recruits he could get. As for the women and the sane men, Kavi would get word to the nearby villages to take them in.

In the Hrum Empire, he'd been told, the government kept track of folk and all their kin, since they had to know who was to be drafted and who was to be taxed. But here in Farsala they'd barely begun working up their tally of the populace. If someone claimed this woman as a niece or that man as a grandfather, they'd have no reason to suspect a lie.

The first side of the two wagons Kavi was working his way down proved easy enough, for the wagons were parked close to the edge of the road, and the Hrum guards, even when they carried the wounded to a resting place, had stayed on the other side, where there was level ground and space. They were settling in for a wait now, arguing about whether they'd have enough time to build a fire and brew tea.

The lock on the last shackle on this side yielded to Kavi's probing. He was getting better, swifter with his picks, for all the locks were similar—the last lock had only cost him half the time the first one had. But it was still taking too long, and here, at the head of the wagon line, he was only half done.

He couldn't see Hama, but he knew she hadn't been caught, and a message passed up the slave line told him she was doing fine. The slaves had developed a fairly efficient system of communication, and fortunately for Kavi, their guards felt confident enough to ignore it. Unfortunately, he still had to unshackle the slaves on the side of the wagon where the Hrum were gathered, and there was hardly any chance they could miss that. But he had to try.

After a careful glance to be certain none of the guards were looking his way, Kavi grasped one of the siege tower's beams and pulled himself into the skeleton of the tower. It didn't provide much cover. A startling number of thick beams crisscrossed the tower's interior, some of them serving no purpose Kavi could see, but there were plenty of gaps between them—and Hrum soldiers on the other side of the line of slaves. Several of the slaves were staring expectantly at Kavi, making it even more likely that the Hrum would look in and see him.

Kavi flattened himself onto the wagon's floor as well as he could, since there were a number of beams there, too, and he had to crawl over them on his way across the wide tower. Once he arrived, he rolled thankfully into the cover of the low wall of planks that made up the wagon's side. At least now he wasn't visible to any Hrum who might glance that way—unless, of course, one of them came to see what the slaves were staring at. "Look away from me, Flame take you!" Kavi barely breathed the words; even a whisper would be too loud now. "You'll attract their attention!"

The slave he was watching started and looked away, a movement so obvious it would be a dead giveaway if any of the soldiers were paying attention. Kavi waited, his heart pounding so loudly he thought the Hrum would hear it, but there was no sound of approaching footsteps, no startled shout of discovery.

Evidently the Hrum weren't paying attention. *Good. Get on with it.*

"Turn around, *casually*," Kavi breathed. "Put your wrist over the side so I can reach the shackle. One at a time!"

Three of the four wrists clanked back out of the wagon, and Kavi caught the one next to him before the man could remove it. He set to work on the lock. They were frightened, and small blame to the poor bastards, for the Hrum didn't deal kindly with slaves who tried to escape.

They dealt even worse with traitors. Kavi felt the tattoo the Hrum had scribed over his biceps as if his flesh still ached from the needle. All Hrum officers had rank tattoos. Patrius, the officer who had talked Kavi into becoming their spy, had assured him that the mark they put on their spies was a closely guarded secret that wouldn't betray him but would give him access to any Hrum officer whose assistance he needed. And indeed, the simple band of diamonds on Kavi's arm was nothing like the elaborate insignia the soldiers bore.

But the Hrum's great secret had lasted about as long as most secrets did, in Kavi's experience — word had gotten out all over Farsala within months of the conquest, and that tattoo had almost gotten him hanged.

If he were caught today, it would buy him a traitor's death, instead of the relative mercy the Hrum offered honorable enemies.

His fingers quivered with haste and fear, but the locks answered sweetly to his picks, as metal always seemed to answer him. The touch of it soothed something deep inside him, which was good—it helped to keep his panic in check.

At least the slaves had settled a bit, talking quietly among themselves, trying to behave normally while Kavi crawled out into the wagon bed to get around the junction of several beams. Going around exposed him more than he liked, but he'd have been even more exposed clambering over, and the slaves themselves gave him some cover, providing movements and small noises so that his movement and the noises he made didn't leap to the Hrum's notice.

The soldiers were less than ten paces from the other side of the wagon now, sitting around their fire waiting for the tea to steep.

The day was cool, but sweat soaked Kavi's shirt, and the picks slipped so often that he had to stop and wipe his hands. The metallic snap of the opening locks was lost amid the metallic clanking of the chains as men and women tethered to a wagon tried to move in a normal fashion. Garren's savage cleverness in setting this little snare had proved to be a weakness as well, and Kavi took great satisfaction in exploiting it as one shackled wrist after another came over the wagon's side.

After he finished with that set of chains, he had one of the slaves signal when no Hrum was looking his way; then scrambled to the other side of the wagon and over the rail. With the jumbled timbers of the siege tower and two lines of bodies between him and the Hrum, it was easy to make his way to the next wagon. Climbing in was still a terrifying risk, but once he'd gained the shelter of the wagon's far wall, he was farther from the Hrum than he'd been before, which allowed him to work even faster—though not too fast.

The mastersmith who had taught Kavi his craft had said that careless haste slowed a job even more than laziness. Getting himself caught would bring this job to a screaming halt, so Kavi took care, crawling softly around the tower's joints and trying to keep his flying fingers from fumbling.

His right hand, with its weakened muscles and warped tendons, had begun to ache by the time he neared the end of the last wagon. This work didn't require a strong grip, but it used the small muscles of his fingers hard, and he was no longer accustomed —

The slave woman's wrist twisted in Kavi's grip, almost tearing the picks from his hands. She grasped his own wrist, squeezing hard.

A warning. But what —

Very cautiously, Kavi raised his head to peer over the wagon's low side. One of the Hrum soldiers had abandoned his tea and was walking down the line of wagons, inspecting them — just as a proper guard should, Flame take him!

Kavi dropped into the wagon's bed, his heart hammering. The guard had started at the head of the line, so he was still one wagon away, and his examination of both the slaves and the wagon was cursory. But he could hardly miss seeing Kavi crouched inside! Kavi had to get out, had to flee. If half the Hrum army came after him, then at least there'd be fewer to seize Hama when she was forced to run for it.

He slithered frantically between the timbers to

the wagon's far side, and was about to scramble over it when several slaves reached in and pressed him down to the floor. They wanted him to stay there? Why?

They weren't looking at him, and several were chatting with their neighbors. Still, so many reaching into the wagon in the same place had to look suspicious.

Kavi forced his tense muscles to relax, and the hands holding him down withdrew.

What were they planning? Whatever it was, it had better be good. And happen fast. He was trusting these people with his life, just lying here. . . . But even trusting these strangers to save him seemed like a better idea than trying to outrun a Hrum troop across the countryside.

Kavi willed his thundering heart to slow, and discovered that slowing his heartbeat under such circumstances was beyond his will. A man's voice rose slightly, addressing the guard, but Kavi couldn't hear what he said.

Then more than a dozen hands descended, dragging him out of the wagon like a netted trout, and he suppressed a startled yelp.

He was sitting on the far side of the wagon,

among several other seated slaves, before his head stopped spinning. One man glared a warning, grasped his hand, and raised it to the same height as the others' chained wrists.

In his drab clothes, with the wagon between them and the other slaves to disguise his presence, Kavi would be well hidden. The guard would pass him by and go on to . . .

Hama!

Kavi barely remembered to keep his arm raised as he spun around to search the line of slaves attached to the wagon behind him. She wasn't there.

"You've got to get Hama out!" he hissed to a middle-aged woman seated next to him. "Before that cursed guard gets there!"

"Don't whisper," she said softly. "It'll attract his attention."

Kavi turned again, and felt the blood drain from his face as he saw the Hrum's trousered legs on the other side of the wagon.

"A diversion," he told her with quiet urgency. "Like you used to distract him from me. Have someone over there complain that you need water."

29

Her brows rose. "We stopped for water, and a rest break, just before this started."

"Then tell him you need food! Tell him your feet are sore! Tell him you're putting a curse on all his family, from his grandparents to the newborn babes! Tell him—"

Several of the slaves around him chuckled, and the woman's sudden smile made her look years younger.

"Relax," she murmured. "Diverting the guards from what we don't want them to see is something we do all the time. They've got—"

Before she could finish, a man on the other side of the wagon called the guard back.

"What is it now?" Irritation sounded in the guard's voice, but no suspicion. Peering beneath the wagon, Kavi saw the man's legs turn till he was facing the slave—with his back to the last two wagons.

Kavi turned just in time to see Hama dragged out of the wagon and land among the slaves. To him it seemed that the flurry of movement was guaranteed to draw the attention of every Hrum in the troop. But no alarm sounded. After several aching seconds, he closed his eyes and let his head fall forward against the wagon's rough wood, listening to the conversation between the slave and the guard. He could barely hear them over the pounding of his own pulse.

". . . I'm just saying, if we're going to be stopping here much longer, we're going to be marching after dark." The slave's voice sounded elderly and petulant.

"And I'm telling you that's not your affair," the guard replied. "You'll march where we say, as long as we say. It's not as if the oxen are going fast enough to tire you out."

"Well, I'm just saying . . ."

The old man's voice trailed off into muttered curses. Kavi looked under the wagon and watched the Hrum guard's legs walking away.

Kavi waited while the guard completed his inspection. It wasn't much of an inspection; he missed the fact that half the slaves he saw had slightly open shackles. Though no doubt the slaves knew to turn the open seam away from him.

He waited until the guard had returned to the fire and taken up his tea. Until the slaves, whose watch Kavi was now perfectly willing to trust, signaled for him to climb into the wagon once more.

It still wasn't long enough for the terror racing through his veins to subside, and his fingers were slippery with sweat when he tackled the next lock. If the slaves hadn't been so competent, so quick, he might have been shackled to this wagon himself by now. And Hama with him.

At least his fingers weren't shaking. Yet.

When he reached the wagon's end, he sent a whispered query back down the line and learned that although Hama had freed everyone on the far side of her two wagons, she was only half way down the dangerous side of the first.

Kavi sent back a message that he had finished his two and would deal with the last side of Hama's second wagon himself. He added that when Hama finished with the wagon she was working on, she was to slip out and stand with the slaves, running with them when Kavi gave the signal. He knew she'd obey, with no nonsense about taking equal shares of the risk, for she was a sensible girl. The slaves were being just as sensible, standing or sitting idly, chatting among themselves as the Hrum poured out their tea and dug bread from their packs.

Only Kavi, slipping cautiously into Hama's

second wagon, could feel the tension in the slaves' muscles as he pulled their shackles open, leaving only a crack that wouldn't betray them unless the Hrum looked closely. It was a miracle that none of them had broken and run, and he hoped that the spin he was giving Time's Wheel today would bring them better fortune in the future. Azura knew they'd earned it.

He wondered how best to signal the slaves to run. A shout would do it. But would Soraya have the archers ready to fire? If flaming arrows didn't start falling the moment the slaves were free, the Hrum would chase them. And if a Hrum soldier had his hands on an escaping slave when the fire arrows arrived, and himself duty-bound to save the towers above all else, would he let the slave go? Or just slit a throat and be done with it? Kavi couldn't discount the second possibility, but there was nothing he could do about it except pray that the girl had her archers ready.

The slaves' message relay had already told him that Hama was finished and ready to run. Kavi opened the last lock, drawing a breath to shout as he turned back for a final check on the guards. The breath left his lungs in an unwary squawk as his eyes met the lady Soraya's. She was practically lying on his boots, her expression calm and withdrawn. But at least she was up against the wagon's side, and had evidently managed to get there without alerting the soldiers.

"What are you doing here?" he breathed. "You're supposed to give the signal to the archers!"

"Don't worry about that." Her voice was as soft as his. "I was wondering . . . your peasant informants told us about the towers, even when they were arriving. Why didn't they warn us about the slaves?" She gestured to several of the slaves in question. They were looking out, or at each other, but Kavi knew they were listening.

"How should I know?" She hadn't come down here to ask that question—though now that he thought about it, Kavi wondered himself. She had come because she didn't trust him. And now . . . "How can you signal the archers without getting us caught? You've jeopardized everything! You—"

"All right, all right." She rolled onto her side to pull a piece of flint and a steel striker from her belt pouch, but even as she moved her expression changed—as if some decision had been reached.

34

"Did you know that you were working magic? On those locks just now?"

"What do you mean? I was picking them. You can't set these towers alight with just a spark. It would take you several tries even to set tinder burning, and the Hrum will hear the striker!"

"You were Speaking to the metal," she said, with an emphasis that made it clear that the word "speaking" meant more than simple speech. "Like the Suud do. Speaking to its spirit."

"That's ridiculous," whispered Kavi, wondering how he could get the striker out of her hands without alerting the Hrum. "The Suud are strange enough that I might—might!—believe they could work magic, but no Farsalan can. Even the church is faking its miracles."

"Really?" A smile eased the tension in her expression. Her dark eyes glinted. She raised the striker.

"Lady, don't—"

She hit the flint once, at an expert angle, sending half a dozen sparks to lie on the thick beam. Kavi knew they would promptly go out, accelerant or no.

As the sparks struck the surface, she whispered,

35

"Burn!" Fire sprang to life, and blazed, and grew, eating along the beam so fast Kavi had to pull away.

"What in the . . ." But whatever had caused it, the fire was well started, and growing faster than he'd dreamed it could.

"Run!" Kavi shouted. He scrambled to the other side of the wagon and leaped out, feeling the heat on his flesh.

The Hrum were shouting too: orders about water, about shovels and sand. The slaves were shouting as they fled in all directions, though Kavi saw that Hama was leading a group up through the thick brush of the hillside toward the archers.

The archers were no longer waiting. Arrows wreathed in fire arced through the air and hissed down toward the siege towers. The heavy, rag-wrapped tips threw them off course, and many of them thudded into the dusty road—and, alarmingly, into the dry brown bushes, which promptly began to smoke.

Time to be going. Kavi plunged into the bushes. He had climbed halfway up the hill before he realized that the lady Soraya wasn't behind him. He turned and looked back.

She stood in the midst of a blazing timber cage, for the fire she had started was spreading far more swiftly than those in the other towers. Kavi pulled in breath to scream at the terrible sight, but she wasn't screaming. She inspected the burning wood with the critical expression of a craftswoman examining her work. She nodded once and then climbed out through the tangle of beams, placing her hands and feet squarely on the wood, as if there were no fire. Her feet, Kavi noticed, were bare.

Free of the wagon, she took a moment to pat out a few sparks in her clothing and then pull on her stockings and boots. In truth she had nothing to fear from the Hrum, who were frantically trying to protect the surviving towers from the fire arrows that still rained down.

She climbed calmly up the hillside to where Kavi stood. "Is that a sufficient signal, do you think?"

Kavi gaped at her. There were scorched places on her clothes—he could smell the acrid scent of burned wool—but her hands weren't burned. Nor her feet, if the way she was walking was any indication.

"I . . . you . . . the fire . . ." He swallowed, feeling the beginning of fear—which was absurd, for he'd traveled with her for weeks, and she was no different now from the girl she'd been then. No, she *was* different.

She smiled again. She was enjoying his fear, the brat, and somehow that lessened it. But wonder remained, and she saw that too, and the malice drained out of her smile.

"I Spoke to the fire's shilshadu," she said. "I persuaded it not to burn me. Just as you Spoke to the shilshadu of the metal, persuading those locks to open. Interested?"

~w~

JIAAN

JIAAN RAISED HIS ARM and signaled his troop to rein in. They'd gained a good lead on the Hrum infantry, but all the horses except his own Rakesh were winded—and even Rakesh was blowing, ready to walk for a while. As the horses slowed, Jiaan twisted in the saddle and looked back at the Hrum's mounted scout, who still followed behind them.

The Hrum soldier had already slowed his own horse to a walk—clearly he had no intention of coming within arrow range.

"We could turn, make a quick charge, and take him," said Fasal. "Keep them from following us."

Jiaan wondered how often it was possible for Fasal to forget the plan.

"I want them to follow us, remember?"

"No, you wanted them to track us. That's not the same thing," said Fasal.

"They'll turn back when they see the smoke," said Jiaan.

"Assuming the others manage to set the towers on fire in the first place. What are they going to do about those slaves?"

Jiaan wished he knew. The memory of the men and women chained to those towers still made his stomach sink. Not that he feared they'd come to harm. His half sister was spoiled and arrogant—or at least she had been; Jiaan wasn't certain that was true anymore—but she wasn't that ruthless. As for the peddler, he probably *was* that ruthless—look at all the men he'd gotten killed at the Sendar Wall—but he wasn't in charge of this operation, Azura be praised. Jiaan hoped Soraya had killed the traitor the moment she saw the slaves.

"It doesn't matter," said Jiaan. "Even if they don't burn the towers, the Hrum troops will turn back when they learn that we've remounted. Once they see that we have fresh horses—and for all they know we've arranged for more—they'll know they can't run us down. That's when they'll go back and send for a tracker. That's not what bothers me."

"There's a lot about this plan that bothers me," said Fasal. "I still think we should have brought the whole army and wiped out the Hrum guarding the towers. If we'd done that, they'd be burning now."

Jiaan thought that what bothered Fasal most about the plan was that it was Jiaan's—the first battle plan he'd come up with entirely on his own.

"They may be burning by now," he said, though he didn't see any smoke. "And most of the rest of the army is still being trained in the rudiments of fighting. If we'd attacked in force, we'd have lost more men than the Hrum. And the Hrum can replace their men more easily than we can."

Though he'd wondered about that, too. He'd been told it was some sort of point of honor with Governor Garren to conquer Farsala with only ten tacti—ten thousand men. But the Hrum army was spread thin. Surely it was time for the man to swallow his pride and send for reinforcements.

"Then why can't we see any smoke?" Fasal asked. "If those towers get to Mazad . . ."

The cool breeze ruffled his straight black hair. He looked cheerful, for all his grousing. Fasal liked to fight; Jiaan was good at planning. Together, Jiaan thought sourly, they almost made a whole officer. And if you added Jiaan's eighteen years and Fasal's seventeen, you had someone old enough to command an army as well. What they really were was a couple of inexperienced boys who had found themselves in charge because no one else had survived. But they hadn't done badly so far, Jiaan reminded himself. And their experience was growing. Almost everything had gone according to plan today, which was better than usual. Only two things worried him.

"The towers can burn at Mazad," said Jiaan. "The city guard can shoot fire arrows as well as we can. Assuming the accelerant acts the way the paint mixer said it would, they might get a few men onto the walls, but they won't get many in."

"Assuming," said Fasal, "that the accelerant was added to the paint in the first place."

All right, three things to worry about.

"But if you hadn't thought of that," said Fasal, reading Jiaan's expression with ruthless accuracy, "what are you worried about?"

"That Hrum scout back there," said Jiaan. "Does one man riding up and down the road strike you as a sufficient scouting force for a troop carrying something as important as those siege towers?"

Fasal frowned. "Maybe they were relying on the slaves to keep us from burning the towers."

"But they had no way to know we intended to burn the towers."

Unless, of course, the peddler had told them. Jiaan's blood chilled. He should have killed the bastard when he had the chance. But when you had a war to win, you couldn't yield to revenge. No matter how much you wanted to.

"For all the Hrum knew, we might have been attacking in force, just as you proposed," Jiaan went on, pulling his mind away from the memory of his father's death on the blood-soaked battleground near the Sendar Wall. "So why was their scouting so inadequate? And even more important, why were they carrying their shields on their arms instead of slung on their packs?"

Fasal opened his mouth to reply, then slowly closed it. He had seen enough Hrum troops on patrol, on the march, to know what they carried and how.

43

"They expected to be attacked," he said, finally. "They may not have known exactly when or where—we did surprise them. But they were expecting an attack sometime."

Rakesh lifted his head and pranced, and Jiaan tightened his grip on the reins. "They might have been taking extra precautions because they were transporting the siege towers."

"Then why was the scouting force so light?" Fasal demanded. "If they were expecting attack, wouldn't they have—"

Rakesh inflated his lungs and whickered.

Jiaan, becoming aware of his mount's focused attention, looked between Rakesh's pricked ears at the orchard that filled a small valley to the north of the road. He saw nothing. Certainly he could hear nothing over the thud of hooves and the jingle of the tack—but the wind was blowing from that direction. Had Rakesh scented—

It was only a small flash of sun on metal within the grove, but suddenly everything made sense.

"It's a trap! This way!" Jiaan spun Rakesh off the road and galloped across the open field beside it—a farmer's field, crops harvested, level and relatively clear, perfect for running horses.

Unfortunately, the Hrum had horses too, and they crashed out of the orchard and raced after the fleeing Farsalans. It was the first wholly mounted Hrum troop Jiaan had ever seen.

If anything had been needed to tell him that this was a well-prepared ambush, that would do it. The Hrum infantry hadn't been trying to run them down; they'd been driving Jiaan and his troop into their net. Only Rakesh's keen senses had given them warning.

Thanks to Rakesh, they had a decent lead on their pursuers. Looking back, Jiaan saw that the Hrum's mounts were the sturdy, sure-footed horses their scouts used, not Farsalan chargers. It looked like most of the Hrum were no more comfortable on horseback than his archers were, but they still out-numbered his small force by over two to one. No, they had to flee. The Hrum's horses were fresh, and Rakesh was already breathing deep. If Rakesh was winded, most of the other Farsalan horses would be in even worse shape.

Jiaan's mouth tightened. His plan was falling apart, but he had finally learned—Azura knew it had taken him long enough—that plans did fall apart, and he had a plan in place for that possibility.

"Scatter and regroup!" he shouted to the men beside him, and heard them passing the order on. A few moments later four of the archers, the worst riders among them, pulled their horses out of the troop and galloped off in different directions.

Looking back, grateful for Rakesh's smooth gait, Jiaan saw that he'd been right. The Hrum, trained to fight as a unit, to stay together in the midst of battle and disaster, ignored the handful of fleeing men and remained focused on the larger group. And the Farsalan horses, weary as they were, were pulling ahead of the Hrum. But for all their famed stamina, the chargers couldn't run forever.

They galloped out of the field and onto a rough track that bordered it. Jiaan turned to follow the track, which paralleled the road, for he didn't dare circle back toward the infantry. Five more men scattered out from the group, and Jiaan wondered where he should go next. When the ambush had appeared, he'd instinctively fled into the small flat valley between the low hills, where his horses had room to run. But couldn't the Hrum have predicted that?

They could have, he decided grimly. *So there may*

be another ambush ahead. And the worst riders had already fled.

Jiaan turned Rakesh sharply off of the track and into another field, headed not for the tempting open ground, but for the rough, low hills that bordered it.

Another five men galloped away from the troop just before Jiaan sent Rakesh flying into a shallow gap between the hills. If this small valley ended in hills too steep for the horses to climb, they would be trapped, but Jiaan knew this area, and most of the hills were passable. Passable for a fresh horse, climbing at a walk.

Eight more men shot off into side canyons as they galloped on. Remaining with the troop were the good riders Jiaan had detailed to act as decoys if they had to run for their lives. Mostly grooms before the invasion, their archery was only fair, but their horsemanship was superb—sometimes better than their deghan masters' had been. But however good the riders might be, the horses were beginning to tire.

Jiaan chose the mildest of the hills and urged Rakesh upward, letting him drop to a scrambling walk, for galloping up a rocky slope on an exhausted horse was an invitation to disaster.

The Hrum reached the bottom at almost the same time the Farsalans reached the summit. A few arrows skittered among them, but the Hrum archers were firing uphill, the range was long, and they all missed. For a moment Jiaan was tempted to order his men to return their shots, since the height would extend their range, but all his good archers were gone, and the Hrum force now outnumbered his by almost three to one.

He pulled Rakesh to a halt and turned back to watch the Hrum begin their ascent. Their stocky, agile mounts might have an easier time of it on the hill, but they were tiring too, Jiaan was pleased to see. Before they reached the top, his troop would make it down and gain more distance crossing the next field. Looking at the irrigation ditch on the far side of that field, he knew that would be all they needed.

"So why not fire back at them?" Fasal asked, pulling his sweet-tempered mare up beside Rakesh, black to the gelding's dappled gray. "Aren't you supposed to be good with that?" He gestured to the unstrung bow strapped to Jiaan's saddle.

"Well, it might just make them mad," said Jiaan. "And I'd hate to do that."

"You saw the ditch."

For a moment, Fasal seemed to forget that Jiaan was a peasant-born bastard who had snatched command of the army away from his betters. His grin held only the fellowship of one horseman for another.

"Let's hope the Hrum aren't as quick as you are," said Jiaan, matching Fasal's grin as the last of his men trotted over the hilltop and started down the other side.

Picking their way down the slope was almost as slow as climbing up. The Hrum's horses had gained some ground and were starting down themselves by the time the Farsalans reached the bottom of the hill, where another wide field lay before them.

Jiaan took the lead, holding Rakesh at a canter, for he wanted to save the horse's strength.

The Hrum must have assumed the Farsalan horses were slowing from exhaustion; their horses charged off the hill and into the field, hoofbeats rolling like thunder.

Jiaan turned Rakesh toward the irrigation

49

ditch and let go of the reins, firmly clasping the streaming gray mane. There were very few riders good enough to stay on a jumping horse with only the strength of their legs gripping the horse's body to keep them in the saddle. Jiaan had never heard of the Hrum doing so, though the deghans had made a sport of it. Jiaan, peasant-born, wasn't as good a rider as most deghans.

The banks of the ditch were only a few feet high, but it was five feet across, and most streams in this part of the foothills were deeper than they looked. Jiaan hoped he wouldn't find out about this one the hard way.

Rakesh, who knew more about jumping than Jiaan ever would, quickened his stride to a rapid lope, shortening his paces as he neared the earthen barrier. Then he gathered his muscles and surged upward.

Jiaan suppressed his shout of exaltation, for it didn't do to startle your horse as you sailed through the air, one with your mount, one with the sky. Then, as it always did, the ground arrived.

Rakesh's hooves thudded to the earth, and Jiaan slammed into Rakesh's withers, trying to grip the horse's slippery hide with his knees and mostly failing. Only his fists, clenched on a double handful of mane, kept him from falling—though Rakesh's forward surge into a rocking canter helped him to regain his seat. He glanced aside in time to see Fasal's mare sail over the ditch and land daintily. Fasal took the landing much better than Jiaan had, but Jiaan had no time for envy— the rest of his troop was approaching the ditch. Only three men fell, and they quickly rolled to their feet and remounted, cantering across the field after the others. Jiaan followed the last of them, tracking the Hrum's progress with his ears. When the Hrum neared the ditch, he pulled Rakesh to a halt and looked back.

The idiots tried to jump it. Perhaps they had seen the Farsalan chargers going over and assumed it was something any horse could do. Fortunately, their horses knew better.

Approaching a barrier that had been almost too big for the larger, stronger chargers to jump, with water of unknown depth on the other side and awkward, unbalanced riders on their backs, the Hrum horses planted their feet and stopped.

Several of the Hrum promptly discovered the depth of the water, hurtling over their horses' heads and into the ditch. It *was* deeper than it looked, Jiaan noted—almost five feet deep, and muddy, too. The riders floundering in the ditch were the lucky ones. Other Hrum riders hit the ground when their horses stopped, and the horses behind ran into the horses in front, stepping on the fallen men and unseating their own riders. Only a handful of Hrum, riding at the rear of the pack, managed to remain in their saddles.

Shouts of pain arose amid the storm of cursing, and Jiaan winced. He had fallen off his horse at the Sendar Wall, when the Hrum had suddenly raised a hedge of long lances, and broken his collarbone. It was barely healed even now, and he vividly remembered how much it had hurt.

Then he remembered the slaughter that had followed, and any impulse to sympathize with the Hrum died.

He turned Rakesh and cantered after the others. They would reach their remounts and be gone long before the Hrum sorted out that mess. In fact, with the extra time this had given them, they could probably lead their tired horses instead of having the local peasants return them later. The risks involved in having the horses returned were small, but Rakesh had been his father's horse—Jiaan hated to take any risk with him.

Fasal was waiting for him at the entrance to the valley that led to a track in the foothills—the track that would ultimately take them to the small mountain meadow where their army had been hidden for so long.

"They're not going to give up, you know." Fasal turned his mare to walk beside Rakesh. "This is probably that Hrum officer your peasant spy said was assigned to hunt us down. They'll send the foot soldiers to look for our riders who left the main force. They'll probably find at least a few of them."

"They probably will," said Jiaan.

"But the Hrum will torture them! They'll reveal the location of the croft!"

"I've been told that the Hrum don't torture prisoners," said Jiaan. "But they won't torture our men in any case. I told them that if they were captured and even threatened with physical harm, they were to tell the Hrum where our army has been hiding. In fact, I ordered them to talk if they were threatened."

"You ordered them to reveal our location to the Hrum? Why didn't I hear about this?"

Because you'd have argued.

"I want the Hrum to find the croft," Jiaan reminded him. How many times was Fasal going to forget the plan?

OF COURSE, JIAAN reflected four days later, the reason Fasal kept forgetting the plan was probably because he disapproved of it so deeply.

"No deghan would ever come up with a plan as . . . as . . ."

"Cowardly?" Jiaan suggested coldly.

A bright half-moon sailed high, but he and Fasal lay in the shadow of one of the pines that covered the slopes around the long valley where the new Farsalan army had been created. He would miss this place, Jiaan realized. But so many knew of its location that it was only a matter of time before the Hrum found it. Better to reveal it himself and let its destruction serve his cause.

"Cowardly, sneaky, and dishonorable," Jiaan went on. "A peasant plan that no true deghan would tolerate. But considering how the deghans' plans worked out . . . well, I can hardly do worse, can I?"

Fasal winced, and Jiaan felt a surge of guilt. He might be an inexperienced commander watching the unfolding of his first solo battle plan, but he had no right to take his self-doubts out on his subordinates.

"Your father," said Fasal, just as coldly, "would have said this plan is too complex."

Jiaan's father had died with the rest of the deghans.

Jiaan turned away, gazing down at the army camp that had sprung up around the deserted farmhouse. It was too late for lights to show in the barracks, but wisps of smoke rose from their chimneys. Sentries patrolled; the soft thud of a stamping hoof came from the stables. All looked exactly as it should. But plans hardly ever ran exactly as they should, even simple ones, and this plan . . .

"You're right," Jiaan admitted. "It is too complex. But I couldn't think of anything that would cost us fewer lives."

Even in the dimness he could see Fasal's eyes roll. "The point isn't to save our lives—it's to kill more of them! If we wanted to stay alive we should lie down like dogs and lick the Hrum's hands."

He had a point, despite the ridiculously arrogant phrasing. "There are more of them," Jiaan pointed out. "If we don't—"

The flicker of movement that caught his eye was so small he almost dismissed it. And it could have been a deer, or a jackal, but . . .

"If we don't, what?"

"Shh," said Jiaan, straining to see into the shadows below the trees.

The Hrum burst from the cover of the forest beside the track, shouting, their drums sounding the charge. They'd gotten their whole unit within striking distance of the camp, and Jiaan had barely glimpsed them—and he'd been watching!

"Kanarang take them, they're good!" said Jiaan. His own sentries shouted a realistic alarm and fled as if the djinn of destruction really were on the Hrum's side. "Most of the Hrum I've seen couldn't sneak into a kitchen for a snack, much less creep up on a battlefield like that."

"The Hrum are warriors," said Fasal. "Warriors don't sneak."

"These did." Half a dozen Hrum were already in the farmhouse; Jiaan could hear their muffled shouts, though he couldn't understand them. A trader who spoke Hrum had joined the Farsalan army a few months ago, and Jiaan was learning the language as fast as he could, but he could only pick a few words out of the rapid commands. "I wonder who's leading them."

The main body of troops spread out, storming toward the barracks. Soon they would reach them.

"Well, whoever's in charge," said Jiaan, "we're about to out-sneak the bastard."

He rose to his knees, nocked an arrow, and drew his bow, feeling the powerful pull in his shoulders and back. He had trained as an archer—not even his father, who had commanded the Farsalan army, had dared to raise his peasant-born son to a position of command. But the Wheel his mother's folk believed in had spun, and things were different now than they'd been in the deghans' day.

"Fire," Jiaan called, releasing his own arrow as the word left his lips.

A flock of dark shafts lofted into the sky, almost invisible even when the moonlight struck them. Then they hissed down toward the Hrum.

In the darkness, it would take several flights

for the Hrum to figure out what direction the arrows were coming from, and Jiaan had further confused the issue by placing his archers on two different slopes. Scattered as they were, with murder raining down on them, the Hrum lifted their shields and ran for the shelter of the barracks, swords drawn to fight their way in.

There was no need for weapons, Jiaan knew, as he drew and loosed another arrow. All the Farsalans who weren't here on the hillsides were long since on their way to the new camp in the desert—a camp so well hidden in the badlands' rocky mazes that Jiaan wasn't sure he could find it without a Suud guide.

He fired again. Shrieks of pain told him that at least some of their arrows were finding targets!

Most of the Hrum had entered the barracks now, several dragging wounded comrades with them.

Jiaan smiled grimly and prepared to launch the evening's second surprise.

"At the roofs!" he shouted. Even if the Hrum heard him it wouldn't make sense, and even if they'd understood it wouldn't matter. Jiaan snatched up another arrow, pulled his bow, and sent it up in the high arc that would bring it down on the roof of one of the farther barracks. Ordinarily that would have been an exercise in futility, for the planks of an ordinary roof would stop a light arrow.

But as the Hrum were about to discover, the last act of the departing Farsalans had been to strip the ceiling planks away, replacing them with thin strips of wood that were barely strong enough to support the thin wooden shingles. Of course the beams that supported the roof would still catch an arrow, but the flimsy construction that now lay between those beams would not.

The bellow that arose from the barracks as the first flight crashed through the roof held as many cries of anger and panic as of pain. Jiaan added several more Hrum words to his vocabulary—terms the respectable trader had refrained from teaching them.

Men were emerging from the deceptive shelters now, dashing out into the open, where they could construct their shield wall and then carry the battle to their enemy. Jiaan thought that fewer men emerged than had run in, but in the chaotic darkness it was hard to tell. And letting these men reach his archers was no part of his plan.

"Whistle," he told Fasal. "You can do it louder than I can."

"But they're not even . . . oh, all right."

Fasal raised two fingers to his mouth—the resultant shriek made Jiaan wish he could clap his hands over his ears, but he was too busy firing a last shot and gathering up his bow and quiver. It might take the Hrum a few moments to realize that Fasal's whistle was the signal for the archers to retreat, and Jiaan wanted his whole force mounted and away by the time they did. They were only a few marks' ride from the trail that led down the cliff face to the rocky desert below, and the Hrum, on foot, would never be able to catch them before they reached it. Once they were in the desert . . . Jiaan was grinning as he started up the dark slope.

"We barely scratched them," Fasal protested, falling into step behind him. "We could have done some serious damage tonight! Especially if you'd kept the footmen here to charge while they were so disorganized. This will only make them more eager to follow us!"

"Exactly. I want them to follow us, remember?"

Fasal snorted. "You said you didn't want to make them mad."

"I changed my mind," Jiaan told him. "Mad is exactly what I want right now. Mad will carry them deep into the badlands. Too deep to back out."

"I think you're relying too much on the desert," Fasal grumbled.

"Remember when I told you that you should spend more time talking to the Suud?" Jiaan asked.

"Yes, though why you wasted so much time on those barbarians, I'll never understand. What of it?"

"You should have spent more time talking to the Suud."

CHAPTER THREE

SORAYA

SHELTERED IN THE DOORWAY of Maok's hutch, Soraya listened to the soft thud of a hammer on hot metal as she watched the peddler and his Suud apprentice. It had surprised her, that quiet thumping, for she'd thought metal being shaped would clang. She'd since learned that that was only true when a piece was "cold-worked." Hot metal could be as soft as wood—as soft as dough, depending on how hot it was. She had learned a great deal about metal over the last six weeks. About other things too.

"We have long needed this," said Maok, peering over her shoulder. "It costs us, to trade with others for our knives and spear points. Now we can make our own. It is a good joining gift."

Soraya, who had brought only grain and dried beans for her gift, gritted her teeth and added jealousy to hatred as she stared at the peddler's back. He had taken off his shirt, even though the night was cool, just as his apprentices had shed the striped robes that covered their white skin. His britches left him with more covering than the Suud, who wore nothing but a strip of cloth wrapped around their hips. Once the Suud had looked almost naked to Soraya, but that had long since passed. Now she thought the peddler looked overdressed.

He wasn't working the metal himself—he could grip neither hammer nor tongs with his weakened right hand. She could see that he longed to take over, but he simply watched, and he didn't nag his apprentices either, commenting only when they needed his advice.

Soraya knew that in his place she'd have been muttering things like "keep the strokes firm and steady," even though the middle-aged Suud man was doing exactly that as he pounded three red-hot iron bars into one. No, she had to admit it— the peddler was a good teacher. She sighed.

63

"You're a fool, girl," said Maok calmly.

"For hating him? He killed my father. I have a right to hate!"

"Maybe. Maybe not," said Maok, annoyingly cryptic, as she so often was. "He learned to Speak to the shilshadu of metal fast. Faster than anyone I ever seen. But he cannot work it with his own hands. And I think he is a One Speaker, as many with strong . . ." She waved her hands, as if to pluck the elusive word from the air. "What is 'feeling for a thing,' in your Faran?"

"Affinity," said Soraya, noticing for the first time that Maok was speaking in Faran. It kept their conversation relatively private, for although many Suud spoke a rough Faran, none of them were as fluent as Maok.

"Affinity, yes." The old woman nodded, her silky hair floating around her white face. "He has strong affinity for metals, but no gift for other things. He will not be an All Speaker, as you will. Besides, Duckie is a nice mule."

Even Soraya liked the peddler's mule, but as for the rest of it . . .

"I think I'm only going to be a Three Speaker," she said, though as far as she knew,

'Three Speaker' wasn't a real term. "I'll never reach the shilshadu of that cursed rock."

"Stone's spirit is slow and still," said Maok. "While your own shilshadu is filled with anger you will not find it."

Ah, here was the scolding. Soraya found that she was in no mood to be lectured about forgiveness.

"I'm going to the mine," she said. "Maybe I can reach the stone's shilshadu better if I handle it more."

She crawled out of the low, round-topped tent and stood stiffly. She'd been sitting cross-legged trying to reach the spirit of that stupid rock for so long that her legs were half asleep. The frustrating part was that it did have a spirit: old, deep, and oddly gentle. Soraya was sufficiently adept with the Suud's peculiar magic by now that she could sense it. She just couldn't yield herself to it as she could with fire or water, or, as she had recently learned to do, with air.

Air was easy, once you realized how vast and loose was the spirit that filled it—so easy that just thinking about it made a sudden breeze swirl around Soraya, reflecting the turbulence in her soul.

She damped the connection swiftly, noting Maok's scowl, for control was something else Maok was trying to teach her. But Soraya couldn't suppress her smile. Air's spirit was so merry and open that even an instant's joining lightened her heart.

"Don't go near the smelting oven," Maok told her. "The way you are now, the fire might flare up."

Soraya nodded, turning away. She had no desire to visit the smoldering pit where the ore was cooked—"smelted," the peddler called it.

"It is not that you hate," Maok called after her. "It is that hate blinds you."

At least she'd spoken in Faran, so the rest of the camp wasn't made privy to Soraya's private life.

Soraya was sufficiently grateful to Maok for guarding her emotional privacy that she took care to close off her own ability to read people's emotions as she passed through the camp, walking away from the peddler and the apprentices who clustered around the central fire. A fire that had required only bellows and an anvil to turn into a forge.

Another of the things that had surprised Soraya was how little equipment was needed to turn rock into sword blades. The peddler admitted that the sophisticated blast furnaces in the mines, and the elaborate forges in Mazad, with their array of bellows, tongs, awls, and other tools, were more efficient. But he said that these primitive expedients would still do the job. Perhaps even better when it came to smelting the Suud's iron, for rumor had long claimed there was something special about the ore found in the badlands. Kavi said he didn't want it heated too thoroughly lest whatever made the ore so special "burn off."

The path to the open trench where the Suud mined iron ore led past the crude pit where lumpy packets of ore were baked into an astonishingly soft, spongy matter the peddler called "bloom." The bloom held soft iron, but it was still caught in its matrix of rock. The men who ran the smelter had to beat the bloom until the other elements scattered out and only a lump of iron remained — a very hard iron, which the peddler said would be too brittle to be useful on its own.

Soraya didn't hear any thumping sounds from the furnace, so she guessed they must be heating the ore. But she still obeyed Maok's instructions and walked wide around the smelter pit. It was a new and unsettling development in her magic, that she had become so aware of the shilshadu of things that sometimes they reacted to her presence even when she didn't intend it. Remembering how hard she had struggled to reach the shilshadu of inanimate things—even of live things at first— Soraya could only smile.

Maok said this was a stage most Speakers went through, and that it would pass as she gained more control. The Suud who manned the bellows were protected by the smelter pit's chimney, but Soraya knew that too hot a fire could ruin the ore they worked on, causing the iron to melt out of the rock and form nuggets at the bottom of the fire pit that were so hard and brittle as to be completely unworkable. And while most of the heat from a sudden burst of fire would go up the chimney, some of it might wash back out of the clay pipes where the men who worked the bellows piped in air. The last thing Soraya wanted was to burn someone, so she left the path, picking her way through the bushes that grew near the stream that provided the camp with water.

Everywhere around her the bushes, the grass, and even the spiny plants were shedding old leaves and putting on new growth. Some sprouted buds that would soon be in bloom. She had learned when she lived with the Suud last year that winter, the time of the rains, was the desert's time of growth. It was in the summer, when the sun struck down, that plants went dormant. Now everything hummed with returning life. Soraya couldn't help but sense it, and she too rejoiced.

By the time she reached the mine, she had calmed down enough to greet the workers with genuine good cheer.

When Soraya finally convinced Maok that the peddler might be able to use his gift to create swords as good as those the Hrum used, and that he would teach the Suud smithcraft into the bargain, men who wanted to learn the secrets of making stone into iron had come from all the tribes in the desert. Soraya knew how valuable the ability to work metal would be to the Suud; that was one of the reasons she'd been willing to reveal the secret of their magic to the treacherous peddler. That and the knowledge that if he showed any sign of betraying their secret she could kill him.

But having watched him teaching his apprentices the craft he loved, she didn't believe he would give them away. The peddler was the one person whose emotions she always allowed herself to sense—Ahriman, djinn of lies, could take "magical ethics" where he was concerned! Yet sensing his emotions was allowing her to know him. To know for a fact that he had been as surprised, and even more appalled than she was by the sight of the slaves chained to the siege towers. That was why she hadn't killed him.

She still hated him—she could never give that up, nor did she want to—but she could endure him long enough to make full use of him before she allowed Jiaan to avenge their father's death.

It was because she refused to take orders from the traitor that she had gotten involved in mining the ore. The peddler was in charge at the forge whenever metal was being worked, and he kept a close eye on the smelter as well. But he paid no heed to how the ore was gathered, once he had taught the Suud to identify the iron-bearing rocks.

The men who had come to be trained as smiths all took their turns at digging, and other members of the tribe helped out too. Soraya recognized Abab and several of the others. It was hard, unpleasant work, swinging a pick in the confines of the narrow canyon where they had found the best vein of ore—though Soraya thought "vein" was a ridiculous word for the huge band of rock streaking across the canyon wall. Rock dust covered the Suud's white skin, and small rocks bounced off the thick cloths they had wrapped around their heads to provide a bit of protection. But no one shirked the work. Even the tribe's children were there, carrying baskets of ore off to the smelter, and the children's presence made any task light.

In the beginning, Soraya had thought to supervise the digging, but there was little to supervise, and she found that there was nothing quite as boring as sitting and watching others work. She had tried swinging one of the miner's picks, which the peddler had ordered shipped down to the desert along with the bellows, the anvil, and the load of "soft" iron bars he hoped would mix with the Suud's ore to produce something like the Hrum's famous watersteel. She was strong enough to swing the pick—after a summer spent working as a servant in the Hrum's camp, she should be— but she couldn't swing it as long or as strongly as the men did.

Now she no longer bothered with a pick but went straight to the baskets, filling them with bits of chattered ore and passing them to the children,

71

making sure none of them took too heavy a load. Proud Walking clan was excited to be the tribe that had brought the secrets of metal to their people, and the children were eager to be a part of it.

Dust sifted into her hair. The rock roughened her fingers and tired her arms and shoulders, but Soraya kept working until Abab put down his pick and approached her.

"We're going to rest awhile," he said. "You can't fight the rock all night—it might start winning!"

Soraya laughed, and he pulled her to her feet and led her out of the canyon with the others.

The night air was fresh and cool on her sweaty skin, and the moon glowed like a lamp. Clouds obscured the stars in a few places, but they were small. The winter rains mostly took place during the day, leaving the night skies clear, for which Soraya was grateful. The nocturnal Suud, with their wide-dilating pupils, could see perfectly well by starlight alone. But on moonless or cloudy nights, Soraya was restricted to the firelit camp—one aspect of living with the Suud that she found most annoying.

On the other hand, she liked the fact that only a few men of the tribe were taller than she was, and then only by inches. Abab was tall for a Suud, and he stood eye to eye with her. Growing up Farsalan, she'd become accustomed to being a small woman. When she came to live with the Suud, it had taken some time for her to feel that their lack of height was normal. When she went back to Farsala, she accepted being short again. It was only when she returned to the Suud once more that she realized how nice it was not to have men looming over her.

Abab sat down on a rock, becoming even shorter, and offered her a skin bag filled with water.

"Kavi says they're getting close with the swords. That the metal is good, and the metal-Speakers are making them feel more and more like watersteel. Our smiths have already made some good knives. They don't look like much"—Abab grinned—"and the blades are a bit lumpy. But they hold an edge, and Kavi says the metal is sound."

Kavi says. He had charmed most of the tribe, just as he'd charmed so many Farsalan peasants into aiding Sorahb's cause. And once the slaves he'd freed from the tower told their tale, his reputation—*Sorahb's* reputation, she corrected herself sourly—would grow even greater.

She closed her eyes, letting the soft, change-able shilshadu of water into her own shilshadu, soothing away her anger, sinking herself into the water's mindless pleasure in even the small move-ments it made inside the bag. She took a moment to remind it of cool streams, of melting snow and the cold of the highest sky where it had formed.

The shilshadu of water was the easiest to affect, for water loved to change. When she handed the skin bag back to Abab it was cold.

He smiled his thanks absently, eyes fixed on her face. "Why don't you like him?"

"Like who?" said Soraya.

Abab snorted. "I heard that he killed your father, but I've also heard that your father died in battle against the Hrum. Besides, your father was a great warrior. Kavi can't even grip fire tongs in his right hand, much less a weapon. And he's not left-handed, either. So I have trouble believing that he could have killed your father—in battle or any other way."

A flash of rage surged through Soraya. "Believe what you like!"

She turned and stalked away. In the old days, she'd have thrown something at him, something

74

hard, and he deserved it too! Who was he—

Water splashed on the back of her neck, startlingly cold against her hot skin.

She spun to glare at Abab, who stood with the water bag still raised, ready to defend himself.

"Just helping you cool that temper of yours," he said innocently.

Anger fractured her control, but Abab was one of the people she found easy to read. Beneath his laughter, Soraya could feel his concern like an outstretched hand. She closed off her shilshadu sensing as soon as she noticed it. She agreed with Maok that it was rude to spy into people's hearts without their knowledge. It was only for enemies that she made an exception. And Abab, though he exasperated her mightily sometimes, was far from an enemy. He was worried about her.

Soraya went back and sat down on the rock beside him. For the first time, she realized that he had led her away from the others; if she didn't lose her temper and yell, they would have privacy.

"He didn't kill my father with his own hand," she said. "He did it with lies and treachery."

"But what did he do?" Abab asked. "Exactly."

Soraya's heart flinched from talking about it.

But perhaps it would be good for the Suud to know the details. To know who and what that charming traitor really was.

"My father hired him," said Soraya, taking a deep breath. "Caught him, really. He had committed crimes in the city of Setesafon, selling gold-coated bracelets and other things as if they were solid gold. He tried to sell one to me and my cousin Pari, but my father caught him."

Pari had been taken by the Hrum to be sold as a slave. Soraya worried more about her than she did about her mother, for Sudaba was stronger and tougher than sweet-natured Pari could ever be. And she feared for Merdas more than either of them. He'd be three years old now. Just a toddler when she'd seen him last. After so many terrifying changes, would he even remember the big sister who had taken him on horseback rides and blown buzzing kisses into his baby-soft skin?

Abab's hand settled over hers, his palm as rough and dirty as her own. "Your father caught him," he prompted firmly. He might sympathize, but he wasn't going to let her off. He and Elid and the others had probably decided that talking about it would be good for her. Soraya wondered if Abab had drawn the short straw—although the Suud settled that kind of thing by drawing different-colored pebbles. In any case, it was clear he wasn't going to give up.

"My father could have turned him over to the city guard," she said, "but he was foolish enough to give him a chance. I was going to stay in the croft, to hide from my father's political enemies." Abab nodded, for he knew about that. "Well, my father hired the peddler to visit the croft as a part of his rounds. To bring any supplies we needed and then to take my father news of me. How I was faring."

She had to stop then, to swallow down the lump in her throat. Her father had loved her. It had been the central fact of her existence—the one thing in the universe nothing could ever change. But death changed everything, and the Hrum had brought plenty of death.

"He used his position to go into the Farsalan army camp," she said. "He learned about my father's battle plans, and gave them to the Hrum. So they were ready for the deghans' charge. Just as the Farsalan horses reached their line, the Hrum brought up lances, hundreds of lances, long enough and well enough braced to kill a horse. I was told they killed half our men, and almost all the horses, in the first few minutes of the battle. After that they were on foot, and the Hrum are the finest infantry fighters alive. The deghans' swords broke on the Hrum's watersteel, and anyway, they were horsemen. Without their horses . . ."

She turned her face away. She could see it clearly in her imagination. She'd had nightmares about it.

"Was your father killed by the Hrum lances?" Abab asked. "I can see why you'd hate Kavi for that."

"No," Soraya admitted. "My father survived the charge, survived almost all the battle that followed. In the end—a soldier who saw it told me this—when it was clear the Farsalans had lost, my father drew a circle in the earth at his feet, challenging the Hrum commander to single combat. But Garren didn't fight. He . . . he had his archers kill my father instead. The soldier said my father saw them coming, but he never flinched. He said it was quick."

Tears fell now. Odd, for she hadn't cried for her father in months. She pulled her hand from Abab's to wipe her face. She would have revenge, as she had sworn to. Revenge against the Hrum, and the traitor. That was better than weeping.

"So it was the Hrum who killed your father," said Abab slowly, working it out. "But Kavi made it possible, showing them how to use these lances?"

"Not exactly," Soraya admitted. "They already had the lances. The traitor just told them when and where to use them. And he told them where the Farsalan archers would be, and some other things."

"So what Kavi did . . . he didn't actually kill your father, but he made it easier for the Hrum to win the battle where they killed your father. He helped them."

"Exactly," said Soraya. "He gave aid to the enemy while he was pretending to work for us. That's what treason is."

Abab eyed her soberly. "I can see why you're angry. But have you asked him why he did this?"

"I don't care why," said Soraya, meaning every word of it.

"But he's helping you now, and betraying the Hrum. Doesn't that . . ." He paused to search for words, but Soraya didn't care how he phrased it.

"No," she said, "it doesn't. It only makes him a traitor twice over."

She went back to work then, gathering up rocks from the canyon floor, and soon the others rejoined her. She could feel Abab's gaze on her as she filled the baskets, but he said nothing more, working beside her in silence until they returned to camp for the final meal of the night.

SORAYA WATCHED THE peddler as he wandered from one family's cooking fire to another in the Suud way of eating a meal. He talked more than he ate, she noticed. The camp's food had tasted strange to her once, but now it tasted right—even when the cook put too much belish in the stew, it was something she was . . . accustomed to. The lamplight glowing through the patterned silk that made up the sides of the hutches looked right, and the bouncing babble of the language sounded right to her ears. Watching the peddler's struggles, she realized how much Proud Walking clan had come to feel like home. But she was a deghass. Her home was elsewhere. She remembered the burned-out shell of the manor where she'd grown up, and shivered.

When Merdas returned, when she had her brother back, she could make a home anywhere.

That was worth anything, even tolerating the traitor, as long as he helped keep the Farsalan rebellion alive.

For according to the Hrum's own law, if Garren didn't complete his conquest of Farsala within a year, the Hrum army would leave, and all the people who had been captured and made slaves would be returned. It had seemed absurd to Soraya, when she first learned of this strange custom. Then she spent the summer working as a servant in the Hrum's main army camp near Setesafon, trying to learn where in their vast empire her mother and brother had been sent. She had come to know the Hrum, and above all else they were a people of law. If their law gave Garren a limit of one year to complete his conquest, then one year was all he had. Only four months left now that Mazad had to hold out.

A shadow fell across her, and she looked up into the peddler's—the traitor's face.

"We done one other sword," he said in his clumsy Suud—no doubt to further charm the Suud apprentices who gathered behind him. "We will test sword, dinner is done. I want you to talk for me, if you want."

"I'd be happy to translate for you," said Soraya in her smoothest Suud, though when she'd only been here a month, she'd sounded much like he did now. "Though why you think another broken blade requires translation I don't know. How many swords have failed so far?"

The peddler frowned, trying to work out what she'd said.

"Uvadu," said one of the apprentices, grinning. "But we're just beginners, you know. We're getting better."

"How much 'uvadu' mean?" the peddler asked.

Soraya had finally mastered the Suud's expressions for various amounts—but it hadn't been easy. "Between thirty-two and fifty," she said. "It's only used when you don't have a precise count."

"Uvadu mean between thirty-two and fifty?" the peddler asked incredulously.

"No, U*va*ydu is between sixty and a hundred and fifty. U*vah*du is between thirty-two and fifty."

"You're kidding me," said the peddler, dropping into Faran. And he must have said it before, for even the apprentices who didn't speak Faran laughed.

"Just say 'much' and 'big much,'" Soraya told him. "Why do you need a translator?"

She might be prepared to tolerate his presence to defeat the Hrum and get Merdas back, but she didn't want to be around him tonight.

"This one sword . . ." The peddler groped for words again, then shrugged. "This one right."

"Right?" Soraya raised her brows

"It feels right," he said, lapsing into Faran again. "The shilshadu of it. The trick of watersteel is something to do with the quenching, I think. When metal cools, I can feel . . ." His hands moved again, and Soraya nodded understanding. It was hard to find any words, Suud or Faran, to describe what you found inside the shilshadu of a thing. But she had seen him, standing behind his apprentices as they worked the steel with their hammer and tongs, his hands on their shoulders. Much as she despised him, it was impossible to ignore his skill at his craft. If he said he felt something, she had to believe that he felt it.

"It's like something is moving, swimming in the metal as it cools," he went on. "In watersteel, I finally figured out, it's swimming in lines, in formation along the edges of the blade, but in the middle it's just . . . just milling around. I don't know how to put it more clearly than that," he added. "But I'm certain of it now. And Lupsh here can feel it too." He clapped one of the grinning apprentices on the shoulder. "The sword he just made feels like everything is swimming in the right way, in the right places. Some of the other lads are honing an edge on it now. By the time dinner's over, it will be ready to test."

"I'll be there," Soraya told him coolly. "Though I still think that one more broken blade won't need a translator."

THE SUUD WERE BEGINNING to yawn, and Soraya felt sleep creeping up on her, too. The graying sky in the east showed that soon the sun would rise, but after the meal was over she went with the rest of the tribe to the edge of the camp, where the peddler had sunk a post into the sandy soil. He had bought it from the miners, along with the rest of his equipment, and it stood almost as high as a Suud man—which left it a hand span shorter than his own curly head, and he wasn't particularly tall. About seven inches thick at the base, the wood was rough and unpolished—rougher now, with the sword cuts in it. That ordinary post had broken every sword the Suud had made so far.

The peddler held up the new sword, and the dim light of the soon-to-rise sun flowed over the blade. It didn't look very promising. The hilt was a couple of pieces of carved wood bound with leather strips, and even Soraya could see that some parts of the blade were thicker than others. The apprentice smiths had only sharpened about a third of one side of the blade, leaving the rest dull.

It did display the rippling pattern that marked the Hrum's watersteel, but Soraya had been watching swords that looked very like this one break again and again, so that no longer impressed her.

"*You* have made this sword," said the peddler in Faran. Soraya translated swiftly. "Not just Lupsh who forged it, but all of you—from the men who dug the ore, to the women and children who gathered wood for the fires, and even those who were taking an extra share of work, hunting and cooking, so that the rest of us could work at the forge, the smelter, or the mine."

He looked at their somber, sleepy faces and smiled. "You did this because you wanted to learn the secrets of making metal, which I have taught you as well as I could. And I taught you because I needed to learn the secrets of your shilshadu magic, and how to apply them to my craft. I think this is the sword that will prove how well we've learned."

His smile widened and he held out the sword to Dai. Dai wasn't a smith or a swordsman, for there were no swordsmen among the Suud. He wasn't the strongest man in the tribe either, though he was no weakling. What he was was the only Suud who had proved willing to strike the post with all his strength. For all the peddler's coaching, the others swung the swords hesitantly, reluctant to break something it had taken so much labor to create. Dai tried to break it, striking as if he understood the price that would be paid by a soldier whose sword broke in the midst of combat.

Despite her skepticism, Soraya tensed as he stepped up to the post. He drew back his arm in preparation for the blow that had broken so many blades, then swung with all his might.

The sword sank two inches into the wood, and stuck there. It vibrated, but it didn't break.

Dai let go of the hilt, grimacing, and shook his hand. The crowd's tension dissolved in laughter.

But the peddler wasn't laughing. "Pull blade out straight," he commanded in Suud, not needing eloquence for this. "All sword break if it pull side."

Dai evidently knew that already, for he cast the peddler an exasperated glance and worked the sword out of the post. He seemed to feel he had something to prove; he took the wooden hilt in both hands this time and swung even harder.

A chip of wood flew from the post the sword held. Dai attacked the post as if it were an enemy, swinging again and again, using the dull edge as well as the sharp one, even stabbing with the point. There were times when Soraya could have sworn she saw the blade flex . . . but it didn't break.

Panting, sweat covering his white skin, Dai glared at the blade. Then his glare lightened and faded into a huge grin. He handed the sword back to the peddler.

The Suud burst into cheers, but Soraya waited, knowing there was still a test to come. Ignoring the Suud, who were slapping each other's backs, even dancing in their excitement, the peddler held up the blade and scraped the sharp edge carefully over his arm.

Dai had used that sharp edge almost constantly,

sending fountains of chips into the air. Now, in the slowly growing light, Soraya could see the fine hairs on the peddler's arm fall away from the blade.

He looked up then, his eyes seeking hers. Even if she'd never had a trace of shilshadu magic, Soraya could have read the triumph there—and the message.

We're going to Mazad. Soon.

ON A FAIR AUTUMN DAY, *an elderly smith approached the Farsalan army.*

"I am too old to work," he told them. "So the Hrum cast me out, giving my forge into the hands of younger men. Now I am starving."

"We can give you some food, Grandfather," the soldiers told him. "Enough to help you on your way, but you'll have to find another place. We're here to fight the Hrum, and our own resources are small. We can't feed those who can't work."

The smith turned away, and clouds rushed to cover the sun. Sorahb didn't notice the clouds, but he did see the dejected slump of the old man's shoulders.

"Let him stay," said Sorahb, stepping forward. "His

muscles may be old, but how much wisdom, how much craft has he gained in his years of labor? As all men know, our swords break like green sticks upon the Hrum's blades. Let him stay, and let our swordsmiths learn from his great knowledge."

The clouds slid from the face of the sun as the old man smiled. "You'll not be regretting this, young master," said the ancient smith. "Showing true farr is a thing men never regret."

The smith was as good as his word, for he taught the Farsalan swordsmiths to make blades with the power of the storm's own lightning. The blades they forged were as strong as those of the Hrum, and Sorahb watched their testing with astonishment.

"Grandfather," he said, "you have given us a priceless gift. With these swords, surely we can defeat the Hrum."

"The swords will help, no doubt, no doubt," said the smith. "But to defeat the Hrum there are three things you must do—which I will tell you, if you will listen to the wisdom of a feeble old man."

CHAPTER FOUR

JIAAN

ON THE EVENING of their fifth day in the desert, the Hrum finally shed the last of their armor. The Farsalans had started shedding their silk-padded armor on the first day, along with their vests and everything else they could shed without exposing too much skin to the burning sun. It was the end of Bear, but a warm wind was sweeping over the mountains and the sun beat down. Jiaan would have sworn it was as hot as midsummer, but he'd been in this desert in the summer several times last year, arranging with the Suud to use their territory for a hidden base, and there had been times when he'd thought the sun would roast him alive. These autumn days—which Jiaan suspected would be pleasantly cool on the other side of the mountains—were merely hot.

But heat is hard to deal with when you're wearing a steel breastplate and helmet. Especially if you've spent the last five days marching through a rocky maze after phantoms.

It was Jiaan's Suud advisors who had suggested the trick, though "advisors" was perhaps too grand a title for the dozens of young men and teenage boys who had shown up to get a look at the Hrum.

When Jiaan had first negotiated with Maok and the clan council, he had asked for Suud guides and advisors to be provided for him, and he hadn't understood why Maok laughed. He understood now—the Farsalans and their Hrum pursuers were evidently the best entertainment the Suud had encountered in years. Jesters, to judge by their laughter. Most of the time Jiaan wished he could understand what the Suud were saying, but there were also times he was just as glad he didn't. And he was especially glad that Fasal couldn't understand them either.

When Fasal and some of the other men complained about being the butt of the Suud's jokes, Jiaan pointed out that, no matter how hard they laughed, the Suud's advice was good. The Suud were the ones who'd pointed out to him that although a determined man could walk down a horseman, walking down an unburdened horse was far harder. And walking down horses that have a chance to rest is completely impossible.

The Farsalans had spent their first five days in the desert on rotation: A quarter of their troops, with a handful of Suud guides, would lead half their chargers through the twisting maze of the badlands while three quarters of their troops and the other half of the horses rested to go out the next day.

By now the Hrum were hot, tired, and disgruntled, and the Farsalans, though also hot, were fresh and rested.

Perhaps that was why the Hrum commander had stopped early to make camp in a long, shallow valley between two steep ridges. It wasn't a bad place to camp, Jiaan conceded. There was shade from the large boulders on one side, and a small stream down the center provided water to drink and allowed the men to wash and cool down

No, Jiaan thought critically, *given what he knows, that ravine isn't a bad choice at all.* Of course, the Hrum commander didn't know everything.

Jiaan looked for the commander. In days of spying on the Hrum, both at march and at rest, he had long since learned to identify the man's lean, serious face. But even if he hadn't known what he looked like, Jiaan would have been able to pick the commander out in the crowd—he was the only man still in armor, though even he had unbuckled his breastplate and taken off his helmet. And why not? They'd been in the desert for five days, and all the Farsalans had done was run away.

Jiaan wished he remembered the man's name. The peddler had mentioned it when he warned Jiaan that the Hrum had assigned a tactimian with six centris to hunt down Sorahb and destroy the Farsalan army. The Farsalan army that now included about fourteen hundred men.

But most of those men were still mostly untrained and completely untried, and the Hrum were the best foot soldiers in the world. In a fair fight, on open ground, they could probably defeat all of Jiaan's troops—which was why Jiaan didn't intend to fight fair.

"Are the archers ready?" He spoke to Fasal in a murmur, though the wind was blowing against them and the Hrum below couldn't possibly hear him.

"The archers have been ready for days," Fasal grumbled. His eyes gleamed with excitement, even though he was so bad with a bow that Jiaan had assigned him to coordinate the retreat instead of taking part in the attack. Coordinating the retreat was important too—so important that Jiaan had assigned Aram as Fasal's assistant, to be sure the young deghan didn't overlook something important. Like the fact that they were supposed to retreat.

Jiaan remembered when Aram first approached the Farsalan army, so humbly unsure that a maimed man could be of any use. Without Aram's steadying presence at Jiaan's side, there wouldn't be a Farsalan army today.

Fasal was perfectly aware of his commander's hidden agenda, but not even he was foolish enough to disregard the one-handed veteran's advice. And Fasal had done a good job—he deserved a reward.

Jiaan looked down at the Hrum, who were now setting up their tents. The sentries the commander had posted looked alert, but they were also the only men who were holding shields.

"Give the command," he told Fasal, nocking an arrow.

Fasal shot him an astonished glance, but that split second was the only delay. "Begin!" he cried.

Jiaan bent his bow. He briefly considered shooting the commander, but the commander was still wearing his breastplate, and the range wasn't close enough to hit a man's throat. Jiaan chose one of the sentries instead. Shooting downhill, he only had to aim a bit over the man's head.

Fasal's shout had alerted them, but they didn't know where the attack would come from. The sentry was just turning toward the hissing arrows when Jiaan's shaft sunk into his chest.

His body spasmed, the shield falling from his grip. His hands rose to the arrow as he sank to his knees, then to the earth, still conscious, still alive, though probably not for long.

Jiaan gritted his teeth and thrust a surge of compassion to the back of his mind. On a great battlefield you fired into the massed ranks of the enemy and never knew if your shot went home or missed. Some part of Jiaan, foolishly, had always hoped his arrows missed. Today, he decided, he didn't care.

This is what war is. Jiaan drew another arrow. *And they started it.*

Even as he fired, several score of Hrum grabbed their shields and started scrambling up the ridge toward the archers. The men coming toward Jiaan were safe behind their shields, but the men going up the opposite hillside had their backs to him—and they still wore no armor.

Jiaan fired at one of them, and his arrow knocked the man off his feet to slide limply down the steep slope.

The soldiers charging toward Jiaan were also falling under a hail of arrows, from the other side of the narrow valley. Men in the camp were falling as they scrambled for armor, for cover, for their own bows.

A band of Hrum archers who'd taken shelter in the boulders on the opposite side of the valley floor finally got their bows strung. Half a dozen arrows arced toward Jiaan and the men stationed near him, but the Hrum archers were shooting uphill at a target that was largely invisible—most of their arrows fell short, shattering on the rocky hillside, and the rest whistled harmlessly over-head.

Jiaan smiled and sent an arrow back at them. His shot missed too, but only by inches, and a Hrum archer ducked back behind the rocks without firing the arrow he had nocked.

The Hrum commander had been shouting orders from the start. Jiaan now knew enough Hrum to understand "get back here!" and the Hrum words for "gather" and "middle," but most of the commands were unintelligible. The result, however, became visible when the Hrum formed their shield shell in the center of the valley.

It wasn't yet solid, and Jiaan sent another shot to arc between two sloppily held shields—though amidst the shouted orders and the screams of the wounded, he couldn't tell if he'd hit anyone.

He shot at another man, who was running for the safety of the shield formation. That arrow grazed the man's ribs, but evidently the injury wasn't serious, for he dashed in among his comrades and vanished.

Except when they opened it to admit stragglers, the shields now presented a solid barrier, and Jiaan lowered his bow.

"It looks like we killed more than forty of them!" said Fasal. "And I don't think we took a single casualty. Well done, Commander."

Jiaan stared at him, but there was no irony in his face or voice.

"Shall I order the retreat now?" Fasal asked. "They'll get organized enough to come looking for us sooner or later."

"Yes," said Jiaan. "Get everyone out of here. But send one of the Suud back to me—I'll meet you later in camp."

"You're not coming with us?"

Jiaan shook his head. "I want to see what the Hrum commander does now."

"What can he do?" asked Fasal. "We beat them soundly. There's nothing he can do."

And it doesn't occur to you that it might be worthwhile to see how this man reacts to defeat?

But even Jiaan wasn't certain what he hoped to learn. "I'll stay anyway—you go on ahead. Just send me a Suud guide, or I won't be able to find you myself."

Fasal shrugged. But he had the good sense to crawl back down the hill until he was out of the Hrum's sight before he rose to his feet and trotted off.

Jiaan returned his attention to the valley where the Hrum's shield formation was moving— first to the wounded men, some of whom, he was glad to see, had been picked up when the formation moved on. The dead were left behind. Jiaan stifled a sigh. This was war. Fasal would think him mad to regret the deaths of enemies—and Jiaan wasn't certain he was wrong.

As soon as they gathered up their wounded comrades, the Hrum picked up their gear and marched out of the small valley, maintaining their formation until there was no high ground within arrow range. When they finally lowered their shields, even at a distance Jiaan could see that they were all back in armor, except for the wounded, who were being carried on shields with more shields laid over them for their protection.

"Good good," said a Suud boy, coming up to crouch beside him. He was swathed from head to foot in the tightly woven striped robes the Suud wore to protect them from the sun. Even the ends of the sleeves were tied shut, to keep sunlight from touching his hands. Jiaan had thought their care excessive until, one overcast afternoon two weeks ago when they were trying to get their tents up before the desert's brief, heavy rain arrived, one young man had become impatient and freed his hands to tie a few knots. His blisters were barely healed, and Jiaan reminded himself again to be very careful to protect his "advisors" from the sun. Not that they couldn't protect themselves and their Farsalan allies, too, most of the time. Now the boy gestured to the valley below. "Hrum men not two times do this."

The corpses lay still in the blazing light. The scavengers would be coming for them soon.

"No," said Jiaan. "He won't make that mistake again. How do the Suud dispose . . what do you do with the bodies of the dead?"

"We bury," said the boy promptly. "Under dirt, then rocks, so the jackals can't eat. You want bury the Hrum bodies."

"Yes," said Jiaan, "if you can arrange it." Farsalans burned their dead, and he had no idea what the Hrum did, but anything would be better than leaving them for the jackals. They had been human, whatever else they were.

The Hrum commander might not make that mistake again, but he would make others. Jiaan had planned for it. There would be other bodies, and some of them would be Farsalan. "Yes," Jiaan repeated. "Bury them."

THE FIRST PART OF the next plan was to give the Hrum time to become careless again. The exhausted Hrum army had finally made their camp in the center of a wide valley, far enough from the ridges that no arrow could reach it.

"But we could attack them in the middle of the night," Fasal said. "Charge in on horseback and take them while they're tired. We have a significant advantage now."

"We'd also lose men," said Jiaan. "The Suud have a saying: 'The desert is the strongest spear.' If we wait, the desert will do most of our work for us."

He could almost see the words "a deghan would attack now" flash through Fasal's mind, but for once Fasal had the sense not to say it. Instead he stalked off to air his frustrations among the younger recruits, many of whom agreed with him.

In one sense he was right—the Hrum were tired now. But weary as they were, they had created a defensible camp and posted many sentries.

Their commander had the good sense to let his men rest over the next few days, allowing the lightly wounded to recover. When the Hrum marched out again they went in patrols of only a few centris, while the rest stood guard over the worst wounded and the camp. A camp that was now protected by a ditch and an earthen bank around all its perimeter, except where the stream flowed in and out.

"We should have charged them that first night," Fasal grumbled when he saw the new earthworks.

"And let them hide in the bushes and hamstring our horses from behind?" Jiaan asked. "Or hadn't you noticed how much brush there is in that camp? Enough to conceal dozens of archers, and men who could ambush attackers too."

He took small comfort from Fasal's embarrassed blush, for it had taken several days for him to realize how much cover was provided by the tall, stream-side bushes that filled the Hrum camp. Instead of cutting them back, which is what Jiaan had expected them to do, the Hrum were harvesting the bushes that grew outside their perimeter. They used the branches to create screens that would further conceal their tents and the movements of their men from any archers who might creep near.

A few quick experiments had taught Jiaan

that no fire arrows would set those boughs alight. Laid in the heart of a blaze, they smoldered and smoked for an amazing amount of time before catching fire, and then burned sluggishly. When he inquired, the Suud told him that the thick-leafed branches would stay green for weeks.

The Hrum's brush screens, along with the clearing of the bushes outside their perimeter, made sneaking near enough to the Hrum camp to do any good almost impossible. Impossible, at least, for Jiaan's archers. After watching the Suud trackers for the last few weeks, Jiaan wouldn't have bet that there was anything they couldn't do.

No, his best move was to allow the Hrum enough time to relax their guard and regain their arrogant confidence. So Jiaan assigned a handful of men to accompany the Suud who followed the Hrum patrols, and sent Fasal and most of his men back to their own permanent camp to rest and relax.

He was startled two days later when Isaf, who had gone with the Suud trackers to keep an eye on the Hrum, came running back into the temporary camp.

"Commander!" he gasped, looking around. His eyes were slitted against the brilliant light. "Where's the— There you are, sir. The Suud sent me to get you. The Hrum have captured a Suud hunting party! They were out on a long hunt and had set up their hutches to sleep out the day. The Hrum came around a bend and ran right into them."

Jiaan was already donning his ring-studded silk vest. "I thought all the Suud in the area had been informed about the Hrum's movements. They were supposed to keep out of their way!"

"Well, it looks like some of them didn't get the word," said Isaf, wiping his face.

The long dry spell had broken days ago in a series of afternoon storms, but today was sunny, and it was too hot to run. Another man handed Isaf a water skin, and he drank thirstily.

Jiaan closed his lips over his next question. He considered his options—there weren't many. "Get the men armed and ready to move," he told Aram.

"But sir, we've not more than fifty men here! If we send to the main camp, we can—"

"If we send to the main camp, they won't come in time to do any good," Jiaan interrupted. "They can't get here before the Hrum get their prisoners back to their camp," Jiaan had been told that the

Hrum didn't torture prisoners, but he wasn't certain he believed it. He knew that they took slaves.

He turned to Isaf. "Have the Suud hunters been harmed?"

"No sir, not yet. And when I left the Suud—our tracker lads, I mean—they had their spears out and were ready to attack if the Hrum made a move. But there's only six of them, and the Hrum have three centris!"

Jiaan had only fifty men—and a debt to his allies that was far greater than this.

"Can we ride there?" he asked Isaf crisply.

"No sir, too rough for horses. Almost too rough for men on foot. I had to climb down a couple of cliffs. They're small cliffs," he added hastily, "but—"

"Then we'll climb them," said Jiaan. He raised his voice. "Everyone! Arm and get ready to march."

Rushing through the twisted maze of canyons, Jiaan had time to think that if the Hrum wanted to set their own ambush this was the perfect way to do it. The only thing that kept him running, that made him willing to continue trading caution for speed, was the knowledge that the Hrum couldn't possibly have anticipated finding the Suud hunters' camp. Unless they'd somehow made contact with a Suud clan that would accept a bribe? No, surely not. If the Suud—any Suud—turned against the Farsalans, then Jiaan's army was doomed. All the tribes knew where the Farsalans' main camp was, and all they had to do was lead the Hrum there.

When Jiaan had first come to the desert, he had thought that the Suud gained their tactical advantage by traveling over the tops of the ridges and rocky buttes. But when he, tentatively, mentioned it, the whole clan had laughed at him. After spending almost a month in the desert Jiaan understood why. The ridges and shattered mesas were too disconnected for anyone to travel on for long; if you tried to do so, you wasted all your time and strength climbing in and out of the canyons that lay between them. The Suud's advantage, and it was considerable, was that they knew the best routes through the maze and the easiest passes from one route to another. But easiest didn't always mean easy. To reach the place where the Suud hunting party had camped, Jiaan's troop had to pass over two ridges—and the descent from one of them was sheer enough to leave him panting with fear as well as exertion by the time he reached the bottom.

It might have been a small cliff compared to the great rampart that separated the badlands from the mountains, but it was high enough that a fall from the top would kill. Jiaan's first descent into the desert had showed him that this was no place for someone who didn't like heights. He was only glad that Fasal wasn't there to see him sweat.

When they climbed the ridge that overlooked the valley where the Hrum had stopped, the first thing Jiaan noticed was that the only place they could fire arrows from was on the other side of the valley, and that the slope there was shallow enough that the Hrum could storm it.

The second thing he noticed was that the Suud, far from being shackled or slain, seemed to be having a very good time.

"The Hrum are feeding them?" he murmured to the hooded Suud tracker who met them at the top of the rise.

"They trade," the man said. He seemed fairly relaxed about the whole thing, although his gaze never left the scene below. "Hunter have gazelle. Hrum give bread stuff, take gazelle. Cook."

Jiaan could see that for himself. The carcass

was still mounted on its improvised spit, but a Hrum soldier was carving off slices for his waiting comrades. The Suud, who were clustered in the shade of a tumble of boulders, were already eating their portions. Except for the presence of the Hrum sentries it looked for all the world like a picnic—right down to the easy smile on almost every face.

"I don't understand, sir," said Aram. "This is the Hrum's chance to learn where we're camped. What are they doing?"

"The smart thing," said Jiaan softly. "That's what they're doing. We'll keep watch all the same, but I don't think we have to worry about making a sudden charge."

Just as he expected, the Suud eventually finished their "midnight" feast, and after some further talk with the Hrum commander returned to their hutches to await the night. The Hrum formed up and marched away.

Jiaan sent all but two of the trackers on to continue keeping an eye on them. One he sent to guide his men back to their own camp, though by now they might have been able to retrace the route on their own. The other, who spoke the best Faran of any of them, Jiaan kept to accompany him.

He waited out the long marks until dusk before descending to the valley. No point in two groups of foreigners interrupting the hunters' sleep.

To Jiaan's surprise, the leader of the hunting party was a woman. "She says good people," his guide translated. "Good, because make bargain."

"They made a bargain?" Jiaan asked in alarm.

The translator shook his head. "Sorry, she says *want* bargain. Hrum people want you people. Us help. Offer knives, spears, cloth—much, much."

He grinned at Jiaan. "She says Hrum Faran good good, but her Faran not. Hard talk. Hrum man tell her like you tell, Hrum take man for army. She makes only one trade, gazelle for bread stuff. Not two trade."

The Hrum commander had confirmed what Jiaan had told them about the Hrum's draft, so they'd decided not to switch sides. The draft was the main reason the Suud had agreed to help Jiaan's army in the first place, but that didn't keep his knees from going wobbly with relief.

"Thank her for me," he said. "Tell her that the

Hrum commander told the truth about them taking your young men for their army, and that the Farsalans will never do that. She made the right choice."

But as he turned away he couldn't help but wonder if the Hrum commander, in telling the truth, in dealing honorably with these people, hadn't made the right choice too.

JIAAN WAITED ANOTHER five days before setting his second ambush. This one entailed some risk, as he told his men when he returned to the main camp to gather his forces and ask for volunteers. The Hrum would have to be able to see the bait and follow the Farsalans for some time before they became excited enough to abandon the caution they'd practiced for the last week and a half.

He wasn't surprised when Fasal instantly stepped forward, but he was dismayed at how many of the newer, more hotheaded recruits instantly followed him. Since horsemanship was one of the main criteria for the men posing as bait, Jiaan accepted Fasal, but he inserted many of his sensible veterans into the party as well.

So far, the Suud trackers reported, the plan was

working beautifully. The Hrum had seen the small band of Farsalans at the end of the canyon—only a third of them on horseback!—and dashed off in eager pursuit.

A horse carrying one man, even with two more clinging to his saddle, could outrun men on foot—but as the Hrum knew, a horse so burdened couldn't keep up that pace for long. Crouched atop the mouth of the long, narrow canyon where his trap was set, Jiaan could hear their hoofbeats approaching. They'd dropped to a trot now, and perhaps it was only in his imagination that it sounded like a weary trot. They would be here soon.

Jiaan turned to the young Suud beside him, wishing he could see his face in the enveloping hood. "Are you ready with the rope?"

The Suud snorted. "Are you kidding? All life, boy, man, I want to push this rock. Old ones not let me. Say no need."

Jiaan raised his brows at the easy, colloquial Faran phrase—he could guess where the man had learned it. He had to admit it; the peddler was proving useful. Jiaan still hated him, but he could push hatred aside . . . for a time.

Looking at the boulder, which balanced on a ledge of smaller stones and looked like it should long since have tumbled into the canyon on its own, Jiaan understood the Suud's temptation. He smiled at the man. "We will push it today."

The horses were trotting up the wider valley now, their hides dark with sweat, their sides heaving. Jiaan couldn't yet see the Hrum who followed them, but he saw the glance Fasal shot over his shoulder, and his stomach clenched in excitement. They weren't far behind.

The horses neared the canyon's entrance. It was wide enough to admit horses, and Jiaan had planned for his men to ride them in, even though it would mean killing the horses in the end, for when the rock fell there would be no way out of the sheer-walled trap. But Fasal had refused, claiming that if the horses were tired enough the Hrum wouldn't be suspicious when the Farsalans abandoned them. Since Jiaan had placed Fasal in charge of bringing the Hrum into the snare, he had let him have his way—and had been grateful to do so, truth be told.

From his place beside the huge boulder, Jiaan watched as Fasal leaped off his horse—not his precious mare, not in anything this risky. The others were already running through the narrow gap into the canyon, but Fasal spent valuable moments guiding the horses toward the wider route, slapping their rumps, sending them on down the track that led to a valley where they could be reclaimed.

Perhaps he had delayed so long that the Hrum saw him darting into the crevice. Perhaps they had been tracking the running men so long that the fact that the horse tracks went one way and the men's another wasn't enough to confuse them, even for an instant—though they probably thought that was what the Farsalans intended. Whatever they thought, the only thing that slowed them as they jogged forward was the fact that five men couldn't pass through the narrow gap abreast.

Jiaan watched, impressed in spite of himself, as the left line of the running column sheered off to one side, formed new ranks as the others passed through, and then followed after them. Two hundred men through that narrow crevice in only a handful of seconds with no confusion. Jiaan hadn't even heard any orders. The Hrum were accustomed to moving in formation, but it was still remarkable. He knew his Farsalans, even the best trained among them, couldn't have done it nearly as well.

He looked down to the far end—the dead end of the small canyon. His men might not move well in formation, but they were very competent in other things. The first of Fasal's troop were just being hauled over the lip of the cliff on the long ropes, and even Fasal, who had doubtless insisted on going up last, was halfway up the cliff face and rising rapidly as the Farsalans who weren't archers drew him up.

The archers, Jiaan knew, were already in position, and the stream of silver helmets was already almost fifty yards from the canyon's entrance. Jiaan fought down a desire to wipe his sweaty palms on his britches and turned to the Suud.

"Pull the rope," he said.

They had threaded the rope behind some of the small stones that underlay the forward edge of the great boulder—not a hard task, for if you lay down and looked at the right angle, you could see daylight on the other side.

Now half a dozen Suud, hands and faces invisible in their thick robes, grabbed the ends of the rope and pulled. Jiaan heard a grinding sound, but nothing else happened.

Jiaan waved another eight of his Farsalans to the rope. He'd wanted them there in the first place, but the Suud had said it was their rock and they wanted to push it!

They would soon get the chance. The angle was bad, for the boulder was near enough to the cliff that the men on the rope were only a few feet from the edge—Jiaan was glad he wasn't one of them. But more than a dozen men now had hold of the rope, hauling in unison. The smaller rocks grated, snapped, then flew across the canyon, striking the opposite wall as if flung from a giant sling.

The great boulder seemed so precariously balanced that Jiaan held his breath, thinking it might fall of its own weight—but it simply sat, with the placid immobility of stone.

The Hrum commander had stopped, almost three hundred yards into the narrow canyon, and was gazing up at the sheer walls that surrounded him. "Back!" he shouted suddenly in Hrum. "Go back! It's a *neret*!"

Jiaan realized that he had just learned the

Hrum word for trap, but he had no time to dwell on it.

"Push the rock," he commanded. "Now!"

The men who held the rope dropped it and swarmed back, even though they weren't in the boulder's path. Jiaan sympathized. If something that big was going to move, he'd prefer to be well out of its way.

He stepped back himself, as a handful of Suud and as many of his Farsalans as could find a space behind the boulder ran forward and shoved with all their might.

The rock didn't budge.

The men leaned down and laid their shoulders against the back of the boulder, thrusting with their thighs, and others found spaces to add their hands to the rock and push.

The rock didn't budge, and the Hrum were coming back toward the entrance of the canyon.

"Archers!" Jiaan shouted. "Now!"

The arrows rained down, fast and hard. But the men below were armored, and many had already raised their shields, expecting the attack. There were a few cries of pain, but not enough to stop the troop. The Hrum were about to escape.

"Push!" Jiaan ran to the boulder himself. There was no open space behind it, but he found a place to brace his hands against it, pushing it toward the cliff with all his strength. It was like trying to push the earth itself—not the slightest hint of yielding, no cracking from the fragile stones beneath it. But it looked so precarious!

Jiaan heard the clatter of armored men running. It sounded as if they were right under his feet.

The Hrum were escaping. He pushed on the boulder, the muscles in his back clenched with effort. The rock wasn't moving, and despair sapped Jiaan's strength.

Then one of the shrouded Suud stepped up beside Jiaan and laid his cloth-covered hands on the rock—lightly, not pushing at all.

Perhaps he was trying to feel a hint of motion, some sign that the rock would give way—but there was no motion, no sign. Jiaan was about to step back and order the others off, when all of a sudden the rock shifted.

"Heave!" he cried, his voice all but lost in the grunts of effort around him. It was probably the most unnecessary order he'd ever given, for the others had already redoubled their efforts. Slowly, slowly, the great rock tipped. Slowly, but gathering speed, it overturned, ground its way down the slope to the top of the cliff, and then toppled into the canyon.

The echoes of the crash blended with the ringing in Jiaan's ears, but he heard other rocks falling as well.

He walked carefully to the edge of the cliff and looked down.

The Hrum who had escaped were fleeing down the canyon, perhaps fearing a further barrage of arrows. Jiaan wished he had thought to place archers on those ridges. He couldn't make a precise count of the mass of running men, but it was clear that most of the Hrum had escaped—Razm, djinn of cowardice, take them. It had been such a good plan too!

He walked down the ridgetop and looked at the canyon on the other side. The boulder had not only blocked the entrance, as Jiaan had known it would, it had also brought down several large slabs of the cliff with it, creating an impassable slope—at least for men who would have to make that climb with hundreds of archers shooting at them.

Looking down into the canyon, Jiaan saw that most of the men there had no hope of climbing. Three of them were seated, two clutching blood-stained arrows in thigh and calf. The only man still on his feet was wrapping a strip of cloth around the arm of a third man, where an arrow had evidently passed though.

The man finished with the awkward bandage and then stepped back, looking up at the Farsalan soldiers who lined the canyon. Or more accurately, at the hundreds of bows, arrows nocked and pointed right at him. His shoulders moved slightly, something between a shrug and a nervous twitch. Very slowly, he drew his sword and laid it on the ground. Then he removed his helmet and placed it next to the sword.

"That's the Hrum commander!" Fasal's breathless voice exclaimed. He must have run over the ridgetop at reckless speed to get here so swiftly. "He's surrendering! What do we do?"

"We accept," said Jiaan. "We lower some ropes and haul him and his people out of there." He looked around for the man who had laid his hands on the rock, but the Suud were anonymous in their robes unless you noticed the pattern of the stripes, and Jiaan had been too busy for that.

Fasal, still looking down the canyon, snorted. "He pulled the wounded back when the rocks started to fall. He could have made it out himself, and as commander it was his duty to escape. And now he's surrendering, the stinking coward."

"Sometimes," said Jiaan, "it takes more courage to surrender than to fight." He remembered the night after the battle of the Sendar Wall. Dying had seemed so easy then, and living so hard. Did this Hrum commander feel that way now?

"*Our* commander fought to the death!" said Fasal proudly.

Jiaan made no reply.

CHAPTER FIVE

KAVI

THEY HAD INTENDED to sneak past the sentries at night, but with the early winter storm beginning to build, Kavi had urged them to try it during the rain.

"Sentries who're all wet and miserable aren't thinking about anything except getting dry," he told them.

The girl had been dubious, but the Suud agreed with him.

"Storm noise stop noise you make, and water in eyes much good than dark." Daralk spoke in Faran, out of courtesy to the local farmer who had agreed to act as their guide. The Suud were a courteous folk,

Kavi had found, though he was pretty sure that when Daralk said "you," he was referring to Kavi alone. But if he was making that small joke, Kavi could hardly blame him, for the Suud made no more noise than mice in the dry brush, and the lady Soraya was almost as skilled.

Kavi had been skeptical, then stunned, and finally delighted when the things the girl and Maok had told him about his own gift had proved no joke at all. Working steel again, even if he could only do it with that odd part of his mind that Maok had awakened, had been as much pain as pleasure, especially at first. But if part of his heart ached for his lost craft, another part took consolation in teaching the Suud. They needed steel, and even with the most primitive equipment they had learned as fast as any apprentices Kavi had seen. It had been a relaxed, pleasant time, and he was grateful for it.

But he also knew they had reached the limit of what they could accomplish in the desert. If the Farsalans were to get strong swords in time to do them any good, it would take a town, a metal-working town, to make them.

So now, as the sky opened up and the cold,

dreary rain of a winter storm pelted down, Kavi crouched behind a screen of leafless branches and stared at the sentry standing on the road. Who would have thought the Hrum would post a guard this far outside the city?

"It's the siege camp's new commander," said the farmer softly. "He doesn't know how we were getting food in—they've not learned about the aqueduct—but that bastard Nehar reported to the Hrum whenever we did, and the commander kept pushing his sentry lines out and out, until they ended up between us and the tunnel hatch." He frowned. "We haven't gotten a shipment in for over a month now. The odd lad bringing messages can get through, but nothing like a big load of foodstuffs. With the new taxes, food's getting harder to come by anyway. And there are more patrols out as well."

Rain was beginning to drip down Kavi's face, but he thought the guard should be allowed to get a bit wetter before they tried anything. "What's the food—"

A bolt of lightning flashed and thunder rumbled, loud enough to make Kavi flinch. The winter rains didn't usually have much lightning in them—

slow and sullen they were—but this early storm seemed livelier than most. The girl was studying the sky. She had flinched at the lightning too, and now she seemed tense, but Kavi found her very hard to read these days. She'd been better company after he'd broken her out of Garren's slave pen—gratitude and all. But that was before she'd decided to kill him. Deghan gratitude was a fickle thing.

"What's the food situation in Mazad?" he asked, "if they're not getting any more supplies?"

The farmer rubbed his grizzled chin. From his days as an apprentice in the city, Kavi knew the man. He recognized the mannerism as one that heralded bad news.

"Not so good, I fear," the farmer admitted. "They've still got a lot of their stockpile, of course. But our shipments were never enough to feed a city that size—at best, we were only helping stretch things a bit. And now the stockpile's beginning to run low. I heard that Commander Siddas wanted to start rationing, but the governor won't allow it. Of course, he's got his reasons."

Kavi nodded. "Did they ever find out how Governor Nehar was communicating with the

Hrum? Last I heard, Siddas was planning on catching him in the act, and using that to turn the better men in the garrison against him."

"Oh, they found out," said the farmer. "For all the good it did. Nehar ties a letter around an arrow shaft and has one of his guardsmen shoot it out into the ruins. Some spot the Hrum know to check. But it's been impossible to catch him at it, for he only uses his own lads, the ones whose loyalty he's sure of. And even if anyone thought to question a guardsman shooting an arrow from the walls, why, he saw something move in the ruins and thought he might be spying a Hrum attack. But no one yelled, so it was likely nothing but a rabbit or a cat, and nothing to worry about."

Kavi's brows rose in surprised respect. "That's clever—simple enough it almost can't fail."

A flash of lightning illuminated the farmer's grim face. "Somebody told me Garren himself came up with the notion. And no one's ever called him stupid."

"No," Kavi sighed. The first thing Garren had done, in retaliation for the siege towers' destruction, was to impose higher taxes on every village in the area. He wasn't sure if the Hrum governor had intended it, but gathering food for Mazad had become far harder. Yet it wasn't enough pressure to push the peasants into outright rebellion. Not quite.

"We should try now," said the girl. She sounded more urgent than Kavi thought the situation warranted, though he was certainly wet and cold, and the Suud in their day robes were naught but lumps of sodden fabric.

"I'll draw off the guard," said Lakka, speaking Suud now that clarity was important. He knew Kavi understood the language better than he spoke it. Although that wasn't saying much.

"Are you sure?" the girl asked in the same tongue. "This isn't the *shapulu* you're used to."

"Terrain"? Kavi wondered. *"Environment"?* But Lakka's hooded face had turned toward him for permission.

Kavi looked toward the Hrum sentry. He still held his shield at his side, with one hand on his sword hilt—the approved Hrum sentry pose—but his shoulders were hunched against the rain, and the pelting drops had to be making it noisy inside that helmet.

"Go," said Kavi. "But take care."

Even in the shadow of the hood, Kavi could see Lakka's confident grin. The man crawled off through the underbrush without making any sound that could be heard over the patter of rain, and the farmer's eyes widened.

The girl grinned. "Watch this. The Suud are the best—"

The lightning wasn't close this time, but it silenced her, and even after the thunder finished grumbling she said nothing.

In that silence, Kavi heard the swift drumming of a grouse's mating dance. *In the rain?* He looked over and met the girl's eyes. She was smiling a fierce, deghass sort of smile.

The sentry's head had turned toward the sound. Kavi could almost hear him thinking, *In the rain?*

The drumming stopped.

The sentry shrugged and settled back.

The drumming began again, this time a bit farther from the road. It stopped, then started again. And again.

The sentry was cold, wet, and bored. He went to investigate.

The next time the drumming sounded, it was

even farther off. The Hrum sentry followed it around the side of the hill and out of sight.

"The hatch is in a shallow ravine," Kavi told the girl swiftly. "Just behind that big clump of bushes back there. You and Lupsh and Orop first."

The girl blinked. "You're not coming?"

"I'll come last," said Kavi. "Now go!"

Lupsh and Orop started up, but the girl reached out and caught their arms. "Wait," she commanded.

Kavi scowled. She seemed to be listening, but he couldn't hear—

Lightning filled the road with lurid light, and thunder pealed.

"Now!" She spoke in Suud, and the three of them darted onto the road and across. Soon they were making their way into the bushes on the other side. They made no sound Kavi could hear, but he did hear the drumming of a grouse in the distance.

The farmer's jaw had dropped. "How did she know . . . ?"

Kavi had sworn to keep the Suud's magic a secret, and in truth he had no idea how she'd known when the lightning would strike—storms were no part of his sweet gift. "The Suud are more attuned to nature than we are. They can detect signs that we don't know about."

Of course, the lady Soraya wasn't a Suud . . .

"Humph," said the farmer. "Well, that lad who's playing the bird is certainly good. But he won't be able to pull that sentry off too far—he's supposed to be watching this stretch of road. And if he hears anything back here . . ."

"That's why I'm going last," Kavi told him. "Compared to the rest of them, I sound like an ox in rut. Adalk, Rosu, Marib—go!"

Despite the wet fabric clinging to their legs, the Suud moved over the road like ghosts, fading into the bushes on the other side.

Only Kavi, Daralk, and Lakka were left to cross. Kavi thought Lakka could manage on his own—in fact he could probably manage better on his own.

Kavi grinned at Daralk. "Come on, then."

He let Daralk precede him down the leaf-strewn, slippery hillside and onto the muddy track. Kavi was just weighing the merits of a quick dash against the need for silence when Daralk, who was already halfway across, spun and hurried back, grabbing Kavi's arm and hauling him up the hill.

Kavi opened his mouth to ask why, but then shut it again since the answer was obvious—Daralk must have seen someone on the road, and Kavi had a fair guess as to whom. They barely made it back to the hollow where the farmer lay before the sentry appeared, picking his way over the muddy surface. It was a good thing his attention was on his feet.

Kavi sank down beside the farmer.

"Bad luck, lad," the man murmured.

The sentry resumed his post, and a few moments later Lakka crawled up beside them.

"Hrum not follow bird again," he said. "Other Hrum see him—say bad bad. Other noise make him . . ." He hissed in exasperation as his vocabulary failed.

"Suspicious," Kavi supplied. "And you're right about that. But tell me"—he turned to the farmer—"how many guards are posted behind these lads?"

"None. Not till you get near the Hrum's siege camp," said the farmer promptly.

"So if we could move down the road and get

ourselves past another of the guards, we could make our way back to the hatch?"

The man took a moment to consider. "You could," he finally answered. "Without too much trouble, either. But if some officer just told one of them off for leaving his post, it'll take more than bird sounds to lure the others away."

"That's all right," said Kavi. "I've an idea. At least . . . do the wild ducks still settle in that slow bit of water near the river bend?"

IT SHOULD HAVE BEEN a garland of flowers, but at this time of year a garland of juniper was the best he could do. It was prickly, too, but Kavi managed to twine some thin twigs into a rough circlet. He pulled Duckie's long ears through it and settled the garland on the mule's head. Duckie, who sometimes received the same treatment from giggling village girls, gave Kavi a disgusted look but made no other protest.

"It needs to be brighter," said Kavi. "This won't be getting their attention."

"I thought you wanted me to board her," said the farmer. "In fact, you've already paid me for it."

"Don't understand," said Lakka. "Mule likes ducks?"

"I do want you boarding her," Kavi told the farmer. "I can get the Hrum chasing after her, but if you claim her as your own, they won't be trying to keep her. Especially if—ah, that's the thing!"

"Mule likes ducks?" Daralk asked, laughter shaking his voice.

"That she does, lad," the farmer replied. "And they like her, too. Several men were selling her, once they found they couldn't keep her out of the duck ponds, nor use her for any work without half a dozen of the beasts waddling after her, quacking—and pecking, too. She was on her fifth owner, who claimed he was developing a taste for mule meat, before Kavi took her on."

"Got her cheap because of it," said Kavi, digging busily through the pack where he kept ladies' goods. "Not that it hasn't given me trouble as well." The ribbons' cheap dye might run in the rain, but that wouldn't matter much, and the wet wouldn't harm the brass foals in the least, if he could only find . . . "Here they are!"

He held up the sack of foals some foolish woman had pierced to string for bangles. She'd been astonished when no one would accept them as money anymore. Kavi had taken them in trade, planning to melt them down for the metal, but he'd never gotten around to it. They were still bright, though, and there were lots of them.

"Here." He handed some ribbons to the Suud. "Tie the coins a bit apart, like this. And you," he added to the farmer, "can offer the Hrum the money if they'll help you get her out of the water. It might even save you a bit of wet." He took some of the shorter bits of ribbon and started tying coins into the garland on Duckie's head. It certainly looked odd.

"I'm already wet," said the farmer. But he went to work helping the Suud, and the four of them soon had Duckie's harness draped in a web of bright ribbons. Duckie snorted and shook herself, and the coins clattered.

"Now what?" the farmer asked, over the Suud's quiet hilarity.

"Now for the final touch," said Kavi. A sharp knife sliced a hole in the seam of one of the bags hanging from Duckie's pack. He took out his purse, removed all the silver mares from the pile of smaller coins, and put them in his pocket.

There weren't many, he was sorry to see. The brass went into the bag, and Kavi shook it down to the bottom.

"Hmm." He made the hole a bit bigger, and several coins fell out. "I suppose that's as close as it's going to get."

"You really think that will pull Hrum sentries out of position?" the farmer asked skeptically. "They'd get in more trouble than any brass is worth, if they were caught."

"Which is why they'll never be admitting it happened," Kavi replied, wishing he felt as confident as he sounded. "The Hrum are human, and there's no man or woman born that won't be picking up money if it falls at their feet. All we have to do is get Duckie onto the road. And the Wheel must be turning for us, for the wind is coming from the right direction."

That Duckie would follow the scent of ducks was as certain as rain being wet. They had to maneuver behind the low hills to approach the road without being seen, but even before they reached it, Duckie stopped suddenly, sniffing and sniffing. She drew in a breath, and Kavi reached for her nose, then changed his mind. The Hrum would be seeing a mule soon enough—no harm in their hearing one.

"Hee haw, hee haw!"

The farmer winced. "Loud, isn't she?"

Kavi unfastened the lead rope from Duckie's halter. He didn't need to swat her rump, for the minute she was free Duckie trotted toward the road—the shortest route toward the scent of her favorite companions.

"Come." Lakka gestured to the hill beside them. "Come look." He added a sentence in Suud that Kavi didn't catch, though he thought it equated to, "This I've got to see!"

With the Suud leading they climbed up the muddy hillside, reaching the top in time to see Duckie approach the new Hrum sentry. The man had drawn his sword, and Kavi suffered a moment of horrible doubt. He had meant Duckie to look strange, not threatening, but in the poor visibility of the storm . . .

Lightning flashed, so near that the thunder struck like a blow and the coins on Duckie's barding lit up like candles.

"Holy Mikkrah!" the Hrum exclaimed.

Duckie had shied at the thunderclap, but once

the nasty sound was gone, she continued on her way. She belonged to a peddler who sold knives— a bared blade in a man's hand held no terrors for her. She trotted within feet of the sentry, ears pricked in single-minded determination.

The Hrum simply stared as she went past, turning to watch her go. Kavi held his breath—at this distance he couldn't see the pouch. Had all the coins already fallen out? Was the hole still too small? Duckie was almost around the next bend before the sentry squinted, then stepped forward and picked something small out of the mud. He hesitated for a moment, looking up and down the road, then sheathed his sword and followed.

Kavi heard a distant voice exclaim in Hrum, "What in the . . ." and the sentry's reply: "Grab her! She's carrying money!"

Kavi laughed softly. "Only a fool tries to get between Duckie and ducks."

The farmer grinned. "I guess I'd best be claiming my mule, and getting home from that wedding I went to. My wife will be wondering where I am and all."

Kavi frowned. "Let them know you've a long trip home. Several days' walk, maybe. I wish there were some way to keep them quiet about this. There's a number of Hrum who know Duckie's habits, and they know she's mine."

The farmer shrugged. "If anyone questions me, I'll say I bought—no, borrowed her off a peddler, to give the folks at the wedding a laugh. Charged me high, you did. You'd better be going now, though."

"Not if they're trying to catch Duckie," said Kavi. "We've got plenty of time." He clasped the man's wrist warmly, then followed the Suud down the hill and across the soggy road.

It took time to work their way back up to the ravine that concealed the hatch, though lightning flared occasionally to show them the path— sometimes near enough to be alarming. Reaching the narrow, brush-filled ravine, Kavi wasn't surprised to find the Suud huddled below a shallow ledge—but he saw no sign of the girl anywhere.

"Where is she?" he asked, in his clumsy Suud.

"Under the *odlo*," said Adalk in the same language, gesturing toward a thin trench that undercut the base of the wall. "She's afraid of the lightning. I understand that, for it's been *reksh* very near. But she told us to stay away from her, and I don't understand that. Someone that afraid should want people near."

Kavi didn't understand either. "Wait a moment." He went down the bank to the deepest part of the undercut. Now that he knew she was there, he could see most of her arm and a bit of one hip, but she'd pulled herself as far into the crevice as she could.

"Come out, girl. We'll soon be in the aqueduct, and safer there than anywhere."

The arm twitched, but didn't move otherwise except for shivering. Kavi shrugged, grabbed her arm, and dragged her out. Her muscles tensed, and for a moment he thought she was going to fight him. Under the dirt, her face was as white as a Suud's, and her eyes were wild.

He pulled her against his chest, feeling the cold of her body through all the layers of both their clothing. For another long moment she resisted. Then she buried her face in his shirt and burst into gasping sobs.

"There now, there now." He rocked her as if she were one of Nadi's little ones. "Why didn't you tell me you were afraid of storms?"

"I'm not," she choked. "A deghass isn't afraid of anything."

"Ah well, that explains it," he said, dryly enough to bring her to her senses.

She pushed him away and staggered to her feet, her face flushed now—and cleaner, since most of the mud had been deposited on Kavi's shirt.

"We should go." She cast a nervous glance at the sky, but her voice was cool—the lady returned. Kavi sighed. But he'd have comforted anyone that afraid. And not teased them about it afterward, either.

"So we should," he said.

They hadn't penetrated deep enough into the ravine to find the great hatch, which wasn't surprising. Unless you knew that the ravine widened again, it looked as if it ended in the mass of brush he now led them through.

When the aqueduct was built, this path had been clear, for this was the hatch where they'd removed the stone and earth, and hauled building supplies in—though it had been partially concealed even back then; that old governor had had no intention of providing an easy invasion route into the only walled city in the whole of Farsala. A city the governor's gahn had built walls around because it was the source of all his army's weapons. Now Mazad would provide weapons again, not for the deghans in their proud skirmishing with the Kadeshi warlords on the eastern border, but for the real Farsalans, to rid themselves of the Hrum and then rule themselves for the first time in . . . for the very first time, as far as Kavi knew.

His exalted intentions made the aqueduct no less dark, for their torches were wet, and they sputtered and smoked. Water from the rising river rushed down the channel between the narrow walkways. It was cold.

This time, at least, the tunnel guards recognized Kavi and didn't demand that he bare his arm. He was already known to be marked as a Hrum spy—and even if he'd only been forgiven by the slightest shifting of the Wheel, forgiven by the council he had been, and that was what mattered.

The guards were so startled by the Suud, who had lowered their hoods in the underground tunnel, revealing their demon-white faces and hair, that they might have forgotten to search for the tattoo anyway.

The Suud ventured into Mazad even less often than they did other Farsalan cities, for Mazad's smithies had close ties with the miners, and the Suud . . . well, the Suud didn't exactly fear the miners, who had so often invaded their desert in search of the legendary "superior" ore, but they'd been forced to kill a fair few of them—and been killed by them too, from what Kavi had heard.

Having dealt firsthand with the desert ore, Kavi knew that it had some hardening element in it, but the steel it made still suffered from the brittleness that plagued all hard steel.

He had wondered, working with the Suud, if some ancient smith had persuaded them to use their shilshadu magic on a cooling blade, and had somehow started the rumors of legendary ore that persisted to this day. And now Kavi was bringing the Suud into the City of Forges itself, to use their gifts. He shivered. But if Maok and the Suud council had feared revealing their secret magic more than they feared the Hrum, then they wouldn't have let them go—or Kavi, either.

He repressed another shiver. It was cold in here, Flame take it, even walking. The girl was shivering like a drenched kitten, and so were the desert-bred Suud.

Kavi hustled them up the ladder that led into

a seldom-used warehouse, and then out into the street with little regard for concealment—if no one had revealed the secret of the aqueduct to Governor Nehar and his pet guardsmen by now, it was unlikely anything Kavi did would make a difference. Besides, the rain was keeping folks inside.

Up one familiar street and down another they traveled, the Suud's bare feet slapping the cobbles, for they were too cold to move with their usual quiet.

Kavi opened the gate to Tebin's work yard and herded the others straight into the forge, without so much as a knock before flinging open the familiar door.

The sudden heat was paradise, and the scent of hot metal was home. The clatter of work died as a dozen apprentices and journeymen stared open-mouthed at the sudden invasion of shrouded barbarians. The only sound breaking the silence was that of chattering teeth.

Then Tebin stepped forward, the astonishment on his face melting into laughter.

"As entrances go, Kavi lad, I think you've just topped the one you made when Feroz Butcher set his dogs on you and the little one still had his teeth in your britches as you burst through the door."

It was too colloquial for the Suud to follow, but the girl laughed, and Kavi felt his face grow warmer still.

"I've brought you some apprentices," he said, with all the dignity he could muster. "For they're in need of more teaching than I can give them—and they've a thing to be teaching you as well."

"Oh?" Curiosity dawned in Tebin's eyes, then deepened as he looked at the bedraggled Suud, who were shedding their wet robes—removing more clothing than most Farsalans would have done in public. But with Tebin, kindness always came first. "Well, it seems to me that this learning and teaching will keep till tomorrow, for you're all wetter than drowned rats—and unless I'm much mistaken, these lads are up in the middle of the night! Warm food, warm beds, and then, lad, you and I will be having a chat."

Kavi felt a surge of gratitude, despite the way Tebin's voice had firmed on the final words, but the girl beat him to speech.

"Thank you, sir," she said, as sincerely as any girl might, and not like a deghass at all.

CHAPTER SIX

—∞—

SORAYA

THE SOUND OF METAL striking metal awakened Soraya shortly after dawn. She yawned and buried her face in her pillow—a proper feather pillow, though the mattress was stuffed with straw and very similar to the ones she'd grown accustomed to in the Suud . . . the Suud! Her eyes snapped open. Were they awake? Probably. Soraya, exhausted, had eaten her bowl of hot oats and honey and slept through the evening and a full night. For the Suud, sleeping a whole night through would be unnatural, even if they had been up most of the day before.

And they hadn't been as tired as Soraya was, for

they hadn't been as frightened. She shuddered again at the memory of the storm, at the knowledge that the lightning was somehow attuned to *her*. She wished, passionately, that she'd paid more attention to Maok's lectures. Like the breeze, and the fires that sometimes flared up as she passed them, the storm had responded to her tension, her fear of the Hrum sentries. Unlike a soft breeze, or even a campfire, an aroused storm could prove deadly for her and everyone around her. And if she could do that to a sleepy winter rain, what would happen when the summer thunderstorms raged?

Soraya shivered, and resolved to perfect her control long before the summer came. But now, Azura be thanked, the sun was rising—and her Suud friends might need a translator.

Soraya pulled herself reluctantly from the warm bed. The muddy shirt and britches she'd shed last night were gone, and draped over a chair were a blouse, skirt, and vest—bright with gaudy peasant color and crude embroidery, but better than her wet and muddy clothes. Soraya dressed and ran her fingers through her short black hair. Kavi had cut it several months ago, when he'd disguised her as a peasant boy to help her escape from the Hrum, and the ends still didn't reach her shoulders. It probably looked odd with the skirt, but the skirt itself felt strange after all this time in her comfortable boy's britches.

Soraya shrugged, left the small room under the eaves, and went down the narrow stairs, where she followed the sound of voices to the kitchen.

There were no Suud present, but the peddler and Master Tebin sat at the table, both looking heavy-eyed as they listened to a man in the black and green tabard of the Mazad city guard. A woman was frying stacks of flat cakes at the stove. She looked up at Soraya's entrance and nudged the half-grown girl beside her. The child glanced at Soraya and then reached for a cup and the kettle.

Soraya vaguely remembered Master Tebin saying something about a woman who worked for him. The girl met Soraya as she approached the table and handed her a mug filled with steaming tea. The gangly child, just entering adolescence, was much the same height as Soraya—who suddenly realized where her borrowed clothing must have come from and smiled her thanks. The girl smiled shyly in return, but Soraya's attention had

147

already turned to the conversation at the table, and she sat down and joined the men.

"So when do you think we'll be seeing these wonderful swords?" the guardsman asked. "I find it hard to believe that people who couldn't even make an iron axe last summer can now make a blade to equal the Hrum's." His head was bald on top; the hair that remained to him was iron gray, and, short as he cut it, it still retained a hint of peasant curl. His manner was relaxed, almost kindly, but the eyes resting on the peddler were shrewd, and there was something about his question that demanded an answer.

"It's a trick of craft," said the peddler easily. "Nothing to do with the desert ore. Which is good, for with the Hrum patrols thick as they are, getting large amounts of ore into the city would be impossible. But Master Tebin's got both hard steel and soft right here in the yard that will be fine."

The guardsman frowned. "I know he's been experimenting with folding the metals," he said. "And I know it failed."

"Sorry, I'm not making myself clear," said the peddler amiably. "It's a craft *secret*. At least till we can be making it work."

Soraya blinked. She didn't think she could stand up to the commanding guardsman that firmly.

The guardsman's eyes turned to Tebin.

"Don't look at me," the swordsmith told him. "I've no clue what the secret might be. I'd think the whole tale was moonshine, except that one of those Suud lads has a sword he forged himself, and the steel would match that of any Hrum blade."

"Ah," said the guardsman. "But did he forge it himself? Or did he steal it from the Hrum, and is using it to gain your craft secrets?"

Tebin met the peddler's eyes and they both burst into laughter. "Sorry, Siddas," the smith gasped. "But when you see this sword . . . Trust me, no Hrum would be caught dead with that blade. I can't prove that young Lupsh forged it himself, but it looks just like a sword made by someone who's only been working metal for a few months. No, I'm lying—it actually looks like something forged by an apprentice who's had . . . oh, nine months of training. But from what I saw last night, Lupsh is a talented lad."

"Last night?" Soraya asked, startled.

"Yes," said Tebin, nodding a greeting now that

the conversation had turned her way. "Not being accustomed to sleeping the night through, the Suud woke up again just a few marks past midnight, and having nothing else to do they went down to look at the forge. They tried to be quiet, but the forge . . . well, it's not a quiet kind of place. So when Kavi and I woke up, we went down and joined them. I'm surprised we didn't wake you, lass—ah, lady—with the racket we made."

"I'm surprised you didn't need a translator," said Soraya, feeling a bit left out. "Where are they now?"

"Asleep in the forge loft," said the peddler. "In the other apprentices' beds, though we'll be getting them their own beds soon. We worked out that they'd get up around evening, work from just after dinner into the middle of the night, then go to bed 'early.'" He grinned. "We're putting half our apprentices and journeymen on the same schedule, as well as me and Master Tebin, so they'll have plenty of company. And the forge is kept dark—all forges are, to make it easier to see the true color of hot metal—so they'll be safe from the sun and not have to wear those robes around the fire. That's a blessing in itself."

Soraya had never considered the danger of the

Suud's flowing robes around the glowing embers and hot metal of a smithy, but now she did, and shuddered.

"I'll have some late nights then," she mused aloud. "You'll need a translator."

"Actually, Lady Soraya," said the guardsman. "I have another task in mind for you, if you'll do it."

"Another task?" Soraya scowled. "Who are you, sir, to be giving anyone tasks?"

"Ah," said Tebin hastily. "Forgive me. Lady Soraya, this is Commander Siddas, in charge of the *loyal* city guard. Commander, the lady Soraya."

He didn't add "of the House of the Leopard," as a formal introduction would demand, but Soraya didn't care.

"Commander. I've heard of you."

What she'd heard was good, but as the light-brown peasant eyes studied her, she wasn't so sure.

"I'm told," said the commander, "that you're wanting to defeat the Hrum."

They'd been talking about her? Soraya stiffened. "You were told truly. What of it?" And why did that arrogant note in her voice make him smile?

151

"I want you to spy on Governor Nehar for me," the real commander of Mazad's defenses said bluntly. "We think he'll betray the city to the Hrum soon, but we don't know when, or even more important, how. If we present you as a refugee, the governor's wife will likely take you into their household."

Soraya blinked. "She probably would. But don't you have other people spying on the governor?"

"We do," Siddas admitted. "But not among his family—the folks he speaks his heart to. And we need more information than we're getting."

"But . . . but I need to translate for the Suud. They're alone here."

"Not completely alone," said Master Tebin. "And they all speak a bit of Faran. We managed well enough last night."

Looking at his plain, gentle face, Soraya realized that she could leave the Suud safely in his keeping. And for all his faults, she knew the peddler wouldn't let them come to harm. But to spy on her own people? To go into a deghan household as a guest with the intention of betraying them? She'd spied on the Hrum last summer without a qualm, but they were the enemy, so that was different. Or was it? Nehar was a traitor. He no longer deserved the honor one deghan owed another.

She picked gently at the embroidery on her skirt. "How could we explain my presence in the city? How did I get in?"

"Smuggled in, blindfolded, with the Suud," said the peddler promptly. "We'll never be able to keep them a secret anyway. We'll put it about that they want to learn smithcraft, for they fear they'll be fighting the Hrum themselves, soon. And the Suud came in with another big food shipment."

"What food shipment?"

"The one that came in with the Suud." Mischief brightened the peddler's eyes. "The one we hope will convince this new Hrum commander that posting that many guards is a waste of manpower."

"He may respond by putting out even more guards," said Siddas, before Soraya could point that out herself. "But there's also a chance that if he does, he'll post most of them somewhere else. He's moved his forces after other shipments have come in."

Soraya's gaze went to the stove where Tebin's servant was making flat cakes—plenty of cakes, enough for all the hungry young men who worked there. But flat cakes with no meat to go with them, and no fruit on the side—just a handful of dried berries mixed into the batter. It wasn't starvation, not even close . . . but someday it might be. Someday soon.

Soraya's gaze fell to the bright embroidery on her skirt. "All right," she said. "I'll do it."

If nothing else, it was time she returned to her true self. She had lived with the Suud for so long, she'd all but forgotten how to be a deghass. Soraya sighed.

"WHAT WAS IT LIKE, living with the savages?" The lady Armina bounced on the thick feather bed that was to be Soraya's that night and many nights to come. "Do they eat raw meat? Do they run about naked? Are they really the descendants of men who bred with demons?"

The lady Armina, at least, had the excuse of being only nine. As for Governor Nehar, who had made much of the honor of succoring the daughter of the House of the Leopard and then discreetly set out to discover whether she knew what had become of her family's wealth, Soraya didn't excuse him at all. After learning that as far as she knew the Hrum had seized everything, he had left her to his wife and daughters.

"No, no, and no," Soraya told the little girl calmly. "They cook their meat just as we do. They wear fewer clothes than we do, because the desert is warm, but by the standards of their own people they go properly clad. And though it's true their skin and hair are white, as the demons' were said to be, I think that's because they only go out at night. And they can't go out in the day," Soraya added, forestalling the next question, "because their skin is so fair that the sun burns it within moments."

"But you just said that the reason their skin is white is because they don't go out, and now you say that they don't go out because their skin is white. Which is it?" That question came from the lady Nayani, who was a year older than Soraya— seventeen, though you wouldn't have suspected it from her conversation, Soraya thought sourly.

"Both, I believe, Lady Nayani, growing from—"

"Oh, call me Nayani," said the girl impatiently. "And I'll call you Soraya. We're stuck here together, after all. I can't believe that your own father sent you to live among the savages!"

"And I can't believe that the lady Soraya wants to discuss such a devastating experience," said the lady Mitra firmly. "We'll drop the topic now, if you please. We all want to help her forget."

Both her daughters pouted. It was the lady Mitra, Soraya thought, who wanted to forget her guest's disreputable past. Governor Nehar's wife seemed to be a woman who put proper behavior above all else—and living with the Suud wasn't proper by any deghass' standards. But Soraya hadn't known how else to explain her whereabouts during the last year; that her father had hidden her with the Suud was the easiest, most plausible explanation. More proper, too. If Lady Mitra was offended at the thought of her living as a guest of the Suud, she'd have fainted to learn that Soraya had worked as a servant in an army camp—and a Hrum camp to boot!

Soraya knew that her own mother, wherever she was, would be just as appalled, though Sudaba would never have been as silly about it as Lady Mitra. Had Soraya once been that silly? Surely not!

She was about to dismiss the lady Mitra as

completely shallow and self-centered when the woman reached out and gently tucked a too-short strand of hair behind Soraya's ear.

"You are welcome in our house," she said, "for as long as you wish to stay. Remember that."

"Thank you, Lady," said Soraya, fighting down a flash of remorse.

"We'll get you some decent clothes, my dear," the lady added. "Once you're dressed, we'll do something about your hair, and you'll soon feel like yourself again."

It was kindly meant, Soraya told herself, trying not to grind her teeth. But she had a feeling that in a few days, far from "feeling like herself," she'd be going mad from boredom and exasperation. She was halfway there already!

SORAYA DIDN'T GO MAD from boredom, though it was a near thing. She'd forgotten how tedious it was to do nothing but gossip and embroider, and in a city under siege it was impossible to hunt or to ride out. At least Mitra ascribed the clumsiness of Soraya's embroidery to lack of practice instead of lack of talent, which was the truth.

The thing that saved Soraya's sanity was her

promise to spy, for there were shreds of interest mixed into the gossip.

Armina was filled with youthful determination to beat those wicked Hrum—preferably by going out on the walls with her father's big sword and leading the guards to victory herself. This seemed a normal and proper ambition to Soraya, at least in theory.

But Lady Mitra scolded Armina—and not for her unladylike blood thirst, which was why Soraya's own mother had scolded her for similar fantasies about fighting the Kadeshi. Lady Mitra's lectures focused on charity, kindness, and not hurting other people, which to Soraya seemed an odd attitude in a city that had been under siege for so long. And Sudaba's lectures, at least when Soraya was nine, had held an undercurrent of indulgence: *She'll grow out of it soon enough.* It was only when Soraya didn't outgrow her tomboy ways that the disapproval had become firmer. Lady Mitra's reproofs sounded more serious, and more nervous, than they should be. And charity, kindness, and not hurting other people were qualities conspicuous in their absence when she described the local craftmasters' wives who passed for society here in besieged Mazad.

158

But that was a small hypocrisy, which Soraya would have ignored if it hadn't been for Nayani's hints. Like Soraya—only a year ago?—her main ambition was to marry, and marry well, and behind her mother's back she'd dropped hints that her marriage might take place sooner than Soraya would think.

Soraya frowned in puzzlement. There were a couple of young deghans, Kalind and Markhan, attached to the governor's staff, but as far as Soraya could see Nayani ignored them with the proper contempt of an heiress for landless men. And they seemed to be too busy with their duties to have time for girls at all. Some wealthy craftmaster's son?

"Of course not!" Nayani exclaimed. The two girls were strolling—in a ladylike fashion—in the enclosed courtyard at the center of the manor. The flower beds were turning brown and dormant, but the air had been scrubbed clean by yesterday's rain, and the rising sun was bright.

After almost a year on her own, living first in the isolated cottage, then as a Hrum servant, and finally with the Suud, the circumscribed life that was proper for a young deghass felt unnatural to Soraya—like trying to cram her feet into shoes that no longer fit. This would be her life again, she realized, when the Hrum were defeated and her mother returned. She winced.

It won't be this bad, she told herself. She could live in the country.

Even in the country, a garden courtyard with a fountain in its center was typical architecture for a deghan's manor, but it was different there. Remembering the courtyard in the house where she had grown up, Soraya smiled even as her heart ached. Except when her father had important guests, it had been full of gardeners, grooms sitting out to polish tack in a good light, maids fetching water or gossiping while they folded clean clothing or linens . . . When Merdas escaped his nursery, the stables were his favorite destination, but the courtyard was his second choice.

The courtyard within the walls of Governor Nehar's manor was smaller than that of Soraya's country home; in the crowded confines of a city, such courtyards were a rare luxury. But it was the silence of the place that struck Soraya. Perhaps Governor Nehar's servants chose to remain indoors. This sunny morning was cold enough that she and Nayani wore cloaks, and no one wanted to be outside in the afternoon rains that were now falling with dreary regularity—none of them, Azura be praised, as wild as that first storm had been. Soraya wasn't sure if that was because her control had returned once she was safe, or if she'd simply imagined that that other storm had responded to her shilshadu, or if being inside helped dampen any effect her shilshadu might have—but whatever it was, she was grateful.

"The world has been overturned, Soraya," Nayani continued. "But that doesn't mean a deghass should forget her place. A *craftsman's* son?"

Her tone would have suited the idea of marrying a Suud barbarian—but perhaps all ineligible men were equally ineligible in Nayani's eyes. Nayani was the kind of proper young deghass that Sudaba had approved of, and for the thousandth time Soraya was grateful that her father had taken an interest in raising his daughter. Thinking of her father hurt less now, but it still hurt, and Soraya dragged her mind back to Nayani's gossip.

"So who are you marrying?" she asked. "I suppose if the Hrum send back all the slaves they captured there will be a few deghans among them, but none of them is going to be rich. Not like before."

"There are other ways of gaining wealth," said Nayani. "High-ranked army officers often got rich raiding the Kadeshi." She giggled.

This was the kind of gossip that had always bored Soraya silly. "Well, all the army officers left in Farsala are here in Mazad. And none of them look rich to me."

"Then I'll just have to learn Hrum, won't I?" Nayani giggled again.

Soraya caught her jaw as it started to sag. "But what about the rebellion? If Farsala succeeds in resisting the Hrum—"

"Soraya, you can't believe that peasants can resist an army that defeated deghans. The world has changed. We have to . . . well, everyone has to do what they can, I suppose. And it's not like . . . I mean, I wouldn't marry *too* low. The stable boys are definitely out of consideration."

If Soraya pushed now, Nayani would pretend it was a joke—so Soraya pretended it was a joke as well, though she couldn't bring herself to laugh.

How could a deghass, even one as shallow as Nayani, agree to marry an enemy? Soraya's whole heart revolted at the thought. But really, what choice did Nayani have? By deghass standards there was no one left worth marrying *except* one of the Hrum. To marry, and marry well, was what a deghass did.

A deghass was also supposed to obey her father or husband and take his loyalties as her own. If Soraya's father had gone over to the Hrum, instead of defending Farsala to the death as his honor demanded, would he still be alive?

Her heart tightened with pain. Given the choice between seeing her own father alive and dishonored, or honorable and dead . .

That choice had been given to her father, not to her, and he had made it. But if he'd decided differently, Soraya knew she would have married anyone she had to in order to support him.

Azura be praised, she'd never been faced with that. And maybe she was wrong. This whole supposition was based on no more than an offhand comment and a giggle.

LATER, IN THE WARM solarium where the women gathered to embroider while the rain fell outside, Soraya mentioned that the Suud had traded with the Hrum, and that the Hrum, hoping to smooth the path of trade, had given the Suud much information about themselves.

It was easy to bring the subject up, for the Hrum were attacking the walls that afternoon. Nothing was audible over the drumming of rain on the roof except for a distant roar, which rose and fell unexpectedly, and Nayani told Soraya that the Hrum attacked "all the time now." Still, it was impossible to think about anything else.

When Soraya started talking about the Hrum, Armina decreed that the Suud who dealt with them were traitors, "'cause no one should help the Hrum at all." But both Nayani and Mitra instantly set about picking Soraya clean of all the information she admitted to having about the Hrum.

Soraya was grateful for the warmth of the fire, even though her growing chill sprang from the heart rather than the flesh. Had Nehar really agreed to wed his eldest daughter to a high-ranking Hrum officer?

NOT WANTING TO MAKE them suspicious, Soraya waited until breakfast two days later before telling

Mitra that it was time she went to see how the Suud were faring.

Mitra grimaced. "Must you, Soraya? It seems so . . . I mean . . . they're Suud."

"They sheltered me from my father's enemies, and after the invasion they kept me safe from the Hrum, even though my father could no longer pay them," said Soraya. "I cannot abandon them in a strange city without sometimes going to see if they need my aid. It's a matter of honor. Isn't it, Governor?"

"Hmm? Ah yes, I suppose." Nehar spoke absently, his attention divided between the document he was reading and his plate, which was filled with slivers of honeyed ham, groats with raisins and sweet curd, and an apple pastry of which even Soraya had taken a second helping. His chef was excellent. Sudaba would have approved.

Mitra frowned, but her husband's consent was sufficient for Soraya. She fled the table as soon as the meal was done, donned her cloak, and left the house without even stopping to change into street wear. Mitra was kind to Soraya, treating her as if Soraya really were a member of her own family, but she kept finding subtle ways to try to "save"

Soraya from the bad influences she'd been exposed
to. It would be like her to come up with some
errand or event and insist on Soraya's presence —
which as a guest she couldn't refuse.

If you didn't know about the siege, Soraya
thought, the cobbled streets, with their shops,
houses, and work yards, would look quite ordinary. But even someone not trained in the Suud's
magic might have picked up the underlying tension that escalated the quarrel between a woman
who'd thrown a bucket of wash water out the door
and the man whose boots she'd splashed. The bar-
gaining at the butcher's shop lacked its usual
aggressive good cheer. The price they settled on as
Soraya passed seemed high to her, leaving the
buyer sullen and the butcher himself not very
happy for a man who'd just gotten a whole brass
foal for a pound of chopped . . . something. The
name of the meat was never mentioned, and
Soraya thought that odd too.

Compared to the governor's mansion the
house attached to the smithy seemed small and
shabby. When the woman who answered the door
saw the subdued gleam of Soraya's robe under the
fur-lined cloak she stiffened, but when she recog-

nized Soraya her alarm faded into a smile.

"Come in, Lady, come in. Master Tebin told me you'd be coming to check on your friends."

"Are they doing all right?" The Suud were more capable of looking after themselves than Soraya had admitted to Nehar's family, but she did worry about them.

"Well, one of them, that lad Marib, picked up a minor burn the other day. But that's common around here, and it wasn't bad enough to be sending for a healer. They're getting on well with the other men." The woman led Soraya into the house and back to the kitchen as she spoke. "And Kavi explained to the younger apprentices that playing tricks that would lure the Suud into the sun could really hurt them, so even those imps are behaving better than usual. Can I offer you bread and tea, Lady? Both are made, since it's all we're having for mid-meal. The commander asked the townsfolk to start rationing themselves, voluntary-like, and Master Tebin agreed."

"I just ate," said Soraya, and watched the woman's face fall. "But tea would be welcome. Did your daughter get her clothes back? I asked the servants to return them."

167

"They did, and thank you for thinking of it, Lady." She handed Soraya a steaming mug. "I'll go and get the master for you now."

Tebin was awake? But when the woman returned, it was the peddler who accompanied her.

"Tebin's attaching a hilt and can't be interrupted," he said, coming in and taking a seat across from her. His gaze rested on the rich silk of her gown, and his lips tightened. His own clothes were sweat-stained and dirty.

"I thought you were going to work when the Suud did," she said. "What are you doing up this early?"

"We've found the Suud are all right on their own at night—we've just set a few journeymen to help them. For making swords it works best if the rest of us start the blades in the afternoon, so they can work shilshadu magic on them in the evening. Then we can attach hilts and do the sharpening the next morning."

Soraya's eyes widened. "You're actually making the swords? Watersteel?"

"Of course." He was trying to sound casual, but a smile tugged at his lips, and crept into his voice as he went on. "We've the beginnings of a fine armory. It was only a matter of getting the lads who can . . . can talk everything into swimming the right way while the blades cool, and putting them together with lads who can actually make a sword. In fact, I'm beginning to think there's a trick to the cooling that would make things swim the right way even without someone Speaking to the steel."

Since he couldn't make swords, the search for that secret was probably why he was up early—but his presence would save Soraya some time. She had thought she'd have to write the commander a letter.

"I think that Governor Nehar has promised his eldest daughter in marriage to a high-ranking Hrum officer," said Soraya. "That's what I came to tell you, so you could pass it on to Commander Siddas." She went on to describe what she'd heard and what she'd deduced.

"That's it?" said the peddler when she finished. "That's all you've got?"

"I've only been there for six days," Soraya protested. "And what do you mean, 'all'? He plans to marry his daughter to the Hrum—to make a blood alliance!"

To a deghan there was nothing more binding,

169

more important, than a blood alliance. But she wasn't talking to a deghan.

The peddler snorted. "We're still getting news from the outside, you know. Peasants in villages all around Mazad are sabotaging the Hrum every way they can, despite Garren's taxes and his threats. Commander Jiaan is fighting battles with the Hrum in the desert. And you're telling us wedding gossip about Nehar allying with the Hrum? That was obvious the moment we learned he was going to betray Mazad!"

"What do you mean, 'we learned?'" Soraya demanded. "*I* was the one who learned he was a traitor in the first place. I told you about it!"

Astonishment swept over his face. He'd forgotten that—Golbad, djinn of envy, take him.

"Yes," he admitted. "You did. I suppose it's different now that you're back with your own folks."

"What do you mean by that?" Soraya demanded. "I said I'd spy, and here I am. With news!"

"Not much news," said the peddler. "Seems to me that when you were spying on the Hrum you were willing to take a chance or two."

"I spent the whole summer with the Hrum,

learning their language and blending into the camp, before I did anything but listen—and the moment I started taking chances I got caught! Besides, I don't see you taking any chances. You're not spying on anyone!"

Which wasn't entirely fair, since it was more important for him to make swords than anything else he might have done. But he wasn't being fair either. She'd only been there—

"Ah, lost your taste for risk, have you?" The peddler's voice was mostly controlled, but anger blazed in his eyes and burned against her shilshadu senses. Anger and . . . grief? Curiosity tugged at Soraya, but she was angry herself by then.

"I've done what I came for. Report it to Commander Siddas." She stood, knowing she looked and sounded regal enough to make Sudaba proud. But she found she was too furious to depart in dignified silence. "Or perhaps," she went on, "you'll use the information to buy some safety from your other *friends*. It wouldn't surprise me."

His expression didn't change, but his raw emotions were open to her. The surge of shame and pain surprised her, for she'd never before sensed any remorse for his betrayal—at least not much. But whatever had touched him, it was swallowed by fury.

"Deghass bitch." He all but hissed the words, and only the pride of twenty generations of the House of the Leopard kept Soraya from stepping back. He might not be tall, but he was far stronger than she was.

"Arzhang-spawned traitor," she replied.

That insult didn't move him, but he too rose to his feet. Before she had a chance to feel more than the beginning of fear, he turned and stamped back to the work yard, leaving Soraya to find her own way out to the street.

Clouds were building for the afternoon rain, and a cold wind tugged at the hood of Soraya's cloak, but she barely noticed. What in the name of Gorahz was the matter with the man? It was clear that the djinn of rage was driving him. But she'd only been there a week! He could hardly expect Governor Nehar to suddenly reveal all his treacherous plans to a strange girl thrust into his household by accident. It was completely unreasonable! And that, Soraya realized as physical activity slowly drained her own anger, was odd in itself. Although she'd avoided him whenever she could, she'd spent enough time with the peddler to know that he wasn't unreasonable. Not really. Could he have been . . . no, it was ridiculous to expect her to have learned anything of importance after so short a time. She'd done well to discover as much as she had! But it did occur to Soraya, as the high, carved walls of the governor's manor loomed before her, that she really hadn't taken many chances.

FOUR NIGHTS LATER SORAYA crawled out onto the roof tiles. They were damp from the afternoon's rain, but they'd dried enough not to be slippery, for which she was grateful. Looking up at this roof—only two stories above the ground—it hadn't seemed nearly as high as it did looking down.

It was the night after her quarrel with the peddler that Soraya, unable to sleep, had opened the shutters on her bedroom window and looked out over the rooftops to the distant walls where the guardsmen patrolled—only visible as dots of darker shadow moving against the dark horizon. She stood and watched them for some time before she realized that farther down the manor's wall, lamplight glowed around the shutters of another window.

Leaning out to count the windows between them, Soraya deduced that the light was coming from the bedroom of the governor and his wife.

Couldn't they sleep either? Had they retired late? Soraya had thought they'd gone to bed at the same time as the rest of the household, but perhaps they'd been working in the outer room, which opened off the second-story landing that circled the courtyard. All sections of the long rectangle that formed the house were two rooms deep, but only the family and noble guests had the two-room suites that fronted the street. The servants, who slept on the other side of the courtyard, had only one room each—sometimes shared with one or even two of their fellows.

Yes, the governor and his wife could have been conducting private business in their outer room long after everyone else was abed—but they'd have had to conduct that business quietly, for those windows opened onto the landing where anyone walking past could overhear. Bedrooms on the outer wall were prized because they gave a couple privacy . . . so what were they doing with the lamp lit?

Even as Soraya watched, the light vanished, leaving the edges of the shutters in darkness.

Whatever the governor and his wife discussed, there was no way she could learn about it, for the wall was sheer, voices wouldn't carry as far as the street below, and the door to the outer room would be latched from the inside. There was no way . . .

Soraya looked up at the eaves jutting over her own window. The dark beams were barely visible on this overcast night, but she knew what they would look like: big and thick to support the tile roof above them. Easily strong enough to support the weight of one slim girl as well. Could that possibly work? Perhaps it could. After all, there had to be some reason the activity she was considering had earned the name "eavesdropping."

The next morning Soraya told the others that if she couldn't ride, she needed to walk at least. She found a used-clothing shop where she traded an old vest Nayani had given her for a boy's shirt, britches, and a warm sheepskin vest. They were much like the clothes her father had provided for her exile to the croft. Soraya swallowed the lump in her throat and traded without complaint, though she knew that the exquisitely embroidered silk was worth far more than the clothes she purchased. But even she noticed that after all this time under siege, the shop's wares were running low. In Mazad these days most people wore their clothes to rags before discarding them. Food might trickle in, but wool or flax for spinning simply wasn't to be found. Soraya wondered how the weavers were surviving—but that, at least, wasn't her problem.

She smuggled her "new" clothes into the house by tucking them under her skirt. It was easy to steer her conversation with the maids to the question of how a chimney sweep would get onto the roof—easy because Soraya had been chatting with the maids about all manner of things since her arrival. In truth, she preferred their company to that of Mitra and Nayani—the work of caring for a great house wasn't so very different from that of caring for a great army, and those were tasks with which Soraya was very familiar.

Thus armed, with proper clothes and the knowledge that the hatch to the roof opened out of a storage closet not far from the room where she slept, Soraya spent the next three nights watching the lamp in the governor's bedroom go out almost exactly when those of the rest of the household did—sometimes before.

But tonight the lamp had stayed on . . . and

on. Soraya eased over the tiles with the patience of the hunter her father had taught her to be. She tried to keep her weight spread as evenly as possible, to prevent the planks from creaking, but she soon realized that the manor was old enough that the heavy boards had settled into their final resting places.

Still, she held her breath as she crawled down the fortunately not-too-steep slope and edged her head over the side. She hoped she wouldn't overhear anything . . . intimate. She really hoped she wouldn't get caught! It was embarrassing enough that she was spying on her hosts in their bedchamber, even when they didn't know she was there.

"Come to bed, Mitra," Nehar was saying. "You've already gone over those things a dozen times." His voice sounded distant, but the words were clear.

"Well, there isn't much space," said the lady Mitra. From where Soraya crouched on the cold tiles, her voice was louder but less distinct. The lady must be near the window, speaking toward the room, while her husband, when he spoke, was looking toward the window.

"You say the groom can only carry what we'll

need for one evening, and that doesn't leave much room," the lady went on. "I still don't see why we can't take our maids."

What groom, carrying what? And why couldn't they take maids? The governor's wife could take a maid anywhere she wanted.

"We're only supposed to be going for an afternoon and a state dinner," said Nehar. He sounded as if he'd said it many times before. "We can't take a chest. A small bundle of fine clothes at the most. Though with all the buying I've been doing, we may need a chest. Prices are incredibly low, now that no one has any use for luxury fabrics."

Buying? *Fabrics?* What would Nehar be doing with fabrics? Was he entering into business like a common tradesman?

"But if we're supposed to be dressing for a state dinner, then I *should* have a maid," said Mitra, her voice a little louder.

If they weren't going to a dinner, where were they going?

"And my girl is the only one who ever gets my hair exactly right," Mitra continued. "You know how hard it is to find someone who can handle fine hair."

Soraya stifled a sigh. In ballads, when the bold young deghan went to spy on the Kadeshi warlord—or in older tales on the demons' council—their enemies had the courtesy to discuss their battle plans when the hero showed up. But what was Lady Mitra doing? Soraya had thought that her maids did everything for the woman except eat and defecate. And wherever she was going, why couldn't she take a maid to help her dress? It was common practice for deghasses to bring their own maids when they visited other great houses. Was this a visit to the home of some wealthy weaver or fabric merchant, whose family the governor didn't want to embarrass? A dinner with—

Soraya barely managed to silence a gasp. You wouldn't take a maid to a dinner—a state dinner—in a Hrum siege camp!

"You'll find another girl to do your hair, my dear." Despite his sympathetic words, the governor sounded bored. "Perhaps you'll be able to keep her after . . . well, afterward."

After what? And even more important, *when?* Soraya was already leaning forward as far as she dared.

"It's the waiting that's worst. Lady Mitra's

voice was so soft, Soraya could barely hear it. "Everyone is so tense. I just . . . I just want it to be done. Finished."

"Not much longer," said Nehar. "A few weeks at the most. Probably less than that. Come to bed now."

Mitra must have turned toward the window, for her sigh was audible. The lamp went out.

Soraya waited on the roof until Nehar began to snore, and then she waited longer. Her feet were cold, her hands were frozen, and blood pounded in her lowered head, but somehow she knew that Lady Mitra was lying open-eyed in the darkness beside her husband. She would hear Soraya's movement. Soraya thought that if she tried to open her shilshadu to Mitra's emotions, in the still darkness the lady might detect that as well.

What did Mitra think of her husband's treason, deep in her heart? It was clear she wasn't prepared to betray him. And she'd have a much better chance of getting a maid who could properly dress her hair as the wife of a high-ranked Hrum official than as a Hrum slave. But still . . .

Nehar was a coward and a fool, but Mitra, for all her propriety, was neither. She was a *deghass*. A deghass wouldn't, *couldn't* betray her people!

What was Soraya doing now, if not betraying Lady Mitra?

Yes, Nehar was a traitor, but Mitra had been kind to Soraya by her own standards. Kind by any standard.

But they'd turned traitor first! Were they still her people? And if they weren't, then why did betraying them *feel* like treason?

It had seemed so simple, in Tebin's warm kitchen, agreeing to spy on a traitor and his family. But when you met the people in question, came to know them, earned their trust . . .

Had the peddler once faced this conflict? Felt like she did now? Soraya thrust that thought aside.

I am a deghass, she told herself fiercely. *A true deghass. That's the difference.*

Besides, her decision had been made long since, when she first agreed to spy.

Eventually, moving as if the stag she hunted were grazing in the brush beside her, Soraya crawled up the roof and made her way back to her room. She hadn't learned much. Probably not enough to satisfy the peddler, and certainly no battle plans. But if something was going to happen in the next few weeks, she thought Commander Siddas should be warned about it. Soon.

"I'M SORRY, LADY, but Kavi's quite busy now, so I hope you can be making do with me." Master Tebin's polite words were belied by the twinkle in his eyes.

"You mean he didn't want to talk to me," said Soraya. "Which is fine, because I don't want to talk to him either. I haven't learned much that's new, but the governor told his wife that something is supposed to happen—that the waiting will be over—in just a few weeks, at most."

"A few *weeks*?" Tebin's eyes widened.

"At the most," Soraya confirmed grimly.

"I don't . . . I'm not in Siddas' confidence, but I don't think he expected anything that fast. I don't suppose you know what's going to be happening?"

Heat flooded Soraya's cheeks. "They said something about a dinner."

"A dinner?"

"A state dinner. With the Hrum, I'm guessing. I know how it sounds, but I assure you that's what they said."

"Don't sound so stiff, lass," Tebin said absently. "I'm believing you, no matter how odd it sounds, and I'll pass it on to Siddas at the council meeting tonight."

Tension Soraya hadn't realized she felt eased out of her muscles. "I wondered, last time, if *he* even bothered to pass on my report."

"Oh, he'd never neglect something like that." Tebin waved his hands in vague apology. "You caught him at a bad time, is all. He'd a friend who was wounded in the Hrum attack last week, and he'd just died the day before. Kavi was angry with the Hrum, with all the world, I think, and it . . . well, it woke the old anger as well. Not that it ever needs much waking." Old sorrow filled the swordsmith's open face, and Soraya frowned.

"Why does Kavi hate deghans so much?" The name felt odd in her mouth, but it would sound strange to Master Tebin if she called him "the peddler." She had used his name, in something approaching friendship, before she'd known what he was.

"You don't know that story?" Tebin sounded startled. "Well, I don't suppose you could, for Kavi wouldn't be telling it. Not to you."

"It doesn't matter," said Soraya hastily. "I just—"

"You're wrong about that. It matters a lot." But before he continued, Tebin went to the stove and poured two mugs of tea, setting one before her. It tasted weaker than it had the last time.

Soraya wasn't even sure she wanted to learn the peddler's history, but somehow the offer of tea trapped her there. Had Tebin known it would? He was a kind man, but he wasn't a fool.

"Kavi was the best apprentice I ever had," the smith began. "One of the best I've seen. At least, the best at his craft. In some ways he was one of my worst apprentices."

"Why did the butcher set dogs on him?" The question had been nagging Soraya.

Master Tebin threw back his head and laughed. It was an easy, well-used sound, and Soraya smiled.

"Hmm," said the smith when he finished. "I should probably let Kavi choose whether or not to tell that story. I'm likely sharing more of his business than he'd care for as it is."

Soraya's brows rose. "Let me guess—the butcher had a daughter?"

"Ah . . . no. In fact, the butcher had a son who fancied the daughter of one of our journeymen. She didn't fancy him, but he couldn't accept that, so he kept coming around. Made a nuisance of himself. And you needn't feel sorry for him—he was an arrogant lad, who couldn't believe that any girl he cast his eye on wouldn't want him. In fairness, he's a good-looking man who will come into his father's shop. But Lalia had the good sense to want none of him. I was about to speak to his father about it, but Kavi and a couple of other apprentices took it on themselves to . . . discourage him. Though you shouldn't feel too sorry for them, either. Their motives might have been good, but . . . well, let's just say that if I was Feroz Butcher, I'd have set the dogs on them myself. And Kavi played plenty of pranks when his motives weren't noble in the least. He was a mischievous boy, and took longer than he should have to outgrow it. Indeed, I'm not certain he's completely outgrown it yet! But skill at his craft, and the love of it, those he had in plenty. Maybe that shilshadu thing he's got has something to do with it."

"Maok, my teacher, said that the gift might

have grown out of love of the craft," Soraya told him. "But what happened?"

The lingering humor left Tebin's face. "What happened is that I took on a job I shouldn't have. A man, a deghan, commissioned a sword—demanded the best I could make and said he'd pay only if the blade was 'worthy.' You could see he was trouble." Tebin sighed. "But the truth is, I didn't mind making a fancy sword. I thought that when he came and found it unworthy—which I figured he would, no matter how the blade turned out!—he'd offer me a fraction of the price, and I'd teach him a lesson by turning it down. It might take me a while to find another buyer, but I'd sell it eventually, and meanwhile it could serve as a showpiece. If he surprised me and paid fair, well, I'm in the business of making blades. And it's not the best idea to refuse a deghan. If you've a worthy cause the guild will back you, but to refuse just because I didn't trust him? I should have, though."

"It's not your fault," said Soraya. "No matter what happened."

"Isn't it?" said Tebin. "A job I agreed to, and a lad—a fifteen-year-old boy—who was in my charge?"

"So this deghan claimed your sword wasn't good enough?" Soraya already knew that Tebin's sword would have been magnificent.

"No. No, he'd a worse scheme than that in mind." The smith's voice was so soft that the low crackle of the fire almost drowned it. "I was out of the shop that week, gone up to the mining camps to buy iron. We'd finished the blade early—the man was supposed to come for it days after I got back. Most of the lads were working in the yard, and Kavi was minding the shop. He said the deghan didn't even try to sneer at the blade. He tried it on the post and it tested out—it was a lovely piece. But the man said he'd one final test for it, and he'd pay when the sword passed that."

"He took the sword without paying anything at all?" Soraya frowned. Outright theft was a bit much, even for the most arrogant deghan.

"And Kavi tried to stop him," Tebin confirmed. "He grabbed the blade, trying to take it back, and the deghan pulled it. Sliced his palm almost through the bone. He was lucky not to lose his hand completely."

"I see," Soraya's throat ached. She hated the peddler, and always would, but she'd seen his gift with metal. She understood what that sword stroke had cost him. "I trust the deghan suffered for it?"

"Not in the slightest," said Tebin. "He killed the cousin who'd inherited the money he thought was coming to him and used his inheritance to bribe the temple to get him off. Then the bastard had the gall to come back and pay me for the sword—full price. He even threw in three gold eagles 'for the accident to your apprentice.' Kavi threw that back at him. Would have attacked him, even though his hand was only half-healed at the time and we still had hopes . . . Anyway, that's why he hates the deghans so—not just the bastard who maimed him, but all of them for letting him get away with it. Though maybe I should say that's why he hated them, for I think that's finally changing."

"Since he got his revenge," said Soraya coldly. "Killing them almost to the last man with his betrayal. Even the ones who didn't allow it, who would never have done such a thing or allowed it if they'd known."

"Kavi would say that they all supported the gahn who allowed it," said Master Tebin softly.

"But you're right. Hate's a bad thing. Anyway, now you know."

THOUGH SORAYA DISLIKED to admit it, as she walked slowly back to the governor's house, it did make a difference. It didn't, couldn't, excuse what he'd done, but he had sufficient cause to hate.

She dredged up a smile for the maid who opened the door, but it faded swiftly as she made her way to the solarium for the afternoon's embroidery. It promised to be even more excruciating than usual, since she would have to listen to the lady Mitra's complaints about a deghass being forced to translate for Suud barbarians, even if they did have questions about the terms of their apprenticeship! Surely someone more suitable could have been found . . .

In fact Lady Mitra only brought up Soraya's improper behavior twice, for she seemed to be disturbed by some other worry. She sewed silently while Nayani and Armina chatted, once even stitching in the wrong color, so she was forced to pick it out and do it over.

Despite her curiosity—would she find herself out on the roof tonight? Nervous as Mitra seemed, she wasn't likely to sleep!—Soraya was relieved when the time came to change for dinner. But as she left the room, Mitra stopped her with a hand on her arm.

"Soraya." She hesitated, looking after her departing daughters uncertainly.

"Yes, Lady?"

Mitra took a breath and seemed to make up her mind. "Soraya, I haven't asked what happened to your family's wealth. But I don't . . . well, I would think that a prudent man would have sent some jewelry or coin along with his daughter, even if he was sending her to live with the savages for a time. After all, if some emergency occurred . . ."

"Lady, my father sent nothing—"

Mitra held up her hand. "I don't care," she said. "I mean that. But now, with your family gone, you'll need anything you may have. So if you do have any . . . keepsakes, let us say, I'd advise you to keep them packed and ready to take at a moment's notice. That's all."

The lady Mitra turned and hurried off, leaving Soraya gazing after her open-mouthed.

It was going to be soon. The lady Mitra was

packing up her jewelry and valuables with her own hands, so the maids wouldn't guess that the governor's family planned to desert the city. And if she was warning Soraya to do the same . . .

It was going to be soon, and Soraya still had no idea what Nehar was planning.

Could she find out? In time?

A deghass would find a way. A deghass wouldn't betray her hosts. A deghass . . .

Soraya sighed. She hadn't found a way, and she *had* betrayed her hosts. In some ways she had never felt less like a deghass in her life, but another part of her heart welcomed familiar people, familiar clothes. . . . Even the familiar boredom had been tolerable in a world where so much was changing. Where *she* had changed so much, she scarcely recognized herself.

But if she wasn't a deghass, what was she?

"TO DEFEAT THE HRUM," *the old smith told Sorahb,* "the first thing you must do is hold the city of Mazad, for if it can hold for a year the Hrum will retreat. Besides, the people there have resisted bravely and do not deserve to be taken into slavery for their courage."

"This I have already planned to do," said Sorahb. "But I will go to them now, for at the same time as I assist them, they will be able to help my army."

Sorahb went then to the city of Mazad. The country folk smuggled him, along with the men the old smith had trained, into the city, though the smith declared himself too old for such adventures.

In Mazad, Sorahb rallied the siege-weary people

to the city's defense and set his men to teach Mazad's skilled smiths to make the lightning swords.

Hammers rang throughout the days and nights, and a new determination arose in the hearts of Mazad's citizens, to fight to the end and beyond if need be, for the legendary Sorahb had come to lead them.

But one man in the city was not pleased. Several loyal guardsmen brought word to Sorahb that the governor of Mazad was himself in league with the Hrum and plotted to bring the city down.

CHAPTER SEVEN

KAVI

THE GIRL WAS RIGHT, Kavi thought, watching the Hrum guards watch him as he hiked up the road to the siege camp. He hadn't been doing enough spying lately. He was out of practice—or perhaps his memory was failing him, for he didn't remember being quite this scared the last time he pulled a stunt like this.

"Halt and state your business," the guard demanded.

Kavi thrust fear to the back of his mind. Just an honest peddler-spy—nothing to worry about.

"I've business with the commander," he said. "It's not urgent, but if you'd be fetching your decimaster I can tell him what it is."

The two sentries looked at each other. No doubt they resented a mere peddler questioning their authority, and Kavi was prepared to spend as long as they wanted arguing about it. The Hrum army's proper procedure claimed that anyone had a right to request to see the centrimaster who commanded the current watch, but Kavi knew that in reality few guards wanted to take the trouble to track down their commander, and no decimaster wanted to bring his superior some minor matter that the guards could have taken care of themselves. With luck Kavi could pass several marks here at the gate, listening in on conversations as others came and went and chatting with passersby.

"You wait here," said one of the sentries. "I'll get the decimaster."

The man trotted off, almost before Kavi recovered his wits enough to shout, "It's not urgent!" at his retreating back. He turned to the remaining sentry. "I wouldn't want to pull the decimaster from something important," he added apologetically.

The sentry shrugged. "He's commander of this watch unit. He's supposed to be ready to attend such matters."

Kavi's brows rose. "He's maybe supposed to be, but I've never seen a watch commander who didn't have better things to do—or at least claimed he did."

The sentry grinned. "Not under the new substrategus command, they don't."

Kavi swore silently. He'd been present as a witness at the meeting where Garren had reassigned command of the siege camp, and he had judged from Patrius' expression that Tactimian Laon was at best only slightly better than the idiot he'd replaced. The new efficiency of the patrols and guards had shown Kavi that Laon was more competent than Patrius had believed, but who'd have thought any crony of Garren's would run a camp this strict?

Kavi just hoped that when the old commander, Substrategus Arus, left he had taken all of his men with him. If anyone here recognized Kavi as the merchant who'd sold the camp drugged beer last summer . . . The centris were supposed to move with their commanders, but the way the Hrum were shuffling men around these days, it was hard to be certain.

Memory of the protest that at that same meeting had gotten Patrius assigned to the thankless task of chasing down Sorahb's army made Kavi wonder how his friend was doing. It felt odd to be hoping passionately for the man's personal safety, while at the same time hoping equally passionately for the total failure of his mission. But the truth was that Kavi liked the Hrum officer far more than he liked Commander Jiaan. Of course, Jiaan had been trying to kill him since they first met—with only a brief hiatus while they escorted the lady Soraya to the hidden croft—so the comparison wasn't really fair.

But Kavi still wouldn't be able to forgive himself or Jiaan—unfair as that might be—if Patrius died. The worst thing about this spying business was that eventually you came to care for people on both sides—and only one could win.

Was the lady Soraya perhaps coming to care for the deghan family who had taken her in? He hadn't been entirely fair to her, either, Kavi admitted. He was tired of betraying people, but he saw no other choice—not if he wanted *his* folk to finally come out on top.

Kavi put down his dusty pack and sat on it, with the relaxed air of a man with plenty of time.

"So, are you making any headway with this siege of yours? You've been here more than half a year now . . ."

THE DECIMASTER TOOK one look at the tattoo on Kavi's arm and immediately took him in search of the centrimaster, despite Kavi's protest that his news wasn't urgent. Once when he really *had* had urgent news, he'd had to argue his way through half a dozen officers to reach this level. Now that he wanted nothing more than to spend a few days here, the decimaster led him through the siege camp at a pace so brisk that he couldn't observe anything without making his interest obvious.

They were working on more ladders, but then they'd had their ladders when Giv was wounded — killed, really, though it had taken him several days to die. Kavi saw no sign of the battering rams Siddas had told him to look for when he'd approved this insanity, but the rams might be in another part of the camp. Or maybe Nehar had gotten word to the Hrum about the barrels of pitch Siddas was holding in reserve for the day a ram showed up, and they'd adopted other, less desperate plans. Looking for rams was one of the reasons

Siddas had agreed to let Kavi do this. Another was the chance to smuggle a message, and the first bundle of watersteel swords, to someone who would take them to Commander Jiaan.

But it was really the hope of learning something—anything!—about Nehar's plans that had brought Kavi here. However, if he was going to learn anything, he'd have to stay for at least a few days.

The centrimaster listened attentively to Kavi's account of the rumor that Sorahb had taken all his army and fled into the desert.

"I believe the commander knows that already," he said.

That's why I'm telling it to you.

"But I'll take you to the command tent, and as soon as he has a spare moment you can tell him about it. The substrategus may have some questions that I haven't thought to ask."

Kavi blinked. "But I don't know any more than I just . . . Wait a moment. I thought Tactimian Laon was . . . well, a tactimian. Did he get promoted?" He stopped walking, forcing the centrimaster to stop too.

"Tactimian Laon was removed from command

over a month ago. Substrategus Barmael has replaced him. And I don't intend to keep him waiting, so if you'll follow me?"

"Yes," said Kavi, forcing his feet into motion. The man's approval of his new commander showed, even through the impatient formality of his tone. "That explains . . . I see."

His mind spun. Barmael was Patrius' immediate commander, and Patrius had told Kavi a bit about the man—all of it good. No wonder the security of the siege was so much improved. But from the hints Patrius had dropped, Barmael was one of the officers who *opposed* Garren. He was also one of the Hrum's most competent battle commanders. Garren had said something, in that tense meeting Kavi had witnessed, about replacing Laon when the time for the assault drew near. A chill raced over Kavi's skin, and he struggled to keep his expression relaxed as he followed the centrimaster through the muddy, bustling streets. The assault was going to be soon. It was going to be soon, and Garren, despite his personal dislike of the man, had sent one of his best battle commanders to lead it. *Never underestimate that man,* Kavi reminded himself. *Never.*

He'd known he would need at least a day or two to get the troops talking in his presence—to put together the information he needed without arousing suspicion. He'd thought it would take several days, perhaps even a week, before Tactimian Laon would deign to interview a humble spy who was reporting a rumor he already knew to be true. But now . . .

Half a mark later Kavi was ushered into Substrategus Barmael's presence. Somewhat to his surprise, he recognized the stocky, red-bearded man who had questioned the governor with such startling directness at the meeting Kavi had attended several months ago.

"I understand that the rebel Sorahb has fled with his army into the desert," Barmael's voice rumbled. Kavi noted that Sorahb had been promoted from bandit to rebel, at least under Substrategus Barmael's command. "Where did you first hear about this?"

Question followed question, some of them alarmingly shrewd, as Barmael sought to determine Sorahb's troop strength, plans, and how he was supplied. To most of them, Kavi replied truthfully that he didn't know. Commander Jiaan had told him nothing he didn't have to, and the rumors that circulated about the Farsalan army were vague. Sometimes they even contradicted each other.

A few of the questions were more difficult. "*Alliance* with the Suud?" Kavi echoed, stalling for time to get his wits in order. "Not that I've heard. But then, I've never heard of anyone allying with them."

"They haven't attacked our forces," said the substrategus, which told Kavi that Patrius' reports back to Garren probably passed through this man's hands. "Even though I've been told that the Suud attack all outsiders who go into their territory."

Kavi shrugged. "That's what the miners say, but if you listen close, you'll hear that the miners were also attacking them. I've talked to others, not many but a few, who said that as long as they didn't trouble the Suud, the Suud didn't trouble them. Kept watching them, always, but they didn't interfere."

With any luck the substrategus would pass that information on to Patrius, although Kavi couldn't see Patrius attacking the Suud . . . unless the Suud got careless and were seen helping Jiaan, and

Patrius realized that there *was* an alliance, and . . .
Caring about people on all sides was hard.

Eventually, even Substrategus Barmael ran
out of questions. "You have nothing more to
report?"

Kavi, who felt like a cloth wrung dry by a
washerwoman, shook his head. "You've already
learned more than I thought I knew."

"Our thanks to you, then," said the substrategus. "The centrimaster here will take you to
the accounts clerk, who'll see you paid. Then you
can go."

Judging by the way Barmael's camp was run,
the centrimaster would see him past the sentries
and down the road as well!

"I paid for three days' stabling for my mule,"
Kavi protested. "I didn't expect to be able to see
you so soon. I thought I'd be able to do a bit of trading here in camp." He gestured toward his pack,
which he'd dropped by the door at the tent guard's
request when he entered.

"You can do business in the town where your
mule is," said the substrategus. "The longer you're
here, the greater the chance you'll be revealed as
our spy."

Trust this man to be the first Hrum commander to care about that!

"But the rain's starting, and, ah . . ."

A commotion at the door of the tent interrupted Kavi's racing thoughts—but far from trying to stop the intruder, the guards stiffened to attention.

Governor Garren, the strategus who commanded the whole Hrum conquest of Farsala, pushed the tent flaps aside and entered abruptly. "We're moving our plans forward," he announced. "As quickly as possible."

Substrategus Barmael rose to his feet, eyes widening in surprise. The centrimaster straightened and laid his clenched fist over his heart in the Hrum salute. And Kavi took a step back, hoping to avoid the governor's notice.

Unfortunately, although Garren was more agitated than Kavi had ever seen him, he wasn't a careless man. His gaze touched Kavi's face and stopped. "You. I know you. You're Tactimian Patrius' spy. What are you doing here?"

Kavi fought down the impulse to say, *Spying, of course.* This wasn't a man you teased. "I came to report a rumor. About Sorahb's army having gone into the desert."

Cold eyes studied him intently, and Kavi suppressed a nervous urge to fidget.

"It seems to me that you've reported a great many rumors," said Garren slowly.

Kavi shrugged. "That's what spies do, mostly. Have I ever been wrong?"

Given that he had only reported information the Hrum already had—in some cases information about his own activities, though well after the fact—Kavi was certain of the answer. Garren might not know that his reports were always good, but he clearly knew of no instance when Kavi had led them astray. "Very well, you may . . . No, stay here in camp. This is too important to risk any leaks."

"I report rumors—I don't spread them," Kavi lied indignantly. "I'd be pleased to stay for a few days, but I'm a peddler. I've rounds to keep."

"Don't worry," said Garren dryly. "We won't detain you for more than a week. After that, it will no longer matter."

He turned away, clearly dismissing both Kavi and the rigid centrimaster, who took his arm and all but dragged him out of the tent.

Fortunately for Kavi's straining ears, Barmael's deep voice carried. "We won't be ready in a week,

Governor. And as I told you, beginning this battle before we're certain we can win, no matter what happens with . . . other plans, is courting disaster."

Garren's higher-pitched reply was lost in the noise made by a camp full of men rushing to get things inside before the rain.

"Well," said the centrimaster. His shoulders sagged in relief at having escaped the presence of a governor and a substrategus who were clearly about to start the kind of fight no lower-level officer wanted to get caught up in. "It seems you'll spend the evening dry after all, peddler. Let me introduce you around before the storm starts."

He meant, curse his efficient soul, that he would introduce Kavi to the men who held the watches so they'd know his face—and know not to let him leave the camp.

"Will you have time?" Kavi asked. "It sounds to me as if you're going into battle soon."

"Not with Substrategus Barmael in command," said the centrimaster. "He won't send us into battle until we're ready, so I think you can count on being here for more than a week no matter what the . . . Um. Plan on being here for a while."

Kavi looked back at the men who guarded the

substrategus' tent. They were there to keep eaves-
droppers out of hearing distance, as well as to protect their commander—standard policy for an
army that campaigned in tents. But judging by
their intent expressions, they were getting an ear-
ful. They would never reveal anything truly
secret, but perhaps . . .

"Lead on," said Kavi cheerfully. "If I'm going
to be here for over a week, I'd like to make some
friends."

THE GOOD NEWS WAS that Substrategus Arus had
taken all his men with him when he was dismissed.
At least none of the men that Kavi met looked familiar, and none of them showed any sign of recogniz-
ing him. The bad news was that now he wouldn't be
able to simply stroll past the sentries, pretending
that his business was done—but there were ways
around that. And with the centrimaster introducing
him to so many men, and the rain keeping everyone
who had a choice in the matter inside, it would be
easy to get a dice game running.

BY THE TIME THE GUARDS who'd stood watch outside Substrategus Barmael's tent came off duty,

Kavi's one game had become half a dozen, clustered at the end of the big meal tent. The noise
level was both loud and merry enough to do his
advertising for him; Kavi had seen to that by introducing a new rule to the game, a Farsalan rule
whereby every winner chipped in half his pot to
buy beer for the losers. And if Farsalans, who had
barely heard of dice before the Hrum came, would
have been astonished at such a custom, well, the
Hrum liked it fine.

Kavi watched the two guards, biding his time
and pretending to drink, as the men picked up
their meals and ate. There was always a chance
that neither of them cared for dice, though to Kavi
it seemed that most soldiers had a passion for the
complex games of battle dice. He hoped these men
did, for it would be harder to get them talking
about the events of the morning if too much time
had passed.

The time Kavi spent waiting wasn't wasted,
though. He learned from several soldiers about one
of Garren's new edicts: that resistance in Farsalan
villages and towns would now be punished in kind.
If Hrum barracks burned, a merchant's house
would be reduced to ashes. If supplies were stolen,

the livestock in the village nearest to the theft would make up the price.

A chill ran down Kavi's spine. What if a Hrum soldier was killed? he asked.

Oh no, the soldiers assured him. Imperial law required proper judicial proceedings for any execution, even in time of war. And while Substrategus Barmael was enforcing the other aspects of this new policy, he was doing so, . . selectively. Particularly in cases where it wasn't possible to determine which peasant, or at least which village, was guilty.

Despite his relief at that news, Kavi wondered how the other Hrum commanders scattered about Farsala were reacting to Garren's orders. There had been deghans, he knew, who wouldn't have balked at executing innocent peasants. Especially enemy peasants.

But whatever the past had held, tonight the Wheel was turning well for him; one of the two soldiers he was waiting for left the tent after his plate was clean, but the other came over to one of the dice games and pulled out his purse.

Kavi gave him a bit of time to settle in and start playing and drinking. Then Kavi lost, badly, three times in a row, cursed his luck, and declared his intention of trying another table. The fact that he'd been losing, which he complained about quite loudly, was enough to make him welcome in any of the other games.

The game in which the guard was playing was fairly intense, and for almost a mark no one discussed anything but strategy and the vagaries of the dice. But once the round was over, everyone relaxed, and the winner went off to fetch another keg of beer.

"So what brought the governor here in so much haste?" one of the soldiers asked. "Not you, Arex—I know you can't talk about it. But one of the grooms who took their horses told me the beasts were overtired. And the governor came on his own, with only a few deci of guards. That's got to mean something."

"Maybe it means we'll be setting about this great, secret plan we've been waiting on, and finally get something done here," another soldier grumbled.

"Come on, Ham. Do you *want* to assault those walls?"

"Yes!" said Ham, with the intensity of the

slightly drunk. "Get us a ram going, and we'll break right through those gates and get this over with. Then we can get back to a city with some women in it! More women, I mean," he added, as one of the female soldiers glared.

"Get plastered with flaming pitch, you mean," one of the more sober soldiers said. "I'm in favor of the plan—whatever it is."

Kavi tried to look drunk and indifferent as his mind raced. Evidently the common soldiers didn't know what was planned either, which meant he was probably wasting his time. On the other hand . . .

"So what do you think brought Garren here, all hasty-like?" Kavi asked, pulling the talk back from the subject of women, where it showed every sign of lingering. "He wasn't happy when he came into Barmael's tent, that I know."

For a moment they all stared at him, assessing his presence almost as if they were sober. "That's right," said the guard—Arex. "You were with the substrategus when he arrived." He giggled suddenly. He wasn't sober.

"Yes," said Kavi. "I'm working for him, you know." That wasn't exactly accurate, so he gave them no time to dwell on it. "But I've met the governor before, and I've never seen the man so upset."

Easy, easy. Don't tug the line. From the look on Arex's face he had news he was wanting to tell. *It shouldn't take much . . .*

"He's got plenty of reasons to be upset," Arex admitted slowly. "For one thing, there's been another governor sent back from Dugaz."

A couple of the more inebriated soldiers snickered, but the others looked grim.

"What is it?" Kavi asked. "Why does it matter if a governor is recalled?"

"They're not being recalled, exactly," said one of the more sober soldiers. "They're being *sent* back. By the citizens of Dugaz. In pieces."

"Oh. Ah, you said 'governors.' Might I ask how many . . ."

"This is the third, I think," said Arex. "But it's not the citizens of Dugaz who're doing it—it's those brigands who hide in the swamps. Which means the strategus is going to send even more centris after them, and where he's going to find them . . ."

He shook his head, blearily.

"Well, that's not our problem, Hieramos be

praised," said one of the soldiers. "But can you tell us if we ought to be sharpening our swords for tomorrow—or maybe even getting sober?"

The others laughed.

"We don't need to get sober," another soldier said confidently. "The substrategus will see that we get sufficient warning before *he* sends us anywhere."

"I can't tell you about that," said Arex. "But I think tomorrow will be as good a day for a hangover as any. I wouldn't be surprised if the governor has one himself. He's in a bad spot, poor bastard."

There was no sympathy in his voice, nor in any of the faces around him—in fact, a few held something approaching glee. Kavi took a moment to note that Garren wasn't popular with his subordinates.

The guard lowered his voice confidentially. "You know why the governor's here—because of his father and all, I mean. Why we've only got ten tacti to conquer this place, and no more coming."

Everyone around the table nodded bitterly. Kavi took another chance—it seemed to be common knowledge, after all. "*I* don't know," he told

213

them. "Though it seems odd to me. I mean, there's thousands of Hrum soldiers sitting over the border in Sendan, and here you are, spread thin as thin and working like dogs."

It wasn't entirely true, for the governor of newly conquered Sendan seemed to have no more troops than he needed—but he also had no fewer than were necessary. Between Jiaan's army in the desert and the Dugaz swamp rats in the south—not to mention every hotheaded village lad prepared to strike a blow for Sorahb as soon as the Hrum's backs were turned—Garren's army in Farsala was spread very thin indeed.

"We've only ten tacti, just ten thousand men, when we could have used three times that many! And all because . . . well, let's just say that the governor needed a bit of high-up help to achieve his exalted rank," one of the soldiers told Kavi.

Ham, who seemed a bit drunker than his comrades, snorted. "What you mean is that if his father wasn't a senator, he'd never have been promoted past decimaster—that's what you mean."

There was a moment of silence, the kind that follows a bluntly spoken truth.

"That's not really fair," one of the soldiers said.

"He's very smart, and competent for most things. I think he'd probably have made it all the way to, oh, tactimian on his own."

"I don't understand," said Kavi plaintively, though in truth he was beginning to. Rank among the deghans had often been achieved in the same way.

"The truth is that Garren was only granted a chance at conquest because his father insisted on it," said another soldier. "Everyone knows it. The high strategus argued against Garren's promotion to strategus in the senate itself! But Garren's father had 'favors' coming to him, and now we're stuck with the problem."

"That much I knew," said Kavi, stretching the truth, for he'd only heard hints of this before. "What I don't understand is, if his father's being so powerful, why isn't Garren sending for more troops?"

And why did smiles dawn on all the faces around him? "What?" Kavi asked plaintively.

"Well, peddler, Garren's father isn't the only one who can maneuver in the senate," said one of the grinning soldiers. "He was trying to defend his son—told the senate it was jealousy that turned the others against him. He said his son could conquer this land with just ten tacti, and the high strategus took him at his word. The deal is that Garren gets ten tacti and the usual year. If he fails to conquer Farsala without sending for more men, then he resigns in disgrace, *and his father resigns from the senate!* That's why the rest of the senate agreed to it, we think, because they usually support the high strategus and the council of strategi when it comes to things like assignments and promotions. And since he knew that Garren had a plan to shatter your army in that first fight, the senator agreed to those terms. Now they're both stuck with them. Can you imagine how that cold bastard must have felt when he realized that your people meant to go on fighting even after your army was gone?"

"And that's not the best of it," Arex chimed in. "Or the worst of it, from Strategus Garren's point of view."

The others stared at him expectantly. "Ah, I might as well tell you about this—if it's a secret at all, it won't be much longer. It seems Garren had an idea for getting around the limitation on troops. He requested a huge sum of money—some from his father, but even his family couldn't pay it all, so he requisitioned the rest from the imperial treasury—for the conquest of Farsala, right and proper enough."

Kavi saw his own puzzled frown echoed on several faces.

"What's he need that much money for?" a soldier asked. "We're already funded for all our equipment, aren't we?"

"Yes, but he doesn't plan to use it for equipment," said Arex, dropping his voice to a murmur. "He's going to bribe the Kadeshi warlords to send him men."

Kavi's heart sank. If that worked, Garren would get all the men he needed. Mazad would fall, and Commander Jiaan's amateur army—

"But we're fighting in Kadesh next," a soldier protested. "Isn't giving them a big sum of money kind of stupid?"

Arex was nodding. "Especially when it hasn't been authorized. That's what's got the governor peeing himself. The senate heard about how much money he requested, and they've sent a committee to find out just what he's planning to spend it on and how his conquest is going so far. If they don't consent to the bribe, that ends that plan. Not to mention the fact that we've only five months left, and half the country is still fighting. That's what the senate committee's going to see, no matter how many centris Garren throws into those swamps. That's where the committee's landing—in Dugaz. And there's no way he can slide that big a bribe past them, either. Not imperial auditors. That's why I told you," he added a bit guiltily. "With the committee coming to investigate, it will be common knowledge before long."

"The whole country's not fighting," said another soldier slowly. "It's just those bandits in the swamps, the rebels in the desert, and this city."

"And that's why Garren's here now," another soldier guessed shrewdly. "He's going to see this city fall as quickly as he can make it happen. Then he can leave just a few centris to garrison it, and send the rest of us to help in the other trouble spots. If we crushed those three forces, the rest of the country would stop fighting. We're going to be taking those walls, my friends, and soon—no matter what Substrategus Barmael might prefer."

The atmosphere of drunken good cheer had

vanished. Arex's eyes were lowered, and he was silent. If he knew what their plan for taking the city was, he wouldn't reveal it.

Kavi let the conversation go where it would, and the game resumed. He allowed several marks to pass before he lost again, and then wandered off to a third table. Most of the Hrum were heading for their beds now; the ones who remained were either die-hard players or very drunk. It wasn't hard for Kavi to select one of the latter, a guard to whom he'd already been introduced, and start winning . . . and winning.

He waited until the next afternoon to confront the soldier, who was still wincing at sudden noises. He winced again and then turned slightly green when he saw Kavi—it turned out he didn't have the money to pay his gambling debt, poor lad. And the Hrum took that seriously, too. It could stop his promotion if it got on his record. Couldn't Kavi give him a bit of time?

Kavi was deeply regretful, but he was a poor man himself—a peddler who would be missing his rounds because Governor Garren's paranoid suspicions had him trapped here. He had to make up his lost profit somehow, and if that meant calling in gaming debts, then that was what he'd do. And even that wouldn't make up for the loss of his customers' trust . . .

It took a fair bit of time to get the hungover fool to figure out he could let Kavi out of camp in exchange for forgiving his debt, but Kavi didn't begrudge it. If Kavi had suggested that solution, the man might have been suspicious, but since he came up with the idea himself, well, there couldn't be any real harm in it. His own centrimaster had introduced him to the peddler, after all, and assured him that Kavi was on their side.

The actual escape was almost too easy. The guard Kavi had suborned was stationed behind the privies that evening. Kavi simply paid them a late visit and then kept on walking into the dark hills beyond. His cloak—all men were wearing cloaks in the drizzle—even concealed his pack from any but a close examination, and no one was looking at him anyway. The guard kept his back carefully turned toward Kavi at all times so he wouldn't see him pass.

Kavi hoped the man wouldn't get into trouble—though if he'd been a guard in Mazad, Kavi would have felt very differently. But with any luck the folks who didn't see Kavi again would just assume that he was spending time in other parts of the great camp; it might be days before anyone realized he was missing. In fact, unless Garren checked on him, only the centrimaster would think to look. When he found that Kavi had vanished . . . well, no one had actually assigned him to the task of keeping Kavi in the camp. If Barmael had been the only one involved, the centrimaster might take the news to the substrategus, whom he clearly trusted—but given Garren's likely reaction, just ignoring the whole matter and hoping the governor forgot about it would undoubtedly seem like the sensible thing to do.

Yes, it might work out that way . . . but it also might not. Kavi wouldn't dare to return to any Hrum camp, for if Garren did learn of his escape, the governor's sensitive suspicions would be well and truly roused. No, his ability to stroll into Hrum camps and gossip was gone for good, but perhaps his news was worth it. Garren clearly meant to take Mazad soon, and Siddas and the others needed to be warned. Whatever their mysterious plan was, Barmael would give Mazad a much tougher fight

than they'd have gotten from someone like
Tactimian Laon.

But as to *how* they meant to take the city, Kavi
had had no more luck in discovering that than the
deghass she-bitch had.

CHAPTER EIGHT

JIAAN

IT'S AMAZING," said Jiaan, gazing at the fortifications around the Hrum camp. The Hrum had evidently decided to make a permanent camp there—or at least stay for some time. Once that decision was made, they had set to work with a will. The earthen dike that surrounded the camp was more than six feet high, and the ditch the earth had come from was full of water diverted from the stream. The area outside the fortifications where the brush had been cleared was so large that only the strongest archers had a chance of reaching the camp, and then only if the wind was with them. And though the tough, twisted stems of the desert scrub might not lend themselves to building palisades, the Hrum had sharpened short lengths and driven them into the sides of the earth banks, eliminating all possibility of horses charging over them.

"Which puts an end to both my plan of harassing them with archery day and night and your plan of galloping in on horseback and rolling over them," Jiaan told Fasal. "I can't believe they got all that up in less than two weeks! It's—"

"Don't you get tired of saying that?" Fasal asked sourly. "I assumed that with their commander taken, they'd be more . . . confused. Slower to react. That's why I thought a charge would work."

"I thought the same," Jiaan admitted. "About them being confused for a time. But whoever's in command now . . . well, if he's confused about anything, I don't see any sign of it."

Perhaps the knowledge that he would be succeeded by a capable subordinate had created some of the calm disdain that showed in the captured Hrum commander's eyes whenever he looked at Jiaan's ragtag army. He hadn't said anything insulting—he hadn't said anything at all, except to ask for what he needed to tend the wounded prisoners. But

Jiaan had seen the cool, almost amused contempt in his face as he watched Jiaan's men going about their duties. Jiaan was having trouble holding his tongue and his temper with the man, so perhaps his silence was a good thing.

"The walls are open where the stream goes in and out," Fasal mused, staring at the Hrum camp.

He and Jiaan were some distance from the Hrum camp, perched on a low rise, with half a dozen soldiers sheltered behind it. It was the only elevated ground in the area, and it gave them a partial view into the parts of the camp that weren't concealed by the bushes the Hrum had left intact — for shade as well as cover, Jiaan now realized. It might be midwinter, but the sun was hot. On the other side of the mountains, he knew, it was raining almost every day. Here in the desert it seemed to run in spells — it had been dry for the last two days, and only the nights were cold.

"Maybe that stream is a weakness we can use," Fasal went on thoughtfully.

Jiaan snorted. "You think you can gallop chargers up that streambed? The bottom will be sandy, rocky, and full of holes, like as not. And you'd have to go through the gap one or two at a time. They'd cut you down in an instant. Even those," he gestured to the sword at Fasal's side, "won't make you invincible."

The watersteel swords had arrived a few days ago, and when tested against some of the captured Hrum blades, they'd proved as strong or stronger. They were beautiful swords too—not fancy, but perfectly balanced, and sunlight ran over the patterned blades like a caress. There were only a few dozen of them, so Jiaan had passed them out to the best swordsmen in his army—which was why Fasal carried one and Jiaan didn't. He shared Fasal's desire to use them—to finally fight the Hrum with weapons as good as theirs! But they needed more of those swords, and more skilled swordsmen to use them too, so . . . "No," said Jiaan firmly. "No charges up the streambed."

"I was thinking," said Fasal dryly, "of poisoning them."

Jiaan stared at him in surprise. That was the kind of sneaky peasant scheme he'd never have expected from Fasal. He almost made a comment to that effect, but he was trying to encourage Fasal to think like that.

"I thought about poison too," he admitted.

"But it wouldn't work. Not in moving water. We'd have to have hundreds of gallons of poison to have a chance of affecting them, and even then the stream would clear in a few marks. And we can't dam it either; the valley's too wide. Their food supplies are limited. All we have to do is wait and starve them out. When they're forced to move, that's when they'll be vulnerable."

"But they know that too, don't they? So what are they planning?" Fasal asked.

Jiaan wished he had an answer, but he was spared having to fumble for one by the sudden appearance of a Hrum soldier on top of the earthen wall. The man stared at them.

"They've seen us," said Jiaan redundantly. "I wonder what they . . ."

The Hrum soldier stuck out his tongue.

"Is he . . . ? You're kidding me," said Jiaan.

Four more Hrum scrambled onto the wall, shouting, "Come and get us! Come and get us, coward boys!"

"Coward boys?" said Jiaan. "They can't do better than that?"

The Hrum proceeded to do better.

"I can't quite hear him," Jiaan murmured. "I

think . . . my father conceived me in . . . in . . . ah. You know, their Faran is pretty good. Anatomical."

"Do they really think we're going to fall for that?" Fasal's cheeks were flushed, but Jiaan couldn't tell if it was from annoyance or amusement.

"Probably not," said Jiaan. "I'd guess they're just enjoying themselves."

One of the Hrum pulled his britches down and his tunic up and waved his bare ass at them. Jiaan felt his own cheeks heat, but his voice was level, holding nothing but the amused contempt he so often saw in Tactimian Patrius' eyes. He was proud of it. "Now that just cries for an arrow."

He waved Aram up to join them. "Who's our best archer?"

Aram rubbed his grizzled chin with his remaining hand. "Besides yourself, you mean, sir?"

"I mean the best we have with us," said Jiaan, in the dry tone his father had used to repel flattery.

Aram grinned. "That'd be Tus. I'll fetch him up to you."

Tus arrived with a promptness that told Jiaan that he and Fasal weren't the only ones watching the performance. More than a dozen Hrum had followed their comrade's example.

"Any preference, sir?" Tus asked, nocking an arrow. His bow was already strung.

"You choose," said Jiaan, gesturing to the line of pale rumps in the distance. "I know the range is long, but . . ."

"Don't mind that, sir," said Tus gently. He raised his bow, aiming for loft, then hesitated, trying to guess what the breeze would do to his shot.

The bow snapped and the arrow hurtled into the sky. Jiaan watched it rise and rise, and then rush down. It missed one plump, white rump by a hand span, but the man's squawk of dismay as he leaped from the wall was audible even from that distance. He wouldn't land well either, not with his britches around his ankles. Jiaan grinned.

"Sorry, sir," Tus sighed. "I was hoping to puncture more than their pride."

"Don't worry about it," Jiaan told him. "Their pride is enough for now. We're going back to our camp. If they're going to rest for a while, we might as well do the same."

THAT WAS EXACTLY what the Hrum did for several days. The Suud grew bored and asked Jiaan's permission to go back to their clans for a while. Jiaan agreed, for as matters now stood his own men could keep watch, and when the Suud returned they could bring him news from his original base camp. He had taken all his veterans to fight the Hrum, but the trickle of peasants who were coming to join his army had recently turned into a small stream. Jiaan had instructed the Suud to lead the newcomers to his original camp, where a handful of veterans remained to train them. Without that training they'd be more hindrance than help, but soon . . .

It was Garren himself who was swelling the ranks of Jiaan's army so effectively. According to the men, who were now arriving almost daily, none of the Hrum commanders were executing civilians, but other reprisals occurred with increasing frequency and severity. If a man's farm was burned, what else could he do but join the resistance? Or at the least send some of his sons.

The Hrum weren't barbarians, but they were still conquerors. The Farsalans resented them, and Garren's edicts were only making matters worse. Garren's edicts combined with the efforts of the peddler, who was convincing the peasants to go ahead with their acts of sabotage.

Jiaan scowled. He had to admit it; the traitor was effective. On the other hand, if he hadn't connived at the massacre of the first Farsalan army, this one might not have been necessary.

Most of the new men wouldn't be ready to fight for months, but a report on their progress would still be welcome. When the Hrum's wounded had healed enough to march, then the Suud scouts would return. That was when he would need them.

TWO NIGHTS LATER, Jiaan was awakened from a sound sleep by a voice shouting, "Wake up! Wake up! They're coming! The Hrum are—"

The *thunk* of an arrow striking flesh stopped the voice, waking Jiaan far more effectively than the shouting. His heart thundered as he clawed free of his blankets and grabbed his bow and quiver. The Hrum? But how? He'd posted men to watch the Hrum camp!

Other voices were shouting now, cries of warning and alarm, and underneath them, in the stillness of the night, Jiaan heard the hiss of arrows.

Jiaan burst from his hutch in a scrabbling

231

crawl and looked around. The half-moon had emerged from the scattered clouds, gleaming on the armor of what looked like the whole Hrum army, or at least several centris, jogging briskly up the broad end of the valley. Their ranks were in perfect order except for their archers, who had fallen out to the sides to fire.

What had happened to the Eblis-possessed fools he'd had watching their camp? There was no time to invoke the djinn of sloth now, but part of Jiaan's mind was still swearing as he added his voice to those shouting alarm. He bent his bow against his foot and strung it.

All his men were crawling out of their hutches now, most of them dressed at least, since the nights were cold enough that men slept in their clothes. But even those who owned some form of armor weren't wearing it, any more than Jiaan was wearing his—and like Jiaan, most had neglected to put on their boots.

They all held weapons, though, and Jiaan knew they outnumbered the Hrum—they must, for he'd kept more men here than the total force the Hrum had brought to the desert.

But they were the ones who were outmatched,

as the Hrum swept into the Farsalan camp and began to fight.

"To me!" Jiaan heard Fasal shouting. "Swordsmen, rally on me!"

Jiaan couldn't locate the young deghan's black hair in the chaotic darkness, but he did see a Hrum archer taking aim at that firm voice.

Jiaan sent an arrow into the man's side, and the Hrum's shot flew awry. Dangerous as it was to draw attention, he knew that Fasal had the right idea—they had to bring some organization out of this mess, or his men would all be slaughtered.

"Archers to me!" Jiaan cried. One of the perimeter guards, engaged in a desperate, defensive duel with a Hrum soldier, tripped over something and fell. Jiaan's arrow pinged off the Hrum's breast-plate, but at this short range that was enough to knock the man off balance, distracting him long enough for his victim to stumble to his feet and run—forgetting his sword, Jiaan noted, though he found it hard to blame the man. At least he had tried. Quite a few men were simply running, running into the narrow, dark mouth of the canyon where the stream emerged, where the Hrum would have to break ranks to follow . . . where Jiaan's soldiers might gain an advantage, if their idiot commander could get them organized!

"Archers, rally on me; swordsmen on Fasal. Archers on me; swordsmen on Fasal!"

Fasal had already gained a sufficient force to take the fight to the Hrum. He shouted a battle cry and ran forward, barefoot, the swordsmen he had trained running with him. Jiaan shot another Hrum archer who was aiming at Fasal, in the throat this time, but he couldn't even spare a second to watch his victim fall, for the other archers were gathering around him.

"Shoot any Hrum who gets past our line," he told them. Fasal's embattled men had formed a ragged line. "Shoot any who seem—"

Before Jiaan could even finish, an arrow sped from another man's bow, raking the face of a Hrum soldier who'd been about to cut off the arm of one of Fasal's swordsmen. Other arrows flew as well, at the Hrum archers, at men who seemed to be in command, at any Hrum who was threatening a Farsalan swordsman.

Jiaan's archers understood their job, and it looked like Fasal's training with the swordsmen was paying off as well, for the Hrum's advance came to a halt. The Farsalan army was holding its own.

Jiaan knew that couldn't last. The Hrum fielded the finest infantry in the world, and the Farsalan camp had been taken by surprise. They had to fall back into the canyon, gain the high ground.

"Noncombatants, evacuate the camp!" Jiaan bellowed. "Fall back into the canyon. Archers to the canyon mouth. Cover the retreat."

Those who hadn't fled were already obeying his orders—the grooms had untethered the horses and were slapping their rumps, driving them into the dark, narrow passage. Under the direction of the middle-aged innkeeper Jiaan had appointed to run the camp kitchen, a handful of cooks gathered up bundles of food and hurried to follow the horses—except for one man, a one-handed man, who left the dark fire pits and moved against the stream of fleeing men, running toward . . . toward the prisoners!

Jiaan's gaze flashed to the sheltered undercut that some long-past shift of the stream had carved in the canyon's wall. He hadn't given the prisoners a hutch, fearing that a guard in that confined space would be vulnerable to attack, but he'd allotted them the shallow cleft. It was deep enough to keep the rain off, and the hutches were only barely warmer than the out-of-doors, so with suf-ficient blankets the prisoners had fared no worse than his own men did.

Only one frightened-looking guard had lin-gered, but he'd kept the prisoners under control. They lay on their bedrolls, face down, their hands spread wide on the ground except for Tactimian Patrius—someone had taken the time to bind his hands behind his back before fleeing.

Aram ran up, grabbed Patrius' hair in his only hand, and yanked the Hrum commander to his knees. Then Aram drew a kitchen knife from his belt, braced the Hrum commander's head against his body, and laid his knife against the prisoner's exposed throat.

"Stop," he shouted in clumsy Hrum. "Stop fighting, or I kill man."

For a moment Jiaan would have sworn that the clangor of battle lessened, that the Hrum hesitated.

Then Patrius shouted, also in Hrum, "Do not stop! Do not obey him. Fight and go on fighting, whatever he does. That's an order! Do not stop!"

The sounds of battle rolled on. Aram's lips moved, and then, even as Jiaan opened his mouth to forbid it, he drew the knife across Patrius' throat.

Jiaan stared in astonished horror as streaks of blood, black in the moonlight, flowed down from the knife. But only streaks, not the spurting flood of severed arteries. And though Patrius flinched back against Aram's thighs as far as he could, he never stopped shouting.

Aram, seeing his bluff fail, swore again—or at least Jiaan assumed he was swearing. He might have been giving orders instead, for the remaining guard seized Patrius' shoulder and dragged him to his feet, herding him toward the canyon with blows from the flat of his sword.

Aram turned toward the other prisoners, but Jiaan knew he'd have no luck getting them on their feet—the two who'd been shot in the leg still couldn't walk, and the man with the wounded arm had developed an infection and looked to die despite all Jiaan's healer could do for him.

Something jarred Jiaan's head, and a burning pain shot from his scalp. Even as he ducked and swore, clutching his head, Jiaan knew that the injury wasn't serious—for all that he felt as if someone had rapped his skull with a hot poker, he wasn't even stunned—but scalp wounds bled. Heat flowed through his hair, around his left ear, and over his throat and face.

Jiaan straightened, wiping his eye clear, and smiled in spite of the pain at the horrified expressions on the faces around him. "I'm all right," he told them. "But I think it's time we were going. Has everyone cleared the camp?"

"Yes sir," said one of the men. "All but the prisoners. Aram saw they couldn't move, so he just left them there. Didn't even cut their throats." He sounded disappointed.

"We'll leave them," said Jiaan. "They'll be more hindrance than help to the Hrum anyway." He could see for himself that everyone else had gone. The Farsalan camp was deserted, except for his archers and Fasal's embattled force. Despite the archers' support, more than a dozen swordsmen had fallen. Jiaan, suppressing a pang of grief, knew they were failing.

"Half of you down the canyon and up that narrow path that leads up to the top," he ordered crisply. "When the Hrum come into the canyon, slaughter them. The rest form up just inside the canyon, against the walls. We're going to have to shoot everyone in the Hrum's front line to get the swordsmen out, but the range will be close enough."

Close enough, in the confines of the canyon, for even a mediocre archer to put arrows into the throats and faces of armored men. Close enough for his archers to force the Hrum back while the beleaguered swordsmen made their escape.

The best climbers among his men were already sprinting for the canyon. The path up to the top was little more than a wrinkle on the rock face that would have made a sensible goat think twice, but it might be less dangerous than facing down the Hrum army, at that. Jiaan turned toward the swordsmen.

"Retreat!" he shouted. He wiped away the blood that still flowed into his left eye, and nocked another arrow. "Retreat, Fasal. Into the canyon!"

Fasal, for all his hot deghan blood, wasn't really a fool. His swordsmen were already inching back, step by step, over the cluttered maze of the abandoned camp, while the Hrum struggled furiously to hack through their lines.

Jiaan saw a sword, one that hadn't been replaced by Mazad's steel, shatter under a Hrum's.

His arrow took the Hrum in the thigh before he could step forward and slay the man whose sword he'd broken. Although another Hrum did slice open the man's chest and arm with a raking slash, the disarmed man was able to stagger back and flee, while his comrades closed ranks and took his place.

Jiaan, firing as rapidly as his blood-blurred eyes could find targets, realized that he hadn't given Fasal enough credit. The swordsmen, whose line was narrowing as the canyon narrowed, were holding back the best infantry in the world. They took grievous losses as they did, but by Azura they were holding them back!

Fasal and two others were the last into the narrow canyon mouth, where Jiaan and his small army of archers waited for them.

As the canyon narrowed, only three Hrum could enter at a time.

"Fire," Jiaan ordered, and his own arrow sprang from the bow to bury itself in a Hrum soldier's throat. The moment his string snapped, he and all the archers in the front row fell to their knees to give the archers behind them a clear shot.

Fasal and his soldiers backed up a step, and

then another, as the Hrum in the lead hesitated.

Jiaan didn't hesitate. "Fire."

More Hrum fell. The swordsmen turned and ran past him, through the massed archers, Fasal the last of them. His golden-brown skin was pale with exhaustion.

Jiaan heard the archers behind him thud down. "Fire," he ordered, and more arrows raced out. He had another arrow nocked himself, but when he looked for a target there was no one in the mouth of the canyon. Looking farther, he could see the Hrum retreating toward the wider valley, their shields raised to protect themselves from the arrows that rained down from the canyon's rim.

But looking over the bodies that lay on the blood-soaked ground between them—far more Farsalan bodies than Hrum—Jiaan knew that the Farsalans hadn't won. They had been lucky to survive.

JIAAN DIDN'T LET THEM stop until they reached the hilltop he remembered—big enough for his whole force to camp, yet steep-sided enough that the Hrum would be at a significant disadvantage

241

charging up. If they had to carry every drop of water they needed up that hill, then so be it.

"We were careless," he told Fasal, dropping down to sit beside the weary deghan. They'd had to mount the swordsmen, double, on the chargers just to get them this far, for they were too weary to walk. In some ways the swordsmen were now better off than the many who'd been forced to march through the dark rocks and prickly plants without their boots. Jiaan thought his feet hurt worse than his head, but his heart hurt worst of all, aching with the poisonous grief of guilt. "Careless, and lazy, and worst of all *arrogant*. What happened to the men who were watching the Hrum camp?"

"Dead or prisoners," said Fasal. "I thought about that too. It was foolish of us to assume the Suud were the only ones who could sneak through the desert. The Hrum will have scouts too. They probably waited until the clouds covered the moon, then crept through the open ground. After so many nights when nothing happened, the guards would have been bored, and sleepy. I just hope they haven't paid too high a price for it."

"I almost hope they have," said Jiaan bitterly.

"Azura knows *we* have. Where's Aram? I need a count of the missing."

Aram would have it, Jiaan knew. Even in the middle of an unplanned march after a battle, both of them in the dark. He had come to rely so deeply on the one-handed man who had feared he wouldn't be of any use.

Fasal was silent. Jiaan looked around. "Where is Aram? I don't see him."

Fasal's closed eyelids tightened. "He fell. After he tried his trick with the prisoners, he came to tell us to retreat to the canyon when you called for it. That's why we were ready to move. Some of the Hrum . . . I guess they were angry. I don't know." Tears streaked the grime on his face.

A cold fist gripped Jiaan's heart, but he took a deep breath, struggling against it.

"So he's a prisoner. That's too bad, but the Hrum will just make him a slave, after all. Even one-handed, he's a useful man. He'll come back with the others after we win."

Fasal turned, anger blazing in his tear-bright eyes. "Don't be such a wretched coward! He's *dead*. The Hrum broke though our line, and he was a one-handed man armed with a kitchen knife.

243

They hacked him to bits. He killed one of them while they were doing it, but Aram is dead."

He buried his face in his arms.

Jiaan laid his hand on Fasal's shoulder—it shook with silent sobs. He sat beside Fasal, staring dry-eyed into the darkness.

NEXT MORNING, WITH the few men who'd snatched up their boots scouting ahead for any sign of ambush, Jiaan led a party of soldiers back to their old camp to retrieve their gear. Most of the food was gone, of course. Jiaan could replace it from the supplies at their base camp, but what they had lost would add several weeks to the time the Hrum could hold out. Somewhat to his surprise, the Hrum hadn't lingered to burn the rest of the Farsalan equipment. Perhaps they were too busy licking their own wounds. Jiaan hoped so.

Fasal, grim-faced, silent except for the low-voiced orders he gave, organized the gathering of bodies and the cutting of wood for their pyre. Jiaan left the task to him. Almost a third of Fasal's swordsmen had fallen last night, dead or so badly wounded that it would be months before they fought again, if ever.

Farsalan deghans believed that the spirit, freed by the dissolution of the flesh, rose to Azura's realm with the smoke of the burning. Farsalan peasants burned a body to symbolize the Flame of Destruction that takes all things when Time's Wheel turns, and then turns again so the Tree of Life can grow in the ashes. It was also, as Jiaan's peasant mother once said when she thought he wasn't listening, a practical and cleanly way to dispose of a corpse, which was a practical peasant attitude. Watching the smoke rise, Jiaan didn't care who was right. It gave men a chance to remember and grieve — the last offering they could make to Aram, to all the dead, before gritting their teeth and getting on with the job.

But it was hard to turn his back on that fire and walk away.

THE SUUD FOUND THEIR new camp soon after dusk, shocked and clearly feeling guilty for having abandoned the awkward strangers who were in their care. Jiaan pointed out that the Farsalans *weren't* in their care, and that the fight they had died in was a war they themselves had carried into the Suud's desert, but that seemed to make little difference to the Suud. They had already checked on the Hrum camp, they told Jiaan, and if he would send the order, the Farsalans who were watching there could return. The Suud would not let even a mouse leave the Hrum fortifications without reporting to him the moment it happened.

The Suud scouts had already found three mounds of fresh-turned earth, topped with stones, on the outskirts of the Hrum camp. Roughly where Jiaan had posted his guards. There had been eight men on watch that night. He hoped the other five were prisoners, and well cared for. The Hrum were good for that much. Jiaan was avoiding the one prisoner the Farsalans still held—if he looked into the Hrum officer's eyes and saw contempt there, he would punch the man in the face.

THE NEXT MORNING, Jiaan himself went out to watch the Hrum camp. "They must have some weakness," he told Fasal, whom he was leaving in command. "If we watch them long enough, we'll see it."

Ordinarily he would have left Aram in charge and taken Fasal with him, but the young deghan had grown up a lot lately—perhaps it was time.

And Aram was gone; someone had to take his place.

Jiaan spent the chilly, overcast morning staring at flashes of movement in the brush behind the earthen walls, wishing that the Hrum had been foolish enough to cut those bushes down. He'd hoped to see some sign of prisoners, but he didn't. He couldn't even see enough of the tents to determine which one held the commanding officer, though there had to be more men coming and going from there. Would the officers' tents be in the center, where the brush was thickest? That would conform to the Hrum's usual method of laying out their camps. But even if they were, what of it? Jiaan couldn't attack any part of that camp without losing far more men than the Hrum would.

No, he'd been right before. Wait till starvation forced them to leave the desert, and ambush them on the way out. Perhaps the Suud could show him the paths the Hrum were most likely to take, and he could plan assaults along each route. He also had to make certain that the Hrum could never again surprise him as they had two nights ago. Or maybe . . . could he set some sort of trap, using his own camp as bait? But how? Perhaps Fasal would have some ideas, or the other squad leaders. Even Jiaan's father hadn't done all his planning alone. He should—

The sound of pounding hooves interrupted his thoughts, and Jiaan turned to see one of his squad leaders galloping a charger toward the rise.

Jiaan's heart froze. There was news, and bad news judging by the grim expression on Hosah's face. The young squad leader was one of their early recruits, a peasant born and bred. He'd been a stonemason before the Hrum had threatened to draft him and eventually his three younger brothers into their army. As he'd said to Jiaan on joining, "Better for me to fight with you now than have all of us going off to fight for the Hrum later." He had a broad, freckled face, surrounded by a peasant's light curls, and his speech was slow and deliberate—slow enough that Jiaan had assumed his wits worked at the same pace. But Aram, who usually preferred veterans like himself, had favored the man—that was why he was a squad leader now.

Hosah tumbled off his horse. He rode like a sack of grain—a sack that had been attached to the saddle by someone who didn't know his knots.

Most peasants rode like that. Jiaan's worry deepened, and he started down the rise. Most peasants preferred not to ride, for precisely that reason, so whatever was wrong must be urgent. But if that was the case, why had this man carried the news instead of one of the grooms who rode well?

"What is it?" Jiaan demanded as Hosah approached. "What's happened?"

"Well, it's not happening yet," said Hosah with his broad accent. "At least, I hope it isn't. But I thought you ought to know, sir." His usually open face was closed—almost sullen. And for someone who'd arrived in such haste, he was certainly taking his time getting to the message.

"What is it?" Jiaan asked again. "Get to the point, please!"

Hosah took a deep breath. "The lord Fasal," he said, using the title most of the men had dropped. "He means to torture the prisoner."

"*What?*"

"He means to torture the prisoner," said Hosah. "Heating up the fire pokers and all. He says that this man knows the Hrum's weaknesses if anyone does, and if he's . . . 'asked properly,' I think Lord Fasal put it, he'll spill them like water from a cracked cup. But I didn't think . . . that is . . . I thought you ought to know about it. Sir."

"You thought right," said Jiaan grimly, stalking past him. "I'll take your horse. I hope you don't mind walking back."

"Not at all," said Hosah. "Grateful for it."

A smile touched Jiaan's lips at Hosah's heartfelt tone, but it faded an instant later. He vaulted up to the saddle, clapped his heels to the horse's sides, then clenched his knees around his mount's smooth barrel as it broke into a gallop. The horse was sweating but not yet winded; it could maintain this pace for the short distance back to Jiaan's camp without foundering. But Jiaan would have pushed the horse to gallop till it dropped if that would have gotten him to the camp in time. It wasn't for the tactimian, either. As far as Jiaan was concerned, Tactimian Patrius wasn't worth the life of a good horse. There were other things at stake here. Things that were worth everything.

HE COULDN'T GALLOP the weary horse up the slope—it would probably have fallen and broken both their necks—so Jiaan ran into the camp on his own feet, panting and sweating from the rapid

climb, and probably not looking at all commanding. It might be important to appear commanding,
but Jiaan was too angry to care.

Looking around the camp, it was easy to see
where the trouble was—a large group of men clustered in a circle on one side of the rise, milling
uneasily, and the others were scattered at the opposite side of the camp, as far away from Fasal and his
hotheads as possible.

Jiaan wondered, stalking up to him, why
Fasal hadn't used the cooking fires to heat the
hooked iron pokers he had taken from the kitchen.
Perhaps the innkeeper had refused to allow it.
Perhaps Fasal himself had felt that torture and
food preparation went badly in the same place.
Whatever the reason, forcing Fasal to build his
own fire had delayed him long enough to save
Tactimian Patrius' hide—and the honor of Jiaan's
army as well. The irons were still lying with their
ends in the coals, though Jiaan could see that the
metal was beginning to glow.

Fasal's men had driven a thick post into the
ground, and the Hrum officer sat with his hands
tied behind it, facing the fire. They'd taken his
shirt, but his skin was unmarred except for a few

old scars. The Suud had once bound Jiaan and Fasal in a similar position. Had it been that memory that inspired this? But the Suud never had any intention of carrying out their threat, while one look at Fasal's blazing black eyes told Jiaan that he wasn't bluffing.

Fasal opened his mouth to speak, but Jiaan beat him to it. "You will not do this. Not under any circumstances."

Fasal's jaw tightened, but his voice was quiet, almost casual. "Why is that, Commander Jiaan? Have you already determined the weaknesses in the Hrum fortifications by sitting and staring at them?" He picked up one of the irons and examined the tip critically.

A murmur of agreement rose from the crowd around him, and Jiaan stiffened. When Fasal had defied him before, the common soldiers had backed Jiaan. But those soldiers had been led by Aram. A pang of loss shook him, but this was more important than grief—more important even than keeping his command, because if he lost this battle, none of the others would matter.

"No, I haven't figured it out yet," said Jiaan. "But we will, eventually, between us. Now I have a question for you: Are we better than the Hrum?"

It wasn't the question Fasal had expected. "What do you mean?"

"Are we better for Farsala than the Hrum?" Jiaan demanded. "Or are you just fighting so that you can be a deghan again?"

Anger flared in Fasal's face. "That has nothing to do with it! And you know it too."

"Then is it because you're pissed at them? For killing your father and all your family?"

"No. Yes! They've killed all of us, enslaved those left alive, and stolen our country! Now they want to draft our men to fight in their wars, paid for with the taxes they take from us. And if you don't think that's cause enough to fight, cause enough to die as my swordsmen did, then maybe *you* shouldn't be here!"

It was a cry from the heart—but Jiaan had learned to think with his head, even as some part of his soul bled for Fasal's anguish.

"All right, they tax us—but we've always paid taxes. And the Hrum provide good roads, and an army that will protect Farsala even better than the deghans did. And the Hrum don't torture prisoners. It's against their laws. So how are we better than the Hrum?"

"We're having no draft," one of the Farsalan soldiers chimed in. "That's what I'm here about. I'm not being hauled off to leave my business and fight in Kadesh for the next five years!" A rumble of agreement rippled through the crowd. But some men were silent—the men who'd come, slowly, from the other side of the camp to stand behind Jiaan.

"You're here now," Jiaan pointed out. "Fighting a war in the Suud's desert, away from your business. And there are no deghans left. Even if the Hrum vanished tomorrow, someone would have to fight off the Kadeshi at the border. So you and your brothers, some of you at least, will still have to fight. And the Hrum don't torture prisoners."

"Well, we don't keep slaves," another man said.

"No," said Jiaan. "We don't. But we're torturing prisoners. Ask that man." He gestured to the silent Hrum officer, tied to the post. He looked remarkably composed; only the pallor of his face revealed his fear. "Ask him if being a Hrum slave doesn't look good to him right now. The Hrum don't torture slaves, either. So if we do this, we're no better than the Hrum."

"I don't care who's better," said Fasal coldly. "I just want them out of my country. If the first step toward that is torturing this man, then I'm not afraid to do it. He has information we need to win! Information that might save our own men's lives! How can you not see that?" The cooling iron swept through the air in a gesture of furious frustration.

"That doesn't matter," said Jiaan. "What matters is that we have to be better than the Hrum. We have to be. Because if we're not, then it's all been for nothing. All the fighting, all the deaths. For nothing, unless we're better than they are."

"Your father wasn't better," said Fasal. "Your father wasn't too cowardly to order the torture of prisoners, if that was what it took to win."

Was that true? It could have been, Jiaan realized. Torture hadn't been forbidden by the deghans' laws. But even if it was true . . .

"That doesn't matter either," said Jiaan. "It's not about my father. It's not even about the Hrum, in the end. This is about *our* honor. We have to be better than they are, or it doesn't even matter whether we win or not."

Fasal didn't understand. Jiaan saw it in his face, and in the faces of the men around him. But some of them did. Hosah, still panting and red-faced from having run all the way back, did. And that too mattered. As for the rest . . .

"I order you"—Jiaan raised his voice—"to release this man. Neither he, nor any prisoners we may take in the future, will be harmed by any Farsalan, beyond what is necessary to keep them from escape. Any man who chooses to disobey this command will be cast out of the Farsalan army."

He made no attempt to imitate his father's command voice. This was his own voice—perhaps the first time he had used it.

Fasal's voice was very soft. "And if we all choose to disobey? What then?"

"Then," said Jiaan, "you'll have to find a new commander." It wasn't even a threat—it was too true for that, like stating that rock is solid. For a moment he thought it would become reality, but Fasal's eyes dropped. He tossed the iron back into the fire and stalked away, pushing soldiers from his path. Several of the surviving swordsmen fol-lowed him. The others returned to their own tasks, leaving Jiaan standing alone beside the prisoner.

"It's not over for him," said the tactimian quietly. "It can't be until he stops grieving for the men he lost. For him it may never be over, though fighting would ease his heart for a time."

Jiaan remembered that this man, too, was a commander.

"I'll deal with it," he said shortly. He wouldn't discuss Fasal's grief with their enemy. Privately, though, he agreed with the man's assessment—the sooner he gave Fasal a chance to fight the better. Jiaan cut the rope that bound the Hrum to the post, then drew him to his feet. "I'll post a guard for you," he added. The man's expression was still composed, but beneath Jiaan's hand his muscles quivered with the shock of relief. "Men I'm sure of," Jiaan continued. "This won't happen again."

"I thank you," said the Hrum officer.

"Don't bother," said Jiaan. "I didn't do it for you."

"I know," said Tactimian Patrius. His face was still pale and stiff, but his eyes were full of curiosity—and dawning respect.

———

CHAPTER NINE

SORAYA

CITIZENS OF MAZAD," said Governor Nehar, in a voice that carried for blocks without sounding like a shout. "You have fought long and courageously for your city, and never failed it. You have proved worthy of the highest honor any man might receive, and I honor you!"

He paused, clearly expecting a burst of applause. But except for his own household, and a handful of guardsmen who stood at the front of the crowd, most people greeted his announcement with something that sounded more like a mutter of suspicion.

The lady Mitra had offered Soraya a place on the balcony, from which the governor spoke to the mob that filled the square on the south side of the manor and spread into the narrow streets beyond. It was one of the highest honors the lady could offer, and Soraya felt more guilty than ever as she declined. "I'm not a member of your family, Lady Mitra, for all your kindness. It's your place, and your daughters', to stand beside him today."

Despite the cold that seeped from the cobbles through the soles of her shoes, Soraya preferred the place where she now stood, among the upper servants and the loyal guardsmen. She hoped her own silence wasn't too obvious—she thought it would pass unnoticed, for in truth, even the stewards' cheers were halfhearted. The grooms, cooks, and maids who stood in the next rank back were almost as subdued as the citizens. Only the guardsmen cheered with enthusiasm.

"But for all your courage, my citizens," Nehar went on, sorrow somehow tingeing that booming voice, "the land outside our walls has fallen. Yes, we might hold out for a full year and more—but what then? Our gahn is dead, and his child heir is the Hrum's prisoner, as are all the natural rulers of

Farsala except for my own family, standing before you. We have dedicated our lives to fulfilling the ancient bargain—to your protection!"

He allowed less time for applause now, which was just as well, since even his own guardsmen could only summon tepid cheers. Governor Nehar had never gone near the walls, so it was pretty cursed clear who was protecting whom.

Even little Armina seemed to understand that much. Her expression grew more sulky—and she had been sulking all morning, ever since her father had told her that he had no choice but to negotiate with the "wicked Hrum," and that she could stand beside him and support him like a true deghass or spend the next month confined to her room! So there Armina stood, but her expression and posture made her own views on the matter clear to anyone who looked at the child.

Mitra and Nayani, in contrast, displayed the distant, queenly dignity that Sudaba had tried so hard to instill in Soraya. If Nayani knew what her father had planned, she was too shrewd to reveal it to Soraya, and in more than a week of eavesdropping, all Soraya had heard Nehar tell his wife was that his "purchasing" was going well.

"My citizens," said Nehar, "I fear that the time has come for Mazad to acknowledge the reality that exists outside our own stout walls, so well defended by your stout hearts. It is time to negotiate with the Hrum."

The reality that existed outside the walls was that the rest of Farsala was rebelling as hard as they dared. They were depending on Mazad to hold out—and the townsmen knew it.

Soraya struggled to keep the contempt out of her expression. She might feel bad about betraying Mitra and Nayani, but Nehar deserved it.

The governor raised both hands to quell the rising babble of protest.

"It distresses me as much as it does you," he cried. "More than you, for mine is a deghan's heart! But I didn't say surrender; I said negotiate! I intend to demand—demand!—the return of our gahn's heir, and all of our people, in exchange for allowing the Hrum to move their armies through Farsala."

Which was a lie. Soraya knew that the Hrum only negotiated such terms with independent, allied realms—never with those they had conquered. And as for Nehar's "deghan's heart" . . .

261

The governors of strategically important cities such as Mazad had been exempt from the imperial summons that brought all the deghans in Farsala to the Sendar Wall. But most of the governors had left a deputy to rule their cities and joined her father anyway.

"I will not betray you, my citizens!" Nehar shouted. "I will never betray Mazad. I will negotiate our lives and freedom out of the Hrum's iron fist, or I will die trying! My own family will remain within these walls to govern and defend you. And if I fail, if the Hrum seize me as hostage, then I bid you, fight on! Fight on even if they slay me, for in the end it is your courage on which my success depends!"

Which made no sense whatsoever, since he couldn't succeed if he were dead—but it sounded good as long as you didn't actually think about it. Soraya's lip curled in a sneer that Sudaba would have approved. There was no chance of the governor seeing it, for he had chosen to end his speech on that lofty note, and left the balcony swiftly, perhaps hoping that if he did so the crowd's silence wouldn't be too obvious.

If she'd been in their shoes, Soraya thought,

she'd have cheered when he talked about the Hrum slaying him! Contemptible traitor. And without the peddler's excuse, either. Soraya sighed. She had nothing to report, but maybe she ought to report that? It was the best excuse she had to approach Master Tebin and Commander Siddas—to discover what was going to happen, and perhaps, somehow, find a way to help. Some other way, for as a spy she had failed.

She told one of the maids that if the lady Mitra asked for her, she had gone to the Suud, to explain the situation and reassure them of their safety. But she doubted that Mitra would notice her absence. The governor had left his wife in charge, not only of the city but of his own plans, whatever they were. The poor woman was so tense, Soraya thought she'd snap like an overstressed bowstring if anything went wrong.

She'd been forced to choose between her husband and her honor. A year ago, Soraya would have despised her for the decision she'd made. Now . . .

She sighed and set out for Tebin's smithy. Like Lady Mitra, she had made her choice.

The citizens of Manad, judging by their

comments as Soraya walked through the crowded streets, did not consider themselves to be Nehar's citizens.

"We've fought and worked and bled, and that soft bastard's going to give it all away!" proclaimed a furious man in a cobbler's apron, who seemed to be trying to rally his own crowd. He had no more success with that than Nehar had had with his speech, which didn't surprise Soraya. The terms of that ancient bargain—peasants to serve and farm; deghans to rule and fight—were deeply ingrained in the Farsalan soul. All Farsalan souls, deghan and peasant alike. Except for the peddler, who in his anger had broken that ancient bond.

No, she couldn't forgive him. But she was beginning to understand.

It was that understanding, when Tebin's servant woman ushered her into the small, warm kitchen where Tebin and Commander Siddas sat with the treacherous peddler, that let her step forward in silence and take a seat. Though she sat as far from him as the table allowed.

"Are you certain you saw no rams, lad?" Siddas asked. "Just the ladders you mentioned, and no more?"

"Yes," said the peddler. "Though they might have had rams in some other part of the camp, or concealed in a tent—or even being constructed elsewhere, ready to ship in like they did with the towers. But the soldiers I talked to didn't think they were planning on using rams either."

Thunder rumbled, heralding the rain, and Soraya shifted uneasily on the hard bench. But as long as she was indoors when they started, she'd found that the winter's milder storms seemed to ignore her—Azura be thanked!

"Maybe," said Siddas, turning his tea mug in slow circles. "A ram is a simple thing, not like those towers. It's just a big log with handles attached. There aren't any large trees in the immediate vicinity, but there are some that would do within a day's march. If the Hrum wanted a ram, they'd have it, so they're not planning to ram. But how do they intend to get through the walls, then?"

It was clear that he didn't expect an answer.

"You went into the Hrum camp?" Soraya asked the peddler, impressed despite the fact that she knew he'd done it before—he was marked as one of their own, after all.

"Yes, but I learned no more than you did," the

peddler replied. "Well, a bit more. It seems our Garren's in a tight spot. I'll tell you about that later. You'll enjoy it."

"He did fine," said Siddas. "And I've to thank you for adding to our knowledge as well, Lady. But I've already received both your reports. I just came today to find out when the next batch of those new swords would be ready, and thought I'd see if I could pry a few more details out of Kavi here. Are you certain, lad, that all the Hrum carpenters were working on scaling ladders, and nothing else?"

"I saw nothing but ladders," said the peddler patiently.

Soraya turned to Master Tebin. "*Batches* of swords?"

"Batches," he confirmed. His expression remained serious, but a spark of delighted pride lit his eyes. "We finally figured out the trick of 'making everything swim the right way,' as the sorcerer here puts it. You have to cool the center of the blade slowly and let the edges cool faster. Mind that's easier said than done, and I'd give a year off my life to know how the Hrum smiths do it, but having learned that, we've got every smithy in the city making watersteel swords now. The Suud lads are wandering from shop to shop, giving the blades a final touch of Speaking as they cool."

"They've armed most of my guards," said Siddas. "And we even smuggled a load to young Jiaan and his army. The next time the Hrum throw their ladders up the walls, our swords will match theirs. But they've tried coming over our walls before, and even when our swords couldn't hold up we beat them off. I can't believe their only plan is to try the same thing again."

The front door banged open. Tebin's brows rose, and his servant went to see who it was. If Tebin, even assisted by all the smiths in this metal-working city, had armed the whole guard with new swords, then Soraya understood why both he and the peddler had dark circles under their eyes.

"When did you find time to go to the Hrum camp?" she asked.

"Almost a week ago," said the peddler. "Under the circumstances, I'm surprised it's taken Nehar this long to make his move. I don't suppose you've heard anything, anything at all, no matter how trivial it — "

He was interrupted by the entrance of two

young men in the black and green tabards of the Mazad guard—tabards that were bordered with the gold insignia of the governor's household. Soraya shrank instinctively, though she had a perfectly good excuse to be here. Unless, of course, the lady Mitra thought to ask a few questions and discovered that there wasn't a Suud tribesman in sight. Soraya was groping for some way to distract them from this awkward fact when Siddas spoke.

"Ah, the last of my spies. Commander Jiaan loaned them to me, for which I owe him a great deal more than I expected at the time! Lady Soraya, Kavi, have you met Markhan and Kaluud?"

"Yes," said Soraya. "In passing." They were part of the governor's staff—of his loyal guards! They were spying for Siddas?

"No," said the peddler, looking at black deghan hair and young deghan faces suspiciously. "No, we haven't met."

"Then meet them now," said Siddas. "Markhan, Kaluud, Kavi is another of my spies. He's the one who brought back that last report from the Hrum camp."

And why did that make them look at the peddler with such startled respect?

"A pleasure," said the one Soraya thought was Markhan, though in truth she'd paid them as little attention as they'd paid her. "But we probably don't have time for that, Commander. After the governor rode out for the Hrum camp, Commander Birzan—finally!—told all the squadron commanders about the governor's plan."

Soraya's heart leaped and began to pound.

"So we'd be prepared," Kaluud added bitterly, "and not carousing in a tavern when the time comes. That's what most of them do. Well, you know, sir."

"I do," said Siddas gently. "And I know how hard it's been for the two of you to listen to my men sneering at you. I honor you for it, and they will too, once they know the truth."

They both looked grateful, and proud, as well. Soraya suddenly remembered that Kaluud and Markhan had once been among her father's aides. Clearly they had transferred their loyalty to this lowborn man. But Siddas was worthy of their loyalty, Soraya knew, just as her father had been—and they had proved worthy of his training. Pride in her heritage, a pride that Nehar's treachery had tarnished, glowed more brightly. These were real deghans.

The peddler frowned, but at least he was listening. He should, for they'd succeeded where he had failed!

"Well," said Markhan awkwardly. "Anyway, the governor plans to negotiate with the Hrum for three days. He'll say he's negotiating for the city, but what he's really negotiating is a position of wealth and rank for himself. On the morning of the third day he's going to send a message that the negotiations have gone well, and that he wants his wife and daughters to 'honor the Hrum with their presence' at a state dinner to celebrate their success."

"Remembering the limitations of Hrum army cooks, I hope the lady isn't expecting dove hearts in saffron," Soraya murmured. The peddler's lips twitched. Kaluud shot her a repressive look.

"When the lady Mitra and her daughters ride out," Markhan continued, "the Hrum will send an 'honor guard' to meet them—a big honor guard. Commander Birzan says they'll carry scaling ladders, disguised, though I don't know how they'll do that. They'll get as close to our walls as they can, salute the lady and her daughters as they pass through their ranks, then turn and charge, hoping to take us by surprise."

Siddas was frowning. "That's not much of a plan."

"That's not all of it," said Kaluud. "Birzan is going to arrange for the governor's guard to be assigned to the gate at the time."

"He's not in charge of assigning units," Markhan added, watching Siddas stiffen, "but he knows the commander who is, and there's no reason for him to object if the guardsmen wish to see their governor's lady and his daughters safely out. It will look suspicious if he refuses. They're going to wait till the battle is well started and everyone's attention is fixed on their opponents—then they'll open the gates. The Hrum who are nearby will be ready for it, and they'll rush in and hold the gates until the centris the Hrum have been holding in reserve can charge across the open area and into the city. After that, their whole army will be able to come through."

Soraya's heart chilled at the thought—Hrum soldiers sweeping through the cobbled streets, slaying any who tried to fight. All the people of Mazad had resisted their conquest. The Hrum would take every man, woman, and child into slavery . . . including her Suud friends. Thunder cracked and Soraya flinched, then willed herself to calm, shutting off her prickling awareness of the storm.

"But what Commander Birzan and Governor Nehar *don't* know," said Markhan, "is that Kaluud and I have been talking to some of the other guardsmen—very quietly."

"You could tell who wasn't happy with the way the governor was handling the defenses," Kaluud added, "though they couldn't complain— all the squadron commanders are loyal to the governor. Markhan and I were careful to approach the guardsmen slowly, but a lot of them have come over to our side."

Markhan nodded. "Almost a third of the men Nehar thinks are loyal to him are actually loyal to Farsala. Nehar never pays any attention to his inferiors, so Kaluud and I were able to gain their trust. They've pledged themselves to our—to your command, sir. When that morning dawns we will hold the gate, for Mazad and for Farsala!"

His voice rang with deghan steel and deghan pride, and Soraya's eyes blurred. The peddler, she noted, looked sour. Well, let him! It was deghans, true deghans, who had discovered

Nehar's plans—and would thwart them too!

"Your loyalty," said Commander Siddas, "and that of your followers, is a fine, rare gift, and I accept it with pleasure. But you say that only a third of the governor's guard will side with us?"

Kaluud and Markhan exchanged glances. "Not quite a third," Kaluud admitted. "But almost."

"We can't be sure how many of us will be assigned to the gate, either," added Markhan. "Kaluud and I will be there, because we've pretended to be the governor's men from the start. But the others . . . we approached those men because we could see they weren't pleased with Nehar's attitude, and I'm afraid Commander Birzan noticed them too. He has to assign some of our people to the gate, or he might not have enough men to open it and hold it till the Hrum get there. I think he's betting they'll obey their officers, since they won't have time to think. But few as we may be, our swords are yours to command, and we will die to a man before we fail you."

This is honor. Soraya's heart swelled. *But still . . .*

"The odds against your lads will be at least two to one," said Siddas, rather dryly. "Maybe even worse. I'm honored to command your swords, most truly, but I'd rather see you alive and succeeding than dead and trying."

"What else can we do?" asked Markhan. "Birzan is watching the placement of units. If you start shifting other troops in toward us, he'll know that you know. And he said something about contingency plans. I think they have a backup plan in mind if this fails, to let the Hrum come over the walls in some other place. The gate is just their first choice."

"And I can't afford to pull men off any other stretch of the wall," Siddas said. "If the Hrum launch an all-out assault, which they likely will if their trickery at the gate fails, I'll need every man I have fighting at his own post. But what other choice do we have?"

"As to that," said the peddler slowly, "I believe I have an idea."

THE HRUM MARCHED *against Mazad, and Sorahb himself dueled their treacherous governor, drawing the circle of challenge in the earth around his feet and bidding the man to come and fight. When the governor did so, Sorahb slew him—but the death of their spy did not stop the Hrum, who redoubled the force of their attack.*

The soldiers on the walls were sore pressed, and all through the long day Sorahb fought with them. His mere presence lent them courage and strength, for so it is with men when a legend fights beside them.

But late that afternoon, after many marks had

passed, even their great hearts began to fail. Sorahb saw this and despaired, knowing that only a miracle could save them. Perhaps the prayers of a legend are greater than those of ordinary men.

CHAPTER TEN

KAVI

THE LADY MITRA and her daughters rode toward the gate, the silk of their embroidered overrobes streaming in the cold breeze. The afternoon's rain was approaching. Mitra was supposed to have left several marks ago, but she'd taken the time to have her hair braided up with expensive glass beads. She'd taken still more time to pack the bundles carried by the horses and the one bewildered groom who accompanied them. It was far more luggage than even a deghass needed for dinner.

The lady Soraya had told Kavi that the woman had packed up the family valuables, but she must have brought more than just her jewelry to make up all those bulging bundles. Even the youngest daughter, her lips pouting in furious rebellion, had a pack strapped to her horse's rump.

It made them look like folks fleeing a disaster, which was why the governor had tried to avoid it. Even their rich clothes didn't detract from that impression. When the people had left the suburbs for the safety of the city walls, many of them had worn their best clothes as well—it was the most practical way to carry them.

In truth, Kavi didn't begrudge the lady Mitra her valuables. The gold and jewels she carried couldn't be eaten, nor melted and reforged as weapons, so they meant little to Mazad—and if the Wheel turned ill for her, she might be needing them herself. Nehar's treachery would soon become common knowledge in Farsala. Kavi doubted that the governor—the ex-governor—would survive it if it weren't for the Hrum's protection.

As for the impression the lady made today, that hardly mattered at all. Fully half the folk who had gathered near the gate to watch her ride out were Kavi's people, and they knew exactly what was going on. Even if he hadn't known them from the time he could toddle, Kavi would still have been able to pick them out—they were the only ones cheering with enthusiasm. Fortunately, there were so many of them that no one stood out.

The men in the tower beside the gate cranked up the portcullis as the lady Mitra's party approached, and then opened the massive wooden doors.

From his place at the back of the crowd Kavi could only see a small portion of the Hrum force that was already marching out to meet her. They had to cross the width of the rubbled plain—which had been a prosperous suburb before the Hrum burned it and then cleared away the wreckage to create a field where they could fight.

"They're carrying long fence-divider things covered with cloth." The lady Soraya stood on tiptoe to see over the crowd, though she was already standing on the steps of the corn chandler's shop, where Kavi had taken his position. "I wondered how they'd disguise the ladders. I think they look pretty suspicious, myself. They're decorative enough, like long banners, but the Hrum don't go in for decoration much."

Kavi looked at the patched skirt the girl had borrowed from a puzzled kitchen maid, and suppressed the comment he'd been about to make, that decoration was more of a deghan thing than a Hrum one. In truth, Farsalan peasants went in for decorating things more than either the deghans or the Hrum. If you had to paint something anyway, why not use a cheerful color and add a bit of pattern to it?

While he was being truthful, he also had to admit that the lady looked as comfortable in a servant's worn skirt and blouse as she had in her silks. She'd looked even more at home in the boy's britches she'd worn among the Suud.

At least she'd had no trouble staying behind. Even the lady Mitra had been forced to admit that she couldn't bring Commander Merahb's daughter to a Hrum dinner.

When Soraya had asked to be present at the gate this morning, Kavi had pointed out that there was little she could do in the coming fight. She'd promptly replied that a man whose right hand couldn't grip a weapon wasn't going to be of much use either.

It was different for Kavi. It was his plan. But he had to admit she was right; there was nothing he could do now except watch the thing unfold and pray that it didn't come apart.

The water carrier was already atop the wall—
he was the only one Kavi had been able to station
there, where his folk would be most needed. But
even as the portcullis rattled down and the great
doors swung shut, Nibbis the soup seller pulled
her handcart and kettle up to the tower door and
knocked.

"Will they let her in?" the lady Soraya asked.

"They should," said Kavi. "She often sells soup
to the men on duty, and it's cold today."

He had asked the woman, whose hair was gray
for all that her body was stout and strong, to yield
her place to her youngest son. He could claim she
was sick. But Nibbis had declared, firmly, that any
change at such an important time might make the
soldiers suspicious.

"Yes, but those men know they'll be fighting in
a few moments," said the girl beside him. "Will
they be hungry? Will they want to encumber
themselves with a woman in that space?"

Kavi shrugged. "Our folk will argue for letting
her in, no matter what the commanders say—and
they can't afford to arouse suspicion either. She's
the only nonsoldier who comes into the gate tower
this time of day."

At least the water carrier on the wall was so familiar that no one would think of repelling him. But the girl was right Nibbis had encountered some resistance. She stood in the doorway, with one of her small, portable kettles under her arm, arguing with someone inside.

But the argument between the street sweeper and the two carpet weavers put her efforts to shame. Those three were the only people involved who Kavi didn't know well. A trio of traveling acrobats, they'd been trapped in Mazad by the Hrum siege when one of the men had sprained an ankle; his brother and sister had refused to abandon him when he was unable to escape before the Hrum arrived. Siddas said that for folk not trained as soldiers they'd done good work on the walls, and they could get themselves up to the top more rapidly than any of Kavi's other fighters.

Those fool deghans and their men would need all the help they could get—when watch assignments were finally announced, the odds against them had turned out to be close to three to one. But neither Markhan nor Kaluud had hesitated for a moment, not that Kavi had seen. He sighed.

He hated the folk they represented, but he couldn't fault their courage.

"You've got to have the street swept," the acrobat wielding the broom argued. His voice carried like that of a man playing for a crowd—which he was, though he wasn't supposed to show it. "You don't want that fine carpet dragging in the muck, now do you?"

"Don't be ridiculous, snapped the girl who carried one end of the carpet. "It's wrapped around this pole—it can't drag."

Kavi had been listening for the Hrum charge, in the long minutes since the lady Mitra had ridden out, but the sound that finally met his straining ears was not the fierce drumbeats of the Hrum's signal, but the soft vibration of hundreds of running feet.

It was followed, barely a moment later, by Farsalan cries of warning and alarm. Given that both Nehar's and Siddas' guardsmen knew about the Hrum's plans, it was probably the most expected surprise attack in Farsalan history. But since both sides had orders to act surprised, it didn't make much difference.

Watching the guardsmen on the walls, Kavi

found he couldn't tell which were Nehar's and which had been subverted by Markhan and Kaluud. They all reacted with brisk competence, pulling out the forked poles they'd use to push away the scaling ladders, shouting down orders to bar the inner gates and for the men in the tower to bring the kettles of pitch—always kept warm—to a boil.

The tower that protected the huge winch that raised the portcullis was where the battle would truly be decided, Kavi knew. Markhan and Kaluud had only been able to get themselves and one of their men assigned inside it. So if Kavi's folk were going to help them, they'd have to clear Nehar's men from the top of the wall and get into the tower fast. But not so fast that they gave away their knowledge of Nehar's plan too soon—it was for the young deghans, who had taken the most dangerous and most important job, to judge the best moment to start the fight inside the tower.

Kavi found that his left hand was clenched into a fist, and his weak right hand was clenched as far as he could close it. He took a breath and tried to relax—just as the Hrum army reached the walls.

They didn't have much effect, as far as Kavi could see.

Farsalan archers fired down, and Hrum arrows arced over the walls as well, but the angle was so sharp that none flew near the steps where he and Soraya stood.

Still, the few ignorant citizens who had come to watch the lady Mitra ride out hurried away now. Some of them would be assigned to assist the soldiers on the walls, and the others would want to see to the safety of their homes—though now that the winter rains had started it would take a near miracle for a fire arrow to set anything alight.

The tower door slammed shut in Nibbis' face. She squawked with outrage and rapped on it, arguing with the men inside that they weren't likely to be in the fighting and could still use a bit of soup. Would they leave an old woman out in the street with an attack on?

It was the acrobats who managed the best performance, though, giving the rest of Kavi's people an excuse to be lingering in the shelter of Mazad's tall, thick wall.

"Out of the way, you . . . you broomy bastard!" the girl who carried the rug was shouting.

"We've got to get to our purchaser before an arrow hits this and wrecks two months of work!"

"But you haven't paid me," the acrobat with the broom whined. "I've been sweeping your path for half a dozen blocks. You're owing me at least two tin bits—a whole foal if you weren't so Flaming tight!"

The crowd around them divided their attention between the quarrel inside and the battle outside, just as they should. If they looked a bit nervous, well, that was to be expected. The Hrum had assaulted the walls often enough that no one was panicking over it anymore, but no one was easy with it either. Especially since the governor was now, presumably, a prisoner in the Hrum camp.

Yes, their reactions were fine. But they might have been doing a ribbon dance or holding an orgy for all the attention the guardsmen on the wall paid them. The guardsmen were pushing over Hrum scaling ladders in a kind of reverse tug-of-war conducted with sticks instead of rope. Though it seemed to Kavi that the Hrum weren't trying quite as hard as they might to hold their ladders in position, and that the men on the wall were as much engaged in shooting surreptitious glances at one another as they were in pushing the ladders down.

"What will they do," Soraya asked suddenly, "about the Hrum's ladders when they're fight—"

A clash of swords sounded from the gate tower. The thick stone muffled it, but the ring of steel on steel was as vivid as a war cry in this battle of ladders, poles, and arrows.

The guards on the wall shouted, and almost as if they'd agreed on the timing between them, turned and attacked each other.

"Now!" Kavi yelled.

The men in the street pulled out the short cudgels they'd concealed and ran for the nearest stair. The acrobats—their fake quarrel dropped in midsentence—unrolled the light rug they carried. The two brothers each took an end, while their sister grabbed the short staff the rug had been wrapped around, stepped into the center, and crouched. As she leaped, her brothers snapped the rug tight, tossing her far higher than she could have risen on her own. They had chosen a place where no one was fighting, which was just as well, since she only caught the edge of the parapet with her free hand—or perhaps that was what she'd intended all along, for she swung one leg over the edge and rolled onto the walk with an ease that seemed miraculous to Kavi.

Her arrival was the signal for the water carrier, who dropped his bucket, pulled out his cudgel, and started cracking backs, elbows, shoulders, any part of a traitor that came within his reach.

The brothers were already unwinding ropes from their waists and attaching grappling hooks when the girl spun toward the nearest of Nehar's men and swung her staff at the back of his knees.

He shouted with pain and surprise as his legs collapsed; then a blow from the flat of his opponent's sword tumbled him off the platform and down to the street. He cried out again when he hit the cobbles—he'd probably broken some bones.

Kavi suppressed a flinch, trying to harden his heart. If the man broke an ankle or two, it would be easier for those who had remained below to disarm and bind him. It was to be a battle that took place here, not a massacre—Kavi'd had a hand in one of those already, and he hadn't cared for it.

The girl whose father had died in that massacre frowned at Nibbis, who was lifting her large kettle off the cart.

"Should we help her? They've barred the tower door."

"She doesn't need our help," said Kavi. "Do you have any idea how much that kettle weighs?"

His point was proved as Nibbis pulled the kettle back and then swung it at the door, just where the latch would be holding it on the other side. She might be old and stout, but she'd been handling heavy kettles most of her life. The tower door burst open. As the thick, hot soup splashed over the steps, Nibbis dropped the large kettle, picked up the small one, and darted into the tower, ladle at ready. A scream sounded within and Kavi winced, imagining a ladle of hot soup striking one of Nehar's guardsmen in the face, in the eyes. Like the rest of Kavi's fighters, Nibbis had been introduced to all of Siddas' men who would be fighting in this area—Kavi hoped she had a good memory for faces.

The screams also told him that some of the portcullis' defenders were still fighting. Not that he'd needed to be told, for the portcullis was still down—not just a barrier, but a reinforcement for the outer gates if the Hrum did bring a ram.

Two guardsmen, the only two Siddas had

spared him, raced into the tower after the soup seller. As Siddas had explained, inside the tower there wouldn't be room for any more. But all of Siddas' men were armed with the new watersteel blades, and even if there were only two, they were the best swordsmen Siddas had.

Kavi's grin died as the water carrier cried out and toppled from the parapet. The acrobats, moving like the team they were, managed to catch him and break his fall. The man was unconscious as they lowered him to the cobbles, blood flowing from a sword stroke that had opened his shoulder to the bone.

The two brothers handed him over to the people Kavi had dubbed his "ground team"—he'd made sure there were healers among them. Then the acrobats tossed up their ropes; they were climbing to join their sister on the wall almost before the grappling hooks had set.

Several of Nehar's men saw them coming and cried a warning, but they were too busy with their own fights to intervene. There was nothing Kavi could do to aid the fighters, but he might be able to help the healers somehow. He was moving off the steps when Soraya's fingers dug into his shoulder.

"Ladders!" she cried.

Kavi looked up as two more Hrum scaling ladders thudded onto the ramparts to join the one she had seen. He shouted his own warning, but the guardsmen were already aware. One of them, next to one of the ladders, bellowed in anger and determination and launched a furious blow, not at Nehar's henchman, but at the man's sword.

Kavi, frozen despite the urgency of the moment, watched the watersteel descend. He could feel the ringing clash as the two swords met, not only in his ears, but vibrating through his skull, his bones. The shattering of the traitor's sword felt as if it were echoed in his own flesh.

He had time to marvel—as Nehar's guardsman fell from the wall, his wrist shattered along with his blade—at the strange ohilshadu gift old Maok had opened for him.

But not much time. The soldier who had broken his opponent's sword snatched up a pole and knocked down one ladder, and the two acrobats saw to another, but a Hrum soldier threw himself over the top of the third and vaulted onto the wall. His own watersteel blade carved patterns in the air before him—defending the ladder so his comrades might climb.

The men on the wall, Siddas' guardsmen and Kavi's civilians, surged toward him, and the Hrum struggled to beat them back. But Kavi's attention was suddenly captured by a sight so horrifying that the battle on the wall was forgotten: a tiny twitch of movement in the great iron portcullis behind the gate. It quivered again, then jerked and started to rise.

"On the portcullis!" Kavi yelled, running across the street to leap onto the grid. It sank as he added the weight of his own body to that of the iron, then rose again, carrying him with it. "On the portcullis, men!" he cried again. "We need weight!"

He suspected there was only one man inside the tower cranking the winch, which was supposed to be a two-man job. But that winch was designed to lift an amount of iron that made Kavi's weight irrelevant, and the man on the crank was desperate. The grate beneath him lifted a foot, and then another.

Three of his ground team, big, muscular men, leaped onto the portcullis. It fell back to the ground, almost jolting Kavi's right hand loose, though his left held firm. Then the portcullis shuddered and started to rise again, but more of Kavi's folk were coming now, and he climbed higher up the grid to make room for them.

Craning his neck, he saw the lady, still standing on the steps, her teeth clenched in her lower lip with the desire to help, somehow, anyhow— but knowing that with her light weight she'd just be using up space better given to a heavier man, like those who were now climbing aboard.

The wooden gate beyond the portcullis shook, banging into Kavi's toes. The Hrum on the other side were getting impatient, but without a ram they'd have trouble breaking through the wooden doors; with the portcullis reinforcing them, they had no chance. As long as the portcullis stayed down . . . But it wasn't moving now, not even a quiver. Kavi saw some of his men, his ground team, going into the tower, helping out blood-spattered men in the black and green tabards of Mazad's guard.

Nibbis came out, her bright blouse and skirt stained with blood from several cuts. Kaluud, who was limping, had hold of her arm—though who was supporting whom was open to debate. If Kaluud had abandoned his post, then the fight for the winch was over.

Kavi climbed down from the grate, his hands aching with the sudden relaxation of his grip.

Despite the blood, the pain, and his horror at the injuries his own folk and even his enemies had sustained, he felt a fierce pride at how well they'd fought. If the deghans hadn't forbidden it, his folk could have ruled and defended themselves. Always! He wasn't wrong.

But looking at the lady Soraya's strained face, holding to her post because it was the sensible thing to do, and at Kaluud, helping an old peasant woman into the hands of the healer before seeking attention for the bloody gash on his thigh, Kavi knew he hadn't been right, either.

He walked forward on shaking legs, praising the men he passed for their effort, for their courage. He took some consolation from the grins they gave him and in the knowledge that the tower door was barred, braced, and guarded. The Hrum were gone from the wall now, and the handful of traitors who still fought wouldn't be opening that gate, not today. It was his people who had made that possible, and they knew it too.

But Kavi also knew that if the battle for the gate had ended, the battle for Mazad had just begun.

——∽——

CHAPTER ELEVEN

SORAYA

SHE HAD TO GET HIGHER in order to see. The peddler had done a magnificent job of rallying his people, and they had won the gate. Kaluud limped out of the tower, assisting the soup seller—still alive, both of them, however badly battered. Within the tower Soraya could see Markhan, evidently not so badly hurt, for he was giving orders to the men who remained, sending the enemy wounded out to the healer and securing those who had surrendered.

The fight on the walls was all but over too. The female acrobat sat on the walkway, rocking in pain, clutching a leg that even from her angle Soraya could tell was broken. If it healed badly, it might mean the end of the girl's career, but if the Hrum won she could lose far more—and the Hrum could still win. Especially with Substrategus Barmael in charge.

Standing idle while the peddler and his people fought for their city, Soraya found that though her eyes gave her the most information about the battle in front of her, it was her ears that told her what was happening in the battle farther down the wall. The sound of war was a demon hymn of cracks, thuds, shouts, and screams, blended by distance into a dull surf roar—but by now her ears were sufficiently accustomed that she could hear the change in pitch as word passed that the attempt on the gate had failed. The Hrum were fighting harder, no longer waiting for the gate to open so they could march in. But even as the Hrum turned their full attention to the fight that lay before them, something nagged at Soraya's consciousness. This still didn't sound like . . . like the desperate determination she'd have expected in an all-out assault. Yet Garren had to win today, so why . . . ? Of course! They were waiting for the reinforcements that would join them at the walls as soon as Barmael realized that Nehar's plan to open the gate had failed.

She had to see, Soraya realized abruptly. She had to see not only more of the walls and more of the battle—she had to see more of the sky.

The storm was nearly there; a small, soft winter rain, the kind she had learned how to flee. More important, the kind that everyone, townsmen and Hrum alike, had learned to fight through with only mild irritation at being wet. But perhaps Soraya could change that—if she had the courage.

The doors of the corn chandler's house were open as the townsfolk carried in the wounded. All the homes and businesses near the wall were accustomed to sheltering and caring for the injured after a battle—the owners often doing the nursing themselves until a healer could come. This time, along with the guard, the townsfolk would be caring for some of their own.

Soraya bit her lip, winced, and deduced that she had bitten it before without even being aware of it. If these peasants could fight so hard for Farsala after their deghan governor had betrayed them, how could Soraya do less?

Holding fast to her courage, Soraya slipped into the house, following some men who were carrying in a guardsman, unconscious and covered with blood. Soraya didn't know if he was a traitor or loyal, and the people the peddler called his ground team had cut up the man's tabard to bandage his bleeding ribs.

The peddler had done well here. In fact, he had probably saved the city. Markhan and Kaluud had been willing to die to defend the gate, but after watching the fight this morning Soraya knew that without the peddler's plan, they would have died. And the city would have fallen. Kavi had earned the name the peasants attached to his exploits, never knowing that the man they called Sorahb was the familiar peddler who sat before them, drinking beer, as he himself gossiped about the legendary hero.

The stairway was at the end of the hall, where she'd expected to find it; one girl, climbing quietly out of the chaos below, could go up unobserved. On the second floor of the house she would have been noticed, but there was no one on the second floor—they were all downstairs dealing with the terrible aftermath of battle.

For a moment Soraya's resolve weakened. She could go back down the stairs and assist the healers. Surely if she did that—such a useful, urgent task—no one could call her a coward. If the storm's lightning found her, not even the best of healers would be able to do anything for her charred remains. In fact if she didn't go below and help, they would call her a coward—a useless lady-deghass who wouldn't dirty her hands even with the blood of men fighting for her own cause!

But if she went on, if she faced the storm, far fewer men might bleed, and more would remain to fight again. It had nothing to do with what people called her, Soraya realized. Not even with what she knew in her heart to be true. It was about Farsala. About her three-year-old brother growing up a Hrum slave, and all the other children, men, and women enslaved with him.

Soraya gritted her teeth and climbed the last flight of creaking stairs. The third floor was smaller, the ceiling slanting beneath the pitch of the roof. At the end of the corridor Soraya saw a door, which she found opened on to a small balcony. It would give the servants and clerks who slept in the chambers under the eaves a place to look out and judge the day's weather. Barely large enough for three people to stand on, it was bright with peasant paint, and stray arrows had gouged the wood of the railings and door. If the Hrum shot more arrows over the wall, they might kill her before the lightning could. But the balcony gave Soraya the view she needed.

The Hrum reinforcements hadn't yet marched out of their camp, but looking over the wall she could see them ordering their ranks in the field in front of their tents. They carried many more ladders now, and Soraya, looking at the battle that raged along the wall, felt a fresh chill of fear. The Farsalans were already hard-pressed.

The tattoo with which Garren had hoped to humiliate her when he declared her a slave had not ached in months, but Soraya found herself rubbing it and snatched her hand away. She had concealed it from the lady Mitra and her family—easy enough in long-sleeved winter garments—for she knew they would have been horrified. Soraya had never minded the mark, for she saw it as a badge of honor. She had never been a slave, whatever the Hrum might have thought—she had been a rebel and a spy. But what if she became a slave in truth? She might, along with all of the townsfolk of Mazad, if the Hrum won today. Soraya turned to the sky.

At least she wouldn't have to call this storm to her; it swept in on the cold, damp wind with the relentless ease of the winter rains. Soraya's shilshadu senses touched it, feeling its smooth, restless energy. Soraya drew a deep breath and opened herself to the storm.

It seemed to flow into her as easily as it flowed through the air that formed it; the light trance claimed her with no effort at all. Soraya had always had an affinity for storms, she realized, much like the peddler's affinity for steel — but that didn't mean the storm wouldn't slay her, any more than he was immune to burns from the hot metal. That was the last human thought to slip through her mind before the storm claimed her.

It was an odd sensation, for she still looked through her own eyes, watching the Hrum troops rush across the muddy ruins that surrounded the walls from the same position as she had before. But she saw them as the storm would see them, less than ants — for to a human ants are alive, and to the storm they were nothing but bits of landscape that moved.

The storm favored them more than earth that didn't move, for the storm was all movement, flowing without effort through the warm and cool currents of the air, using them to build its energy. Build and build, for it was born of air and the energy air generated. Water gave it weight and mass, and it gloried in its own power and existed for nothing else.

But the part of the storm that was Soraya did care for some of those moving bits of earth, and she willed the storm to stop, here, above them. Stopping was no part of the storm's nature, and the alien thought almost pushed Soraya back into herself. So instead she drove the storm into motion, motion that swirled around itself, motion that was not stopping, but simply moving in the same part of space.

The storm's charged air was unbelievably slippery. Trying to twine it around itself was like trying to knit with wisps of unspun wool, the strands escaping in every direction at the whim of the storm—and Soraya was even worse at knitting than she was at embroidery. But soon the storm found that when it twisted on itself in a certain way, its energy grew, and it followed those paths as eagerly as water flowing downhill, for it loved growing upon itself.

The loose clouds became denser and formed thunderheads, large and black, stretching into the cold of the highest sky. More water added mass, creating its own energy. Lightning was born in the swirling currents of the wind, and it blazed and struck, illuminating the moving things in the darkness below.

Soraya laughed in delight, for the part of her that was the storm, by far the greater part, had no more fear of the lightning than she had of her own hands. Some part of her that was still Soraya didn't dare to grasp the liquid fire with hands and mind made of mortal flesh. But she urged it to be born and rejoiced when it struck, struck again and again in the city, the camp, the countryside. She cared not where, for the earth meant nothing to the storm, and now, deep in her trance, she was almost wholly inhuman.

Her body didn't feel the cold drops pelting her clothes and flesh. Instead she felt the rain as a great release of pressure, of weight, like grain slowly spilling from a basket she had carried for too long. It felt good to drop the rain, and she dropped it faster and faster. Only her human eyes saw water pouring from the gutter spouts, running over the cobbled street in rushing streams. Only the smallest, most buried part of her mind knew what this dense rain would do to the already sodden earth around the walls. Carrying a ladder through that sea of sticky mud would be like dragging logs through a swamp. Raising a ladder, as its legs sank and slithered in the muck, would be impossible. So the human part of her laughed at the deluge, and lightning cracked in echo, and she laughed at that, too. When the Hrum army retreated, she didn't even know it, because the storm didn't care.

EVENTUALLY THE STORM, having shed its energy, dissolved into the wind and dissipated, and Soraya came slowly back to herself. She was lying on the balcony, one cold cheek flattened against the wet wood, the other covered with strands of dripping hair.

But she wasn't as cold as she should have been. Stirring, she discovered that though her clothes were wet, she was tightly wrapped in several wool blankets, which were almost dry since an oiled-silk tarp had been wrapped around them in turn.

She was chilled and damp and spent . . . so spent that she felt almost as insubstantial as the last wisps of the storm, as if she too might dissolve into the air. But she wasn't freezing.

It must have been the peddler who had wrapped her up and left her there; no one else would have recognized the shilshadu trance. The others would have carried her in and tried to wake her. Remembering the storm, the vivid seeking of the lightning, Soraya knew that that would have been disastrous.

She had hidden herself from the lightning, she slowly realized, by burying herself in the storm. It hadn't been attracted to her because she had barely existed.

In one sense, she supposed, that was cowardice, but she was too tired to care. And despite her exhaustion a deep satisfaction welled within her. If the peddler had had time to come looking for her and bundle her up like an infant, then the Hrum had been beaten off. And if their all-out attack had failed, failed badly, Soraya didn't think even Garren would be able to try again before the senate committee arrived.

Her lips were almost too stiff with cold to smile, and she realized she'd better move. It was a struggle to extract herself from the blankets. When she finally crawled through the door, she collapsed on the floor as soon as she was inside. Usually working the Suud's magic gave you more energy, but the storm had stolen hers away. In a few minutes, Soraya resolved, she would recover enough to stand. Then she would go downstairs, resting a time or two along the way, eat a huge meal, topple into bed, and sleep for a week.

Surely she would have at least a week before Governor Garren made his next move.

CHAPTER TWELVE

JIAAN

URING THE DAY, with so many eyes upon the prisoner and the men guarding him, Jiaan had no fear that he would "disappear," even if the guard were distracted for a moment. But in the darkness . . .

"There's no help for it," he told Hosah grimly. "He'll have to sleep in my hutch. No one would dare try to get to him there."

Jiaan had spent the rest of the day among the soldiers and squad leaders, mostly listening. He now knew that Fasal commanded the loyalty of less than a third of them, and even those men preferred that there be no power struggle between their two leaders. But they did see the army as having two leaders, not one commander and several subordinates, and that was dangerous. If they could distract the guards and get their hands on the prisoner, they would do so—more to uphold their chosen commander's authority than out of any need for information. But in Jiaan's own hutch the prisoner would be safe, for no one would go so far as to fight Jiaan for him. Not yet.

Less than four months, he thought. *If I can hold this army to its purpose, keep some part of Farsala free of the Hrum for four months, then Fasal can do whatever he likes.*

Yet his heart ached at the thought of abandoning his men, the army he had created. For all the stress and irritation that were daily parts of the job, he knew he was good at it—better than Fasal would be anyway!

Hosah, who seemed to have attached himself to Jiaan, promptly provided one of those irritants—subordinates who questioned his decisions. "Are you sure about that, sir? I thought you said that inside a hutch they'd be close enough to take a guard by surprise. And there's not enough room in your hutch for you, a guard, and a prisoner."

"The guard will stand outside," said Jiaan patiently, "with orders to cut his way through the walls the instant he hears anything suspicious. If we shackle the prisoner's right wrist and ankle to the posts and keep anything that could be used as a weapon out of his reach, what can he do to me, even in my sleep, with just one hand?"

Hosah thought it over, and his troubled frown lightened. "That'll do, sir. I'll get shackles from our stores and see that your hutch is prepared and the prisoner settled before you're ready for bed. That way he won't be disturbing you."

"He'd better not," said Jiaan. "Or I might change my mind."

He had saved the man, but that didn't mean that he liked him, and the thought of sleeping under the eyes of an enemy officer was . . . disturbing. But it seemed the only way to make sure that the man stayed safe—and that Jiaan's army remained under his control.

HE HAD PREPARED HIMSELF, as he left the circle of men who gathered around the big cookfire shortly after the winter's early sunset, but it still felt odd to enter his own hutch and find a man chained there.

309

The silk walls admitted enough light to see that Hosah had stacked the chests that held Jiaan's personal possessions at the foot of his bedroll, binding the prisoner by his wrist and ankle on the other side of the small hutch—with rather short chains, Jiaan noted. He might, if he stretched as far as possible, be able to touch the chests with his free foot. But he couldn't reach behind them to pull them toward him, and if he kicked them over it would wake Jiaan and alert the guard.

There was nothing within reach of his left hand except the blanket and pillow of his own bedroll, and just possibly Jiaan's. If he tried to smother Jiaan in his sleep with just his left hand . . . Jiaan found a small, malicious smile tugging at his lips and banished it. It was as wrong for him to want to take out his rage and grief on a helpless prisoner as it was for Fasal—worse, for he hadn't even the excuse of seeking information. And, he reminded himself, this man had had nothing to do with the attack where Aram died.

"Are you comfortable?" Jiaan asked shortly.

"Perfectly," said Tactimian Patrius even more shortly.

Jiaan eyed him. He didn't look comfortable.

The thin bronze circles clasping his wrist and ankle probably wouldn't be too burdensome, if not for the chain linked through them and fastened to the strong, deep-driven poles that supported the hutch. Jiaan himself had once been tied to one of those poles, and he knew how immovable they were.

Patrius had only one hand free to tuck behind his head, and perhaps six inches of movement for his right wrist and ankle—but the blankets covered him, so at least he'd be warm. Even when the Hrum kept their slaves imprisoned, which they seldom had to, they kept them in iron-barred pens where they had plenty of room to move, to sleep in whatever comfort they could find. On the other hand, if the man said he was comfortable, Jiaan wasn't inclined to press him further.

Without another word he unfastened the belt that held his sword and dagger, laying them with his quiver and bow, which Hosah had put behind the stack of chests. Jiaan might have trouble reaching them swiftly—usually he left his weapons right beside his bedroll—but they were well out of the prisoner's reach.

Jiaan stripped off his outer clothes, shivering in the chill air, and sought his blankets, which

were cold too. But as he lay listening to the soft
conversations of the men who lingered by the fire,
his blankets slowly warmed.

He was very aware that another person
shared his tent—aware of his breathing, of the
small movements that made the chain rattle. As
his father's aide Jiaan had often shared tents with
the other aides, many of whom despised him as a
peasant-born half-blood, and some of whom he'd
disliked in return.

But he hadn't caused any of them to be held in
chains.

In a way the distraction was a good thing, for
it kept him from thoughts of Aram, which might
have made him weep. He was relaxing toward
sleep when the Hrum commander said softly,
"Your officer was wrong, you know."

"He's wrong about a lot of things," said Jiaan,
and then remembered that he should uphold
Fasal's authority before this man. "I mean . . . to
what are you referring?" His voice became coolly
formal on the final words, but the prisoner
laughed, a bare puff of breath in the firelit dimness.

"I meant that I don't know of any weaknesses

in my force. He'd have learned nothing from me, no matter what he did."

Jiaan snorted. "Of course you expect me to believe that?"

"I can prove it," said Patrius. "At least, after a fashion. Tell me, if you were aware of a weakness in your command that we could exploit to defeat you, what would you do?"

"Fix it," said Jiaan. "Immediate . . . Oh."

"Exactly," said the Hrum officer. "If we have weaknesses, you can be certain that I'm the one person who *doesn't* see them. Or they wouldn't be there anymore."

Jiaan fell silent, for the man's logic was irrefutable. He was wondering if he could get Fasal to see it, when he finally fell asleep.

He spent the next few days observing the Hrum army with the sullen Fasal at his side. He said nothing to Patrius during the day, and no more than a few words each night. The Hrum officer watched him, without a trace of the reserved contempt that had previously been so marked in his expression.

By the third day Fasal was bored enough to start complaining. "If we could see anything, then

there might be some use in it. But those Ahriman-
spawned bushes are so thick, all you can see are
men darting in and out of them. They're beginning
to turn brown, but as far as I can tell they haven't
lost a single leaf. Unless the Hrum are doing something obvious, like leading mules to the stream or
carrying a basket of clothes to wash, you can't
even guess what they're doing!"

It was yet another truth Jiaan couldn't deny.
"They are thick," he admitted. "Very . . ." His
heart began to pound. They *were* beginning to turn
brown. The green boughs hadn't burned well, but
he hadn't tried to burn dried ones.

"Very what?" Fasal asked impatiently.

It was too soon to talk about it, especially with
Fasal. "Very thick. So we'll just have to watch a bit
longer."

That evening, after dinner was served but
before men started drawing near the heat of the
cookfire, Jiaan wandered into the hills. It took
some time to find dead branches on live bushes,
but eventually he came across a place where a
recent rock fall had broken several limbs. It
looked like they'd been dead somewhat longer
than the ones in the Hrum camp, but it was prob-

ably as close as Jiaan was going to get. He built a small fire, laying the dried boughs in the flames with hands that shook with hope.

Even dry, it took a while to get them started— but once they began to burn, they burned very hot. The bushes in the Hrum camp were still green, of course, but the Hrum had made so many screens and shelters with the branches they had cleared around their perimeter that there might be enough fuel to set even the live bushes alight! Jiaan resolved to gather more dried boughs the next day and do some experiments.

"I WAS WONDERING about the Hrum," he said to Patrius that night. "You seem very organized. Prepared."

Jiaan knew how lame it sounded, how suspicious after several nights of silence. But he couldn't think of any way to start a conversation that wouldn't sound suspicious, and if he could get the tactimian talking about the Hrum's preparedness in general, he might be led to discuss the preparations they took against fire.

Chains jingled as Patrius rolled onto his back. "We try to be efficient. It's the only way to handle armies the size of ours. If you aren't well organized, in almost every aspect of life, you get bogged down." The words came easily, but his tone was reserved—wary. He knew Jiaan was fishing for something. But he had answered. Jiaan pressed on.

"Well, you're certainly not 'bogged down.' How many countries have the Hrum conquered in the last few centuries? Thirty?"

"Twenty-eight," said Patrius. "And there are three allied states. That's what you want, isn't it? Independent, allied status?"

"What other choice have we?" Jiaan asked bitterly. "Except to be swallowed whole?"

"You could be independent and nonallied," Patrius told him. "Ban our troops from ever crossing your soil, forbid all trade, close your borders to our scholars and engineers. An independent state is free to do that. But none of the countries who've proved too strong for us to defeat without spending far more than their conquest was worth has ever chosen to do so. Do you know why?"

Jiaan kept silent, but he did know why. His own father had spoken of the advantages, the wealth that came from alliance with the Hrum.

His father had intended Farsala to become an independent ally from the start.

"Those same advantages," Patrius went on, as if Jiaan had spoken his thoughts aloud, "go to the countries we conquer as well. In many of the countries we invade, the people welcome us—even throw off their overlords and fight on our side."

"Well, that didn't happen here!" Jiaan snapped. But he remembered the Kadeshi swordsmith he had spoken to, when he was searching for the secret of that beautiful watersteel—a secret that the Suud and Mazad's swordsmiths had now mastered. The Kadeshi smith hadn't known the secret, but he had told Jiaan that if he did, he wouldn't reveal it—that he would do nothing that might delay the Hrum's invasion of his own land. The Kadeshi would be far better off under Hrum rule than that of their own warlords—slavery and all. In fact Hrum slaves, protected by law, were treated better than free Kadeshi peasants, who had no laws to protect them from their harsh and rapacious rulers. But Farsala wasn't like that! Even the Farsalan peasants were resisting the Hrum.

"You would have those advantages," said

Patrius when Jiaan fell silent, "as citizens of the empire. And you could spare all the lives that will be lost if this war continues. Why not give up now, and gain the advantages without losing the lives?"

"Because your citizens pay a price for their advantages," Jiaan replied. "We aren't prepared to send our young men into your army, to die making your empire richer and stronger."

"And safer," said Patrius. "That comes with the wealth and the strength, you know. And if you're conquered, it would be your empire too, and you would share in the wealth, the strength, and the safety. And many of us *choose* to go on in the military after our years of service are over. It's really not that bad."

There was humor in his voice, for the tactimian himself had made that choice. But he had said something else, as well.

"If," Jiaan said softly.

"If what?" Patrius asked.

"You said, 'if you're conquered.' Not when. You're not certain you're going to win, are you?"

The silence lasted so long that Jiaan thought Patrius was going to stop talking, but then he sighed. "Governor Garren suffers certain . . .

handicaps when it comes to conquering this land."

"Like the fact that he can't send for more troops or his father will be dismissed from the senate?" Jiaan asked. A messenger from Siddas had brought that information just that morning.

Patrius sat up, the chains rattling as he yanked them. "How do you know that?"

Jiaan said nothing, for Patrius must have guessed that the Farsalans had spies. One of whom, much as Jiaan hated to acknowledge it, had discovered an incredible amount of information. At considerable risk, from the sound of it.

Did Patrius know about the committee of senators that was coming to pressure Garren even further? He probably didn't—the Suud said no messengers from the Hrum had reached Patrius' forces, and Jiaan thought the Suud would know.

The tactimian settled back into his bedroll. "All right, I'll admit it—that's why I'm not certain you'll lose. But I should warn you, he may be handicapped by the terms his father accepted, but they also make him desperate—more desperate than any Hrum commander should be. Do you know the story of Perapolis?"

"You conquered them," said Jiaan. "In the

end. But they fought so hard and so long that they almost beggared your empire and destroyed your army. And by the time you took them, the land was so damaged as to be worthless. That's why your commanders are only given a year—so that won't happen again."

"Exactly," said Patrius. "We've learned that sometimes you can lose so much in the fighting that in the end victory isn't worth the price you paid."

"So? That's good for us, isn't it?"

"Maybe," said Patrius. "But only if you learn from it yourselves, instead of having to learn it the hard way, as we did." He rolled onto his side, facing the wall of the tent. He couldn't roll the other way.

Jiaan lay on his back, staring at the hutch's leather roof for a long time.

THE NEXT DAY Jiaan cut a dozen big branches off the bushes and spread them by the stream. If he kept carrying them back to the cookfire, soon there would be questions, and how well they burned in an established fire wasn't what he needed to know. He would give the first branches three days to dry, he decided, then return with a candle and see how hard it was to set them alight with a small flame.

He also decided that it would be better to initiate a less direct conversation with Tactimian Patrius. Looking back on their talk, Jiaan realized that the one topic they hadn't discussed was the specifics of how the Hrum organized or prepared for anything—and he didn't think that was an accident. He still wanted to know about their standard defenses against fire in a camp, but he knew that Patrius would say nothing if he approached the subject directly. However, if Jiaan got him into the habit of talking, perhaps in a week or so he could steer the conversation, subtly, in the direction he wanted.

He began that same night, as soon as his blankets started to warm.

"I thank you," he told the Hrum tactimian, "for your warning about Governor Garren. You did intend to warn me, didn't you? As well as trying to talk me into surrendering?"

For a moment he thought he'd taken the wrong approach, because Patrius hesitated before replying. "It was a warning. But you needn't thank me. I didn't do it for you."

"Ah." How odd, that they should have that in common. And how difficult it must be to have the person who sought to sully the honor of your army as your superior instead of a subordinate you could command. "I heard that you were assigned to the thankless task of hunting us down because you argued with Garren."

He hoped that was vague enough to conceal the fact that his source of information had been present at the meeting where it was decided — though it sounded like the peddler was doing a pretty good job of wrecking his cover on his own.

"He doesn't punish people for disagreeing with him," Patrius said. "Not yet. But I worry that he might come to that. The Hrum learned long ago that to truly conquer a country, to hold it and make it a working part of your empire, knowing how to use mercy is every bit as important as knowing how to use force — more important, in the long run. Even Garren knows that, but this situation makes him even more likely to favor short-term results . . . and he wasn't much for thinking about the long term in the first place. That was why so many questioned his promotion to strategus and governor. He isn't stupid, or incompetent, or even foolish, but . . ."

"We've seen that," said Jiaan dryly. "Though the Hrum didn't show much mercy . . ."

. . . *to the Farsalan army.* But that had been Garren's plan, and perhaps that was the kind of thing Patrius was talking about. Had Garren crossed the line into dishonor? Jiaan knew that his father, as a commander, would have agreed to implement that plan. And the plan slowly forming in Jiaan's mind wasn't much kinder, except that he expected to take most of the Hrum forces prisoner. So instead he said, "You didn't show much mercy to the slaves you chained to the siege towers. Or at least, you were risking a lot on our mercy. If we'd been ruthless enough, we might have burned the lot of them to death. And that ambush was your doing, wasn't it?"

"Yes," said Patrius. "But the slaves were only there to disrupt your plans. To force you to reveal yourselves. If they appeared to be in danger, their guards had orders to pass out keys so they could release themselves. And I didn't know," his voice was dry, "that the towers had been coated with an accelerant."

Jiaan hoped the darkness would hide his grin. Then a thought struck him. "How did you know we were going to attack? You even knew the day, for the slaves weren't there the day before."

"You think you're the only one with spies?"

"No, but . . ." In his forces? Among the peasants who'd helped the peddler, or among their neighbors and friends? Surely not one of his men! Jiaan knew that none of them bore the rank mark the Hrum tattooed onto their spies. On the other hand, surely the peddler's peasant forces were checking for that mark too.

"I thought all your spies were marked." Jiaan touched his own arm. "So they could approach any officer and be identified and believed."

"Not since they threw our spies out of Mazad, and we discovered that the mark was known to you," said Patrius. "We're proud of our service to the empire, but we're not stupid. Surely your Commander Sorahb guessed that much."

"I'm sure he has," said Jiaan blankly. There could be spies among his men. In fact, there almost certainly were! The first thing Garren would have done was send men to infiltrate Sorahb's army. Fear crept through Jiaan's soul. But at least here, isolated in the Suud's desert, no spy could send out a report. The Hrum had stopped sending couriers to Patrius' force after the Suud had captured the first few. But a clever spy *could* communicate with the Hrum camp—by the simple expedient Nehar had used to get messages out of Mazad, if by no other means. Jiaan's mind was so full of the security measures he would have to implement—tomorrow!—that he barely caught Patrius' next comment.

"But the mercy your commander showed in Mazad wasn't a bad thing. The commanders who've fought against that city haven't executed any of the farmers they caught trying to smuggle in food either. If Mazad's commander *had* executed the spies . . . Sieges are the most bitter form of battle, you know. Anger is born on both sides, not only in the hearts of the besieged."

"I didn't know you'd caught anyone," said Jiaan, his mind still reeling with the implications. His camp could be full of spies!

"Oh, yes," said Patrius. "Even before Tactimian Laon replaced that . . . replaced Substrategus Arus."

"What happened to Arus, anyway?" Jiaan asked, more to give himself time to think than because he cared.

"Demoted in disgrace," said Patrius. "And sent to chase bandits in the Dugaz swamps—a more thankless task even than mine. Some of his senior centrimasters were demoted with him, but the junior ones who had no say in anything were kept in Setesafon with their centris. Though why you'd take a proven incompetent and set him to a difficult and vital task, no matter how unpleasant it . . . Never mind."

Jiaan smiled. "That's the kind of thing you meant, isn't it? The reason your high command didn't want to promote Garren in the first place."

"Exactly," said Patrius. "In a way that's why. . . . It pleased me—for more than one reason!—when you showed that you also understood that without mercy, without honor, an army is just another band of thugs. Garren . . . he called Sorahb and his army bandits. But when you protected me, you proved that—for all you're not very . . . polished—your army is an army that defends a nation. That was a commander's decision—not a thug's."

Was that why the contempt had vanished from Patrius' eyes?

"You're Sorahb, aren't you?" the tactimian added casually.

Of course Patrius had his own agenda—

things he sought to learn from their conversations.

"No," said Jiaan. "I just command the army for him. Sorahb is the one who coordinates all the Farsalan defenses."

"He's in Mazad then?" Patrius sounded surprised.

"No," Jiaan repeated. The firmness with which he spoke was prompted by a sudden vision of Commander Siddas' head on a Hrum pike—though the Hrum didn't do that, either. For Sorahb, Garren might make an exception. "How could he send out orders if he was trapped in Mazad? I won't tell you where he is, though."

"I don't expect it," said Patrius calmly.

Jiaan couldn't tell if his half lies had been believed or not.

HE SPENT THE NEXT few days ensuring that none of his men would get a chance to fire a message arrow into the Hrum camp—at least not without their comrades seeing and reporting it. He brought Fasal into the planning of the new security procedures, and even that small amount of action cheered the young deghan enough that when Jiaan set him to training more swordsmen he only glowered for a moment before doing as he was bid.

Jiaan knew he should go further—that if he confided his growing plan, he would gain Fasal's full cooperation. But given his new awareness of the need for secrecy, he wasn't prepared to do that yet. In light of that need he took Hosah into his confidence, setting him to experiment with the slightly dried boughs because Jiaan feared his own movements might be watched. Hosah reported that once the dried boughs were ablaze, they would eventually set the green bushes alight. And although it took a lot of dried boughs to start the fire, once the green bushes were blazing, they were almost impossible to put out. Jiaan remembered the thick brush screens that shrouded the Hrum camp, and rejoiced.

Jiaan was finishing dinner that evening, with ideas for getting fire into the dried brush in the Hrum camp floating through the back of his mind, when the guards reported that several Suud were escorting a horseman up the hill—and that by his clothes he wasn't one of Siddas' men. In fact, they said, he didn't look to be Farsalan at all.

Curious, Jiaan abandoned the remains of his

meal and went to greet the small party of travelers as they came over the hill's crest. When he saw the horseman, Jiaan's brows lifted. The messenger had donned Farsalan clothes, and his peasant guards might not have recognized the breed of the sturdy, rough-coated horse, or thin, arrogant cast of the man's face, or even the long band of embroidered silk the man wore like a sash across his chest, proclaiming his status as a messenger under safe conduct. But any of Jiaan's veterans would have recognized a Kadeshi courier.

Why in Azura's name were the Kadeshi sending a message to him? Jiaan folded his arms and waited. Half his mind was curious, but the other half was filled with growing distrust.

"You are Commander Jiaan?" the man asked in good, if accented, Faran.

"Yes," Jiaan admitted. He could hardly deny it, though some part of him wanted to.

"I have a message for you from Warlord Siatt, with who you once offered an honorable alliance."

"He turned it down," said Jiaan. "And I told him that any force he sent into Farsala would be regarded as an enemy army."

He saw no need to tell this man that by the

time he had ridden through the impoverished misery of the Kadeshi countryside and spent just one night in Siatt's rich palace, he'd been relieved that the warlord had refused his offer. Relieved—and perfectly aware of how easy it would be for Farsala's ancient enemy to turn against Jiaan's exhausted army once the Hrum were gone. Given a choice between the Hrum and the Kadeshi warlords, Jiaan would take the Hrum any day. So would the Kadeshi peasants if they were given the chance.

"Ah. Well, Warlord Siatt has reconsidered your offer," said the courier. "If I might speak with you in private, I have much to reveal."

Jiaan started to say that he concealed nothing from his men, then remembered possible Hrum spies and thought better of it. "Come with me," he said instead. "My men will care for your horse."

Switching to his still-clumsy Suud, he addressed the hooded shapes that had escorted the messenger. "Go to the fire. My cook will find hutch to shade you, bring you food. You are much kind, to waste sleep to bring man here."

"It was fun," one of the bundled Suud replied, the humor in his voice making him seem less mysterious. "We led him in circles that would make a bird dizzy—even blindfolded him part of the time. We don't want the build-on-hills people to come here. Not ever."

"You are wise," said Jiaan.

He led the messenger to a flat rock, far enough from the camp that no one would overhear them, and sat down. "Well?"

The Kadeshi looked around. Clearly, the accommodations were rougher than he was accustomed to. The futility of protest was equally clear. He shrugged.

"Warlord Siatt has been approached by the Hrum governor, Garren. The Hrum have offered us alliance—and they too have need of our warriors, to come to their aid."

Yes, there was a subtle insult buried in that sentence, Jiaan decided. He didn't care. Siddas' last letter had warned him about Garren's plan to bribe the Kadeshi. Jiaan wished them the joy of each other.

"I know about that," he said, and had the petty satisfaction of seeing the man scowl as his shocking announcement failed to shock. "I also know that although the Hrum offer gold, they won't promise not to invade Kadesh. If Warlord Siatt wants my advice —"

"The warlord needs no advice!"

Jiaan's father had told him that Kadeshi messengers were often impoverished relations of the warlord they served, and they gained much status from that relationship, even if they seldom got rich.

"He knows full well that the Hrum will next invade Kadesh," the man went on. "But the Hrum offer reveals that they are weak."

"So he's turning them down?" Jiaan asked. "That's wise." More wisdom than he'd have expected from the old snake.

"No," said the messenger promptly, restoring Jiaan's faith in his own judgment. "The warlord is more subtle than that. He will take their gold, yes, and supply them with the many men they ask. But instead of warriors he will send peasants. Farmers, whose only use is to till the dirt. Shepherds and goat-boys."

"No slaves?" Jiaan asked.

The messenger blinked. "Slaves are expensive."

"I should have known," said Jiaan dryly. "Siatt is a thrifty man."

"Peasants replace themselves with great abundance," the messenger agreed. "And they will be no threat to you or to us."

"I'm not so sure about that," said Jiaan. "The Hrum army is built of peasants. They are expert at turning farmers and goat-boys into soldiers."

"Does not the warlord Siatt know this?" the messenger demanded. "He will let the Hrum train these little men as best they can. But when the warlord sends them the signal, they will turn on their Hrum comrades, even in the midst of battle, and attack them! Surely this, coming as a surprise from the midst of their own ranks, will disrupt even the mighty Hrum army and grant their enemies an easy victory."

Jiaan snorted. "Why should the peasants betray the Hrum? It would almost certainly get most of them killed right on the spot, and all of them killed if the Hrum win. Why should they obey Siatt at all, once they're out of his hands and trained to fight?"

"Because," said the messenger, "peasants have families. Families who will be working on the warlord's land, within his reach."

The chill that swept through Jiaan's heart was so intense that he wrapped his arms around himself. "Siatt will kill their families if they defy him? Even though obedience will end up killing them?"

"Of course," said the messenger. "The peasants know it, so they will obey. And they might not die if the Hrum lose the battle, so they will fight hard."

"You've never fought the Hrum," said Jiaan. "And it shows. Why is Warlord Siatt going to so much trouble to tell me this?"

"Because," said the messenger softly, "there is still one question to be resolved in his plan. In what battle will the warlord use this mighty weapon? In a battle where the Hrum fight his own forces . . . or one where they fight yours? When you came to beg for troops, you told him that it would profit him if the Hrum were stopped in Farsala—if the battle for both our lands was fought on your soil alone. This he agrees to. Yet if he is to place a weapon of such power into your hands, he would require a suitable recompense."

HE WAS NOT RESPONSIBLE for the lives of Kadeshi peasants, Jiaan told himself for the dozenth time as he entered his hutch that night. He couldn't see

Patrius' face in the dimness, though he sensed the tactimian's welcome. Jiaan remembered a Kadeshi peasant girl who had hiked up her skirts to flee at the sight of an armed man; he remembered the lean—too lean—look of the adult male villagers. If Jiaan could help them without hurting his own people, his own cause . . . But how? For the Kadeshi, he could see nothing in Siatt's plan but grief, death, and the kind of choice that no one, no matter what rank or nationality, should ever be forced to make.

"What's wrong?" Patrius' voice was soft and worried. Jiaan suddenly remembered that Patrius was a prisoner—if there were something wrong, he'd be at his captors' mercy.

"It's nothing," said Jiaan. "Nothing that concerns you. At least, not directly." Though if Warlord Siatt's plan worked, it might cost the Hrum a battle. And what if that battle would free Farsala? Did Jiaan have the right to throw away such an advantage—any advantage—when the odds against them were so high?

And yet if Siatt's plan won the day for them, if some of the peasants and all their families happened to survive, would Jiaan then be able to fight off the warlords? Warlords who would already have an army, trained by the Hrum, inside Farsala's borders?

"Whether it's nothing or not," said Patrius, "there's no point in standing in the dark with your cloak and boots on. If it doesn't concern me, do you want to talk about it?"

Jiaan started, suddenly realizing how long he'd been standing there. "Yes," he said, dropping onto his bedroll to pull off his boots. "I think I do."

It did involve Patrius, in that it might make a difference if the Hrum learned of Siatt's treachery, but since Patrius was going to spend the duration of the war in the Suud's desert it didn't matter what he learned.

"I went to Kadesh, a few months ago," said Jiaan. "I was trying . . . um . . ."

"Trying to find an ally? We expected you would. In fact, Substrategus Bar—ah, someone whose opinion I respect was surprised that they hadn't come to your aid."

Jiaan grimaced. "He shouldn't be. When you know the warlords better, you'll find that they don't even care about their own people—far less anyone else. When I rode through their countryside . . ."

There was no reason at all to share this with an enemy officer, but the memory flooded his heart.

"Their peasants are half-starved racks of bone, while the warlords feast off gold plates. In some ways the Kadeshi's slaves are better off! They may be covered with whip scars, but they can be sold for coin, so at least their owners feed them."

Jiaan paused, remembering the misery he had seen—and his own aching shame at riding past, helpless to do anything about it.

"I talked to one man," he went on. "A weapon-smith. He actually wanted you to invade."

And Jiaan had agreed with him.

"Why not?" Patrius asked. "Many of the peoples we conquer are better off in the empire. Most of them, in the long run. Though it looks like Farsala might not discover those advantages."

"I don't think I can count on that," said Jiaan grimly. "Not anymore. Garren has found a way to get more men. A lot more."

Chains jingled as Patrius moved sharply. "That's impossible! The senate would never grant him more tacti. Not when . . . no, not even if he somehow replaced the emperor with his own man. That bargain was made on the senate floor, and it's public knowledge. Nothing . . . nothing *has* happened to the emperor, has it?"

"Not to my knowledge," said Jiaan, noting that the position of a Hrum emperor might not be as secure as it seemed from the outside. "Garren found another way."

He told Patrius the story of Garren's bribe, of Siatt's plan, and even about the arrival of a senate committee to investigate the amount of money Garren was spending.

"Well, that's a good thing," said Patrius. "The emperor will have given them the authority to overrule Garren if he seems to have gone too far. Defending the empire's honor is part of their charge."

"Will they care enough to keep him from bribing Siatt?" Jiaan asked hopefully. That would save the Kadeshi peasants—if Siatt wasn't paid he wouldn't send them, and he could hardly punish the men or their families for it either.

"I'm not sure," said Patrius slowly. "They won't allow Garren to cheat—but is this cheating? It's not exactly winning with ten tacti, which was the main stipulation the senate imposed, but they also agreed that he could purchase whatever he needed. And if they do forbid it, then Garren's father might say that the senate is breaking the terms of their agreement and get out of it that way. The committee is going to think about that, too."

"So they'll let him take those men?" Jiaan asked. "Even if it means that either they or their families will die?"

"But they don't know about that!" Patrius exclaimed. "If they did, they wouldn't allow it. To help people like these men and their families, to bring them into the safety and prosperity of the empire is . . . is what our army is for, when you come to the bottom of it."

"What about those who don't want to be brought in?" Jiaan demanded.

"They may resent us for a time," said Patrius calmly, "but they're grateful for it within a generation or two, no matter how hard they fought at first."

Jiaan snorted. *Grateful? Or just having no other choice, and accepting that?* But Patrius' voice held so much certainty that he knew it was useless to argue.

"The committee doesn't know about Siatt's

plan," Jiaan said, "so they might allow Garren to go ahead with it?"

"They might," Patrius admitted. "I'm not sure."

"And the Kadeshi . . ." Jiaan closed his eyes in anguished sympathy. "The Kadeshi will turn on the Hrum someday and die, either on your swords in battle or executed for treason later."

"Yes," said Patrius. His voice was quiet, but beneath the tactimian's surface calm, Jiaan heard the same grief and horror he felt. "Another commander, hearing their story, knowing why they'd done it . . . but I don't think Garren would listen. And even another commander might not allow them to escape the consequences of that. A man who turns on his comrades in the midst of battle . . . there is no worse crime. Not in military law. If the committee learned the truth, they'd stop it. Our army is a wall to protect such men, not to topple and crush them."

"Are you going to tell me that the committee would believe Sorahb, if he sent them a message?" If Patrius said yes, Jiaan would know that the man was lying.

"No," said Patrius. "Any message from the enemy would be assumed to be a ruse. They'd be more wary of the Kadeshi troops. They might even learn the truth from them, but that wouldn't help the Kadeshi families. Even if I told them myself," Patrius went on bitterly, "they'd say that my information came from you and was part of the ruse. Revealing the truth isn't enough. It might save our forces, but it wouldn't save the Kadeshi and their people."

Patrius cared about that too. Men who were willing to make their own bodies into a wall to protect their empire would care, Jiaan realized. For they were their empire's wall, just as the deghans had been Farsala's. As his own men were now, he supposed. They seemed so frail, these walls of flesh and will—but to be without such protection, like the peasants who lived under the power of the warlords, would be terrible indeed.

There was nothing Jiaan could do to protect the Kadeshi either.

JIAAN SENT SIATT'S courier back to his master the next morning with his refusal of the warlord's "generous" offer.

"You may tell the warlord that I have no more money now than I did last time we spoke," he told the messenger. "And the other things I said then still hold true. My master, Sorahb, will regard any force of Kadeshi coming into Farsala as an enemy army and react accordingly. The Hrum were foolish enough to underestimate Sorahb. Ask Warlord Siatt and his friends if they really want to do the same."

It was true—Jiaan hardly had any money at all. The Farsalan army's food came from sympathetic villages, slipped through the mountains to the desert by young men hiding from the Hrum's draft. Jiaan might have been able to raise some coin— perhaps enough to give Siatt his excuse to betray two armies, both of them his enemies, at the same time. That alone was sufficient reason to turn him down. But the real reason Jiaan did so was because he refused to be the one who sealed the Kadeshi conscripts' fate. He could have tried to betray Siatt in turn, using those men against the Hrum and then keeping the warlords from using them against him. Allowing the Hrum to execute them after the battle was the easiest way, but Jiaan refused to do it. Patrius was right. There was a line an army couldn't cross, not if it was to remain a wall instead of becoming a shackle around the throat of its own people. Jiaan might not be able to help the Kadeshi, but he refused to make Farsala a part of their destruction. Destroying the Hrum, on the other hand, was his job.

JIAAN WAITED TWO more weeks, till the dark of the moon, before he attacked the Hrum camp. He'd worried about the delay, for the one thing Patrius never said a word about was the Hrum's food supplies, and Jiaan thought they had to be running low. Hunger might force them to flee, and moving in formation, ready for attack, the Hrum would be far less vulnerable than if they were taken by surprise in the middle of the night.

But Jiaan had wanted all the darkness he could get, mostly to aid the Suud spearmen, who now crept over the open ground the Hrum had cleared around their walls. Despite the Suud's assurance that they could do it—easily!—and despite the fact that his archers had managed to crawl into arrow range of the Hrum camp, Jiaan had wondered if the Suud could really cross so much space unseen. They had to get very near the walls to throw their burdened spears as far into the camp as his plan required.

But the Suud had been right even looking at

the area where he knew they must be, Jiaan couldn't see them. And as far as he could tell, none of the Hrum sentries had even twitched.

"Now that I'm knowing them," murmured Hosah, who lay beside Jiaan in a hollow they had found, "I know it's not true. But you can see why the miners swore they'd been bred from demons."

Much as he liked the Suud, Jiaan had to admit that there was something uncanny about their ability to vanish into the desert. Especially hauling bundles of spears and big skin bags of oil. Still . . . "Nonsense," he said firmly. "You've been working with them for months now. Have you ever seen them do anything magical?"

"No," Hosah admitted. "Though I've heard they worked some magic on those swords, turning them into watersteel."

"Well, if they did, it's a magic that's now being practiced by every swordsmith in Mazad," Jiaan reminded him. "Not to mention the Hrum. So I hardly think—"

The whisper of spears in flight interrupted him. Many spears—and the way they coordinated that first volley in the darkness truly did seem like magic, even though Jiaan knew that the Suud could see in the dark.

Jiaan could barely make out the Hrum sentries on the distant wall—they hadn't been so foolish as to ruin their night sight with torches—but he heard them shout as the spears passed over their heads. The warning wouldn't do them any good, for in the darkness they couldn't see the small sack of oil each spear carried. Even if a drop of oil from a bag's loose seam fell on someone and they guessed the truth, there was nothing they could do about it—not in time.

The delay—as each Suud took his large, tight-stitched skin, filled the next small sack, and tied it to his spear—seemed very long to Jiaan. But eventually the second volley arced up and over the Hrum's heads.

The camp was rousing now, but the Hrum's enemies were invisible. If Jiaan was lucky, every man in camp would head straight for his post on the wall and be there when the real show began.

Six more flights of spears followed. The earthen banks that shielded the Hrum camp were packed with soldiers, most still donning their armor and boots, from the sound of it. Jiaan was willing to allow them boots and armor, though it was more mercy than they had given his camp on the night that Aram died. That was the only mercy he would show them.

"Kindle," he called softly, and heard the command being passed from one group of archers to another.

It was Hosah who dropped a handful of dried grass and small twigs into the thick clay pot where they had carried the embers. He blew steadily into the pot's wide mouth.

Fire burst forth. Jiaan nodded grimly and held out his first arrow, watching the flames lick the pitch-soaked strip of cloth tied to its tip. He didn't need to say another word—his arrow would be the next signal. Jiaan nocked it. The fire rippling at its tip hurt his dark-adapted eyes as he pulled his bow and let the arrow fly.

It streaked through the dark like a comet, and dozens of others followed from all around that side—the upwind side—of the Hrum camp. Jiaan was already kindling his second arrow when the first one fell.

They had experimented over the last few weeks. The thin leather bags didn't always burst when they hit the ground, but the oil—all the oil Jiaan had been able to gather—seeped swiftly through the loosened stitches. The Suud had sent their spears into the most dense patch of brush in this end of the camp, but it still might take a while for an arrow to find oil, and until that happened, they wouldn't accomplish much. The fire arrows might ignite a partially dried branch, but they usually didn't burn long enough to ignite green bushes at all. To make matters worse, it had rained two nights ago—a long, soaking rain that lasted almost until dawn, while Jiaan huddled in his blankets and cursed.

He had considered waiting a while longer, but any winter night in the desert might bring rain, and the moon would soon be growing brighter.

Jiaan fired another arrow. All his archers were firing as quickly as they could, since there was no point in trying to coordinate a volley. The oil wouldn't dodge.

Jiaan kindled and fired almost a dozen arrows, knowing as he waited for each set of pitch-soaked rags to light that at least some of the Hrum were running for buckets and shovels, preparing to fight the fire they now knew was coming. Patrius had finally told Jiaan how the Hrum were trained to deal with fire in their camp. Even as he watched a distant flame flicker to life, Jiaan felt an ache of guilt for betraying his friend. Patrius had become a friend, he suddenly realized. But Jiaan wouldn't let that stop him.

The flame leaped and grew, reaching into the bushes around it with greedy fingers.

"That will do," said Jiaan with satisfaction, lowering his bow. One of the things they'd learned in their experiments was that the green bushes might be slow to catch fire, but once they were burning well they were almost impossible to put out. "Everyone move to your next position."

Getting himself to the downwind side of the camp was hazardous, and not because of the beleaguered Hrum. Jiaan fell twice during the first part of the journey, and the second time he rammed his leg into a prickly plant. He stopped immediately and pulled half a dozen spines out of his flesh—working by touch was no handicap for that task—but even though he got them out swiftly, the irritant that coated their tips had set to work, and his muscles ached and throbbed as he went on.

Moving was easier now—the fire was so big, so brilliant, that even hundreds of yards away its light touched the rocks and plants of the desert floor. When Jiaan looked toward it he was almost blinded, and tears streamed down his face.

The Hrum camp was burning.

Men rushed about at the far end, where the fire hadn't reached. Some still held buckets and shovels, but more were hastily gathering bundles of whatever they thought it made sense to save. Still more, Jiaan was glad to see, were carrying stretchers to the farthest unburned end of the camp, where they could be extracted quickly when the army was forced to flee.

Their departure was inevitable now. This fire would be stopped by nothing but the earthen walls the Hrum had erected and the cleared ground beyond them—both of which were perfect for containing the conflagration Jiaan had released. He had pointed that out to the Suud when they had expressed reservations about setting the desert ablaze.

The orange light painted everything, making it look as if the whole of the wide, flat valley were on fire. It shed enough light for Jiaan to see the

Hrum's pack mules skittering over the barrier and racing across the cleared space. Enough light for him to watch as two centris burst over their walls, reforming their formation even as they ran down the left side of the small stream. They probably hoped that a sudden assault could burst through the Farsalan forces, creating an escape route from the cleared ground that had once spelled safety and now formed a deadly trap.

The arrow fire started immediately. Despite the drifting smoke, in this light the archers Jiaan had stationed downwind could hardly miss. More arrows were arcing in from behind the Hrum as well. Most of Jiaan's forces, less clumsy than their commander, had already reached their next position.

With arrows coming from two sides and their shield wall abandoned in their haste to reach the enemy, almost half the Hrum had fallen even before Fasal and his men rushed out to meet them.

Jiaan had suggested that Fasal ride his charger. He wouldn't have been very effective on horseback once his lances were gone, but Jiaan trusted the well-trained mare to keep him safe, and frankly, he was worried about Fasal.

But Fasal had coldly refused to take the deghan's traditional role, preferring to fight on foot beside his swordsmen, and Jiaan had yielded. Fasal might be in more danger that way—Jiaan thought that was part of what he wanted—but it was a commander's choice, and Jiaan could only respect him for it.

Jiaan himself was still too far from that end of the cleared ground to recognize faces in the seething mass of men, though the clamor of metal on metal, the screams and shouts, reached his ears even over the buffeting roar of the fire.

He couldn't recognize faces, but the swords that flashed in the light were red with blood. He saw men fall and others stand over them to shelter them from their enemies. He saw a Hrum soldier stagger out of the battle, his breastplate glowing in the light, a cut just below the line of his helmet pouring blood into his eyes.

Jiaan, remembering the terror of being blood-blind in the midst of combat, couldn't blame the soldier for fleeing; until he could see again, the man was nothing but a danger to his comrades. But then another man followed him, a man who was whole as far as Jiaan could see, and then another, and another, until the Hrum's whole advance force was running back toward the bulk of their army.

Many of them saw that Fasal—following orders for once, Azura be praised—did not pursue, so they paused to pick up and carry back their wounded. Jiaan's men were gathering up the wounded at their end of the field as well. He had no doubt that the older, more reliable veterans he had seeded so liberally into Fasal's forces would pick up the Hrum wounded and tend to them along with their own.

By the time Jiaan limped up to join Hosah on the familiar rise he had designated as the command post, the Hrum were evacuating their camp. They marched clumsily down the streambed, their shields forming the best wall they could manage. But fleeing a fire, laden with gear, in eight inches of water rushing over smooth stones, was not conducive to maintaining formation.

Through the gaps in the shield wall Jiaan could see that they carried more men on stretchers than they had gathered before they fled their camp, and that some men carried not bundles of food and arrows, but men on their backs.

More wounded than they have stretchers to carry, and no time to make more. They won't try another attack tonight.

Even as the thought crossed Jiaan's mind, the Hrum in the lead staggered out of the stream onto a patch of clear, flat ground—out of reach of the fire, but far enough from the edges of the cleared area that any arrow that reached them wasn't likely to be accurate.

"I still think we should take them," said Fasal, coming up to join Jiaan. "Disorganized as they are, a charge would break their formation. We could pour over them like a wave over rocks."

"Rocks that have the wave outnumbered," Jiaan pointed out. "Rocks that are still the best infantry in the world. My way takes a bit longer, but it will work. In fact, I'm betting it will work tomorrow morning."

"Really? How much?" Fasal asked.

Jiaan laughed. "One brass foal."

"That's not much," said Fasal critically. "Even for someone as poor as you are."

"I'm not a big gambler," said Jiaan. Which wasn't true, for he had already bet far more than mere money on his plan.

"Well, I'll take it." Fasal shrugged. "A foal's a foal, after all." In truth, he had no more money than Jiaan did.

Fasal's padded silk armor was bright with fresh blood under the stained steel rings, but none of the blood seemed to be his. Even more important, the wild anger of grief and guilt that had underlain every expression on Fasal's face since the Hrum's ambush was gone. Jiaan had almost forgotten what Fasal looked like when he wasn't angry. Patrius had been right—it was combat Fasal had needed. He might need it again, but for now his pain was lightened.

"How many did you lose?" Jiaan asked.

"Just two dead, but another sixteen wounded, three of them badly. They may not fight again. The healers tell me it's too soon to be certain, but they think they'll live. The Hrum took worse losses. A lot worse."

Despite the good news—the losses were incredibly light—grief clenched around Jiaan's heart. When Aram was alive, Jiaan had gone to him for the tally of wounded and slain. When Aram was alive, it wouldn't even have occurred to Fasal to make the count himself.

So we both have to grow up and get on with it.
Perhaps it was time.

IN THE MORNING a handful of Hrum marched into
the blackened, smoldering ruin that had been their
camp. Jiaan let them go, to learn for themselves that
there was nothing left. He already knew that their
water supplies were low; in the dawn's gray light he
had seen them straining the ash-choked water of the
stream through their tunics before they drank it.
They couldn't have much food, either.

He rose to his knees, then to his feet on the
low rise of the command post. Hosah hissed in disapproval, but if Jiaan saw anyone raise a bow he
could drop behind the ridge fast enough. For some
reason he felt it was important for the Hrum to see
him, even if he was too far off for them to read his
expression.

Jiaan cupped his hands around his mouth.
"You have no gear," he shouted. He had expected
his voice to sound thin, but the dawn air was so
still that it boomed across the valley. He had no
doubt that the Hrum could hear him. It was a
good thing they all spoke Faran.

"You have no clean water; you have only the

355

food you salvaged; you have no mules to carry loads for you. And you have many wounded—some of whom won't survive a march."

He let those truths echo for a moment before he went on. "You are four days from the great cliff by the most direct route—and you don't know that route. If you march straight toward the cliff, you'll run into the rock maze, where a man can wander for weeks without finding the path through it. While you try, our archers will shoot at you from atop the rocks, where you can't reach us."

Before they had settled into their defensible camp, the Hrum had spent some time tracking Jiaan's Suud-guided army through that rock maze. If it wasn't entirely impossible to find routes through it, it would be nearly so for men being misled by Suud trackers.

"If you go south to bypass the maze, it will take you almost two weeks to reach the cliffs, marching through narrow valleys with my archers shooting down at you. If you march north, out of the rocks into the great desert, you will find no water. And we will be waiting when you return."

Jiaan didn't bother to add that under any of these circumstances only a handful of Hrum would escape the desert alive, for they knew that too.

"If you surrender," he called, suddenly impatient to get to the point, "you will not be killed. You'll not be harmed in any way, and we'll help your healers with your wounded as much as our medical supplies will allow."

He prayed they wouldn't need much, for his healers' supply of medicines and salves was running painfully low. Fortunately, the Suud had good herbalists among them. They'd been teaching Jiaan's people about the desert's medicinal plants, many of which were surprisingly effective.

"You will be fed and treated well," Jiaan went on, "though you will be held prisoner until the end of the conflict between Farsala and the Hrum. However, that conflict will end, one way or the other, in just four months."

Also true, for if the committee decreed that Garren had completed his conquest, Jiaan's rebels would suddenly become not Farsalan fighters but civil criminals in a land awash with soldiers who would enforce the law. *Governor* Garren, confirmed in his post, could bring in all the tacti he needed. The thought of being under

Garren's governance for the rest of the man's life sent a chill through Jiaan's heart and roughened his voice on the next words.

"If you don't surrender, we will hunt you relentlessly, with archers, never giving you a chance to strike at us. You'll be lucky, very lucky, if even one centri of you leaves the desert alive."

He stood for a moment, straight and proud, then turned and walked regally down the hill. The moment he was out of sight he spun and crawled back up, raising his head just far enough to see what they did.

The Hrum clustered in small groups, discussing his demands. But they had also lowered their shields, clearly considering that his offer meant that some sort of truce existed between them—at least temporarily.

"Pass the word," Jiaan told Hosah. "Anyone who fires an arrow now will *deeply* regret it."

"They already know that," said Hosah. "But I'll pass it along. You know, the odds are three to one against them surrendering this morning."

Jiaan's brows rose. "I thought only Fasal and I were betting."

"Not anymore," said Hosah cheerfully. "Even

your own men think you're being . . . optimistic. Surrender without a fight? Without even trying to get out? These are the Hrum!"

"So they are," said Jiaan. "But if you want some advice, put your money on me."

Hosah snorted. "Why would that be, sir?"

"Because I've learned something talking to Tactimian Patrius these last few weeks," said Jiaan. "The Hrum are human too."

"That hasn't made them eager to surrender in the past," said Hosah dubiously.

"No, but in the past . . . Those men are probably loyal to their emperor, in the abstract, but their emperor's not here. Most of them have never even set eyes on him. I'd guess that they're very loyal to Tactimian Patrius, but he's not there either. So let me ask you a question: as a human being, Hosah, would you be willing to fight, and probably die, for Governor Garren?"

HALF A MARK LATER, the Hrum army lay down its swords and surrendered.

RAIN STILL FELL *on the city of Mazad as Sorahb stumbled toward the house where he lodged, almost too tired to walk. He had nearly reached his destination when he came across a pregnant woman wandering through the streets in soaked and ragged clothes. Sorahb knew that many of the townsfolk, the women and elders who could not fight themselves, had come out to support those who fought, carrying food, arrows, and even stones for them to throw down upon the Hrum. Seeing that the woman was as exhausted as he was, Sorahb took her arm, and questioning her gently, he helped her through the dark streets to the door of the small, dilapidated house she claimed as her home.*

"I thank you, sir," she said as they climbed the low

steps to stand before the door, "for both myself and my unborn babe. You've aided the both of us tonight."

"If I have done you a small service," said Sorahb, "it is less than nothing compared to the service you have done for your city. And even that is little compared to what your city does for Farsala."

"You have served too," she said. "And I see you are weary with it. I only wish I could assist in the next task that will fall to you."

"What task is that?" Sorahb asked. He prayed she was not about to request some further aid from him, for his bones ached with weariness. But the soaked cloth of her skirt outlined the bulge of her belly, and he knew that just as she had done all she could to fight for her city this day, it behooved him to do what he could for her.

Something of his reluctance must have shown, for a sudden, impish smile lit her face. "Your next task, sir, is to defeat the Hrum army in the desert."

With that she went into the battered house and closed the door. Sorahb stood on the step with the rain running down his face, and for the first time he realized that he was dealing with the god Azura in disguise.

SO SORAHB DEPARTED *from the city of Mazad, knowing it would be safe until the Hrum could bring* reinforcements. He went into the desert and dealt with the Suud tribesmen. The Suud were wild and fierce, but they still bowed before the divine farr that Sorahb possessed in such measure.

Once they agreed to follow him, Sorahb showed them how to harass the Hrum. When the time came, he led his army to the Hrum's desert camp and, with the assistance of his Suud allies, defeated the Hrum with flood and fire.

As Sorahb stood upon the charred wreckage of the battlefield, dealing with the duties and problems that arise from victory, a small Suud boy drew near. When the last who had petitioned Sorahb for aid had left him, the child approached. Sorahb was about to ask how he could help the boy, but the glint in the child's eyes was too ironic for any mortal's years. It seemed oddly familiar as well.

Sorahb folded his arms. "I would offer you help," he said, "but I doubt that you need help from any man. You have come to lay another test on me, have you not?"

The boy laughed, light and clear as any child. "All folk need help," he said. "These tests are set by the Hrum, and not by me; I merely advise you which to take next, although I believe this will be the last of them."

"And this test would be . . . ?" Sorahb's voice held the politeness that is half insult, for no man likes to be befooled, even by a god.

"Your last test is to abandon force of arms and use gold against the Hrum instead," said Azura calmly. "When men serve only for gold, it forms the beating heart of their army, and becomes their greatest weakness, as well."

Sorahb frowned. "But I have no gold! My army lives on the charity of the country folk, who have little enough to share, though they have supported us generously. How can I use gold against the Hrum!"

"That," said the boy as he turned away, "is for you to find out. That's what makes it a test."

CHAPTER THIRTEEN

JIAAN

THEY RETURNED TO CAMP late that afternoon. The prisoners carried the wounded, to encumber them, and Jiaan's men carried the prisoners' weapons. Only when they arrived did Jiaan learn that Tactimian Patrius had escaped.

"He was talking at us, sir," the guard complained. "All the time! We were watching the fire—we could see it from here—and trying to figure out how things were going, and he just wouldn't be quiet. So we finally tied him in one of the hutches, just like you did when you went to sleep, and he never escaped from you."

So it's all your fault, the aggrieved undertone in

the man's voice proclaimed. But how could Patrius escape his shackles without help? Hosah had sworn that all the men he recommended could be trusted with the prisoner. Was Patrius foolish enough to accept aid from someone who might be part of Fasal's faction? If they'd offered to help him escape, he might have taken the risk, hoping to escape from them later. Jiaan's heart began to pound, but he kept his voice level.

"Show me the hutch where you held him."

One look resolved the mystery.

"We tied his hands to one post and his feet to another," said the guard. "Just like in your hutch, and he never escaped from you."

"I didn't tie his hands to the post," said Jiaan mildly. Relief flooded through him—it was impossible to be angry. "I used chains. I especially didn't tie him in a position where he could reach the knots with his teeth."

"Oh." The guard blushed. "I didn't think of that."

Hosah, who had come up to join them, sighed. "Five minutes' thought would have told you. Five seconds with another man, but with you . . . I'm sorry about this, sir."

"I understand," said Jiaan. "We needed every man we could muster for the fight. It was really the fact that the camp was empty that gave Patrius his chance."

Alert guards could have made up for that, but Hosah had clearly left his least capable men behind to guard the prisoner. In truth, Jiaan would rather have had them here than blundering around on the battlefield in the dark. But with them guarding Patrius, the result was a foregone conclusion.

Looking at the scuff marks on the earthen floor, it was clear that Patrius had simply lifted the cloth at the far side and rolled out, so the only question was . . . "Did he take any weapons from this hutch? Any gear?"

"No weapons," the guard replied, looking a little less embarrassed. "I'm not fool enough to leave a prisoner alone where there are weapons. But he did take my water skin and a thick cloak."

"I wonder if he took time to look for a weapon elsewhere, or if he just seized his chance and ran," Jiaan mused aloud. "I'll ask the cooks if any knives are missing. But if he found a weapon, we'll know it soon enough. Right now, what we need is a Suud tracker."

THE SUUD DIDN'T SET out on Patrius' trail till after dark. They'd already been up for a night and most of a day, and like the rest of the army they needed some sleep. Besides, they told Jiaan, the trail left by Patrius' boots would be child's play to track. And sooner or later the Hrum would have to sleep too.

Jiaan wanted to go with them, but he knew he couldn't. The details of holding a group of prisoners that still outnumbered his own force, even with the whole Farsalan army assembled on the hilltop, ate a commander's time. The only thing that made the task possible was that Fasal and his supporters, their grief and shattered pride soothed by this annihilating victory, made no trouble. The Hrum, so unaccustomed to losing that they almost seemed to be in shock, made even less trouble than Fasal.

Still, as Jiaan instructed the Suud to lead small parties to completely enclosed crevices, where they could lower the prisoners by ropes and leave only a handful of men to guard them. As he arranged guard shifts, food for the prisoners, water for the prisoners, and medical care for their wounded—almost a dozen of whom might die, even with the best care Jiaan's healers and their own surgeons could offer. As he sent a request to the Suud council asking if their tribes could hold his prisoners, at least for the next four months, Jiaan received reports on how Patrius fared.

"He's not a fool," said the Suud woman who came to report to Jiaan the next morning, just before dawn. "He's staying near the streams and doing his best to keep warm and dry at night, but he doesn't know desert terrain at all. We took the hatchets you gave us and cut some bushes, right at the base. When he gets close to one of the passages out of the maze we block it with bushes, very thick, and erase all the tracks going in. When he comes he sees brush too thick to pass and no tracks, and walks right on by. He never seems to wonder why he finds bushes thick in some places and hardly any in others that look just the same."

"He would not," said Jiaan in Suud. "He is taught to see land to fight on, not to think of bushes." In fact Jiaan, whose training was similar, wasn't sure *he* would have noticed—

especially if the Suud had done it well, and the Suud did things like that superbly.

"Well, it won't be much longer," said the woman. "He's already tired, and we're going to start driving him away from water tomorrow."

TWO NIGHTS LATER she reported that Patrius had lost his water skin to a Suud spear.

"Onock says he was aiming for the flask," she said, "but I think he just got lucky. None of us were trying to hit that close to the man, just near enough to drive him away from the stream. But now that he can't carry water with him, it should only take two more nights."

IN FACT PATRIUS LASTED four more days. At the end of the fourth night another Suud came for Jiaan.

"He may not be smart," said the Suud youth, Abab, "but he's tough. Six nights—days for him, I suppose—with no food and four with little water, and walking all the time. But then he just sat down, and he's not moving. He's not far off, if you'd like to go there. I don't think he'll fight you now."

369

"Yes," said Jiaan. "I'd like to . . . I'll go to him."

Jiaan told the yawning night guards where he was going, and after some deliberation left Hosah in command of the camp. Fasal would probably be insulted, but even though he'd calmed down considerably since they defeated the Hrum's force in the desert, Jiaan wasn't sure he trusted him with prisoners. Besides, Fasal might see it as a sign that Jiaan feared his influence and be pleased instead. If he didn't see it that way, could Jiaan point it out to him? Subtly enough to keep Fasal from realizing that he was being manipulated? Probably not. But Hosah was in command, so how Fasal felt didn't really matter, did it? Jiaan knew that his father had commanded deghans he didn't like, some of whom had actively plotted against him.

I am not my father.

Jiaan sighed and put aside the squabbles of his officers as he followed the Suud youth out of the camp. The sun hadn't yet risen, but the sky in the east was fading from black to gray, and there was enough light for him to avoid the prickly plants if he didn't walk fast.

Soon the sun flooded the desert, illuminating

the gold, orange, and gray of the rocky spires. Abab stopped in the shade of one of the rocks and hastily donned his robe, pulling the hood over the white skin of his face and tying the sleeves closed to protect his hands.

Having seen the burns they risked at the slightest touch of the sun, Jiaan was often amazed by the courage it must take for the Suud to move around in the day, even though they kept to the shadows as much as they could. Abab's pupils had shrunk to pinpricks, making his pale eyes look blind, but Jiaan knew that the Suud could see in daylight, though not as well as they could at night.

They set off once more, and soon reached the sheltered bend in the small canyon where Patrius sat, wrapped from head to foot in the thick cloak he had taken from the guard's tent.

He sat upright on the rock, though his eyes were shut, and the lower half of his face bore a scruffy, half-grown beard. The Hrum, like Farsalan men, were clean-shaven, and Jiaan had allowed his prisoners to maintain that small dignity, though under close supervision from their guards.

He now realized how much it had mattered. Even chained to the posts of Jiaan's hutch,

Tactimian Patrius had possessed the authority of a Hrum officer.

This ragged, exhausted man had lost that sometime in the last long week. For the first time Jiaan realized that Patrius, in his late twenties, wasn't that much older than Jiaan at eighteen — though there was a time, less than a year ago, when that gap would have seemed huge. But Jiaan was no longer a boy. In some ways he felt older than the man before him as he walked up to him and sat down.

"I'm sorry," he said gently.

Patrius opened his eyes, studied Jiaan's face, and closed them again. His skin above the bristling whiskers was almost as pale as Abab's.

"I thought I could make it. I knew the Suud would mislead me if I followed their tracks, but I thought if I ignored the tracks and concentrated on getting out . . ." He stopped and shook his head, and Jiaan let the silence lengthen. The next question was the hard one. He would give Patrius time to summon his courage.

"We lost, didn't we?" The tactimian's voice was rough.

"Yes. Thirty-two of your men died, and fourteen more are severely wounded, though the healers think they'll survive if their wounds escape infection."

Jiaan saw no reason to mention the two prisoners who had died of their injuries over the last few days, simply including them in the count of the slain.

The muscles around Patrius' closed eyes tightened. "I thought we had. The guards were talking about your plan. I could see the fire, even from your camp. I thought if I could get out . . . a rescue force . . . It was my decision, you know, to leave all those bushes in place. To add screens of branches from the bushes we cut down. Cover from those infernal archers of yours." He stopped speaking and swallowed. His pale skin sheened with sweat. He toppled off the rock slowly as his balance gave way. He wasn't quite unconscious when Jiaan lowered him to the ground, but he wasn't exactly conscious, either.

Jiaan sighed. Patrius' expression of it was quieter than Fasal's, but it was just as destructive, and Jiaan was tired of dealing with command guilt.

"He looks pretty bad," said Abab, staring down at the Hrum officer. "He'll need nursing to get enough water into him. Do you want to take him back to your camp, or should we take him to our healers?"

Jiaan looked up at him, startled. Four other Suud were emerging from the surrounding rocks.

"Is your camp close to here? I thought it was much days walking away."

"We moved it," said Abab. His voice was gravely polite, but laughter at Jiaan's alien ignorance danced in his eyes. "We move around a lot, especially in winter when we're replanting the stream banks. Now we're sun from there"—he pointed to the sky, then swept his hand through a thirty-degree arc—"to there farther from your camp than from ours. At least, I think it's about that long. It's harder to tell time with the sun than it is with the stars."

"Tell time with the *stars*?" Jiaan asked.

He chose the Suud camp, not only because Abab was right about Patrius needing nursing, but also to keep him out of Fasal's reach. As the Suud bundled Patrius into his cloak and cleverly rigged rope handles to make the cloak into a sling in which it would be much easier to carry him, Abab told Jiaan that the Suud had no units of time like the Farsalans' candlemarks. If they wanted to coordinate some activity, they would choose a star that would touch the horizon at the moment they wanted to designate and say something like, "I'll meet you at the twin rocks when the Lizard's Eye touches earth." To specify a given amount of time they'd say, "It'll take from the Needle's first star to the second star of the Goat's Horns to repair that basket."

"It's more accurate than your system," Abab added smugly. "Because candles burn at different rates, no matter how hard you try to make them alike, but the stars always move at the same pace."

"What about when it rains?" said Jiaan. "You can't know time then, not at all."

"And you can light a candle in the rain?"

Even with all five Suud and Jiaan carrying the sling, the tactimian's weight seemed to increase with each passing mark. Jiaan was sweating when they reached the Suud's camp in the early afternoon.

Jiaan hesitated to awaken them in the middle of their "night," but Abab swiftly summoned several healers. Soon Patrius was carried into a hutch, while the others went for water and herbs.

Jiaan was about to follow the tactimian, when

a cloth-covered hand grasped his arm and stopped him.

"They will care for him." The Faran was fluent, if accented, and the voice was familiar. Maok's voice. Jiaan was pleased to see her again, but . . .

"I should be there," he said. "He's still a prisoner. He'll have to be guarded."

Maok snorted. Her face was invisible under her hood, but Jiaan had seen her impatient-with-fools expression before. "The healers will do more for your friend now than you can."

"He's not—"

"Besides," said Maok. "I have your answer from the council."

"About keeping the prisoners? What do they say?" His voice had risen, and Maok clucked her tongue disapprovingly.

"We will talk away from here. Come."

Before Jiaan could apologize or protest, she led him down a trail beside the stream to a stony bend some distance from the sleeping camp. The old woman found a flat rock in the dense shade of the canyon wall and seated herself, pulling back the hood to expose her wrinkled face and flyaway milkweed hair.

"Can you take this much exposure to the sun?" Jiaan asked, slipping gratefully into the Faran she had spoken all along. "Even in the shade?"

"In the shade, yes," said Maok. "For a time. It is so harsh, this light." She gestured to the sun-drenched rocks on the other side of the stream. "No softness. No place to hide."

Jiaan knew he should let her take the conversation where she wished, since she probably would anyway — but he needed to know. "Can you hold our prisoners for us for the next four or five months?"

Maok sighed. "A sunlight question, so I will give you a sunlight answer. No, not for even four months. They eat too much for us to feed them if they do not hunt, and if we give them weapons to hunt . . ." She shrugged. "Soon they are not prisoners."

Jiaan's heart sank. He had hoped not to have to deal with keeping those men himself. It would take men away from his forces, men he might need desperately. The next force Garren sent into the desert would be far larger, and in more of a hurry to win. Even with the Suud on his side . . .

"You have done good, very good, riding the tumbling of the world so far," Maok said, interrupting his circling thoughts. "You have won a great victory, with few deaths even to your enemies. Do not lose your balance now. We can hold your prisoners for several weeks. Maybe two months, if you give us some food for them."

"If we gave you enough to feed them, could you keep them the whole time?" Jiaan asked.

"Maybe," said Maok. "We are separating them among our tribes, so they will always be much fewer than we are. If they try to escape, we will let them. As your friend found out, the desert is the best guard. So little trouble for us. But can you get food for all these men, for four months?"

He couldn't. The villages that supported them were sending all the food they could spare, and Jiaan could barely feed his own army. If he had enough money, he could have had food shipped in from all over Farsala. But he hadn't enough—not nearly enough. The last of the exhilarated triumph of his victory vanished under a tide of responsibility. Who would have thought that victory would be even more complicated than the fight? *I hate command.*

"Do not lose your balance now," Maok repeated firmly. "It's not often the Creator Spirit kicks the world this hard, and you've done good so far."

"The Creator Spirit what? Oh!" The quaint myth she'd once told him surfaced in Jiaan's mind. "Yes, I remember. Your god gets bored, and he kicks the world to shake things up."

The blind-looking eyes studied him, soberly. "It has been kicked hard this time," she said, ignoring his smile. "Change is always coming, but some are harder than others. There's only one thing men can do when the world changes."

Jiaan's humor dropped away. "Survive it?" he asked bitterly.

"Not quite," said Maok. "But you're close. Change, world-kicking change, has come several times to the Suud. We remember those times, for it is not a thing that people forget."

Jiaan had other concerns on his mind, but he knew better than to ignore anything Maok wanted to tell him. "Go on."

"The first time even we do not remember well. It is said that we were once day dwellers. In the earliest of our stories the Suud lived in the land on the other side of the mountains, though—"

"The Suud lived in Farsala?" Jiaan knew he was interrupting, but he was so startled he couldn't help it. He'd never heard anything about this.

"I am telling you," Maok said calmly. "But the land on the other side of the mountains was much different then. The marshes that now are only near the sea covered most of the land, and it was filled with great and terrible animals who killed our ancestors. But these animals were day dwellers too, so the wisest of our ancestors went into caves during the day, where they could defend themselves, and only went out at night when the animals slept. Long and long passed, and our skin grew pale, and our eyes came to see in the dark.

"Then the Creator Spirit kicked the world again, and it trembled and trembled for many years, and the land tipped, and the swamps drained into the sea, and it grew colder, so all the great animals died. But the Suud, in our caves, were warm and safe. With the swamp gone the grass grew, and the cliff that splits the land rose up, and it became as it looks today."

Jiaan knew that she and other Suud had traveled in Farsala often enough. It shouldn't have surprised him that she described it so well, but somehow it did.

"Why didn't the Suud come out of their caves and become day dwellers again?" he asked. "Hunting is better in the day now, and the . . . the great animals are gone."

He wasn't certain he believed in the "great animals," but it was her story.

"We might have done," said Maok, "after long and long had passed. But before that, change came to us again. This time the Creator Spirit's kick set the people of the world moving. Two groups of people, traveling together, came into the grasslands, fleeing from a common enemy on the other side of the great desert. One group had light hair and eyes; they tilled the soil and made houses. The other had herds of goats and horses, planted little, and lived in tents like the Suud do now. Their eyes were dark and their hair straight and black."

Despite the inaccuracy of that—for the Farsalans had never fled before any enemies, but had always lived in Farsala and defended its borders—Jiaan recognized his own people. However, this story was obviously false.

"How could they have crossed the great

desert?" he asked. "No one who's explored it has ever found water, or any life at all out in the sand. No one even knows what lies beyond it. Unless . . . have your people crossed it?"

"No," Maok admitted. "But maybe the outer desert was less harsh then, for cross it these two peoples did. They were not friends to each other, though they had chosen to flee together. The dark-haired people fought long and long before they brought the light-haired ones under their control. We knew this because we watched from our caves, and hoped that their quarrel would keep them from fighting us."

"Wait—you're saying that the deghans . . . conquered the peasants? That's not true! They made a bargain—peasants to serve and farm; deghans to rule and fight!"

"Maybe they did reach this bargain in the end," said Maok indifferently. "I do not know what let them cross the desert as allies, or why they fought later. All I know is that we asked only for the night, offering them the day, but they both turned as one to fight us. I think . . . the stories do not say this, but I think that turning against us was what finally brought them together."

"But . . ." There were no Farsalan stories of deghans fighting peasants; there were no stories of crossing the desert. But the very heart of Farsalan legend began with the time when champions fought the demons who inhabited Farsala in those ancient days. Fought them until Rostam cast down their king and drove them out. Demons who had skin and hair as white as the face of the moon, who were creatures of the night and could not endure the light of Azura's sun.

Demons who might, just might, have lived in Farsala before the Farsalans did?

"I don't . . . I didn't . . . I don't know what to say," said Jiaan. "I'm sorry."

"You should not be," Maok told him. "Not for a thing that happened so long before that only memory remains. Those old Suud rode the tumbling of the world, just as we try to now, and we came into the desert, where our ability to see in the dark and live in the night helps us much. But do you see the point of all this change, Young Commander?"

"Um, no. Not really."

The old woman was too subtle to roll her eyes or sigh in exasperation, but the exaggerated patience in her voice got the message across. "The point is that people cannot stop change, but they can shape it to be for good—or at least not so bad. Change is not a one thing complete—it brings choices. When your people came to the land on the other side of the mountains, my people could have chosen to fight to all their deaths. Some did fight and die. But the wisest of them retreated to the desert, and your people who followed could not beat us, and we have lived long in peace and happiness because of it. These wise ones did not fall down when the world tumbled—they thought about the change, rode the tumbling of the world, and made things better. Just like your sis—your people in Mazad are doing."

Jiaan frowned. "What happened in Mazad?"

"You didn't hear? The messenger was just . . . ah, he would have reached your camp after you left, for he spent the night with us. There have been several victories happening against the Hrum. The Hrum leader sent two centris to hunt some men in the swamp place called Dugaz, but the men they hunted killed almost all of them."

Jiaan's heart leaped—the swamp rats had been forced to fight! "Good for them!"

Maok eyed him skeptically. "Don't sound so happy yet. The swamp men lost many of their own lives in this fight. The messenger said that one of them had told the Hrum where their camp was hidden. The swamp people sent this man to the Hrum, after the battle. In very small pieces."

"He was a traitor," said Jiaan.

If they hadn't been at war with the Hrum, he would have approved of someone who betrayed bandits to the authorities. But they *were* at war. And now that he thought of it, Shir, the bandit chieftain, was another person who had the good sense to want the peddler dead—and that was enough in itself to win Jiaan's approbation.

Maok sighed. "Well, if that news pleases you, this you will like even better. Your people in Mazad have made a great victory, bringing the storms in the sky to help them. They beat the Hrum army so bad that they will have to bring more men before they fight again."

The relief that welled through Jiaan's heart was so intense, tears came to his eyes. "Yes! Let the senate committee see that! But what do you mean, the storms helped them?"

Maok's eyes glinted. "The messenger said that a

big storm came up to the city and stopped right on it, and that it rained much harder there than anywhere for far and far. He said that the people around the city saw the clouds stop in one spot, like a hand held them, and grow and grow. They say that Sorahb did it, and they whisper that he is a sorcerer and call him 'storm-bringer.' That is what the messenger said."

Jiaan laughed. "It helps to be lucky, too. A good storm would have run off the city cobbles and made the ground outside the walls a sea of mud. That's wonderful!"

"And so," said Maok, "the people of Mazad rode the tumbling of the world until it rolled them a storm and gave them victory. What will you do with your prisoners, Commander Jiaan?"

IT WAS ALMOST DUSK when Jiaan returned to the Suud camp, tired and very hungry. But there was no point in returning earlier, for the Suud wouldn't begin cooking until after they rose, at sunset. And before he ate, Jiaan had something to settle. He went to the hutch where Patrius was being tended and asked the hooded Suud who stood guard outside if the prisoner was awake.

Yes, the guard replied, his friend was awake and doing better, too.

Jiaan, who had already identified Patrius as his prisoner, sighed.

When he went into the hutch, he thought that the tactimian looked better—still tired, but at least his skin held more color than that of the healer beside him. There were lines of pain around his eyes, but the grief and guilt that had marked his expression earlier had vanished under his usual cool control. Perhaps Jiaan could ease those emotions, or at least distract him.

"I've got an idea," he said abruptly. "You say that neither Garren nor the committee is likely to reject Siatt's offer. But once they've accepted, would they be willing to trade those Kadeshi peasants to me in exchange for more than five centris of Hrum prisoners?"

Patrius sat up abruptly, then clutched his head and swore. Jiaan winced in sympathy—he had become dehydrated on one of his early visits to the desert, and the resultant headache had been one of the worst he'd ever suffered.

"You'd trade us for the Kadeshi? Of course Garren will do it. A skilled soldier is worth more, than four untrained men. Our training methods are good, but we couldn't get far with them in the few months Garren has left. But neither will you, no matter how many peasants you've trained to fight."

Yes, he would have learned where Jiaan's army had come from. Jiaan wondered what else the Hrum officer had deduced, and how Garren might use it against them. For a moment his resolve wavered, but then it firmed. This was the right thing to do, and if Jiaan couldn't figure out a way to make it work for him, then maybe he should step aside and let someone else command.

"The Suud can't feed you," said Jiaan, "not for four months anyway. Neither can I, so letting you go is no hardship."

"But there will be more of the Kadeshi than of us," Patrius protested. "Probably a lot more."

"Yes, but they could hunt and . . . never mind. I'm not worried about that part of it." Actually he was, but his nascent plan to mix the Kadeshi conscripts with his troops, scatter them throughout the countryside, and have them all attack the Hrum as Garren's time limit drew near was still largely unformed. Even if it had been honed to a fine edge, he wouldn't have shared it with a Hrum officer.

"The point is that if they're fighting for us, Siatt probably won't kill their families," Jiaan went on. "Why should he? The men will still be fighting the Hrum, which was what he wanted, more or less. They won't have had any choice in the matter, so killing their families would be a waste of good labor. If he blames anyone, it will probably be me—which I'd consider an honor. And instead of five hundred plus prisoners who have to be fed and guarded, I'll have a huge number of men who, no matter how ill-trained, will fight on my side."

There were advantages for the Farsalans. And if this plan came perilously close to collaboration with the enemy, then so be it. If he could save the Kadeshi peasants and their families, it would be worth it.

Did the peddler think that, when he first decided to help the Hrum?

But that was different! Kavi *betrayed* the Farsalan army, and the deghans weren't nearly as bad as the warlords. This was a good plan, even if . . .

"Taking a large force of potential traitors off his hands will rid Garren of a huge problem," Patrius pointed out. "Do you want that?"

"It doesn't matter," said Jiaan. "The sacrifice of those peasants is one weapon I'll never use. You wouldn't either, and we both know it. What I'm wondering is, would Garren pay attention to a different warning? If you told him that Siatt's only goal is to weaken us both, so that he'll have an easy time conquering whoever remains, would Garren listen to that? Listen and take precautions against any offer Siatt or the other warlords might make? I think that Siatt is acting on his own now—the warlords fight each other as often as they band together to fight us. But if they had a chance to conquer Farsala . . . If we have an army of Kadeshi warlords inside our borders when this ends, I'm not sure either of us could kick them out. And even if we could, the cost would be very high."

Patrius rubbed his forehead, but Jiaan could see that he was thinking despite the pain. "Yes," he said slowly. "The committee will heed that warning even if Garren ignores it, and I think Garren will pay attention to this. It's how his own mind works. I'll carry your warning to the committee, and I'll convince them too."

The words 'I promise' hovered in the air between them, but with Patrius there was no need to say them aloud. The tactimian could be trusted. It was strange, Jiaan thought, to be so certain of the honor of his enemy.

CHAPTER FOURTEEN

KAVI

ANVILS WERE GOING to be the worst problem, Kavi realized, gazing around the shed where Tebin stored broken tools and things that weren't in frequent use. Tongs, punches, chisels, hammers—almost all the tools a smith needed were there in plenty, most needing only minor repairs before the Suud could use them. But anvils . . . *We'll just have to be casting some*, Kavi decided. The Suud deserved to have the townsfolk of Mazad, especially the smiths, give the Wheel a spin in their favor. Without Suud magic to guide them they'd never have figured out the trick of cooling different parts of the sword at different rates—though half the journeymen in town were now claiming to have come up with it first, and soon, Kavi feared, the Suud's assistance would be almost forgotten. But no matter who forgot their aid, Kavi would see to it that the metalsmiths of Mazad did not forget their debt.

He picked up a wire puller and examined it critically. A bit rusty, and the wooden handle was cracked, but nothing that couldn't be fixed.

The Suud were becoming restless—homesick, in truth, though they had promised to stay until the conflict between Farsala and the Hrum was over. Less than four months now, one way or the other. When the Suud left, the town would be sending them home with proper tools to practice their new trade—though hauling seven anvils over the mountains and down into the desert would be a rough job. If the new smiths weren't quite finished with their training—and to be honest, they weren't nearly finished—they would continue to improve with practice and could always return when they needed further lessons. If they continued to refine the use of Speaking on steel, who knew what they might eventually—

A soft rap on the door interrupted his thoughts.

"Come in," he called, and suppressed a smile as the lady Soraya entered. Time was, she'd never have knocked on any door, much less that of a peasant's toolshed, but now she did it without thinking. Kavi didn't delude himself that the last few weeks of living under the kindly hand of Tebin and his housekeeper had brought about the change either. Something in her had finally broken her out of her old mindset and into a new one.

Though that didn't mean she'd like to see him smiling at her. She was tolerating him better these days, but he wasn't forgiven. He didn't expect that—forgiving a father's death was too much to ask of anyone, no matter how they'd grown. And speaking of forgiving . . .

Commander Jiaan followed her into the shed and Kavi grimaced. He'd hoped to avoid the man for the rest of the war, and beyond it too, if Jiaan couldn't be persuaded to abandon his resolve to kill him as soon as the Hrum were defeated. Now that Kavi had helped to create watersteel swords to arm his men, perhaps Jiaan would settle for a flogging or a bit of maiming?

Jiaan wasn't even looking at him; he was talking to a third man, who was dressed as a country farmer. But this man was no farmer, nor a countryman at all.

The wire puller fell from Kavi's loosened grip and thudded on the dirt floor. Soft as it was, the sound caught Patrius' attention. He looked up, squinting in the dim light of the shed. Then his eyes widened.

"You!" It was the first time Kavi had seen the composed tactimian taken completely off guard.

The girl's brows rose. "You two know each other?"

"All too well." Kavi picked up the wire puller, wiped the dust from it, and hung it back on the rack. "Don't be fretting about it, Lady—I pretty much ended my days as a spy when I escaped from Barmael's camp."

"But you were spying for us!" Patrius exclaimed. His voice was high with outrage, but even as he finished the sentence Kavi saw a glint of humor enter his eyes. At least, he hoped it was humor—it could also have meant that the tactimian had come up with some horrible and appropriate revenge.

"Who gave you permission to go to the Hrum's camp?" Jiaan demanded.

No humor in that one at all.

"I don't need permission," said Kavi coldly. "I was trying to find out a bit about Nehar's plans, and I didn't, though I did learn something of interest. Did Siddas tell you about the committee that's coming to inspect our Governor Garren?"

"I vouched for you," Patrius murmured—but there was laughter in his voice, as well as despair. He looked Kavi up and down as if the peddler had suddenly turned into a stranger, which Kavi supposed he had, but in his eyes Kavi saw the dawning of respect. It was an expression he'd never seen on the tactimian's face before, for all they'd worked well together.

"I'm glad you're all right," he told Patrius. "I was worried about you—and not just that you might be winning, either."

Patrius' expression closed down in sudden, private pain. "It seems you needn't have worried about that at all," he said.

For all his sudden coolness he was alive and whole. A commander who couldn't recover from losing a battle, at least eventually, would be worthless—and Patrius was far from worthless. He would regain his emotional equilibrium soon enough. The tight and painful knot in Kavi's heart loosened as they went to find Tebin and arranged for one of the storerooms to be furnished as a small but reasonably comfortable cell. Patrius was a trusted prisoner, but a prisoner nonetheless. Which meant he would be out of the fighting for the rest of the war, and Kavi need no longer wake up in a cold sweat from dreaming about the tactimian's death.

After Patrius was locked away, Jiaan asked about swords, so Kavi took him out to yet another shed to show him the newest batch and discuss future numbers. They had armed every man in Mazad's guard, and had almost two hundred more swords ready for Jiaan's forces.

"Unfortunately, those may be growing soon," said the commander grimly. "Or maybe it's fortunate. I'm not entirely certain. Can we speak privately here?"

"I think so," said Soraya, looking at Kavi for confirmation. Jiaan had asked her the question, though he had to know Kavi could answer it better than she could. It looked like Commander

Jiaan wasn't ready to settle for flogging yet—which meant that Kavi had to defend Mazad from the Hrum's final attack, free Farsala, and then escape Jiaan's revenge afterward. It seemed a lot to ask.

"We can talk here," said Kavi. The clatter of metal on metal from the smithy was muted by the walls, but it would be hard for anyone outside the shed to overhear them—not to mention the fact that no one could have anticipated this unscheduled meeting of the commanders of the Farsalan defense.

And that, Kavi realized with a chill, was precisely what the three of them were. Even Siddas was thinking of Mazad alone—that was responsibility enough for any man! Only the three of them had thought of all Farsala from the beginning of the invasion.

How did I get into this?

"I know that you two know about the committee, and about Garren's plan to bribe the Kadeshi warlords," Jiaan went on. "You're the ones who discovered it."

Kavi realized that Jiaan, too, had changed. The hatred was still there, but this assured voice was the voice of a commander, who for all his youth had defeated the army sent against him. A small army, perhaps — but escaping Jiaan's revenge after this was over suddenly didn't sound as simple as it once had.

"What you don't know," Jiaan continued, "is what the Kadeshi are planning in return."

He told them about Siatt's offer, about a horde of peasants whose families would die if they refused to sacrifice themselves. Even in the midst of his own anger, Kavi noticed that the girl was almost as furious and appalled as he was.

"Thinking of taking them up on it, are you?" he demanded. If the bastard was, swordsman or no, Kavi would pick up a hammer and smash out his brains. His grip might be weak, but if he used both hands and a big hammer —

"No," said Jiaan coolly. "And I'd consider myself insulted, but I'd expect you to think of something like that."

Heat surged in Kavi's face as that insult struck home. He took a moment to breathe until he was calm enough to speak quietly.

"I'm sorry. I was angry at that . . . that sorry excuse for a man, much less a ruler. But I shouldn't have let my anger spill onto you."

Jiaan nodded, but Kavi noticed that he didn't apologize in return.

"As a matter of fact," the commander went on, "I have an idea that might save them—some of them, at least, and all of their families. I'm going to offer to trade Garren my Hrum prisoners in exchange for his Kadeshi troops."

The lady Soraya frowned. "But those men are just peasants. And Garren hasn't even paid his bribe yet, so they won't be coming for at least a month and probably more. Can you train them enough to be useful in the time that remains?"

Jiaan shrugged. "Not very useful. But I'd rather have them on my side than have to kill them. Or watch the Hrum kill them, knowing that their families will die if they fail. I can't allow that, not if I can prevent it. Besides, resistance is growing throughout Farsala now, and Garren is exacting harsher and harsher reprisals. With this committee putting even more pressure on him . . . The Hrum might refuse an order to execute civilians, but Kadeshi troops would do it."

A grim pause followed. The young commander's quiet voice broke it.

"Finally, I can't feed my prisoners for more

than another month, so giving them back in a way that might help us is the only thing that makes sense. I won't let them starve."

"But wouldn't it be better to keep Garren from bribing this warlord in the first place?" Soraya asked. "If the Farsalan army captured the committee and stole the gold, it would certainly prove that Garren doesn't control Farsala. We could even hold them for ransom. And if you had the gold, you could buy food for your prisoners—and anything else you need as well."

Kavi knew what his expression looked like, because Jiaan's face bore the same look of stunned stupidity.

"I don't . . . I didn't . . . why didn't I think of that?" the commander of Farsala's army stuttered.

"Probably because it's more subtle than two armies bashing each other," said the girl tartly. She didn't add *Men!* but the thought was there. Kavi might have resented the implication, but he was wondering why *he* hadn't thought of it.

"We don't know when this committee is arriving, do we?" Kavi asked. "That could make it hard to capture them. They'll be well guarded, too, carrying all that gold." Though likely not so well

guarded that they could fend off the whole
Farsalan army.

He could see Commander Jiaan running the
same thoughts through his head, with a better
understanding of things like ambushes and troop
movements behind them.

"I don't think it will work," he said finally. He
sounded so regretful that Kavi knew it was an honest estimate, not a rejection of another's plan just
because it wasn't his. "The first problem is getting
our army across the width of Farsala without the
Hrum realizing it. I know they are Farsalan peasants, but that many people moving in the same
direction is going to be noticed by any Hrum commander with half a brain, and most of them aren't
stupid. It will be reported to Garren, and he's not
stupid either. He has to know that both the gold
and the committee are a target. Even worse, there
might be—there probably are—spies in my own
forces." He told them what Patrius had said and his
own conclusions.

"If the Hrum aren't marking their spies anymore, they could be anywhere," said Soraya, thinking it through. "We can't trust anyone."

"That's not entirely true," said Kavi. "Mazad's

been closed off by the siege, so there can't be any spies here. But in the countryside . . ."

There was no way to know, he realized. Any peasants he dealt with, even if they were honest, might have friends, or neighbors, or cousins who had decided that the Hrum were here to stay and they might as well profit from it. Some of them might even work for the Hrum because they preferred them! Kavi had made that choice himself, not so long ago. And he couldn't expect others to see, as he had, that the Farsalan peasants might get a chance out of this to rule themselves. There could be spies anywhere.

"I wouldn't put it past Garren to use the committee sent to investigate him as bait to trap us," Jiaan went on. "In fact, from what I've heard about him, that's exactly the kind of thing he'd come up with."

That was true. The lady Soraya, who'd also dealt with the governor, nodded agreement.

"If he guesses you've pulled your army out of the desert to attack the committee," said Kavi, "the first thing he'll do is bring in a large force to take Mazad. He's probably going to do that soon anyway, but I know Siddas is counting on your help when they come for that final attack."

"He is," said Jiaan. "We've spoken of it. So I can't pull my army out of position. I'm sorry, Lady Soraya. It's a good idea, but I don't see how we can manage it."

The girl's shoulders slumped. Not for the first time, Kavi was struck by their strange relationship. These two were half brother and sister, but they had grown up as lady of the house and bastard page, and it was clear that that was how they still regarded each other—even though Soraya's only surviving family had vanished into the vast Hrum empire, and, as far as Kavi knew, she and her missing brother were the only kin Jiaan had left. They didn't look alike, but Kavi could see their father in both of them—not in their hair, or eyes, or the cast of their features, but in their straight spines and the way their minds worked. They thought alike. And in fact the girl's idea was a good one. If only . . .

"Why do we have to do it?" he asked softly.

"What do you mean?" said Soraya.

"Why does the army have to capture the committee? I mean, your soldiers are wonderful and all, but they're not the only men in Farsala."

Jiaan frowned. "You're talking of the villagers? The senate committee will have a huge guard, and most of the villagers who are willing to fight are with me already. Besides, there's even more chance of spies—"

"I'm not talking about the villagers," said Kavi, though he thought they might be more effective than Commander Jiaan believed, if they were properly organized. "I'm talking about a group of people even less likely to have spies in their midst than we do at Mazad, for in a way they're even more isolated. And more willing to fight than any men left in Farsala. I'm talking about those mad bandits in the Dugaz swamps. Let them capture the committee for you. They're even landing there!"

The committee hadn't much choice, coming by ship; Dugaz was Farsala's only deepwater harbor. It was perfect! Kavi wondered why he hadn't thought of it the moment he'd learned of the committee's existence.

Jiaan's frown deepened to a scowl. "They're not interested in helping Farsala. They don't care about anything but—"

"They don't have to want to help Farsala,"

Kavi interrupted impatiently. "They'll be helping themselves. Or don't you remember how much gold that committee's bringing with them?"

Jiaan's expression brightened, and the girl nodded. "I'd rather we got the gold," she said. "But I'd rather see the bandits take it than see Garren get his hands on it."

"But who will tell them about it?" Jiaan asked. "I have to stay here with the army because . . . in case Garren moves faster than we expect."

That wasn't what he'd started to say, but Kavi knew better than to press him.

"Well, I can't go," said Kavi. "Last time I saw Shir—he's their leader," he added, noticing the girl's puzzled expression. "Last time I saw him, he wanted to kill me."

"He probably hasn't changed his mind, either." Jiaan smiled. It was the first time he'd ever smiled at Kavi, and Kavi hoped it would be the last.

"I'll go," said Soraya. "I'm no use here. Not anymore."

"I'm not sure you'd be safe," said Jiaan. "In fact, I'm sure you wouldn't be. Not alone. And with you gone, who'd watch *him*?" He didn't even glance at Kavi, but his tone made his meaning clear.

"I'll take him with me," said the lady Soraya with a bit of her old arrogance. She didn't look at Kavi as she spoke either. "He can protect me if it's necessary, but I'm pretty good at looking after myself these days. Do you really think they'd put a higher value on raping me than getting their hands on Garren's gold?"

"But they'll kill me," said Kavi.

"Maybe not," Jiaan answered Soraya, "if you use knowledge of the gold to protect you. But—"

"But they'll *kill* me!" Kavi repeated, his voice rising.

"So?" said Jiaan, "That will save me the trouble. Are you certain about this, Lady?"

"Yes," said Soraya, though to Kavi's ear she didn't sound certain. "If the committee is captured and held to ransom, it will be the best possible proof that the land isn't conquered—or at least that it's not under Garren's control. And that's important. We're running out of time."

Kavi looked from her determined face to Jiaan's troubled one and updated his list for the next four months: Survive Dugaz, defend Mazad, free Farsala, and then escape from Jiaan. Even at the top of the Wheel's turning, the Tree of Life wasn't likely to produce that much good fortune. Kavi sighed.

~

CHAPTER FIFTEEN

SORAYA

A MESSENGER ON A fleet horse, on dry roads, could go from Mazad to Dugaz in six days. Traveling on their own two feet, in the midst of winter's mud and rain, it took Soraya and the peddler almost three weeks to reach the edge of the great marshes, and another day to reach what the peddler claimed was the best path in.

"I was here in the summer," he told Soraya, eyeing the shimmering sheet of water that covered most of the path and all the rest of the land between the thick clumps of leafless mull bushes. "It was drier then."

"If we'd taken horses we'd have been here

faster," Soraya grumbled. They'd both wanted to avoid the extra notice the Hrum gave people who were mounted. Though after passing through the countryside, listening to the tales people told about the harassment the understrength Hrum garrisons had suffered, she wasn't sure they'd have bothered with a pair of harmless-looking travelers. The Hrum had too many real troubles to attend to.

Soraya pulled her sheepskin vest tighter. They were near enough to the sea for her to catch its scent on the whipping wind, and it was cold, too. Soraya looked at the wet, muddy path and sighed.

"It wouldn't have been any drier a week ago," the peddler pointed out. "And it's not like we've never been wet before. I don't suppose . . ." He gestured to the ranks of dark clouds streaming in from the sea. Clearly most of Farsala was going to get rain today, and from the look of things Soraya and the peddler would be joining them. At least she had been able to wear her warm, comfortable boy's clothes for this venture.

Despite the frequent rain and muddy roads, Soraya had enjoyed being outside the walls of Mazad. She hadn't realized how restricted she'd felt, surrounded by those narrow, stone streets, until she was out in the grassland, with nothing to contain her except the horizon and the low clouds that filled the sky.

She could see that the peddler enjoyed it too, striding out in his wet boots as if the simple act of moving through the world allowed him to possess it. He had greeted Duckie, after months of separation, like a long-lost love.

Which didn't mean he had enjoyed being rained on almost every day anymore than she had.

"No," said Soraya shortly. "I told you that before, remember? I haven't a clue how to stop it from raining."

He sighed. "It'll be a mess in the swamp, then, but I doubt it will be any drier tomorrow, so there's no use putting it off."

He had accepted her denial of ability to change the weather without pressure or protest, for which Soraya was grateful.

They'd been traveling through the farmland outside Mazad for several days, giving news-hungry peasants the town's version of the battle. In return they heard the country folk's tale of the "miraculous" storm Sorahb had summoned, which by now had gathered out of a clear blue sky and dropped so much rain—only on the Hrum, mind, none in the city at all—that the whole Hrum army had been washed away.

That was an exaggeration, though not by much. The Hrum's official explanation for the storm that had mired their troops, collapsed their tents, and almost drowned some of their wounded in its mud was "bad luck."

That same bad luck, she'd later learned, had destroyed Governor Nehar's whole fortune. Rain had soaked clear through the bundled packets of expensive dyes he had purchased in the beleaguered city for so much less than their true value. All of it, ruined in the storm.

Mitra still has her jewelry, Soraya told herself firmly. And the Hrum would continue to protect even a failed traitor, if he had committed his treason in their cause. But protection and work were all they had offered him. When she thought of the haughty Lady Mitra as the wife—and Nayani as the daughter—of a low-paid army clerk, remorse tugged at Soraya's heart.

I had no choice.

"It sure would be nice," the peddler had said,

on the fourth morning of their journey, "if Sorahb Storm-bringer could do something about the rain that's about to fall on our heads. It would save us time, not to mention the soaking."

Since he was the one who had found her deep in the shilshadu trance, she could hardly deny the title. Memory of that awakening, covered and warm, softened her impulse to snap at him. "No, thank you. Sorahb Storm-bringer doesn't know how to stop the rain. In truth he doesn't dare use that magic outside of dire emergencies. It's dangerous."

Her sudden shiver had nothing to do with the damp wind, and she thought he understood that. His voice was easy as he went on, "According to the Suud, only the best, the strongest of their All Speakers, can be working the weather. It's a gift they prize in that dry land of theirs. But I don't remember them saying it was dangerous. Perhaps you've just tackled it too soon."

"Perhaps," said Soraya. "And perhaps I should never have 'tackled it' at all."

"Hmm," said the peddler, declining to commit himself. "The thing that's surprising me is that no one's trying to attribute it to the Suud. Folks know

413

they're in the town, helping the smiths deal with the 'new ore,' but we're not hearing any rumors of Suud sorcerers or Suud demons. It's Sorahb getting the credit."

"All the better for the Suud," said Soraya. "I know that Maok didn't want their magic to become common knowledge. I think . . . I think people don't want the Suud to have magic. If they had a power we didn't, if they weren't simple barbarians, we'd have to stop looking down on them and start fearing them."

"Maok's right," said the peddler. "That would be bad. But you could be claiming the credit yourself, if you want it."

"I don't need people fearing me, either," said Soraya. "Let Sorahb have it. Besides . . ."

If people knew that she had brought the storm, they might expect her to do it again.

". . . besides," she went on, "I don't see you claiming to have commanded the battle that saved the gate. Sorahb's getting credit for that, too."

"Ah, but Sorahb, poor fellow, is made of nothing but words and moonshine, so he needs all the rumors he can get. I've got flesh, so I don't need words to hold me together," said the peddler cheerfully as the rain began to fall. "Even wet flesh is better than none."

Now Soraya watched him stepping down the muddy path, letting the mule take the lead, she noticed, and sighed. But he was right—they'd both been wet and muddy before.

She didn't like the swamp, she soon discovered. The bare twigs were still thick enough to block her view, almost as if she were wandering through a maze, and the mud that clung to her boots was as heavy and far more smelly than the mud of the road. The only saving grace was that it washed away whenever the deep, somewhat clearer water covered their path. Her feet were soaked before they'd gone a hundred yards, and the water was now creeping up the legs of her britches. "This is awful," Soraya complained. "How are we going to find anyone? Are we even on the path?"

As far as she could tell, the path, such as it was, had vanished less than a quarter league into the swamp, although the mule acted as if she knew where she was going. Having traveled with the quirky beast several times, Soraya was fond of Duckie—but she wasn't sure the mule was a qualified trail guide.

On the other hand, she enjoyed watching the ducks. A flotilla of more than twenty surrounded them at the moment, paddling around the mule and quacking companionably.

"It's better now than when it's hot and full of bugs," said the peddler. "Trust me on that. The risk of fever's down in the winter too. As for finding anyone, we're just giving them a chance to find us."

Soraya stopped for a moment to unfasten her vest from a twig and then hurried to catch up, splashing in the ankle-deep mud. One of the ducks muttered, as if it were commenting on her performance — and the comments weren't flattering.

"What if they don't want to find us?"

"Then we try again tomorrow, and maybe the next day to make certain, then we give up and go back," said the peddler. "No one finds the men who work this swamp when they don't want to be found. But don't worry," he added gloomily. "I'm sure we won't be that lucky."

Soraya had her doubts. If she'd been a swamp bandit, making her money picking silk cocoons from these bushes when there were no travelers on the road worth robbing, she'd have seen no reason to deal in any way with the impoverished peasants she and the peddler appeared to be. Now that she was splashing through the swamp, she completely understood why the Hrum had failed to find the bandits' camp—it was a wonder they hadn't all drowned. She'd already skidded into one shallow sinkhole, straying off the trail the mule chose, and she knew there must be deeper ones.

But the peddler proved correct again. Several marks later, just as Soraya was deciding that she'd had enough of the Dugaz swamps to last several lifetimes, the ducks started quacking and skittered away like flower petals in a sudden gust of wind.

Soraya stared after them in bafflement, but the peddler stopped in his tracks and held his hands out from his sides, away from his knife.

"We've come to see Shir," he said, a little too loudly for the calm he was trying to project. "We've information he'll be wanting. Information for which he might reward the men who bring the messengers."

A muddy, bearded man came from behind one of the bushes. Soraya supposed she couldn't blame him for the mud—she and the peddler were splashed from hand to thigh, and solid mud from the thighs down—but this man looked as if it had been years since he'd been clean. On the other hand, when you looked that tough, you probably didn't hear critical comments about other aspects of your appearance. Soraya decided to let the peddler do the talking, but it was the man who spoke next.

"Oh, Shir'll be rewarding me, peddler-who-carries-messages-from-Sorahb. He's been wanting to see you again for quite some time."

To COMPLETE THEIR misery it started to rain before they reached the bandit camp, so Soraya was soaked and shivering as well as filthy and exhausted when the bandits pushed them through the tent flaps and into the presence of their leader. At least the floor, a wooden platform raised above the mud, was dry, and several braziers made the big tent almost warm. But the rain pattering on the oiled-silk roof brought a damp chill with it, and the sight of the lean man lounging in the great chair made Soraya feel no safer, though he was both clean-shaven and relatively clean. He looked at her and the peddler with the analytical gaze of a cook selecting the plumpest chickens for the pot.

"Peddler! You're a rude young man, you know. You enjoyed our hospitality last time and departed without so much as a by-your-leave. If you hadn't left gold"—the bandit leader gestured to the thick buckle that adorned his belt—"I'd have been so disappointed in you, I don't know what I'd have done. And you're not carrying gold today—you or your girl."

He would know that they had nothing. His guards had searched them for weapons and wealth with a chilly efficiency that had discovered Soraya's gender but hadn't taken time to exploit it, not even with rude comments. That was probably a good thing, but she found it frightening, too—almost unnatural.

"I'm not carrying gold today," the peddler said. "But we've news of a fortune to make you rich. Rich enough to leave this swamp, if you so choose, and take up a life elsewhere."

Looking at the ruby that hung from the man's ear, the bright silk of the cushions on which he lounged, and the expensive glaze under the soot on the braziers, Soraya knew he was already rich enough to leave the swamp. If he'd gotten it from the peddler, she had had a doubt about the big gold buckle, but most of his jewelry appeared to be real.

"I'm always interested in money," said Shir, leaning back in his chair and crossing his ankles. But he wasn't, Soraya realized. Not today. Today he was frightened.

"They're pressing you, aren't they?" she asked. "The Hrum troops. You may have fought off one force, but you know it's just a matter of time."

The bandit chieftain's face froze. He rose from his chair like a panther and slapped her face, once. The blow was so quick, Soraya barely saw it coming and had no time to dodge. She was sitting on the floor with her ears ringing when Shir resumed his seat.

The peddler, ungallantly, had made no move to stop him—though in fairness the man with the drawn knife who stood behind him might have had something to do with that.

"The Hrum will never take us," said Shir. "I allow no one to doubt that. No one."

The tension in the tent did not come only from the bandit leader, Soraya realized; the guards were stretched tight with it too. If the Hrum really were pressing him, if his men were leaving him because

420

of it—and why wouldn't they? The Hrum had a short way with bandits—then she'd probably gotten off lightly with just a slap. She had misjudged this situation. Badly. Still . . .

"I'm quite certain that no one could find you if you didn't choose to be found," said the peddler, with the smooth flattery that seemed to come naturally to him, especially in emergencies. "But it would be better for all of us if the Hrum were gone, now wouldn't it?"

His easy, soothing voice had its effect. The bandit leaned back in his chair.

"I'll certainly admit that," he said. "I don't know anyone who'd deny it. Except, perhaps, a man who is marked as a Hrum spy."

The peddler didn't flinch, though Soraya thought he wanted to.

"That's old news to everyone now," he said. "All the Hrum's enemies know it. You might—might—get a few brass foals from the Hrum for confirming their suspicions. Assuming you dare get near enough to a Hrum officer to hand me over." He shrugged, suddenly impatient, and reached down to help Soraya to her feet, ignoring the way their guards twitched around them.

"He's right," Soraya told Shir. "You can't make much from turning him over to anyone, or from killing him. But alive he and I can provide you with information that will not only make you rich, it might help get the Hrum out of Farsala!"

Her cheek stung and throbbed.

"And what of you, lady?" Shir asked softly. "Perhaps the lad's worth no more than a few foals, but surely the family of such a lovely deghass would pay well to get her back, whole and unharmed."

Soraya snorted. "How many rich deghan families do you think Farsala has left? If I belonged to one of the families that are serving the Hrum—and they're the only ones with money, I promise you—would I be here trying to talk you into fighting them? My father died at the Sendar Wall, and my mother and brother are slaves somewhere in the empire. I've been working as a kitchen servant and hiding among the Suud for most of the last year. Do you think I'd do that if my family had a fortune to spend in ransom?"

Shir scowled. He rose from his chair again—not quite as pantherlike this time—reached out, and took her hand, running his thumb over the roughened skin, the calluses that still lingered despite the softer weeks in Mazad. It was no longer a lady's hand. Shir dropped it and sat down.

"You're talking about the gold the senate committee is escorting, aren't you, sweetheart?"

Despite her resolve to reveal nothing, Soraya felt her eyes widen. "You know about the committee?"

"And the gold," Shir confirmed. "I have spies too, you know."

"Then you must see how much you could accomplish if you take them! It would prove better than anything else that Garren hasn't conquered Farsala!"

"And that being the case," said Shir, "he'd send all his troops to hunt us down and crush us, to be getting his precious committee back. Or hadn't you thought of that?"

"But you'd only have to hold them for three months—less than that now," said Soraya. "I didn't think you were . . ." The aching bruise brought caution. "I'd think a few months' effort would be worthwhile, if it rid you of the Hrum forever. And there is the gold."

"So there is." Shir sighed. "Or so there was, I

should say, for that cursed committee landed in Dugaz over two weeks ago."

"They're here?" Soraya exclaimed. "Already?"

"Here and gone, sweetheart. I gallantly anticipated your commands and tried to capture them too—not to mention their gold—but their guard was too strong. They left the swamp, putting themselves out of our reach, over a week ago. So you can hardly blame me for trying to find out what sort of profit remains to be made from the two of you."

Soraya barely heard him. "Over a week? They'll almost have reached Setesafon by now. Why didn't we pass them on the road?"

"Because they'll have taken the river," said Kavi. "Barge up to the Trade Road, then cart into Setesafon. It's by far the easiest way, especially carrying a heavy cargo in winter mud. That will slow them, by the by. They'll not be in Setesafon yet, though they'll arrive before we can get there."

"Well, at least they were attacked on the way," said Soraya. "That should help convince them Farsala's not completely subdued, don't you think?"

"Excuse me," said Shir, "but—"

"Not as much as relieving them of all that gold

would have," said the peddler ruefully. "I wonder if they came early on purpose, to take Garren by surprise. I know he wasn't expecting them this soon."

"Excuse me," said Shir, "but we were discussing the small matter of your ransoms. Which is closely related, I might add, to the even smaller matter of keeping the two of you alive."

Soraya didn't understand how he managed to sound both sinister and amused at the same time, but he did.

"If you ever want to be rid of the Hrum, then you shouldn't take him out of the fight," she said, gesturing at the peddler. "He's Sorahb's liaison to the peasants who support the rebellion. He's arranged help for Mazad, gained recruits for the army, fostered acts of sabotage . . . If you want to be rid of the Hrum, you don't even want to delay him. We've wasted too much time on this already!"

Furious frustration leached into her voice, giving her last statement the unmistakable ring of truth. But everything she'd said was true, she realized. If the Hrum were defeated, it would be in large part because of the peddler. It didn't, it couldn't, excuse what he had done at the Sendar Wall, to her father, to her family. But he had done as much to make up for his betrayal as any man could have. She could never forgive him, but all his actions since then had to count for something, didn't they?

She shook her head slowly, her thoughts spinning. Could you hate someone and respect him at the same time?

"Then that leaves you as my only source of profit," said Shir, looking her up and down. "Unless you're the one who's going to be taking on the Hrum army single-handed? Or are you working for Sorahb too? His liaison to kitchen maids? A band of deghass warriors in silk skirts?"

"She's your liaison to the Suud," said the peddler, before Soraya could think of a reply. "If she's being harmed, or even held, they'll leave you to rot. But if you do all you can against the Hrum, which it sounds like you already have, the Suud's healers will try to find a cure for the swamp fever. They say they'll try, mind—no promises of success. But it's a better hope than you've got now, which is no hope at all if the fever takes you."

Shir frowned. "Suud healers? What makes you think they could cure anything? The Suud are so primitive, they can't even make knives!"

426

"That's changing," said the peddler. "And you're not fool enough to think it matters. The desert is full of medicinal plants, and the folk who live there know how to use them."

"He's right," said Soraya. "Their healers are very skilled." Even when they didn't use Speaking to enhance their medicines. "But they can't guarantee anything—they've never seen a case of swamp fever. The best they could do is try."

Had the peddler spoken to the Suud about curing swamp fever, or was this a lie crafted out of invention and need? Not that it mattered—Soraya had known enough Suud healers to know they'd try if she asked them.

"So you want me to give up whatever profit I might be making, on the slim chance that he can help Sorahb defeat the Hrum, and the even slimmer chance that some Suud herb-picker can cure swamp fever?" Shir asked. "That's not much, friends."

"You'd not be getting much of a ransom for us either," said the peddler apologetically. "So that's probably fair."

"So you say, but . . . ah, Flame take you, get out of my sight. If there's no profit in you, then you're wasting my time."

"You want us to let them go?" one of the guards asked incredulously.

"Unless you can think of a way to get more money out of them than I can. We might get a little work out of the one, and a little pleasure out of the other, but that's hardly worth the trouble of keeping them prisoner," said Shir. "And dead we'd have the labor of burying them. Their claim that they might be getting the Hrum off our backs, or curing the fever, is probably moonshine, but it costs us nothing. Let them go."

"I'll ask them," said Soraya impulsively. "The Suud healers. But I can't make you any promises."

"If you'd promised," said Shir, "I'd have known you were lying. And if you annoy the Hrum half as much as you've annoyed me, that's almost as much profit as a decent ransom right there. At least it will make me feel better, and these days, that's something."

"THE HRUM MUST BE pressing him hard," said the peddler, following the mule's round hindquarters between the muddy hummocks of grass and brush. "Time was, he wouldn't have let us go half that easily."

"You call that *easy*?"

It was still raining, and Soraya struggled to keep her teeth from chattering, though she suspected half her shivering was born of relief. Until she had left their camp, until the ducks' return had told them that their invisible escort had finally abandoned them, Soraya hadn't dared to admit how frightened she had been. "Did you really ask the Suud healers about a cure for swamp fever?"

"Not the healers," said the peddler. "How could I? None of the lads in Mazad are healers, though they have friends who are, and they said they'd likely try. If healers didn't like curing folk they wouldn't become healers in the first place."

"So you prepared that tale in advance? To get us out?"

The peddler shrugged. "I've met Shir before. I knew I'd be needing all the bribes I could get."

But he hadn't used his lie to ransom himself—he'd used it for her. Despite the cold rain running under her collar and soaking her shirt, despite her frozen hands and feet, something hard and cold in Soraya's heart began to thaw—as if the peddler's lie carried sunlight inside it.

SORAHB CREPT ALONE *into the Hrum's camp and stole enough of their uniforms to garb himself and a band of loyal men.*

Then Sorahb led them into the city of Setesafon, into the old gahn's palace, the very heart of the Hrum governor's lair. There he and his men reft away the gold that was the lifeblood of the Hrum army. But as they fled with the treasure, disaster struck.

CHAPTER SIXTEEN

SORAYA

THE PEDDLER SENT a message asking Jiaan to meet them in Setesafon. The winter rains were finally letting up with the onset of spring, so they'd made better time returning to the city. But the peddler said they all needed to learn what the committee thought of Garren's progress, and what they intended to do, as soon as possible. Soraya agreed with that, though she had her doubts about the peddler's motives: When he talked about the gold, there was a gleam in his eyes that she didn't trust. It wasn't greed, either. She'd have felt better about greed, for greed was usually predictable, controllable. The glint in the peddler's eyes was mischief, and she didn't trust that at all. She sighed. At least he had the sense to hide it from Jiaan, who had arrived last night, muddy, tired, and in no mood for mischief.

"I'm thinking," the peddler told him, "that we should still be regarding that gold as our target. The committee is so well protected now that we've no hope of taking them, and it's always harder to make off with a shouting, struggling man than a chest of inanimate stuff. Besides, judging from the comments the servants have overheard, Shir and his ruffians did a decent job. The committee, so I'm told, is none too pleased with the governor." He reached for the teapot, realized his mug was still full, and set it down again, but that was the only sign of nervousness that showed.

Soraya had hoped to rent a room for this breakfast conversation, but a private room in a Setesafon inn cost more than the three of them together could afford, so they sat at a table in the tap room, their privacy protected by nothing but the easy chatter coming from the other tables and their own lowered voices.

"That's good," said Jiaan. "But they haven't suddenly stopped guarding the gold, have they?"

"No." A stubborn look came over the peddler's face. "Of course they guard it. I'm just saying we might have a chance. We should at least try to learn if it's possible."

"No matter how great the risk?" Jiaan asked, an unnatural gentleness in his voice.

"The potential gain is worth some risk. That gold's not only for bribing the Kadeshi, you know. There's army supply money in with it, and pay for their troops. If Garren lost it—"

"He'd probably just take what he needs from our merchants, instead of following Hrum law and buying it," said Jiaan. "And as for the risks, well, you wouldn't be taking them, would you?"

The peddler flushed. "I'm known by too many of the Hrum who are fighting at Mazad now," he said. "I was seen by some of the men that were there before them too. I don't dare go near the Hrum."

"No," said Jiaan coldly. "You don't dare. But you're willing to send others in your place."

The peddler drew a deep breath, visibly struggling to control his temper. "If those other men were having a decent chance of success, then—"

"No," Jiaan repeated. "When I heard that

your plan had . . . that the committee beat you to Setesafon, I brought Patrius along with me. I've instructed my people to release him outside the city, just before—"

"You're letting him go?" said Soraya. "Just . . . just releasing him?"

"Why not? Our first plan failed, so now we have to move on to mine. Patrius will warn Garren and the committee about Siatt's treachery, and offer to exchange the Kadeshi troops for my Hrum prisoners. And they'd better agree," Jiaan added grimly, "because I'll have to let those prisoners go in a few weeks—that or kill or starve them."

A brooding silence fell. Soraya wanted to deny that she and the peddler had failed, but they had failed. And while she hated the Hrum, the thought of hundreds of men slowly starving in the narrow rock crevices that made up the desert's natural cells was a horror she would not be party to—and she knew the Suud wouldn't either. Without the gold . . .

"Without the gold, he can't feed the prisoners," she told Kavi. "He's right. We have to trade them for the Kadeshi."

"But if we could get the gold . . . oh, you're

right. At this point we're likely too short on time to be buying food and smuggling it into the desert anyway. If the Hrum got wind of a shipment of food that big, they'd probably try to trace it."

"I thought of that," said Jiaan softly. "I wondered if you had."

"Yes," said Soraya. "We talked about how to buy the food near the passes and smuggle it in in small—"

The peddler's face hardened. "That's not what he means, Lady. He thinks I wanted the Hrum to be following them in."

"It did cross my mind," said Jiaan. "After all, you've already changed sides twice . . ."

"Just once," said the peddler, his voice as soft and almost as deadly as Jiaan's. "I was on the Hrum's side from the start, or at least against the deghans'. And if they weren't—"

Soraya laid a hand on his arm, stopping him, but it was too late. The words "if they weren't all dead" might as well have been spoken aloud. Even with her shilshadu sensing closed down she could feel Kavi's blazing rage and Jiaan's cold hate.

"We can't afford this," she said, her own voice low, for people at the nearby tables were staring.

"We need his spies," she told Jiaan. "He knows the people who've made contacts with the palace servants, remember. He'll be able to tell us, if anyone can, how Garren reacts to your offer."

"And you know that he's right," she added to Kavi. "We didn't reach Shir in time. It probably wouldn't matter if we had, since he attacked them on his own anyway. Our plan failed—it's time to try his."

"I already admitted . . . ah, Flame take it!" The peddler rose and stalked off, leaving Jiaan scowling after him.

"He is on our side," said Soraya softly, "and we need him. Every third peasant in the country-side sends him news. Or at least they send it to Sorahb through him. He's done a lot toward getting rid of the Hrum."

Jiaan's expression didn't change, but his eyes flashed at her defense. This was no longer the humble page boy who had served Soraya's father.

"I know what he's done," said Jiaan at last. He looked tired now, though the anger was still there. "I know we need him. I just wish I were certain we could trust him."

He didn't ask why she was certain, Soraya

436

noticed. After living in close contact with the
Suud for so many months, he had to have seen
some things. How strange, this Farsalan need to
deny that the Suud had magic, and how deep
that need went. If she hadn't woken out of a
sound sleep and seen Maok dancing in the fire,
would Soraya have denied it? Would she be
without it now? She shivered.

"Don't worry," she said, reassuring herself as
much as Jiaan. "I know where he's staying. I'll
stop by every day and ask if there's news."

THREE DAYS LATER there was news, and it wasn't
good.

They met in the same tap room, at the same
dark corner table, but this late in the evening,
past the Hrum's curfew by several marks, the
room was full of men who had settled in for an
evening's drinking. The noise level was so high
Soraya could hardly hear herself think, much
less overhear what was said at another table. She
wondered if all these men had paid to stay at the
inn tonight, or if they were drunk enough to
think they could evade the Hrum patrols—
which wasn't too hard if you were sober. After

almost a week in the city, Soraya was getting adept at it.

"What's Garren doing?" Jiaan demanded. "I haven't heard a word from them. I thought . . . I knew it might take a while to make the arrangements, but I thought he'd answer me immediately."

"In a way you have been answered," said the peddler. "Or at least this is the only answer you're going to get. Garren's not making the trade."

For the moment even Jiaan subdued his anger to attend to more urgent concerns. "How can he refuse? Almost six hundred experienced soldiers for a horde of untrained peasants that he *knows* will turn on his army? He'd have to be mad—"

"Not mad," the peddler interrupted. "Desperate. They say he's recalled Barmael to come and impress the committee with their plan, for they have to be taking Mazad. But they need more men to do it, and Garren thinks that if he pulls men out of any city or town in Farsala, the people there will erupt in rebellion. According to Garren's sources this whole country is just waiting for a chance to rise, cast out the tax collectors, loot army storage depots, and generally rebel."

"Is that true?" Jiaan asked, startled.

"In part," said Kavi, "though probably not as true as Garren thinks. Sorahb has taken on more life than we expected. Folks everywhere are organizing themselves to rise in his name. After all, he's got a great army hidden in the desert, poised to spring out and destroy Garren's whole force as soon as the time is right."

"No, he doesn't," said Jiaan. "We can help Siddas defend Mazad, but that's all. We won't even succeed there if Garren brings in enough troops."

"He knows that," said Kavi. "That's his solution to the problem. He's going to take the Kadeshi—there's near seven thousand of them, by the way," he added. "We've heard from some folk who live near the Kadeshi border, and they say they're already gathering—"

"Seven *thousand*?" Jiaan's voice rose. Soraya started to demand quiet and then shrugged. They were already the quietest group in the room. Two tables away men were singing and banging their mugs on the wooden surface, except for one man who had slipped off the bench and was pounding his mug on the floor.

439

"Seven thousand," Kavi confirmed. "You can see why your prisoners don't look so good to him, can't you? His plan is to use the Kadeshi to flood the defenses at Mazad. He's going to throw the whole lot of them at the walls, with so many ladders the guard will be swamped. And once they're over the walls, the rest of the troops can come in. He's heeded your warning," said Kavi grimly, "to the extent that he'll only be arming the Kadeshi with clubs, so if they do turn on the Hrum, the Hrum will make short work of killing them. But he doesn't think Siatt will tell them to turn on the Hrum troops until they're fighting against Siatt— and that'll be some other strategus' problem. Have you thought about that?" Kavi added bitterly.

Soraya glared at him but Jiaan shrugged off the barb. "How are you getting so much information? This isn't something Garren would talk about in front of Farsalan servants."

"That's true," said Soraya, remembering. "He sent all the servants out of the command tent when he discussed anything secret, and let his men serve themselves."

"Actually," said Kavi. "Most of it's coming from Patrius. Not directly," he said as Jiaan's mouth opened in protest. "But it seems our tactimian is so angry about the governor's refusal to ransom his men that he's taken to muttering about it, complaining to his fellow officers, members of the committee, even their staff . . . and he often does it where the servants can hear him."

"He wants us to know," said Jiaan. "He wants us to save the Kadeshi troops."

"Why?" Soraya asked. "I mean, he's a Hrum officer . . ." Her voice trailed off, for both Kavi and Jiaan were shaking their heads.

"He's a good man, as well as a Hrum officer," said the peddler.

"And in a way he is fighting for them," Jiaan added. "He's fighting for his empire's honor."

Soraya wasn't as certain of this Patrius as they seemed to be. "If he's trying to deceive you—"

"It's not Patrius alone," said the peddler. "Most of the details have come from people overhearing him, but there are other sources as well. The committee's not overfond of Garren's fine plan either, and . . . I'm interpreting here, mind, but it sounds as if they're not going to stop Garren unless he out and out breaks Hrum law, for fear that his father will use their intervention as grounds to get out of the bargain. It sounds like getting rid of Garren senior is as high a priority for the senate as getting rid of Garren junior is for us."

Soraya wondered if Ludo was one of his sources. "So we can't expect the committee to intervene. We have to do it ourselves."

"From Garren's point of view," said Jiaan, "it's a good plan. If he sends seven thousand Kadeshi at Mazad's walls, they'll swamp the defenders. They'll take huge losses, but for Garren that's probably a bonus," he added bitterly. "They'll be less of a threat in the future. And the fact that he's using Hrum troops as a . . . a human sacrifice won't matter because they're not Hrum, only allies. Untrustworthy allies, at that. It's a great plan, if you have no honor and no heart. No wonder Patrius is passing on information."

"But will it be doing him any good?" asked the peddler softly.

"What do you mean?" said Soraya.

"Now that we know what Garren plans, is there anything we can do to stop him?"

Kavi had answered her question, but he was looking at Jiaan.

"I could bring the army out of the desert,"

Jiaan said. "If we attack them before they reach Mazad—they'll be untrained peasants armed with clubs—we could kill a lot of them. Maybe even enough to keep them from making a difference in the battle. Our casualties would be high, but . . . if we kill those men, even if Garren is the one who forced it on us, are we any better than he is? Patrius isn't the only one with an army's honor at stake. Not to mention five hundred prisoners that I'm going to have to release or murder in cold blood if I can't feed them."

He looked older than his eighteen years, and so like Soraya's father that sudden tears rose in her eyes.

"Unless," said Jiaan slowly, "Garren doesn't send for the Kadeshi at all. Unless he can't, because the gold is gone."

Soraya's gaze turned to the peddler. He had anticipated this, she thought. There was a bit of smugness in his expression, but mostly it was sober. She suddenly found herself wishing that the mischief would return.

"When that gold leaves for Kadesh, every guard Garren can spare will be watching it," said the peddler. "And I don't know this, but it wouldn't surprise me if Siatt sent some troops, real warriors, to escort it as well. And the problems with taking your army away from Mazad still apply, don't they?"

He had an idea. Soraya could see it in his face. She and Jiaan stared at him.

"So we'd have to be taking it before it's shipped out—from the very heart of the old gahn's palace, right under the noses of all Garren's guards. What are you staring at me for? I'm a peddler, not a burglar."

Soraya and Jiaan stared at him, and he gave up and grinned. "But I know someone who is."

"WE'VE GOT GOOD information about the way they've organized their security at the palace," said the middle-aged laundress, setting several large rolls of parchment on the table where she folded dried linen. "But it's tight. I don't know how you could even get into the vault, much less be getting anything out."

They were meeting in the laundry instead of in the house next door because the laundress, Nadi, had young children, and she didn't want them to wake up and overhear something they shouldn't know. Hama, of course, already knew everything.

Soraya had only agreed to meet with Nadi in the first place when she learned that the laundress was Hama's mother—and even then she'd had to convince Jiaan. But once Jiaan met Nadi himself . . . there was something in the woman's lined face, a forthright endurance, that all but compelled trust.

The laundry was filled with tubs and long lines of drying linen. The rustling quiet, the shadowed corners where the lamplight didn't reach, the empty, hanging shirts and shifts made the room feel eerie to Soraya. But the great furnace, which was kept burning to help dry the clothes even when it wasn't heating water, made the room warm—and on this dark, dripping night that was worth a bit of eeriness.

Since Nadi's workers had left for their own homes before the curfew, their privacy was assured. The Hrum patrols, Nadi had said, would think nothing of it if they saw lamplight around the shutters, for she and her older children sometimes stayed late to do a bit of mending or mix a batch of soap. The only one Kavi seemed worried might find out about them was someone named Sim. But when Nadi said she'd taken care of that, the peddler had shrugged and taken her word for it.

"I've got an idea for getting the gold out," said Hama quietly. "The governor only moved into the palace when he learned that the committee was coming. It was supposed to be the symbol of his final victory, moving in." A smile tugged at her lips. "When he heard about the committee arriving, he went and declared his victory early. For us that's good," she added. "The Hrum know exactly how to keep their camps secure, but this big, sprawling palace is new to them, and they've had to set up new procedures. I haven't tested them, but I bet there's a lot of confusion. And confusion is something a burglar can always use."

Jiaan looked dubious. He had only met Hama briefly last fall when she had brought Kavi news of the siege towers, and a sixteen-year-old girl speaking so confidently about burglary did sound odd. But Jiaan hadn't seen her slip out of the bushes and onto the cart, as smooth and silent as a serpent, or the speed and deftness with which she'd opened the slaves' shackles.

Soraya smiled at her. "So what's your idea?"

"First, let's consider the obstacles," said Nadi,

unrolling the parchment on the long table. It held a large, wonderfully proportioned drawing of the palace and its gardens.

Soraya caught one corner of the parchment and studied it. "This is incredible. It's as if you were a bird looking down on the palace, except with all the ceilings gone so you can see inside."

"It's a builder's drawing," said Jiaan, pressing down another corner. "How did you come by this, Mistress Nadi?"

"My husband's family were masons," said Nadi. "His grandfather helped build one of the wings of the palace—the new wing, they're still calling it, though it's more than a hundred years old now. I'm not exactly certain how he came by it, but he kept it for its craft, and his pride in having built part of the gahn's own palace. What he'd think of the use we're putting it to . . ."

The peddler laughed. "If he was anything like his great-grandchildren, he'd be cheering us on. What's your plan, lass?"

"Obstacles *first*," said Nadi firmly, and Hama grinned.

"Yes, mother," she said meekly. "The only real obstacle is the guards, but there are a lot of them, even if Garren has been forced to spread them thin. The grounds are so big, he can't cordon them off the way the Hrum do their camps. And why should he care if someone gets into the gardens? Which the town boys are doing all the time, on dares. That's the first bit of good news. If the Hrum who patrol the grounds see someone going out over the wall, or coming in for that matter, they're not going to fill them full of arrows and ask questions later. Hrum or no, they've no desire to shoot down foolish children."

"Good for the town boys," said Kavi.

"Yes, but it doesn't gain us much," Hama went on. "It's around the outside of the palace that the real security begins. You can think of it as a series of rings, though they're not round. The first ring is the guards on the gate and the grounds patrols. The gate guards will ask your business, and if you're on the list of people they expect to see, they'll pass you in and give you an escort to lead you through the rest of the security. If you're not expected, they send a man to whoever you're wanting to see, and you wait till the message comes back before they admit you."

"What about servants?" asked Soraya, who

had been one not so long ago. "And the people who bring in wood and eggs and so on?"

Nadi gave her a look of startled approval, but Hama shook her head.

"Folk like that are allowed in," said Hama, "but only as far as the kitchen, and the kitchen is outside of the palace proper—outside the second ring of security. The building isn't connected to the palace, so the Hrum only keep the servants under casual watch. The Hrum officers who come and go from inside the palace are given new passwords every morning, for they change them every day."

"So that's why the food at the palace feasts was never hot when it reached the table," Soraya muttered.

The peddler's grin surprised her. "The terrible price of power. But it sounds like we could get through this first ring without much trouble."

"That's true," said Hama. "But the next ring is a real cordon of guards around the buildings of the palace."

Kavi's brows rose. "A solid line of soldiers? That's a lot of men for Garren to be keeping on guard duty."

"It's not solid," Hama admitted. "But they're

posted so they can see each other, and they carry whistles so they can call in the roving patrols to help them. They're not supposed to be leaving their posts to help each other," she added. "So if you're thinking about causing a diversion in one part of the line so that someone can slip through in another, you can forget it."

The peddler's expression of chagrin was almost comical.

"I thought of it too," said Hama consolingly.

"This isn't a contest!" Nadi snapped. "It isn't a prank! This is deathly, deathly serious, and if I could keep you from it, lad, be sure I would."

Soraya knew that the first condition Nadi had placed on her agreement to help them was that Hama would not, under any circumstances, assist them with anything but the planning.

"You needn't fear for me," the peddler assured her, with a warmth in his voice Soraya had never heard before. "Enough Hrum know my face that I can't be going among them either."

"Well, someone has to go in," said Hama. "Because the second ring of guards, and all those stationed past them, ask everyone for the password that applies to that security level on that very day. If you don't have the right passwords, you're caught—and outside of the gardens you're likely dead, as well. The inner guards will shoot you full of arrows and be asking questions later," she finished somberly. "According to our sources, you have to have three passwords to get as far as the wine cellar. It's likely more than that to reach the vault, and the cells where the prisoners are kept, but no one we could reach has ever been that far in."

There was a moment of daunted silence.

"So the first thing we need is a day's worth of passwords," said Kavi. "As many as we can get. Could your people bring them out to you?"

"No," said Nadi. "The steward keeps the passwords. He only gives them out if he has to send someone into the palace on an errand, and mostly he goes himself. Our folk have only gotten them occasionally. And if some Hrum guard starts asking questions . . ."

"So one of us will have to go in," said Jiaan. "Someone who is, for instance, marked as a Hrum spy so he can reach a high-up official. An official in the center of the palace, so he'll hear all the passwords on his way in. I'm just wondering if you set it up that way deliberately."

"Then you can stop wondering," said the peddler sharply. "It can't be me. Didn't you hear me telling Nadi that too many of the Hrum would recognize me?"

Looking at their stiff faces, Soraya wondered if they would be able to work together long enough to bring this off.

"But those Hrum are still at Mazad," she said, before Jiaan could say something worse. "Aren't they? The ones who got to know you before you escaped from Barmael's camp?"

"Yes, but that still leaves the ones who saw me when I was selling Arus' camp bad beer," said the peddler. "And there were a fair few of them."

"But they were all sent to hunt Shir's bandits," said Soraya. "So they won't be here either."

Jiaan's corner of the parchment rolled back toward the center, and Soraya glanced at him. She couldn't interpret the expression on his face.

"What is it?"

"Nothing." Jiaan smoothed the parchment back into place. "You told me that all you did was leave Barmael's camp without permission. By the time Garren left, his attack on Mazad had been defeated. Do you think he'd remember to tell his people here to watch out for you?"

"Likely not," said the peddler slowly. "He might not have been told that I escaped, though I'd not care to bet my life on that. But even if he was told, the defeat at Mazad would probably put it out of his head. So all I'd need to worry about are those who met me when I was dealing with Patrius—and odds are they still think I'm a loyal spy."

"What about Garren?" Nadi demanded. "He may not—*may* not—have remembered to warn his people about you, but if he sees you himself . . ."

"Yes," said the peddler thoughtfully. "I'd have to pick a time when our Garren's so busy that no one would even think of taking me to him. And a report that's urgent enough to be getting me in deep, but not so urgent they'd interrupt the governor's business."

"You could tell them you heard folk in the city planning a riot to show the committee that Setesafon's not really conquered," said Hama. "Not killing anyone—that might bring you to Garren's notice—but shouting insults and throwing filth."

"Or you could tell them you heard a rumor that I'm in the city," said Soraya. "Or better yet

that you've seen me, somewhere in the countryside. There's still a reward for my capture, isn't
there?"

Jiaan said nothing.

"Yes, and I wouldn't mind claiming it either,"
said the peddler. He didn't look at Nadi's tense
face, but he laid his scarred hand over hers where
it held the parchment. "All right, I'm the best one
to go in for the passwords. I'll get through all the
layers I can, but I doubt I'll learn enough to get
you into the vault. So how do we reach the gold?
Not to mention carry it off without getting ourselves caught."

"That's where my idea comes in," said
Hama. She let go of her end of the palace
drawing, allowing it to roll toward Jiaan and
Soraya, and after a moment's hesitation her
mother did the same.

"This is a drawing of the cellars." Hama
unrolled the next parchment. "It doesn't show
where the guards will be posted, or how many
there are, but it does show the wine cellar, which
is connected to the vault and cells through this
short corridor, here."

"What's this?" Jiaan asked, pointing to what

looked like a corridor, though it ran onto the map at an angle and ran off the page on the other side.

"That," said Hama proudly, "is the basis of my plan for getting the gold out. Those are aqueduct tunnels, bringing clean water in under the palace and taking sewage to the river."

"Can't we go in through the aqueducts?" Jiaan asked, his expression brightening. "We could bypass the guards entirely!"

"Unfortunately," said Nadi dryly, "the Hrum thought of that too. The aqueduct and sewer tunnels are also guarded—the soldiers complain about that duty, especially the ones who have to take the sewer side. They don't put a lot of men down there, but they all have whistles. If they sound so much as one chirp, you'll have patrols parked at each end of the tunnel in minutes, and they can send in men to hunt you down at their leisure. Once you're in those tunnels, there's no other way out."

"But," said Hama, "if you put the gold in wine barrels, just enough in each cask to make it float a bit under the surface, you could be sending the gold down the sewer tunnel without having to carry any of it out yourselves! We could have fishing boats run out their nets near the sewer tunnel mouth to pick up the barrels as well. They'll likely miss a few, but the barrels would just come ashore somewhere downstream. And even if all the gold goes to the bottom of the river, at least the Hrum won't have it."

Soraya frowned, trying to picture this. "Can you weight a barrel so it will float under the surface?"

"Yes," said the peddler. "It'll take some fiddling with the weight to get the first one right, but after that the rest should go pretty fast. And if the guards in the sewer hear something scraping along the bottom, well, they won't be blowing their whistles for that. Nor wading in to investigate, either—not on the sewer side. Hama, that's brilliant!"

"It still leaves the problem of getting into the vault," said Hama, though her eyes were bright.

"I think I could manage that," said Jiaan. "I'm the one who'll bring you in, Lady Soraya. With a band of my men, disguised as a deci of Hrum soldiers. If we had the passwords, who would even think to question a patrol taking a prisoner, someone known to be wanted, to the cells? We could go straight to the cells and then the vault if we had the passwords."

"And what happens when a guard demands a password you don't have?" Nadi demanded.

Jiaan shrugged. "We'll think of something."

Or not. Soraya shivered. She hadn't really minded being a servant in the Hrum camp, once she became accustomed to the work, but she'd detested being their prisoner.

"Where will you get eleven Hrum uniforms?" she asked, hoping he wouldn't have an answer.

Jiaan reached behind him and pulled forward one of the tunics that hung on the line. "This is part of one, isn't it, Mistress Nadi?"

"It is," said the laundress reluctantly. "I'm taking quite a bit of laundry from the army—I could probably clothe half a centri on any given day. But Hrum swords and armor are harder come by. Not to mention boots."

"We've got enough between us to outfit eleven," Hama broke in eagerly. "You know we do."

There was a moment of silence, while Soraya tried not to think about how the resistance had come by eleven sets of Hrum armor and boots. At least she wouldn't be wearing them. And perhaps she was wrong she hadn't thought the resistance had killed many men

"That serves for disguises," said the peddler. "Do you have eleven men who can speak good Hrum?"

"I speak Hrum best," said Jiaan, in Hrum.

Soraya winced. It wasn't his accent—many Hrum spoke that language with an accent—it was the stiffness, the lack of fluency, that gave him away.

"That won't do," said Kavi. "You sound like a Farsalan trying to pass himself off as a Hrum soldier. You've got to get someone else."

"I speak Hrum better than any of the Farsalan troops," said Jiaan, in Faran now. "We had a trader with us for a while—he was fluent. He was the one who taught us, but he was killed when the Hrum raided our camp. Besides, all I'll have to say is, 'We're taking this prisoner to the cells.' I can practice that till it sounds right."

"But what happens if they give you directions?" Nadi demanded. "Or ask a question, and you can't even understand what they're saying?"

Soraya sympathized with the woman's desire to rein in the whole mad scheme, but . . .

"I can translate for him. I speak Hrum very well," she added in that language. She continued, still in Hrum. "It might be a challenge to rephrase what he needs to know, but I could probably manage. And if it's something he doesn't need to know immediately, I can tell him what was said later."

The peddler nodded, but Soraya's heart sank at the puzzled look on Jiaan's face.

Nadi saw it too. "This is ridiculous. You didn't even understand what she said! You'll make it to the cells, all right—the lot of you! I can't be party to this!"

"There are seven thousand Kadeshi," said Jiaan coldly, "waiting at the border for that gold. If Siatt gets it, they'll march to Mazad in less than a week."

"Closer to two," said the peddler. "These men likely aren't accustomed to marching."

"Two weeks then," said Jiaan. "Another week to get them organized, and then they will take the city. If Mazad falls, what will happen to the resistance in the rest of Farsala?"

Nadi shook her head, refusing to accept it, but Hama put it into words. "Most will be quitting, and you know it. It's because Mazad's held out so long that they've found the heart to fight. And the ones that don't quit . . ."

"Once Mazad has fallen, once Garren is established as governor, he'll be able to summon enough Hrum troops to put down any resistance," Jiaan finished. "We have to keep the gold from reaching Siatt. If this fails, I'll bring my army and attack it en route. But with the guard the Hrum will put on it, I'll probably lose so many that Garren will be able to take Mazad anyway. We have to stop it here—we have to!"

The anguish in his voice made him suddenly sound his age. He was fighting to save his army, Soraya realized, as much as Farsala. Just as she was fighting for Merdas. And the peddler . . . She'd never known what was driving him—her shilshadu sensing only gave her emotions, not thoughts—but she knew it was strong.

"You're young," Nadi whispered. "Young and so stupid with it. You think you're all invulnerable, that nothing can be happening to you."

But that wasn't true, Soraya thought. Losing her father had taught her that she wasn't invulnerable to loss, though it was hard to think that she might die. Jiaan had to have been close enough to death in the last year to know that it could come for him, and as for Kavi . . .

The peddler laid his maimed hand on the woman's shoulder. "You're not trading my safety for Sim's," he said softly. "It's not your choice at all. We're going to be trying this, with your help or without it, but your help will give us a better chance."

Nadi's crumpling face hardened. "Then I'd best be seeing to your uniforms, hadn't I?" She turned and walked away through the tangled maze of damp fabric. Kavi started after her, but Soraya stopped him with a touch on his arm. "I'll go. I need . . ." She shrugged and walked after the laundress, as Jiaan distracted Hama with a question about how the aqueducts branched.

Nadi was standing in front of a line of scarlet Hrum cloaks. Her hands were tangled in the cloth, but she wasn't moving. Soraya came up beside her and was startled to find that her face, though taut with misery, was dry.

"I'm sorry," said Soraya. "But I wonder if you can help me with something. The last time the Hrum captured me, I wore a servant's skirt—very ragged. It made it hard to stand up to them. This time I'd like to be better dressed."

It was the only excuse she could think of . . . the

only thing that would present the woman with a task she could do.

Nadi took a deep breath and turned to face Soraya. "He couldn't have done more for me, for my family, if he had been my son." Her voice was as stark as her expression.

"Then help him," said Soraya. "Because this is something he has to do. I don't understand why, but—"

"I do," Nadi interrupted. "And you're right. I can't be stopping him, so I'd best give all the aid I can. Better dressed, is it?"

SHE TOLD SORAYA that the robes had been brought in for laundering just before the Hrum invaded the city, and they had never been claimed. Soraya wondered if she had known the deghass who'd owned them, and hoped the woman was a living slave somewhere and not dead in the fighting for the city. Her odds of having survived were better than those of the Hrum who'd owned the armor Jiaan and his soldiers would wear.

The robes were a bit big on her, but most women's clothes were. The underrobe was a soft cream, the overrobe a rich brown embroidered

462

with amber and gold. Autumn colors, strange in a robe that had been worn in the spring—perhaps it had been chosen because the colors were flattering rather than for the season. It would have suited her cousin Pari. Soraya thought of Pari, also a slave, she hoped—for if not, then her cousin was almost certainly dead. She felt a surge of renewed anger at the Hrum, and at Kavi, too! How many lives had they destroyed?

And yet . . . She remembered his scarred hand on Nadi's shoulder. The deghans had destroyed lives as well, and had never struggled to make it right again, as Kavi did. Strange as it seemed, she knew she could rely on the peddler to do his part. It was Jiaan, with his hatred and his inexplicable reactions, who worried her now. And it was Jiaan she was trusting with her life.

Soraya stroked the rich robes that might have belonged to a dead woman, and shivered.

CHAPTER SEVENTEEN

KAVI

KAVI APPROACHED THE gate in the low palace wall, walking as easily and confidently as he'd have approached any village where he hoped to sell his goods. If his pulse pounded in his ears, if his hands and feet were cold, no one knew it but him. Even Duckie sensed nothing amiss, and if Duckie couldn't detect his fear no one could.

Truly, he told himself, it was foolish to be so nervous. He was coming to the Hrum as a peddler, selling information instead of goods, and he had done this several times before. The Hrum who might know different were all far from here, with the sole exception of Governor Garren, and Kavi wouldn't be seeing him today.

They'd chosen the day when the governor planned to show the senate committee the city of Setesafon with a grand procession of a tour, ending with Garren giving a speech to the townsfolk. The governor hoped to create a festival atmosphere, offering a public feast in the great square where the pavilion for the speech was being erected, Several oxen were already roasting there, and bread was being shipped in along with dried fruit and cakes that would be given to the children.

Kavi's worst worry was that some would take it into their heads to put on an anti-Hrum demonstration—though if Kavi succeeded in delivering his warning, there should be sufficient extra troops around the square to discourage that. The presence of those troops would also show the committee that Setesafon was far from beaten, whatever Garren told them.

In truth Kavi was afraid of what would happen in the countryside if Garren got control of the Kadeshi troops. The spirit of rebellion had taken root in Farsalan hearts—but that didn't magically transform peasants into soldiers. He wanted to see his people ruling themselves, not piled into early graves.

At least it looked like the weather might help keep people out of the streets tonight. Any townsman could have told Garren that early Raven, right on the edge between winter and spring, was a bad month to rely on doing anything outdoors. So far the rain was holding off, but thick clouds scudded through the sky and the wind was cold. Surely the governor would be too busy putting on his show for the committee, to trouble himself with spies or captured prisoners. That was why they'd chosen this day, though it had given them only a few days to prepare.

But here was the gate guard, looking at Kavi with a question in his eyes. Kavi took a deep breath and pushed up his sleeve, showing the tattoo.

"I need to speak to one of your officers," he said, sounding remarkably normal considering the tightness in his throat. "It's not dead urgent, but it needs to be happening before the committee goes out into the streets."

"Come inside and wait," said the guard. His eyes had widened a bit at the sight of the tattoo, but he showed no other sign of understanding that would draw attention to it. "I'll send a runner for someone to escort you to the watch commander."

Very professional. Efficient. Kavi approved, even when the guard scowled at Duckie and added, "Do you have to bring the mule in too? This is the governor's palace!"

Kavi shrugged. "I could take the time to find a stable and board her, but if I do the committee might be out in the streets by the time I get back. I promise you, that'll be a lot more embarrassing than having a peddler's mule in the gahn—in the governor's garden."

They really were alike, Hrum and deghans. If Kavi were in charge of these gardens, he'd open them so folk could bring their children to play here, eat lunch on the grass, and watch the fountains, pretending to be rich themselves—that's what he'd do. There was somewhat less chance of Kavi owning these gardens than of the sun rising in the west, but the small surge of anger calmed him.

He wasn't averse to the guard drawing attention to Duckie, either. He'd usually had the mule with him when he reported to Patrius, and he hoped that Duckie would reinforce his identity as a Hrum spy in the minds of any who remembered him.

Patrius would have been another person he had to avoid, but the servants had reported that Patrius had made himself so unpopular with Garren that the governor had finally exiled him to the old camp outside the city, where many of the troops were still quartered. Azura be thanked, for Patrius would recognize Kavi instantly, and that would bring the whole mad scheme down on top of them.

With any luck he wouldn't encounter anyone who remembered him at all. The Wheel seemed to be turning his way, because two sets of Hrum troops passed through the gate as he waited. The password for the day was "today." Kavi wondered if tomorrow's password was "tomorrow" and fought down a giggle that would have been far too nervous.

It wasn't long before the watch officer himself returned with the runner, who led Kavi off through the maze of low hedges toward the gleaming marble spread of the palace. "Palace complex" would have been a better description: More than a dozen buildings sprawled over the huge meadow that ended at the low cliff that divided the wealthy sections of Setesafon from the massive city below.

"What's your information about, peddler?" his guide asked, as soon as they were out of earshot of the gate. "If it's really confidential you needn't tell me, but you'll reach the person you need to talk to more swiftly if I have some idea who that is."

"It's not being secret," said Kavi, "though there is some urgency about it. Last night in the tavern where I'm staying, I — oh, no you don't!"

He retrieved the lead rope Duckie had pulled from his hand, and dragged the mule back onto the path — away from the wide lake, where the swans, who belonged there, had been joined by a rabble of wild ducks and geese.

The lake was landscaped where the shore touched the palace grounds, but the banks turned into a reedy, muddy mess where it bordered the merchants' quarter, even though there was a path beside it.

The officer watched Duckie yearning toward the water. "Is your mule thirsty?"

"No." Kavi sighed. "And it's too long a tale to tell. But my news concerns the committee's tour today. I overheard some men talking about showing the senators . . . 'a proper welcome' was how they phrased it. Shouting insults, throwing filth and such. Nothing too serious, but I was thinking the governor might like a warning."

"Yes indeed," said the officer, his brows rising. "I'll take you to the officer in charge of the committee's security. But first we'll stable that mule."

The stables, like the kitchen, were between the first and second ring of guards, so Kavi learned no further passwords on the way. He removed Duckie's pack and latched the mule into a comfortable stall. There was only one groom, a woman who looked to be near Nadi's age, tending the whole place by herself, since the rest were out putting up pavilions in the town square. Kavi warned her not to let Duckie anywhere near the lake unless she kept a tight hold on the mule's tether. He thought he smelled the smoky, metallic scent of a forge nearby, but he didn't ask. Kavi was well satisfied, despite his impatience with the delay. Surely the head of the committee's security would be several layers in.

Shortly after they left the stable, they passed through the cordon of guards that surrounded the buildings of the palace, the watch officer passing through with only a brisk nod and the word "salute." If Kavi hadn't been listening for passwords he might not have noticed it, since the guard saluted as they went by.

Now they approached the main buildings of the palace. Kavi had seen the Hall of Whispers, which swept down the hillside and was used for public events. Like any visitor to the city, he had looked over the low wall at the gardens. He had never been this close to the palace itself.

Even as he thought about the hardworking farmers and craftsmen whose taxes had paid for it, Kavi had to admit that the buildings were beautiful. From a distance the marble all seemed to be a soft, golden tan; up close he saw that many different kinds of stone, in varying shades, made up the arches, the patterns on the portico floor, and the sweeping stairs leading to the carved, inlaid doors. Bronze vines twined up the pillars, and Kavi suspected that in the summer the metal spirals would serve as trellises for real vines. Even now, when only the first green shoots were breaking through last year's dead leaves, the dancing fountains made the gardens feel alive.

The back of Kavi's neck prickled as they approached the formal entrance of what had to be the gahn's—no, the governor's residence. If he encountered Garren, coming back from the privy, say . . .

But the commander led him past the grand entrance, and his pounding heart slowed again.

"Where are we going?" he asked. "I mean, which building?"

"That one." The watch commander gestured to a rambling structure that seemed to drift over the low rise in three graceful levels. "The servants say that was where most of the old ruler's nobles and his high-up guests stayed. Now it's mostly officers' quarters, but there was plenty of room for the committee and their households as well—and by Dagrana's hand, it's fancy enough."

"I see," said Kavi, calming himself with the reminder that all the officers who knew him from Mazad were either still in Mazad or hunting bandits in Dugaz. Not for the first time, he was grateful that Garren was a vengeful fool.

His nerves had quieted enough that he was amused instead of annoyed when the watch commander led him around the building to a small door that was obviously the servants' entrance—who'd ever heard of spies going in the front door, after all? Servants' entrance or not, it was guarded.

One man stood on the stoop at the top of the short staircase, and another was posted a bit further down the wall—far enough apart that no enemy could approach them at the same time, each was able to see whatever happened to the other, and both of them had the slim brass tubes of whistles tucked into their belts.

It was good security. But all Kavi had to do was listen for the passwords as he lied his way in and out. Getting to the vault was Jiaan's job.

The watch commander climbed briskly up the steps. "Mile," he told the guard. It was a Hrum distance measurement, meaning roughly a quarter of a league: a good password, for it had no Faran equivalent.

The guard saluted, the commander stood aside, and as Kavi started up the stairs, the door opened and a man emerged. He wore the tunic of a Hrum officer, with the insignia of a surgeon embroidered on the front, since surgeons wore no breastplate. He walked down several steps before he saw Kavi and stopped, his eyes widening in astonishment.

He was one of the surgeons Kavi had dealt with when he'd smuggled poisoned beer into the siege camp surrounding Mazad last summer.

Even as Kavi cursed the fools who'd told him that Garren had shipped all the men involved in that debacle off to the swamps, even as he cursed this turn of the Wheel, spinning him down into the Flame when he'd been so close to success, he pinned a delighted smile on his face and climbed the steps.

"Surgeon! I'm glad to see you. I didn't expect to find you here."

The blank surprise on the man's face gave way to alarm. He stiffened, stumbling back a step, drawing breath to shout.

Kavi leapt up the stairs and punched him in the stomach.

"He's sick!" he exclaimed, as the surgeon doubled over. It wouldn't confuse them for more than a few seconds, as they tried to reconcile his words with what they'd seen, but those seconds carried Kavi up the last step. The watch commander was staring at the gasping surgeon, so Kavi punched the commander in the nose with all the force he could muster, shoved him into the guard's startled grip, and pushed both of them down the stairs.

They fell together, taking the surgeon with them, their armor clattering on the stone.

Two long strides took Kavi to the edge of the

stoop. Even as he swung his leg over the low railing and dropped into the flower beds below, he
heard the shriek of the second guard's whistle.

He ran for the corner of the building, not even
caring about direction, then across an open space
and around another corner. Other whistles added
themselves to the growing chorus behind him, but
he had a few moments, perhaps. One fast glance at
the half-open courtyard between the two buildings
told him that no one was watching him now. He
made a final dash to a stand of bushes—a species
unknown to Kavi—with handfuls of dead leaves
still clinging to their thick, tangled branches.

Kavi worked his way into the bushes as deeply
as possible and pulled handfuls of leaves over his
legs and tunic, using the tips Hama had given him
about hiding: *Try to break up the shape of your body—
if something isn't man-shaped, folks likely won't see it.
Above all else . . .*

A deci of guardsmen burst into the courtyard,
running toward the shrilling whistles, swords
drawn. Kavi froze, his hands buried in the mulch.
His face was too clean, his head was too high, and
he thought that one booted foot was sticking out,
but . . . *above all else, hold still!*

Only his eyes moved as he watched the running guards through the thin screen of twigs. He didn't dare breathe, for fear the leaves would rustle and betray him. He didn't turn his head as the guards raced out of his field of vision, allowing only his ears to track their progress as they ran . . . right on by, without—as far as Kavi could tell—so much as a glance in his direction.

His taut nerves screamed for movement, but he stayed where he was till they were well past the corner of the building before he crawled out of the bushes. He brushed bits of leaves and mud from his clothes as he walked, tidying himself as much as he could. The leaves came off, but the mud stuck.

There was nothing he could do about that, however, and now it was time for him to take a bit of advice that he'd once given Hama. He moved toward the stables, briskly, like a man with work to do, but not running like a fugitive to draw all men's eyes.

He couldn't get out. As surely as if he stood beside the man, he knew what the watch commander was doing now—sending runners with his description to all the stationed guardsmen, alerting the patrols. But if Kavi couldn't get out himself, he knew someone who might.

He wasn't sure when the plan had come to him—it was simply there, complete, and maybe even possible if he had a bit of time.

Kavi nodded to a guard a few dozen yards away. The man was scanning the grounds for invaders and assassins; he had no interest in the grubby-looking servant who went into the stable.

The groom looked up from a bridle she was examining. "That didn't take long."

"No." Kavi smiled at her. "It didn't."

When she rose to lead him to Duckie's stall, he struck the back of her head with his fist. It hurt his hand, and it wasn't enough to knock her unconscious either, but she fell to her hands and knees. Before she could summon her scattered wits, Kavi was seated on her back, pulling one arm up behind her, setting his knife against her throat.

"Make one sound and I cut," he whispered. The vicious hiss in his own voice startled him, and he felt the vibration through the knife blade as she swallowed.

She made no move to fight as Kavi tied her wrists behind her back and gagged her with some fairly clean rags from a box of items used to polish tack. Finally he shoved her into one of the empty stalls and latched the gate. The woman turned to face him, her expression stiff with anger and fear.

"Keep quiet and you live," Kavi told her. "Start making noise of any kind and I'll come back and silence you the only way I can." His mind said he was bluffing, that he couldn't really kill her, but in his heart . . .

Fear grew in the groom's face, and she nodded. Kavi turned away, fighting down a mad desire to go back and apologize. He couldn't afford to take either the risk or the time.

The smithy was where he had guessed it would be, not only next to the stables but accessible through a door in an adjoining wall. It was even emptier than the stables; presumably Garren had drafted all the outdoor servants to prepare for the festivities in the town square. But the fire was there, as it always was in a forge, banked and needing only the breath of the bellows to bring it to life.

Kavi chose an awl with a long, fine point and left it heating among the coals while he went back to the stable for Duckie's halter. He should have brought the halter with him when he went looking for the smithy in the first place, but he hadn't thought of it. He was too frightened, his thoughts skittering like startled mice, and he couldn't seem to quiet his racing heart—and the awl would need time to heat, anyway.

He looked in on the groom on his way back to the forge. The woman had seated herself in the rear of the stall, still gagged, still frightened into obedience.

Kavi examined Duckie's halter as he went back to the forge. The lead was made of rope, no use to him, but the headstall, the cheek pieces, the chin strap, and the nose piece were all strips of thick leather. The point of the awl was already cherry red—it was small, so it heated quickly, and the wooden handle would protect his hand.

Kavi picked up the awl and burned the letters *T O D A* into the leather before the point cooled too much to write—it was as fast to chill as it was to heat. As the awl warmed among the embers, Kavi thought of another piece of information his messenger needed to carry. When he finished burning in the *Y*, he added the numeral *1* after it, and managed to imprint the *S* and *A* of "salute" on the other cheek strap before the awl cooled.

He thought about trying to scratch or press

the letters into the leather instead of burning them, but if his plan worked, the leather would get wet and muddy before anyone had a chance to examine it—and they'd likely be too upset to notice details. The letters would have to be big and dark to catch anyone's attention.

Two more reheatings, as he listened to the growing sounds of disturbance outside the smithy, gave him the rest of "salute," the numeral 2, and the Hrum word "mile." He didn't have enough heat for the numeral 3, but if they couldn't figure that one out on their own, they deserved for the Hrum to win.

A surge of resentment shook him. Why should he sacrifice his best chance of escape to help a pair of deghans who'd done nothing for him but threaten to kill him when they finished using him?

But he wasn't doing it for them, and there was no time for heart-searching now. The Hrum would be searching the outbuildings soon, and not in a metaphorical sense either.

Kavi dashed back into the stable and pulled the harness over Duckie's nose and ears, pushing aside the thought that this might be the last time he'd stroke his friend's satiny muzzle. This night's worst—likely—result would be for him to end up a Hrum slave alongside the deghans he'd betrayed. And if Jiaan and Soraya succeeded in getting their hands on the gold, that wouldn't last long.

Yes, slavery was absolutely the worst thing— unless Garren decided that the fact that he'd been a Hrum spy made him not an honorable enemy but a traitor, who deserved a traitor's . . .

"We're not going to think about that," he told Duckie firmly. "And I'll thank you not to mention it again. We're walking out of here as if we hadn't a care in the world, got it?"

His hands twitched toward his pack, but it would be foolish to burden his messenger.

Kavi summoned up his nerve and led Duckie out of the stable and down the path toward the gate where they'd entered. It wasn't his real goal, for he knew he wouldn't make it that far, but he had to get Duckie within scenting distance of the lake, and walking as if he had a perfect right to be there was his best chance of doing it. And if his hands were shaking, well, the running patrols and the alert guards couldn't see it.

Duckie had picked up on his anxiety by now, prancing uneasily, ears swiveling and nostrils flared as she sought to discover what had frightened her person so badly.

But the guards paid no attention to a mule in the hands of a groom, strolling calmly down a path in plain sight. A hundred yards passed beneath his feet and Duckie's hooves.

The sun broke through the clouds, then vanished again. The brisk, cold wind dried his sweat-damp shirt, making him shiver. Another fifty yards.

Duckie smelled the lake and took two steps toward it, then swerved back to follow Kavi without even being prompted, unwilling to leave him when his scent must be shrieking that danger threatened.

That would be all he needed!

Kavi took a breath and forced calm into his voice. "Easy, girl. It's not so bad as that. Nothing going on to worry a mule."

As the seconds dragged by, the quiet, familiar voice had its effect. Duckie settled a bit, her ears turning more often in the direction of the water.

They weren't quite abreast of the lake when the shout rang out, "Hey, there he is! The peddler! Stop him!" but it would have to do.

Kavi dropped the lead rope and slapped

Duckie's rump. "Off with you, my friend. Go—"

Duckie, always fickle in the face of temptation, was already turning toward the duck-strewn lake.

Ridiculous tears, of relief, of abandonment, chased down Kavi's cheeks as he ran—in the opposite direction, to be sure no one would capture Duckie before she reached the lake. Once in the water, especially deep water, she'd be impossible to catch till she was ready to come out—no stranger would persuade her to emerge.

They caught him easily, for there were far more of them, and he surrendered the moment they had him surrounded. He might allow himself to be captured for the cause and even enslaved for a few months, but allowing himself to be injured was too much to expect.

"Hah!" the watch commander wheezed, trotting up to them. Dried blood marked his chin and his breastplate, and his nose was swelling. "I don't know what you thought you were doing, rebel, but you've failed. You may even have the privilege of meeting Governor Garren himself, for he's interested in people who work for Sorahb—but not today. Take him to the cells and lock him up."

The cells. The guards must have wondered at his sudden snort of laughter, but he couldn't resist. He'd soon be having every single one of the passwords he'd come for — and they'd not do one bit of good. Even if he survived the Hrum, Nadi would kill him for worrying her so.

As they dragged him into the building that on Hama's map was labeled "armory," which had both the cells and the tunnel to the vault below it, the last thing Kavi heard was a voice shouting, "Someone go in and get that mule! It's only water."

He was smiling as the door closed behind him.

———

CHAPTER EIGHTEEN

JIAAN

I T WAS NADI'S OLDEST son, Sim, who finally lured the mule out of the lake. Nadi had been forced to tell him what had happened, for the story of the mule who swam with the ducks, and of the half a dozen Hrum soldiers who couldn't catch it, had spread through the city like wind. For someone who knew Duckie . . .

The boy had been torn between fury at having been left out and fear for the peddler; that left him better off than Nadi and Hama, who were frightened but blamed no one. Though that would change if they found out what Jiaan had done. None of them knew what had happened, but Jiaan was almost certain that the peddler had encountered one of Substrategus Arus' officers.

He had tried to control it—to acknowledge the good the peddler had done, to work with him, for Farsala's sake. But as soon as Jiaan had set eyes on the man, the hate flooded back.

Besides, if I'd told him what Patrius told me, that some of the officers weren't sent to Dugaz, he wouldn't have gone in.

It was true, too, and if there was even a chance of getting rid of that accursed gold before it was shipped to Kadesh—under heavy guard, no doubt—Jiaan had to try. But now, without any of the passwords . . .

We'll have to capture it before it reaches the border, but that means bringing the whole army out of the desert—away from Mazad. And even if we can get that many men into position near the Trade Road without Garren learning we're there, he'll know as soon as we attack. Then all he has to do is get a large body of troops to Mazad before we can get back. Assuming there are enough of us left to make a difference.

The crowd that had gathered to laugh at the Hrum soldiers' efforts was beginning to disperse. Jiaan watched the dripping boy pull the balky mule up the shore, but his heart was too cold to smile. Attacking a large convoy of guards who expected an assault was the most dangerous thing his fledgling army could do—except, perhaps, fighting a field battle like the one that had destroyed the deghan forces at the Sendar Wall, or making an assault on a fortified city, such as Setesafon had become.

A last determined goose trundled out of the waves after the mule, hissing and trying to peck, but Sim drove it off with shouts and kicks. Jiaan wouldn't have blamed him for wringing the beast's neck; there were bruises on his face and arms where the ducks and geese had pecked him as he swam after the mule. They'd assaulted the Hrum soldiers, too, who swore and flailed at them with great splashing blows. But in the end it was the crowd's laughter that had defeated the Hrum. *Let the misbegotten creature drown! I'm not making a fool of myself any longer.*

Nadi flung a blanket around the boy, and Hama took the mule's lead rope, preparing to take her home—preparing to care for her, for her master's sake, until he returned with the rest of the Hrum slaves and reclaimed her. Nadi had decreed that he would be back—firmly, dubiously refusing to acknowledge that the peddler's failure to return with the passwords had significantly reduced the chance that the slaves would be returning. Though the lady Soraya, standing silent and grim at Jiaan's side, was obviously aware of it. Curse the fellow for failing! Serve him right if the Hrum killed him—it would save Jiaan the trouble! But the Hrum didn't execute prisoners, any more than they tortured them. They did kill traitors, however, and the uncertainty as to which they would consider the peddler had left Nadi's face white and miserable.

If it were up to Jiaan there'd be no doubt—he *was* a traitor, a traitor to Farsala, whatever he was to the Hrum. As far as Jiaan was concerned they could—

The girl, Hama, was leading the mule toward him, which was odd because they'd agreed it would be safer if they pretended not to know each other in this all-too-public place. The crowd was leaving, but . . .

Her face was grim, but her eyes blazed with anguished hope.

"Look at her halter!" she murmured, before Jiaan could complain about the attention she was drawing. In truth, that attention wasn't much—garbed as low-ranked craftsmen, with the lady's deghass-black hair covered with a scarf, Jiaan and Soraya could have been friends or even kin of the girl before them.

It was the lady Soraya who stepped forward, running curious fingers over the wet leather. Then she stiffened. "Salute!" she exclaimed incomprehensibly. "But if that's two, what's one?"

Only when Jiaan came forward and looked for himself did he see the dark letters scorched into the leather. His heart began to pound.

"Not here!" he commanded sharply. "Inside, where no one can overhear us."

Inside turned out to be a small shed attached to the laundry, where Nadi had decided to keep the mule. It was currently filled with casks of soap, coils of laundry line, and bundles of stirring paddles, all of which would have to be moved to accommodate Duckie. In fact there was barely room for all of them to squeeze in beside her—Soraya climbed onto a big barrel to get out of the way—but they couldn't wait any longer. Hama and Sim stripped off the mule's halter and spread it out between them.

"'Today 1,'" Hama read. "That means the first password is 'today,' doesn't it?"

"And 'salute' must be the second," said the lady Soraya. "What's that last one? It's upside down from here."

"Mile," said Nadi, pronouncing the Hrum word awkwardly. "But there's no number after it."

"He probably ran out of time," said Jiaan, the calmness of his voice belying the rapid beat of his heart. How fast had the peddler's heart been beating as he took the time—time he might have spent escaping—to burn those words letter by letter into the straps, knowing that Duckie might succeed where he had failed?

Traitor, perhaps—coward, no.

"That's only three of them," said Nadi reluctantly. "We don't even know how many layers of security you'd have to pass to reach the vault."

"It's better than what we had before," said Jiaan. "According to Hama, this will be enough to get us out of the grounds and into a building. After that, we'll take our chances."

"I'll go with you," said Sim, who Jiaan judged to be all of twelve years old. "I can help."

His mother's mouth opened, but Jiaan beat

her to it. "You've already helped, lad, getting this"—he lifted the damp halter—"into our hands. And I'm afraid you'd look a bit unconvincing in a Hrum breastplate and helmet."

The boy, who had drawn a breath to object, fell silent—though he came up with plenty of other plans in the next few marks, including disguising himself as the lady Soraya, which told Jiaan just how badly he wanted to go. But he wasn't a fool, and when the men began arriving in response to Jiaan's summons, Sim gave up and helped them don their disguises and arm themselves.

Nadi, who had wisely left the task of discouraging her son to Jiaan, was even more helpful. She provided clean tunics and trousers that not only suited the rank of common Hrum troopers, but fit each man as if they had been made for him.

The breastplates didn't fit well, but after a bit of shuffling they got each man into something that wasn't too uncomfortably small or too obviously big. Once they donned their cloaks, discrepancies in the size of the armor were hidden.

Then Hama led the lady Soraya off to help her dress, and Nadi approached Jiaan with a deci-master's tunic and a scarlet cloak over her arm.

"Time for you to get ready, la . . . Commander."

"You can call me lad," said Jiaan. His hands were cold with fear, but his heart was light. This was best. If they could get the gold, even most of the gold, out of Garren's hands, then Jiaan's army could defend Mazad against anything Garren would be able to bring against them. Even if Jiaan failed to return, he knew he could entrust that task to Hosah and Fasal.

"I'll be calling you commander," said Nadi. "For it's as a commander that I want to ask a favor of you."

"You want me to get the peddler out?" It wasn't a difficult guess; all the underground areas, the wine cellar, the vault, and the cells were connected by a tunnel that paralleled the aqueduct. "I can't prom—"

"He has a name!" the woman snapped. "After all he's done for you, the least you owe him is to use it. The *least* you owe him."

Jiaan took a deep breath. "We'll be lucky to get out ourselves. Even if we claim we're taking the lady to be questioned, sooner or later—"

"If you're taking one prisoner to be questioned, why not two?" Nadi handed him the tunic, watching as Jiaan stripped off his shirt and put it on. "Remember to keep those sleeves pulled down, by the by. No one will find that odd, not in this weather, but if anyone sees that none of you have rank tattoos . . ."

"I've already told them," said Jiaan. "And you have to understand . . . oh, all right. If it's possible to get him out, I'll try."

The peddler had earned that much even Jiaan had to concede it. "But getting the gold out of Garren's hands comes first. Before anyone's safety, especially his."

Nadi stopped unbuckling a decimaster's breastplate to glare at him.

"He put that first himself," said Jiaan. "You know he did."

"I do," the laundress admitted. "Though I'm not so blind that I can't see the anger between you. I don't know why you're feeling that way—frankly, I don't care. But let me tell you what lies between Kavi and me."

As she fastened Jiaan into the unfamiliar armor, she told the tale—briefly, though it clearly mattered to her. He understood that. If you were a recent widow, impoverished, with a pile of children both your own and others' to feed, and someone offered you a source of income—no matter how dubious its legality—which allowed you to survive and set yourself up in a respectable business, you would care about that person.

In truth, Jiaan wasn't impressed. Even the greatest villains usually cared about their families. Of course, these people hadn't been the peddler's family then . . . but he was still the man who had betrayed the Farsalan army at the Sendar Wall, and nothing would change that. A part of Jiaan hoped Garren would kill him—though didn't that make Jiaan as bad as Garren? He had told Fasal they had to be better . . .

He thrust the confusing thoughts aside. Still, those straight, careful letters scorched into the leather had to be worth something.

"I'll try to get him out if I can," Jiaan told Nadi finally. "But I can't promise more than that."

"That's all I ask," said Nadi, though she probably would have asked for more if she thought she could get it. "But I'll hold you to that much, *Commander.*"

Jiaan nodded acknowledgment and reached out to take the helmet as the lady Soraya returned.

494

It had been more than a year since Jiaan had seen her dressed like this, in flowing, embroidered silk, with glass beads and feathers braided into her too-short hair. The gasps of the men around him were a tribute to her beauty, but Jiaan had been in her company often enough to see her almost as the sister she truly was. And at least . . .

"Whatever happens," he said, "you'll make a fair diversion."

"That's the point," said the lady Soraya, coolly ignoring the admiring looks of his men. "Shall we go?"

Jiaan thought he heard a quiver of fear in her assured voice—arrogance could be a cover for fear, he had learned—but he couldn't be certain.

THE SUN WAS SETTING as they made their way to one of the palace gates—a deci of guards escorting a deghass prisoner. She was clearly a deghass and clearly a prisoner, her hands bound in front of her, her overrobe artistically ripped. Her gleaming, shoulder-length hair formed a disheveled black cloud around her tense face. She really did look as if she'd fought them, and if Garren knew her at all, Jiaan reflected wryly, that would add verisimilitude. She'd been arguing with Jiaan almost every step of the way.

"Say it again," she murmured in Hrum.

"I say it often, already," said Jiaan in the same language. "I say it again, it will be . . ." He paused, the Hrum word eluding him.

"*Ariapar*," said the lady Soraya. "It means 'suspicious.' Repeat it please."

She couldn't possibly expect to teach him Hrum in just one afternoon—but if she didn't, it wouldn't be for lack of trying on her part. Or on his. Jiaan sighed. "*Ariapar*."

"*Ariapar*. Say it again."

"No," said Jiaan. "It will be *ariapar* if I say it again."

Not that the Farsalan workmen around them were likely to care what he said, especially in Hrum. They were still casting dark glances toward Jiaan and his men, and in the lower city, less than a quarter mark ago, a group of apprentices and journeymen had followed them for several blocks, calling low-voiced insults. The one about needing eleven Hrum soldiers to capture one Farsalan girl had been the mildest of them, and since then Jiaan's men had been marching with drawn swords in their hands.

After that the mob had melted away. No others had dared to take their place, but Jiaan was still nervous.

The mood in the city was odd this evening: half celebratory, for the feast had already begun, and, perhaps unwisely, Garren was handing out beer for the adults as well as sweets for the children.

He and the committee had already taken their places in the pavilion, watching a parade of the cities' craft houses pass through the square before them. Soon the speeches would begin. Jiaan suspected that the peddler had been forced to use his tale about a demonstration of hostility toward the committee, for there were almost as many Hrum soldiers in the square as Setesafon townsmen. That left the rest of the city lightly patrolled, and under the cheer of beer and celebration an undercurrent of sullen resentment bubbled upward. When darkness fell, Garren and the committee might need their guards.

For Jiaan's later, tentative, plans for escape, the swirling, chaotic crowd was perfect—but right now it made being a Hrum decimaster escorting a prisoner a nerve-wracking experience. He was almost relieved to see the palace gate looming before him.

"Today," he said, nodding briskly to the guard who saluted in return.

"Good evening, sir," said the guard, standing aside to let them pass.

Jiaan decided to risk some simple words. "Not out here, it isn't."

The guard looked out at the crowd with a practiced eye. "I can see that. I'll *vressa* you're glad to be coming in."

"Yes," said Jiaan in Hrum, trying to control the quiver in the pit of his stomach. He walked briskly toward the palace, trying to duplicate the Hrum's straight military posture and succeeding, he thought, fairly well. Some of the men who followed him could mimic the Hrum better than he could, but Jiaan spoke it best—and they all, hopefully, understood enough to obey simple commands.

So far their only duty had been to follow Jiaan and look like soldiers, and they seemed to be doing that well. At least no one had pointed at them and either laughed or sounded an alarm.

Jiaan thought there were fewer guards patrolling than there had been that afternoon.

"Are they all at the square?" he murmured to

Soraya in Faran, after a quick glance to be certain there were no Hrum nearby.

"I don't know, but it looks . . . curse it!"

They rounded a bend in the path and came into sight of the building that stood above the prisoners cells, just as the kitchen, according to Hama's drawing, was perched over the vault and wine cellar. The guards patrolling the grounds might have been thinned, but the cordon surrounding the palace, the armory, and the building where the senators lodged had been redoubled and perhaps redoubled again.

The lady's steps slowed and she stumbled. Jiaan caught her arm to set her upright. It gave him a reason to slow as well.

"We've got two more passwords," he reassured both himself and her.

"Yes, but they look awfully alert. Suppose they ask for more than passwords? Suppose they ask you to state your business in a way that can't be answered by 'I'm taking this prisoner to the cells'?"

Sunset lit the bronze decorations on the breastplates of dozens of men scattered through the guard cordon—decorations that denoted officers. They might have been placed there to ask questions, Jiaan realized. Someone had tightened security.

"The kitchen," he said. "We'll take you in through the wine cellar."

Soraya snorted. "Why would you take a prisoner to the cells through the wine cellar instead of straight through the armory?"

"To prevent the committee from seeing you," Jiaan improvised. "Orders from Garren himself."

He turned crisply, taking a path that would lead them to the back of the palace where the kitchen was. Jiaan had spent a large part of the afternoon memorizing Hama's drawing, and now he was glad of it. The guards who surrounded the palace and armory were too distant to have gotten a good look at them . . . he hoped.

"Why wouldn't Garren want the committee to see me?" Soraya asked. He wasn't sure if she meant it, or was asking because she thought the Hrum guards would ask him that, but either way the answer was the same.

"How would I know? I have my orders and I'm obeying them." Sometimes Hrum discipline was a wonderful thing. "How do I say all that in Hrum?"

The lesson kept him busy until they reached the modest building that housed the kitchen. Jiaan could have used more time to master the proper intonations of "I'm taking this prisoner to the cells through the wine cellar; the committee isn't supposed to see her," but he could shrug and say "orders" as well as any Hrum soldier alive.

When they first entered the kitchen, all that preparation seemed unnecessary; only a handful of men and women remained in the long, echoing room, scrubbing a small mountain of pots and pans. The cooks had probably gone to serve at the feast, which was good. The bad news was that if there was a tunnel leading to the wine cellar, Jiaan couldn't see it. He looked at the lady Soraya, who shrugged.

No help for it—he had to try. Jiaan walked up to a woman who was carrying a towering stack of clean pots toward a storage rack.

"I'm taking this prisoner to the cells through the wine cellar," he said stiffly. "The committee isn't supposed to see her. Where is the wine cellar?"

He knew how clumsy it sounded, but he didn't know the Hrum word for 'entrance.'

The woman didn't seem to notice anything amiss. "Over there," she said, motioning with her head toward a far corner. Her next comments were too fast for Jiaan to follow, though he caught the words for "stairs" and "turn." Thank Azura he had a translator.

He nodded his thanks and marched himself, his men, and his prisoner briskly in the direction she had indicated. There it was, in the shadow behind the pillars—a stairway leading down, and a guard standing beside it.

"Password," said the man, saluting casually as he ran curious eyes over the lady Soraya. She glared at him.

"Salute," said Jiaan. "I'm taking this prisoner to the cells through the wine cellar. Orders."

"Why not just take her through the *netalirium*?" the guard asked, though he was already stepping aside.

"The committee isn't supposed to see her," said Jiaan.

"But the committee's all off watching the *garanial*," said the guard.

Jiaan shrugged. "I obey orders."

"And *liassa* as usual," the man sighed, looking at Soraya. "Too bad. She's *aurin varet*."

Soraya recoiled against Jiaan, turning him

away. "Look stern and say, 'Discipline, soldier,'" she whispered in Faran.

Two Hrum words she knew Jiaan knew. "Discipline, soldier!" he snapped in Hrum. The accent might be faked, but the tone of command was real. The guard stiffened. "Yes, sir. Sorry, sir."

Jiaan nodded and herded his troops down the stairs and into the tunnel. It was paved and lined in plain stone, and so narrow that only two could go abreast. The small oil lamps barely produced enough light to see the floor. He felt safer here than he had at any time since they'd crept out of the laundry's back door. He waited until they'd passed several turns before he bent toward Soraya.

"What did he say?"

"He said I was a pretty slut," said Soraya coldly. "Or words to that effect. I hope his kind are never set to guard the slaves."

Not all Hrum were like Patrius.

Soraya took a deep breath and let it go. Some of her angry tension seemed to go with it. "The kitchen maid said that to reach the wine cellar we have to go down the stairs, follow the tunnel to the fork, and then go left. She said the right fork leads to a portal to the sewers."

Jiaan frowned. "There was no fork in the tunnel in Hama's drawing." It hadn't turned as much as this one, either.

Soraya shrugged.

They went on in silence for a time. Jiaan began to wonder if the woman had gotten her directions confused, if they might be following the aqueduct out from under the palace. But eventually they passed around another bend and saw two new guards, stationed half a dozen yards apart so if anything happened to one the other could sound the whistle tucked into his belt.

They both looked bored, but they straightened up when they saw Jiaan and his party. Behind the second guard was a thick wooden door. The wine cellar?

Jiaan marched up to the first guard. "Mile," he said, as the guard saluted crisply. The second guard had already turned to unlock the door. Jiaan's shoulders started to sag with relief, but he caught himself and stiffened. The first guard looked curiously at Soraya.

"Ah, if you don't mind my asking, sir . . . this is the wine cellar."

"I know," said Jiaan in his best Hrum. "I'm taking the prisoner to the cells through . . ." The guard had just told Jiaan it was the wine cellar. "Through here. She isn't supposed to be seen by the committee. Governor Garren's orders."

The guard frowned, then shrugged. Jiaan blessed Hrum discipline yet again and led his small troop though the door and into the cellar. It was a vast, dark cavern of a room, full of barrels, casks, bottles, and even some cloth shrouded furniture — which had been stored there for some time, judging by the dust — but it was empty of people.

The wooden door swung closed behind them, shutting out the guard. Jiaan's knees wobbled with the relief of not being watched. He heard the men behind him all draw breath at once, their armor clinking softly as they relaxed. He turned and gestured urgently for silence — they'd been about to start talking, every one of them.

"They might be able to hear us through the door," he whispered in Faran. "Loud sounds, at least. Keep your voices down."

They had fallen out of formation with the sudden release of tension, but they all nodded. The lady Soraya pulled her wrists free of the loose rope and rubbed her face with both hands.

"It's not over," she said. "We still have to reach the vault, and the peddler in the cells, and then get out of here. It's not over at all."

But they still took a few moments to relax in the dim cellar, locating casks of the right size to float down the aqueduct, exploring the room, and enjoying a moment of respite.

It was with reluctance that Jiaan waved them back into formation and donned his heavy helmet.

The lady worked her wrists into the rope without assistance. It looked tight — Nadi had tied the knots, for she had been the one who insisted that Soraya needed to be able to free herself. Looking at the girl's taut face, Jiaan wondered if that had been because the laundress feared Soraya might need to free her wrists swiftly, or if she simply wanted to give the girl some measure of control.

Jiaan opened the unobtrusive, ironbound door at the far end of the cellar; according to Hama's drawing, it led to the tunnel that led to the vault. This tunnel was narrower than the one from the kitchen to the wine cellar: Two could barely walk abreast, so Jiaan signaled his men to stagger their ranks. And since the vault was somewhere between the wine cellar and the cells, this tunnel was much shorter.

Jiaan was almost startled when they came around a bend and saw the bronze-sheathed door to the vault . . . with one guard standing before it and the other half a dozen yards farther down the tunnel. *Curse Hrum discipline.*

Jiaan marched toward the first guard without slowing, but his mind raced faster than his pounding heart. Would the third password work on these men? Probably not. The vault was far more important than the wine cellar.

This was the point where he'd told Nadi he'd think of something. At the time, safe in the laundry's warm darkness, Jiaan had imagined himself sweeping forward in a burst of action, taking out the farther of the surprised guards while his men leaped to subdue the other. But the tunnel was too narrow for him to pass the first guard without alerting the second, and both guards were as well armed as Jiaan, and probably better trained. As he drew nearer, Jiaan saw another of the side tunnels that led off toward the sewer, almost between the two guards, but he couldn't think of any way to use it.

It was too late to go back; he had to try. Maybe if he told—

"Halt and state the password," said the first of the two guards. He was frowning, clearly wondering why anyone would bring a prisoner through the vault.

So tell him. "We're taking the prisoner to the cells through the wine cellar." Jiaan slowed his pace, though he didn't actually halt. He had to get both himself and his men nearer to the guards if they were to accomplish anything. His pulse thundered in his ears. He was ready for action, ready for violence—but the moment they attacked, the alarm would sound!

"Halt," said the guard again. "Why would you take a prisoner through the vault instead of through the armory? That doesn't make sense."

Jiaan paused for a moment. "I know that," he said, wishing his Hrum were fluent enough to sound casual. "Governor Garren doesn't want the committee to see her."

A puzzled scowl crossed the guard's face, but the hand that rested on his sword hilt relaxed a bit. Had he been about to draw it?

"Why does he care if the committee sees her?

She's just a slave who came into the *regios* to spy."

Jiaan was so startled, he almost stopped walking. But of course Soraya might be recognized. She'd been held prisoner by the Hrum before—it was probably sheer luck, and the fact that all the experienced staff were helping with the feast, that she had passed through the kitchen without seeing anyone who knew her.

"I don't know why," said Jiaan. "I have my orders." He strolled nearer, slow and casual, almost there, almost within reach. He could feel the tension, the readiness, of the men moving quietly behind him.

"She was made prisoner today," he said, as the guard opened his mouth to ask for the password again. "In Setesafon. I don't know what she does there."

The clumsy, simple speech had tweaked the guard's suspicions. "Password," he demanded. "And halt there."

Jiaan stopped—still not close enough. "Mi—"

The lady Soraya slipped past him and bolted toward the guard. He made a grab for her, his hands closing on the strong silk of her overrobe— but she must have unfastened it as they walked,

509

for she slid out of it like an eel and raced down the corridor toward the other guard.

"Stop her!" Jiaan yelled, leaping past the guard after his quick-witted prisoner. The guard swore, cast the heavy robe aside, and joined Jiaan in the chase.

The second guard moved forward to trap her, but she still ran toward him, seemingly oblivious to his outstretched arms . . . until she reached the side passage and darted into it.

"Get her!" Jiaan commanded. "If she reaches the sewer she can escape!"

Even Hrum discipline wasn't proof against a prisoner escaping right under his nose. The second guard followed her into the narrow passage, Jiaan and the Farsalans on his heels. The first guard was right in their midst now, and could surely be taken as soon as —

Jiaan hooked a foot around the first guard's ankle — easier in this narrow tunnel than it would have been in the open, for here only one could pass at a time, and the rough floor slanted down.

The guard fell forward with a startled cry. Jiaan reached down, pulled off his helmet and struck the man's temple with his dagger hilt, in the exact place his father's arms master had shown him only a few years ago, though it seemed like another lifetime.

He didn't strike hard enough to knock the man unconscious, but he was sufficiently stunned for Jiaan to bind his wrists and gag him. Jiaan heard the commotion as the other guard was overpowered, but after one quick glance he left that to his men. He'd almost finished binding his prisoner when Soraya returned.

"Bring them this way," she said. "There's a wider place ahead where they won't be found."

"That was brilliant," Jiaan told her sincerely. "Brilliant, and brave, and wonderful enough—"

"I don't want to be their prisoner again," said Soraya, though she smiled at his praise. Perhaps it was as well that she cut him off before he finished, though the words echoed in his mind: *wonderful enough to make me proud that you're my sister.*

"Bring them along," said Jiaan, and followed the lady Soraya down the passage. Away from the main tunnel there were no lamps, and he had to grope his way forward, but when they reached the sewer they found that someone had placed a dimly glowing lamp in one of the niches—probably to stop people from walking out of the passage and into the water.

It flowed swiftly down the stone canal just a few paces from the end of the passage. It didn't smell as bad as Jiaan had expected, perhaps because the current was so fast, and, as far as he could tell, the water was deep.

"Over here," said Soraya, gesturing toward a place where the ledge that bordered the flowing water had been widened. "You can tie them to that pillar. Even if they make some noise, it shouldn't carry too far—not if they can't shout."

"Especially," said Jiaan, "if we take these." Reaching down he pulled the whistles from the guards' belts. Both of them were at least semiconscious, but they appeared to be too battered to care what he did—in fact, Jiaan wasn't sure the second guard even noticed.

Jiaan handed the whistles to two of his men who spoke better Hrum than the rest. "Go back to the corridor," he told them. "Take the guards' places." He hoped no one would approach them, but even if someone did come down to the cellar, it didn't take much Hrum to say, "Halt. Password."

"What now?" the girl asked.

Jiaan grinned. "Now the gold."

It took time to get back to the great bronze door, realize they needed a key, go back and search the second guard's clothing, and get into the vault itself.

There were, Azura be praised, no guards inside. Understandable, since not all the treasures were locked up in chests. That carved lion with the emerald eyes, that graceful gazelle with the gold-plated—solid gold?—horns . . . both had surely graced the gahn's palace. Jiaan was surprised they hadn't been shipped west with the rest of Farsala's wealth—perhaps Garren intended to bring them out when he was lord here. The small chests that contained Garren's bribe were highly visible among the larger chests and crates stored in the vault. Small because their contents were so heavy that a man could barely carry one. The girl, for all her strength, couldn't lift any of them.

It took even more time to bring the gold back to the sewer outlet, to bring in the wine casks and empty the wine. Time to break the locks on the chests, to figure out how much gold a cask could carry and still float without rising to the surface.

By the time they finally had the weight right, Jiaan and several of his men were thoroughly soaked. The sewer water was cleaner than he'd expected, but it still smelled. Once they knew the correct measure of gold to a cask, the work went more quickly.

Not so long after that, Soraya tipped the last cask into the water. She had retrieved her over-robe from the corridor, and her underrobe wasn't too wet.

Jiaan, who by this time was standing waist-deep in the sewer, tested the cask's buoyancy. It sank to the bottom, but so lightly that he knew the current would carry it downstream with no more than a bump or two. He gave it a kick to set it on its way and hauled himself out of the water.

Soraya stepped back from the splash, but her eyes were shining. "That's it," she said. "More than thirty chests of gold and silver coin. All we found in the vault."

Jiaan smiled at her, at his waiting men. "It feels kind of good to throw away that much gold, doesn't it?"

"Speak for yourself, young sir," said one of his

Farsalan veterans. "I want the fisherfolk to be giving us a share!"

Their laughter echoed in the tunnels, and Jiaan started to motion for silence and then desisted. He didn't think the sound would carry far, but even if it did and some guards posted further down the sewer heard it, it shouldn't make them suspicious of the occasional scrape or bump coming from the murky water. If anything, it would make them suspect some practical joke, and they'd be even less willing to investigate.

Jiaan was still smiling when they went back to the vault, but humor vanished when they finally examined the metal-clad door on the far side of the vault and found that it couldn't be unlocked from the inside.

"That makes sense," Soraya whispered. "No one needs to lock themselves into a vault. And there's no guarantee that the key from the other door would work in this lock anyway."

Jiaan dropped to the floor, where a faint glow illuminated the stone, and peered under the door. All he could see were the heels of two Hrum boots, presumably containing two Hrum feet.

It wasn't likely that quiet sounds would

penetrate the door, but Jiaan signaled the others to move away for their murmured conference.

"There's a guard there," he told them. "And I couldn't see him, but I'm sure there's another guard down the corridor."

"Maybe several guards," said the lady. "This is the vault's main entrance; we came through the back door."

"So when we knock on this door, they'll be surprised," said Jiaan. "And a bit suspicious. And they'll ask for a password before they open it."

There was a long, grim silence.

"So we'll go out the way we came in, and try to get to the cells through the armory, like we planned in the first place," said Soraya.

Jiaan winced, but the thought of explaining his business to an officer wasn't quite as intimidating as it had been. It was worth a try.

"We can say that the governor has returned from the city and wants to question you tonight," he told Soraya. "We've been down here long enough that it shouldn't sound too odd. I'll bet he is back by now, or he will be shortly."

"We'd better not meet him," said Soraya. "Kavi's not the only one he'll recognize."

"So what?" said Jiaan. "We'd just be told to wait till he's finished with you and then escort you to the cells. Someone might even give us the passwords to get there."

Which reminded him that they didn't have those passwords, so getting to the cells was an enormous risk. They'd already stolen the gold. They'd done what they'd come for. On the other hand, he'd promised Nadi he'd try.

Out of the vault, down the corridor, picking up the two men he'd stationed there—to no purpose, it turned out, since no one had tried to pass. Jiaan ordered those two to the front of the troop; they were cleaner than the rest of his men, including Jiaan himself, though his tunic sleeves and trousers were beginning to dry. The body of his tunic, which was covered by his breastplate, would probably stay wet till he took off his armor. With any luck no one would be able to tell where the smell was coming from.

Soraya coached him as they walked, and on the far side of the wine cellar Jiaan rapped boldly on the door.

"Mile," he said. "Let us out. Now the governor wants to see the prisoner."

The door opened on the guard's surprised face.

"That didn't take long," he said. "You *dicedus* just a few *jaur mar*.

Jiaan hoped he didn't need to answer that—probably not, for the girl was silent.

"The governor sent word he was returning," said Jiaan, using the Hrum phrasing they'd agreed on, which would cover them whether Garren was back now or not. "He wants to see the prisoner before he retires."

"Good *ariss*," said the guard, opening the door.

He saluted as Jiaan passed, though his nose wrinkled. Jiaan didn't dare look back, but Soraya did, and she choked down a laugh. Jiaan waited till they'd passed the second guard and were well into the long tunnel before he whispered, "What?"

"After we went by, he smelled his armpits."

Jiaan grinned and his spirits rose. That was the normal reaction to an odd smell—not instant suspicion that the people you were looking at had been throwing gold into a sewer. The Hrum were human, after all. Jiaan was starting to think they had a chance.

The tunnel that had seemed so long miraculously shortened itself on the way back; in no time at all they were climbing the stairs to the kitchen. The guard who opened the door stared at them.

"What are you doing here?"

"The governor wants to question this prisoner before he retires," said Jiaan. "*Salute*," he added pointedly.

"Yes, sir," said the guard. "But I recognized you." He was frowning.

Jiaan wanted to deliver a lecture about always asking for passwords, but he knew his vocabulary would fail him.

"I'll tell the governor what you said about me," said Soraya in Hrum. "And he'll be shamed before the committee by the manners of his pigs of guards."

The guard flushed. "You can tell him what you like," he said in Faran almost as fluent as Soraya's Hrum. "I do my duty."

"She won't see the committee," said Jiaan in Hrum. "Governor Garren's orders. We go now." He gave Soraya a push and nodded acknowledgment of the guard's salute, which was slower and more thoughtful than the usual brisk gesture. Had Jiaan strayed too far from his lines and made the man suspicious? At least he hadn't sounded the alarm.

Jiaan walked away, not too quickly, since his men were still emerging from the passage. Soraya went with him perforce, for he gripped her arm, but perhaps she too sensed the guard's suspicion, for she turned and called back, "No woman, Hrum or Farsalan, would ever marry a pig like you! Men only insult women because they can't attract them! Sometimes because . . ."

Jiaan paid her no further attention. There didn't seem to be anyone in the kitchen now. The only light came from the banked cookfires. The long tables were clear, except for the racks of gleaming knives.

Most of Jiaan's concentration was fixed on listening for his men, the last of whom were still coming up the stair when the guard said sharply, "Wait! How did you all get so wet?"

Jiaan let go of Soraya and spun, but his men were already taking care of it. The nearest of them swung his fist, but the guard had stopped them because he was wary—he leaped back, shouting, and bumped into a rack of pans. It swayed.

Jiaan could see the idea come to the man,

almost as if time had slowed, giving Jiaan leisure to note all that happened around him. The guard's whistle was tucked into his belt—he didn't have time to draw both it and his sword, but this . . .

"Alarm!" the guard cried. One of his hands went to his sword hilt, the other pulled the top of the rack toward him. "Alarm! Intruders! Enem—"

The heavy fist of one of Jiaan's soldiers took him square on the chin, flinging him back—but his hand, still clenched on the rack, pulled it down on top of him.

The smash of breaking crockery was bad enough, but the terrible din as the iron pots and kettles bounced onto the floor was far worse. According to Hama there would be someone posted near enough to have heard the guard's shouts.

"Run!" Jiaan commanded. Snatching up Soraya's arm again he set the example, weaving in and out of the tables like a bubble in a millstream until they reached the kitchen's outer doors.

"We'll get farther if we look like soldiers," said Jiaan. "Hold ranks as long as you can, but if someone tries to stop us, get yourselves out! Understand?"

His men, still sorting themselves into the deci's

unfamiliar marching order, muttered assent. Jiaan had no time for more. He opened the door and started out, his prisoner held properly between the two men who marched behind him. The rope that had bound her wrists was gone, but if she clasped her hands in front of her, no one would notice that unless they examined her closely. They still looked like a Hrum troop escorting a prisoner—as long as no one drew near enough to smell them.

But why would they be escorting a prisoner out of the palace grounds?

"Why are we taking you away from the palace?" he asked Soraya.

"How should I . . . wait, I've got it. There are witnesses in the city who'll confirm my identity."

She repeated it in Hrum. Jiaan practiced it twice under his breath before asking, "Why don't the witnesses come here to—"

"Hey!" It was another patrol, jogging toward them. Just as Jiaan began to panic, their decimaster called, "Did you hear something?"

Jiaan opened his mouth to deny it, then inspiration seized him. "Yes! I think over there!"

He pointed at an angle past the kitchen. The guard they'd tackled would be rousing soon, and the fewer patrols in the vicinity the better.

"Come on!" the patrol leader waved his men forward, breaking into a run. No one would expect a patrol escorting a prisoner to go with them.

"Not bad," said Soraya. "But next time say, 'Shouts and a crash. I think it came from over there.'" She repeated the phrases in Hrum.

Jiaan chose the most direct route to the wall. Forget the gates—if the alarm was raised, he'd never be able to talk his way past the guards. They were only halfway through the gardens when a burst of whistles sounded behind them, shrilling and shrilling. Their cry was taken up by others, both near and distant.

"Sir?" one of his men asked uneasily.

"No," said Jiaan, through gritted teeth. "We keep walking."

His mind knew it was their best chance, though his body screamed for action, for speed.

Two more patrols ran past them, some distance away, giving Jiaan's troop no more than a glance. The wall drew nearer, and nearer still. Jiaan's heartbeat thundered through his body. They were only a few hundred yards from the wall when a shout rang out. "There! Them! Stop them!"

"Scatter!" Jiaan cried. They had planned this in advance, knowing that the Hrum instinctively stayed with their units, so to organize a pursuit that forced them to separate would take time. Jiaan grabbed Soraya's elbow and took off once more, running all out for the low wall. Once she'd pulled up her long skirts, the lady didn't slow him.

He glanced back and saw that one part of his plan had worked properly, for none of the patrol were pursuing his men as they fled in different directions. Instead, the whole troop was chasing Jiaan, who wore a decimaster's insignia, and the girl, who was the other, clearly different member of their party. He reached up and cast off his helmet—it was too late to keep it from marking him, but at least he was free of its weight. The patrol was gaining on them, but they weren't near yet, and the low wall that bordered the palace grounds loomed before them.

In a way, low was a misnomer—the wall's height ranged somewhere between four and five feet, depending on the slope of the terrain.

The lady Soraya was small and slim. Jiaan

picked her up and threw her over the wall as if she were a child—frightened as he was, it wouldn't have mattered if the wall had been twice that high.

Soraya squeaked in surprise to find herself airborne, and vanished from sight.

The hiss and smack of arrows on the stones sent Jiaan vaulting over the wall, hastening away almost before he landed on the other side. He found himself in a shop-lined street that he vaguely remembered led to a minor marketplace. Ordinarily it would have been nearly empty after dark, but tonight, the curfew relaxed for the festivities, there were still people abroad. Several of them stopped to stare at him and Soraya, and a few near the wall who had heard the sound of the arrows shouted a frightened warning.

The patrol must have fired low, Jiaan realized, to avoid sending arrows into the crowd. That was probably why they'd missed, and they hadn't missed by much—an arrow shaft that had stuck in the hem of his cloak was knocking against his leg.

Soraya staggered to her feet and ran to his side. Jiaan put his arm around her waist, pulling her into the crowd, for he knew the wall would slow their pursuers no more than it had them.

Soraya let him lead, since her attention and her quick fingers were focused on the buckles of his breastplate. Jiaan could feel them loosening. He pulled the pin that fastened the distinctive scarlet cloak and let it fall.

Some of the people in the street realized what was happening, and the crowd near the wall began to thicken as the first of the patrol vaulted over.

"Done," said Soraya, and Jiaan felt the heavy steel part on one side like a clam's shell. He worked his arm free and the breastplate dropped to the cobbles with a clang. He swiftly changed direction, walking up the street with most of the other pedestrians instead of directly away from the wall as he had been.

He heard shouts from the patrol as they shoved through the townsfolk who blocked their progress—and hopefully their view, as well. "Where are they?" was the most common question, and if the peddler was right about the mood of Setesafon's citizens, they would get no answer.

Soraya had already shed her overrobe; now she struggled free of the damp underrobe and let it fall to the road. Beneath it she wore a peasant's bright skirt and blouse, with a scarf around her waist. She pulled the scarf free and tied it over her hair.

A middle-aged man stopped for a moment, staring at the Hrum tunic, trousers, and boots Jiaan still wore. They weren't so different from the clothes worn by most Farsalan men, except for the drab color, but this man clearly recognized them.

His eyes shifted to the patrol, who were cursing in two languages as they tried to run through the crowded streets—in two directions, since they didn't know which way Jiaan and Soraya had gone.

One shout would change that. Jiaan braced himself to run. The man grinned suddenly and slipped off his vest. Even in the dim light from the shops that remained open to take advantage of the festival, Jiaan could tell it was dark green, embroidered with red rams and yellow suns. The man handed it to Jiaan and turned away without a word, vanishing into the crowd.

Jiaan put on the vest, tucked Soraya's hand through his arm as if she were his sweetheart instead of his sister, and continued toward the market—strolling now, for there was no need to run. Any member of that patrol could look right at them, and see nothing but a young craftsman who'd taken his girl out to the feast.

"It's people like that," said Soraya, "who make me wonder if he wasn't right."

"Who wasn't right about what?" Jiaan asked.

There were tears in her eyes—something he didn't remember ever having seen in his life. She took a deep breath and wiped her face briskly. "Never mind. We didn't get the peddler out."

"We couldn't," said Jiaan. "We'd have been caught for certain if we'd tried. We got the gold away—that's what's important."

But as he spoke, he felt a pang of regret, so deep it surprised him. Perhaps it sprang from the thought of Nadi's disappointment.

"Besides," Jiaan went on, "he'll be released when we win." Was he trying to reassure Soraya or himself? "And we will win! We crippled Garren tonight. He can't bring down Mazad without withdrawing so many troops that the whole country will rebel. We did it!"

"We did," said the girl, and Jiaan heard the same fierce triumph in her voice. "Though I still wish . . ."

She didn't have to finish the sentence. And despite his own reassurances, and the knowledge that Hrum law truly did forbid the torture of prisoners, it occurred to him that not all Hrum were like Patrius.

AS THEY STOLE AWAY *the gold, one of Sorahb's soldiers made some clumsy error and the Hrum captured him.*

Sorahb was sorely grieved, though he knew the Hrum did not kill their prisoners, and that if he won all those they had taken as slaves would be returned. But Sorahb had reckoned without the desperate arrogance of the Hrum governor. Through their long fight the governor had come to know his enemy, and he saw how he might use this man, and Sorahb's own honor, against him.

The governor sent out a proclamation challenging Sorahb to single combat, saying that if Sorahb did not come to fight, the captured Farsalan soldier would die.

"This is a trap!" one of Sorahb's officers told him.

"He has no intention of fighting—he seeks to bring you out of hiding so you may be slain!"

"I know," said Sorahb. "Yet sometimes a trap can be turned against the trapper."

The officer frowned. "This is no test of the god's devising, Commander. He set you three tasks, and you've accomplished them all. Surely you need do nothing more."

"You are right about the task," Sorahb told him. "This is a test that men set for men. But even so, no man of honor could refuse it."

So Sorahb strapped on his armor and went forth. And Azura watched, taking great pride in this best loved of his creations, who would not shrink from the tests of gods or men.

CHAPTER NINETEEN

KAVI

THE SUDDEN KICK to his stomach brought Kavi out of a sound sleep gasping and choking. The man he sensed standing over him waited till he caught his breath. Till he rolled over and looked up, blinking in the torchlight.

"Where is the gold?" Garren demanded.

Half a dozen flippant responses along the lines of "You've lost something, have you?" flashed through Kavi's mind, but one look at the governor's face told Kavi that doing anything to annoy this man was a really bad idea.

"I don't know." It was the literal truth, but it still earned him a kick.

This time, braced for the blow, Kavi recovered more quickly. There were no windows in his cell, for it was deep underground, but somehow it felt like nighttime. This impression was confirmed by the rich, ponderous robe Garren wore, draped in bands of Hrum scarlet. A Hrum governor's formal garb? Surely he was assuming that title a bit prematurely. Had he just returned from making his speech to the populace to find that all his gold was gone? Good for Soraya and Jiaan!

Kavi's heart sang with triumph, but he struggled to keep it out of his expression, assisted by his aching stomach. Garren-in-defeat would likely prove twice as dangerous as Garren-who-was-winning—and he had never been a good person to defy. There was no way Kavi could resist physically. Garren had brought a middle-aged decimaster and half a deci with him, along with a much younger centrimaster who carried pen and parchment and looked more nervous than someone of that rank should.

"I don't know what you're talking about," said Kavi, regaining his breath. "I came here to offer some information, and then—"

"Don't bother," Garren interrupted him. "I

won't believe you. As soon as you smuggled yourself out of the siege camp we realized you were
working for Sorahb—which was confirmed when
our assault on the gate failed."

"But how could I know about—"

"Then you came to this palace, using a ruse to
get past our guards," Garren went on. "And shortly
after you were captured, another known agent of
Sorahb's . . . who, come to think of it, escaped from
our custody when you were present in our camp.
Anyway, she followed you into the palace, though I
must admit her ruse was a clever one."

A flash of professional appreciation crossed his
face, but when it vanished his eyes were colder
than they'd been before.

Kavi licked his lips nervously. "I don't know
anything about that."

"She and her escort were also discovered, and
fled, though I later found that they'd spent some
time here. Time in the wine cellar and the vault.
And the gold in that vault is missing. Which is
something of a mystery; the vault guards they subdued know they spent time in the sewer access
doing something, but they were too disoriented to
remember what went on there. The guards posted

downstream in the sewer tunnel claim they saw and heard nothing—a lack of vigilance for which they've paid by walking the entire length of the sewer twice. Wherever the gold is, it isn't there. Not any longer.

"You're not going to convince me that your presence at the scene of so many of our defeats is due to coincidence—and short as my patience is tonight, I advise you not to try. For the last time, where is the gold?"

Kavi's mouth was dry; he had to swallow before he spoke. "I don't know."

It was the truth, though there was a lie at its core. He didn't *know* where the gold was, but the odds were very high that it was concealed in the hidden cellar under Nadi's house. The thought of Hrum troops breaking down their door, of the children shrieking in fear, of Nadi, Hama, and Sim hauled off to a life of slavery, frightened Kavi even more than the growing determination in Garren's face.

He'd agreed to take some risks to get the gold, but this was ridiculous!

The governor turned, not to his aide, but to the gnarled docmaster. "Break this man."

The centrimaster, who had yet to take a single note, bit his lip. "Sir, prisoners can't . . ."

"He's a traitor, not a prisoner," said Garren. "But even if he weren't, he stands between me and the conquest of this land. I'd break hundreds like him if I had to."

"Wait!" said Kavi quickly. "I can . . . ah . . ."

"Are you going to tell me where the gold is?" Garren asked.

Kavi drew a shaky breath and summoned all his resolve. "I don't know where it is. But surely we can make some sort of deal. I do know—"

Garren turned and walked out of the cell without a backward glance.

"I have information!" Kavi shouted after him. "Wait! We can deal!"

The centrimaster did look back. The anguished regret in his eyes was even more terrifying than Garren's coldness.

"Tie his hands," the old decimaster told the men who remained.

Kavi tried to resist, which was probably foolish, for there were five of them, and his knees were trembling so hard he could barely stand. His mind wasn't really on defending himself, anyway.

The Hrum are no different from the deghans, after all. A deghan would have said "peasant" instead of "man," but the order would have been the same. So much for the rule of law that Patrius promised. Kavi had been wrong about the Hrum, but his people could still have their chance. He could make it right, make the deaths at the Sendar Wall count for something . . . if he could hold out. His heart was hammering, and cold sweat poured down his spine. It didn't seem a likely thing.

"Ah, don't look like that," said the decimaster calmly. "It won't be as bad as you think."

Kavi blinked in astonishment. "But you're going to torture me, aren't you?" He looked around the cell, noticing for the first time that the Hrum had brought no instruments with them—no pinchers, no knives beyond the ones all Hrum soldiers wore at their belts, no brazier of hot coals . . .

"Well, yes," the decimaster admitted. "But there are things about breaking someone that most people don't know. Especially most Hrum." Kavi suddenly noticed that the man spoke with a pronounced accent. That wasn't unusual in the Hrum army, but judging by his words this man must be from some recently conquered country, a country where Hrum laws were new, and other ways, older ways, might have been practiced in this man's lifetime.

"There you go again, imagining hot pokers," said the decimaster as his men hauled Kavi to his feet. They had to hold him upright, for his knees were wobbling. "You're a smith, aren't you?"

Before Kavi could reply, the decimaster slammed a fist into his stomach and, when Kavi doubled over, hit him in the face with his knee.

Kavi collapsed to the floor, coughing, gasping for breath. On top of Garren's kicks the blow to his stomach hurt, and his face was beginning to throb.

"You're a smith, aren't you?" the man asked again.

Kavi managed to nod.

"So you're used to burns, right?"

Kavi didn't nod this time, though the man was right—smiths were accustomed to minor burns, and he knew that most people feared hot metal far more than he did.

"That's the thing with pain," the decimaster continued. "If someone's motivated, he can withstand it for quite a while—as long as he's rested.

It's only when a man tires that he can be broken. And it's no shame to you, boy, so don't go blaming yourself. Humans are fragile that way. They get tired enough, they'll break from that alone—and every pain and ache becomes bigger. It doesn't matter how courageous or determined you are. So all I'm going to do, mostly, is make you tired."

"Then why are you beating me?" Kavi asked, as the soldiers lifted him again.

"Because fear, a bit of pain, and hunger will weaken you faster."

This time the decimaster hit him twice in the face, then the stomach.

Kavi's ears rang, and he tasted blood on his lips. But the bastard was right again—painful as it was, this wasn't unendurable. He could hold out, Flame take them. He would!

"You think that now," said the decimaster, reading Kavi's face with annoying ease. "But you're fresh now. I promised the governor I'd have his information for him in two days, three at the outside."

"Flame take you," Kavi muttered through swelling lips. He was fighting for Farsala, for his people's chance to rule!

"That's enough for now," said the decimaster. "Get his hand out."

The soldiers untied Kavi's hands, but instead of letting him go they seized his wrists, flattening his right hand against the stone floor.

"What are you—"

The decimaster pulled out a small club and struck Kavi's little finger with it. Pain shot up his arm, so intense it made his shoulder ache. Kavi gritted his teeth and managed not to scream.

"There, just enough discomfort to make it harder to sleep," said the decimaster. "Not that we'll give you much chance for that, but we'll leave you alone for a while."

And they departed, taking the straw pallet and blanket with them.

Kavi leaned against one of the walls and took stock. His stomach ached, his face hurt, and his finger throbbed—but all in all, he didn't feel as bad as he'd expected. He could resist this, he thought, for longer than three days. Long enough for Soraya and Jiaan to arrange his escape? *Jiaan?* Kavi snorted. The commander of the Farsalan army was probably cheering. No, if they hadn't gotten him out when they were in the vault, within one tunnel of the cells, those two wouldn't be coming for him. On the other hand, the gold was in Nadi's cellar, and she'd be applying pressure. And even if worse came to worst, Kavi would be free once Garren lost.

The cold stone floor was even less comfortable than the thin pallet had been, but Kavi was tired. It took some time, but eventually he fell asleep.

HE WOKE WHEN the cell door opened. The sound was soft, but under the circumstances it wasn't surprising that Kavi's eyes snapped open the moment the lock clicked.

He struggled to his feet, wondering if he should fight or if that would only bring him worse punishment. But all they did was take him from the cell and walk him up and down the corridor before pushing him back in and latching the door behind him.

Now thoroughly awake, Kavi rubbed his eyes—gingerly, for the bruises around them were tender. He didn't know how long he'd slept, but he didn't feel rested. If they were going to keep waking him, he should try to get as much sleep as he could.

He lay down on the stone floor again, but just knowing that they'd be coming to wake him soon made sleep harder to recapture.

THEY WOKE HIM AT least once a mark, perhaps more often, though with no window Kavi couldn't be certain. He had water but no food, but he wasn't hungry anyway. His face hurt and his hand throbbed, but the exhaustion was worse. When the decimaster arrived for his next beating he almost wept from sheer weariness. Worse than his fear of the pain was his growing fear that the bastard would be right—that lack of sleep would break him more surely than the beatings.

If he broke, they would kill him as soon as they had the gold. Kavi had no illusions about that, not anymore. He was willing to work for Farsala's freedom, but he didn't want to die for it! The very thought made his stomach twist with terror. He had to hold out. For himself, for Farsala. For everything.

HE TRIED TO HOLD out for Farsala, for its freedom under peasant rule. But sometime after the second beating, that notion swam into the moving darkness that more and more was clouding his consciousness. Then he tried to hold out for his own redemption — in reparation for the bloodstained grass near the Sendar Wall. For a girl, a nice girl, who even now was living somewhere as a slave. To his surprise, that motive lasted longer.

He tried to keep the details of Garren's situation, of why he had to hold out, in the forefront of his mind, but they too kept swimming away — though sometimes they'd swim back and let him look at them before vanishing again.

Only the words he had learned stayed with him: today, salute, mile, serve, deep. He had gotten all five, all five of them, though he'd only been able to pass three of them on. Sometimes he remembered why those words were important, but mostly he just let them march through his mind as the guards walked him up and down the endless corridor. *Today, salute, mile, serve, deep.* He felt as if they'd been burned into his brain, as he had burned them into the leather of Duckie's halter. He sometimes wondered if he'd ever get them out of his head, but mostly he didn't think at all, except to long for sleep with an intensity that brought tears to his eyes. But that didn't mean much, for these days he wept at the slightest provocation.

543

• • •

HE LOST TRACK OF THE passage of days as well as day and night. His only calendar was his throbbing right hand—three fingers now, and the decimaster sometimes beat him without smashing a finger, so as a method of keeping time it wasn't reliable.

All thought of redeeming himself had long since passed into the shifting shadows. He was still afraid of dying, in a distant, abstract sort of way, but fear didn't really touch him, not now. The reason he held out now was because the gold was at Nadi's house, and he wouldn't send the Hrum there to beat or enslave Hama, Sim, and the little ones. And if that meant he never slept again, except in the snatches the guards allowed him, then so be it. He was becoming accustomed to it, in an odd, light-headed fashion. Sometimes he hummed the passwords as he walked.

WHEN THE DECIMASTER came for his next beating he wept, but he wept most of the time now. His body still felt the blows, but he knew he could endure them, because blows that fell on him weren't falling on Nadi, Hama, and Sim.

At some point Garren came into the cell—or perhaps he'd been there all along, and Kavi hadn't noticed him until he interrupted the decimaster. He came to complain, of course. The man was always complaining.

"You said two days, three at the outside. This is the beginning of the fifth day!"

The decimaster shrugged. "He's tougher than I expected."

"Siatt's delegation doesn't care how tough he is—they're getting impatient." Garren's voice held a threat. "I need that gold. Do whatever you have to."

The decimaster sighed. *Amateurs.* "He'll hardly feel anything you do to him now, Strategus. He's holding on to something, holding hard. I doubt he'll break sooner for pain than for weariness. He's almost done in. Just another day or two."

Kavi wondered if they were sufficiently involved in their discussion that he could catch some sleep. His mind understood that Garren wanted him tortured horribly. He should be panicking, but his body was too tired to care.

"That's what you said two days ago," Garren snapped. "I want results!"

"And I'm telling you, sir, that getting the results

you want takes time. Worn down as he is, a serious injury, even shock alone, could kill him. Then you'd never get your information. Besides . . . here, let me show you."

When the guards flattened Kavi's hand on the floor, he was almost grateful, for that signaled the end of the beating, and after a beating they let him sleep a little longer.

The pain rang through every nerve in his exhausted body, and Kavi screamed. He'd given up on not screaming a long time ago.

When the pain departed and thought returned, he was lying on the floor. That wasn't unusual, but there seemed to be more people in the room now, and several of them were yelling.

Kavi almost decided that he didn't care, that he wanted to sleep now. But the phrase "illegal and degrading" caught his attention, and a spark of curiosity stirred. He opened his eyes.

There were far more men in the room than there had been. Some were guards whose insignia looked odd to Kavi. Then he realized that it wasn't their insignia, but the fact that their tunics weren't the standard undyed flax that most Hrum wore, but a purple so deep it was almost black. A substrategus accompanied them, a bulky man with a thick red beard who looked vaguely familiar to Kavi. Barmael, yes, that was the name. The servants had told Kavi he'd been recalled from Mazad, but what was he doing here? If Kavi remembered correctly, this man was one of the officers who disapproved of the governor.

But it was the three men who stood in the middle of the room shouting at Garren who captured most of Kavi's attention, for they wore the bleached-white robes of Hrum senators. Their language didn't live up to the dignity of the robes.

". . . disgusting, brazen jackass. I could have your command revoked right here, right now, for this alone."

"I still have six weeks," said Garren, and for once his voice was hot with anger. "I'll succeed if your cowardice doesn't stop me."

"Cowardice?" a plump senator sputtered. "You call it cowardice to enforce the law? Though since your idea of courage seems to be torturing a helpless boy, perhaps—"

"And if you do stop me," said Garren, overriding the senator's voice with sheer volume, "it will abrogate your bargain with my father."

An abrupt silence fell.

"Our bargain assumed that your conquest would be accomplished within the law," said the third senator. Or perhaps it was the first speaking again. Kavi was having trouble keeping them straight in his mind, though he was tracking the conversation amazingly well—almost gleefully, for it seemed that Garren was going to get . . . something bad, anyway.

"Our bargain assumed it?" Garren's voice was cool again. "You gentlemen may have assumed it, but our bargain was written down by the senate clerks, and I don't believe that the word 'law' appears anywhere in it."

"But . . ." said one senator.

"But that's . . ." said another.

"Morethos curse him, he's right," said the third. "We forgot to include 'acting within the law' as a condition. Stupid of us, considering who we're dealing with."

Patches of red appeared on Garren's cheekbones.

"That's preposterous!" The plump senator was outraged. "If nothing else, conquests that don't follow those laws fail—fail, or we waste generations putting down rebellion after rebellion. There's a reason for those—"

"The bargain stands as it is written," said Garren. "If you remove me from command before my time is—"

Kavi's eyes were closing, and he didn't bother to open them. He didn't have to see in order to listen.

"But our mandate here—ordered by the emperor himself!—is to defend the honor of the empire! This boy will have sleep, medical aid, and decent treatment, and no more atrocities will be permitted."

"I told you, he's a traitor," said Garren.

"Not without a trial, he's not. In the future, *Strategus*, you will remain within the law, or we'll arrest *you*, and your cursed bargain can go into the nearest privy! Do you understand that?"

"You're very clear, sir," said Garren. Why did he suddenly sound triumphant? Kavi made an effort and opened his eyes again.

"I will complete my conquest, within the allotted time and within the law," Garren went on. "Farsalan law! I'll use this pathetic boy as bait—it doesn't matter if he's a traitor or not! I can declare him hostage for his master and challenge this Sorahb to single combat. If he doesn't answer, according to Farsalan law I can kill my hostage."

Deghans, deghan law, reaching out from the grave. They probably owed him an ill turn, at that. Kavi sighed and let his eyes fall closed.

"Is that really their law? How barbarous," said one of the senators.

"It is barbarous," said Garren. "But unless it directly contradicts imperial law, the law itself decrees that local customs prevail!"

"Executing prisoners is forbidden by imperial law," said a senator.

"But executing a hostage isn't," said Garren. "Not if the agreement that binds the hostage is broken."

"But there was no agree—"

"Be quiet!" a senator snapped. "All of you. This is a legal quibble, and I'm not a lawyer. The committee will allow you to issue your challenge, Strategus, but if Sorahb doesn't show up, you won't be allowed to kill this man. You're not governor yet."

"You have no say in the matter," said Garren. "Local laws rule this. But if you allow me to issue the challenge, the question won't arise. I've fought Sorahb long enough to know that he holds to the old deghans' code. If I challenge him, with his follower's life for the stake, he'll come. And when he dies, Farsalan resistance will die with him. My spies tell me that their loyalty, their trust in Sorahb, is the only thing that gives these people the will to fight."

Which was probably true, but there was no Sorahb. The confidence in Garren's voice told Kavi he was plotting something, but what was it? A nonexistent man wouldn't be answering any challenges, so . . . did he mean Jiaan? Did Garren think that Jiaan would accept his challenge? To save Kavi?

Kavi began to laugh. He laughed while the senators and Garren departed, while the guards dragged his pallet and blankets back into the cell and then left, locking the door behind them.

He was still snickering as he crawled toward his bed, though his laughter now verged on tears, and he had forgotten what was so funny.

The thin straw pallet, with its rough blanket and battered pillow, looked like paradise.

CHAPTER TWENTY

Soraya

"AHRIMAN CURSE HIM," Jiaan grumbled, gazing out over the old flags-and-lances field. Garren had set up a platform in the center, where the senate committee sat, overlooking the circle marked on the ground below. "If he'd held the challenge in the city square, like he said he was going to, I could have had an archer on every rooftop and in every window! Why change the location at the last minute?"

"Presumably," said Soraya, "to avoid having to deal with archers at every rooftop and window."

The view from the packed stands was excellent. She and Jiaan perched about halfway up, right beside the railing that kept the audience from falling from the raised seats into the entrance that cut between them. And the stands were packed, despite the wind whipping the banners and the low clouds that promised a storm. Judging by the thunder's distant rumble, this might be the first of the wild spring thunderstorms, instead of the last of the slow winter rains. Either way they were going to get wet, but that hadn't stopped most of the population of Setesafon from coming here.

It was clear that Garren wanted lots of witnesses for whatever it was he had planned, but Soraya wasn't sure that gathering this huge mob was wise. Sorahb had become not only the symbol but the soul of Farsalan resistance. Here in Setesafon, where Garren's power was greatest, the growing disaffection was less obvious than it was in the rest of Farsala—but it was there.

At least the mammoth crowd gave Jiaan plenty of cover for his archers. Unfortunately, they were too far from the center of the field to do any good. Past the stands, past the guards who manned the barrier at the foot of the stands to keep people from coming any closer, there was no cover at all.

The last time Soraya had sat in these stands, she'd been seated in the gahn's partitioned section, watching her father compete. It wasn't the last time she had seen him, by a number of days, but he had been magnificent then, mounted on Rakesh and wreaking havoc among his opponents, even with a wooden practice sword and blunted lance. He'd been happy . . . Tears rose in her eyes, but they felt better than the others she'd shed—as if they held more love than bitterness. Was she finally beginning to heal? This seemed an odd place for it, dressed as a shopgirl, crammed in among craftsmen and townsfolk.

At least the noisy conversations around them assured their privacy. A handful of people looked at Fasal as he rode through the entrance and stopped beside Jiaan, but as far as Soraya could tell no one even tried to listen.

"The archers are scattered through the crowd, all around the field, just as you ordered," Fasal told his commander, in a tone that seemed, to Soraya's ears, to lack the proper respect. "For all the good they'll do."

Definitely lacking respect—but the authority in Jiaan's voice made up for it. "They probably won't be needed—that's what I'm counting on. But even if Garren goes through with it, I'm not letting you accept the challenge. We've been over this before."

In fact, they'd been arguing about it ever since Fasal brought in the archers late yesterday afternoon. Garren had given Sorahb seven days to arrive for the challenge, which seemed almost reasonable until you realized that word of the challenge had to reach Sorahb first. As Nadi had put it, "If the champion's much further off than Mazad, Garren doesn't have a thing to worry about."

It was mostly her concern, Soraya thought, that had induced Jiaan to send for his archers. He made no secret of his own belief that Garren was bluffing about killing his prisoner. Soraya had to admit that it was against Hrum law, it would alienate the population he hoped to rule, and it would gain him nothing at all. It would be stupid, and Garren had never been stupid. Still, Jiaan had managed to get word to his forces in time. And Fasal, against Jiaan's express order, had come with them, hoping to take up the challenge.

"But if I win," he said, as he had so often since yesterday, "it will end this war—right here, right now, No final battle for Mazad. The Hrum gone, the young gahn returned. Farsala would be as it was before!"

Privately, Soraya doubted that Farsala could ever be the same—but perhaps that was because she could never go back to being the girl she'd been. Did she regret that?

"What makes you think he won't cheat?" Jiaan asked, as he'd already asked a dozen times. "Just as he cheated the last time. Look at the guards around that circle."

He had a point. The circle where the combat would take place was surrounded by Hrum soldiers, half of them carrying bows and quivers. She remembered the Farsalan soldier describing her father's death, cut down by Hrum archers after he had challenged Garren to single combat.

. . . shot full of arrows like—um, it was quick, girl. Lady. As quick as death in battle ever can be . . .

Part of her still flinched at the memory, and that same part of her understood Fasal. She *wanted* to see a champion take up Farsala's cause, to see Garren fall, as he should have fallen almost a year ago under her father's blade!

So spoke her heart, but her brain said otherwise.

556

"Jiaan's right," she said, interrupting Fasal's protest. "If you showed any sign of winning, Garren would order your death. He's not a deghan. And I think . . . I think he has more at stake here than his own life."

"Then we should bargain instead," said Fasal. "Tell him that if he kills our man we'll kill our Hrum prisoners. We're out of food for them anyway, and the Suud have already shared more than they can afford."

"I've told you before," said Jiaan, "we have to be better than they are! To kill more than five hundred prisoners because he killed one would— "

"I'm not saying we kill them," Fasal interrupted in turn. "Just tell Garren we're going to."

"The problem with that," Soraya intervened hastily as Jiaan's face darkened, "is what do you do if Garren doesn't believe you? What if he refuses to bargain, demands combat, and kills Kavi when 'Sorahb' doesn't show up?"

"He might do that," Fasal admitted. "But would the committee allow it? I thought they were supposed to keep him from doing things like that."

Soraya fell silent. In truth she didn't know how this strange committee would react. They d certainly responded quickly to the "anonymous" note Jiaan had sent Tactimian Patrius.

It was Hama who'd heard rumors that the governor was torturing a Farsalan prisoner, and that even the Hrum who guarded him were angry and upset about it. She hadn't been able to confirm it, or learn any details, but she'd still come home in tears, full of rash, vague plans for a jailbreak.

It was Jiaan who came up with the idea of sending a letter to Patrius, detailing the rumors, which he might not have heard, since he, along with most of Garren's opponents within his own forces, had been exiled to the old camp.

Exiled or not, they still had some power. Garren's proclamation of challenge had been read in the markets the next morning, and other rumors began circulating soon after that. Some were as wild as Garren threatening to imprison the whole committee and rebel against the emperor, or the committee threatening to have Garren imprisoned, or executed, or . . . But all the rumors claimed that senators had broken into one of the cells beneath the armory and found . . . the rumors of what they'd found had started at appalling, and soon grew so improbable that even Hama and Sim stopped listening to them.

They promptly became a lot more cheerful, for if those rumors were false, then the previous ones had probably been false as well.

Jiaan had doubted the whole thing. As he told Soraya privately, "If they'd put any pressure on that bastard, we'd have had Hrum soldiers breaking down the door days ago. And we haven't, so you can be pretty sure they aren't torturing anyone. On the other hand, that doesn't guarantee they won't start . . . or worse yet, come up with a decent bribe."

Shortly after that conversation, he had arranged for the gold to be moved out of Nadi's house and into the keeping of a member of the resistance the peddler didn't know. Soraya considered that a sensible precaution. She didn't share Jiaan's estimation of the peddler's cowardice, but her father had once told her that given enough time anyone could be broken.

For the first time in her life, Soraya wondered how her father knew that. She shivered, and thunder rumbled in the distance. Was she influencing that storm? She closed down her shilshadu sensing, firmly, as Maok had taught her. Rain wouldn't stop Garren, not today. And neither . . .

"I don't think the committee will stop him," said Soraya slowly. "At least, I don't think we can count on it. Garren was prepared to leave Hrum prisoners in our hands in order to get the Kadeshi troops he needed to win, and the committee didn't stop him. I think there's more at stake for the committee than we know about too."

"Then you should let me answer the challenge," Fasal argued. His voice was calm, but his mare snorted as his hand tightened on the reins. "If I win, the committee has to honor the terms Garren offered. They've endorsed them in the emperor's name!"

That was true. In fact, all ten members of the committee were seated on the dais, with all the officers of the Hrum army who were posted to Setesafon sitting behind them. Even Garren's enemies were there. Soraya saw Patrius, his face stiff with worry, sitting behind Substrategus Barmael, whose red-bearded face showed nothing at all. But Soraya had served in the Hrum camp with the substrategus, with many of the officers seated on the dais, and she knew that Barmael's controlled expression concealed a generous heart.

The committee's faces were harder to read,

since she didn't know them at all, but she thought they looked grim. Almost as if . . . no, surely they wouldn't permit Garren to kill a helpless prisoner, even if "Sorahb" failed to show up. It was against their law, just as Jiaan had said, and Soraya knew even better than he did that the Hrum were a people of law. The odds in Setesafon's marketplace had been running about even on whether the committee would allow the execution if Sorahb didn't arrive, but Soraya had lived among the Hrum and she knew better.

The odds on whether Sorahb would take up the challenge had fluctuated wildly, almost as if the townsfolk were as divided between heart and mind as she was. They knew he might not come. He could be too far from the city to hear Garren's message before it was over, for as everyone knew, he ranged over the entire country. A few people were even bold enough to doubt Sorahb's existence, pointing out that no one they knew had ever seen him, but they were universally shouted down. In their hearts, Soraya knew, everyone wanted the champion to come—just as she did, and she knew "Sorahb Storm-bringer" was a myth.

Some of the people in the chattering crowd

might have come in the low hope of seeing blood-shed, but most of them had come here hoping to set eyes on the legend himself. With any luck both expectations would be thwarted, Soraya thought firmly. If Garren really meant to kill his prisoner, and the committee allowed it, there was no—

Garren appeared abruptly, riding through a gate at the other side of the field. Over a soldier's tunic and armor he wore the deep scarlet robe of a Hrum governor, and the guards around him wore the same color—a color to which, according to marketplace gossip, Garren was not entitled until his conquest was complete.

A mutter of dissent, like distant thunder, greeted his appearance.

A clap of not-so-distant thunder echoed it. The wind was picking up, and Soraya wondered how long Garren intended to wait for the champi-on to appear. If he waited very long, they were going to get drenched. Then the governor's guards led out their prisoner, and the crowd fell silent.

He was on foot, his ankles linked with a short rope, his hands bound in front of him. Two guards held his arms, but even in the clumsy hobbles he walked without their support. That was probably good, Soraya thought numbly, but nothing could belie the dark, almost black bruises that marred his face, or his swollen lips and eyelids. Even across the width of the field, Soraya could see that four fingers on his right hand were also dark with bruising and swollen like sausages.

She shut her eyes, fighting down a surge of nausea. She hadn't been as certain as Jiaan, but she hadn't expected this.

The crowd erupted in a storm of threats, hisses, and jeers. If Garren had ever had any hope that Setesafon might accept his rule, it was now gone. But if the committee had allowed this . . .

"Garren's going to kill him," Jiaan whispered. His face was white. "I thought . . . I didn't think . . . Fasal, get word to the archers—everyone is to make their way upwind of the dais. If this breeze gets stronger as the storm moves in, with enough loft maybe we can make the range."

"You can't," said Fasal.

"We might."

Garren dismounted and climbed the steps to the dais. Kavi, on foot, was still crossing the field. He scanned the crowd intently, as if searching for someone—for rescue? But Fasal was right. There would be no rescue.

"You can't make that range, and you know it," the young deghan said now.

Kavi had reached the ground before the dais.

"I am here today to challenge the rebel Sorahb for this man's life, though by our law he is a traitor to the Iron Empire—" The guards who held Kavi tore his right sleeve down from his arm, revealing the tattoo that almost everyone now knew marked a Hrum spy. The stitches of his sleeve, Soraya realized, must have been weakened so Garren could make his gesture. She saw a flash of cynical amusement cross the peddler's battered face, and knew that he had just realized the same thing. Her heart wept for him.

"A traitor to the empire," Garren repeated, "and thus, by our laws, condemned to death."

"That's his excuse," said Jiaan grimly. "That's how he's getting it past the committee. Fasal, go now! Tell the archers to move!"

"It's too late," said Fasal. "Garren's not waiting."

Thunder cracked, but Soraya no longer cared whether she was influencing the storm.

"But in my mercy, I will give this man's master

a chance to save him," Garren shouted over the rising wind. The guards dragged Kavi up onto the platform—if he was to die, everyone would get the clearest possible view. "A chance to fight for Farsala, as he claims to do—while in reality he hides in the shadows and lets others take his risks."

"Have you got any better ideas?" Jiaan snapped.

"So, if he cares for this country as he claims, let Sorahb come forth!" Garren roared. "If he wins, he wins your independence—by the sworn word of the senate and the emperor. If he is willing to fight for you, let him come forth now!"

"Yes," said Fasal, "I have an idea. If nothing else, it will give you time to get the archers into position." And he kicked his mare into motion, onto the field.

Jiaan dived half way out of the stands reaching for his reins, and missed. "Kanarang take the idiot. Now Garren's got two of my people for hostages!" He squirmed though the railing, half leaping, half falling to the ground, and rushed off to find his archers.

Soraya thought of following, but even though her heart pounded with the need for action, there was nothing she could do. Nothing but stand and watch as Fasal cantered his mare across the field and pulled her to a snorting stop before the circle. She shouldn't have been able to hear Fasal, but the crowd had fallen silent as they too strained to hear. The only sound was the banners snapping in the breeze, not loud enough to drown Fasal's clear voice.

"I accept your challenge, for Farsala and for this man's life."

"You're Sorahb?" Garren asked. He looked completely taken aback—and in that moment Soraya knew that he himself had not believed in Sorahb's existence. His spies, or the men who studied their reports, must have reached the correct conclusion. When Garren had realized that the Kadeshi troops were lost to him, he put together this whole farce—not as an excuse to kill Kavi, but to show the people of Setesafon, of all Farsala, that their champion didn't exist. Or that if he did, he wouldn't risk himself to save one of them.

Garren had never been stupid, but this maneuver was brilliant! He could have taken the heart out of the resistance, all over Farsala, just

when he most needed them to fail! Now...
Soraya suppressed a giggle. Now his whole plan
was thwarted, because a foolish deghan youth
stood before him, shrugged his shoulders, and
said, "Yes. I'm Sorahb."

He didn't sound very convincing. Soraya
knew that Fasal was willing to claim the name
only because he, too knew the truth—that everyone who had fought the Hrum was Sorahb. He
had as much right to that identity as anyone.

The crowd didn't know that. Their roar of
approval, of adulation, made the stands shake
and had Soraya clapping her hands over her ears.
The expression on Garren's face was magnificent, but even he didn't look as dumbfounded as
the peddler—who also knew that there was no
Sorahb—as he stared at the total stranger who
had just ridden up and offered to fight for his life.
A *deghan* stranger!

Soraya's laughter was lost in the crowd's
cheers, but the burst of thunder that echoed it
was not.

Garren looked up at the gathering clouds, his
expression dark with furious thought. He'd had
no objection to waiting in the rain to prove to

Farsala that their champion . . . wasn't. Now his plans were changing. Now there was only one way to kill the myth.

He pulled off his robe and tossed it into the hands of one of his guards. Because he'd had to make it look as if he expected to fight, he had arrived wearing his sword and the steel breast-plate of an officer. As Soraya watched, one of his guards brought forth his helmet, and Garren buckled it on.

Fasal wore a Farsalan deghan's armor of padded silk studded with steel rings. Not as heavy as the Hrum's, but not as strong, either; the deghans had relied on their horses' agility to carry them out of harm's way—an advantage Fasal wouldn't have today. But surely all that steel would slow a man on foot, as well?

Since Jiaan wasn't there to ask, Soraya looked to the peddler, hoping to read something about Fasal's chances in his face. But he was still gaping at "Sorahb" in astonishment. Had he ever even seen Fasal before? Soraya thought not. When they had first encountered the peddler, Fasal had been left behind with her father's command, and after the battle at the Sendar Wall, Fasal had been with the new Farsalan army—which the peddler had done his best to avoid, because he was avoiding Jiaan. He might have met Fasal when he was spying on her father's army for the Hrum, but only in passing— one of the high commander's many young aides. Judging by the expression on his bruised face, if he'd ever seen Fasal in his life, he didn't remember it. To him it must have seemed as if a ghost had suddenly come to life: a legend taken on flesh and breath, and come to save him.

Listening to the excited babble of the crowd around her, Soraya knew that it didn't hurt that Fasal was young and handsome—the picture of a true deghan as he sprang down from the saddle and went to stand outside the circle, facing Garren.

One of the senators was speaking, probably explaining the rules, though no one in the audience could hear him. When he finished, Fasal drew his sword, saluted his opponent, and stepped into the circle. Garren, his expression cool and controlled, did the same. For the first time, Soraya wondered if the governor was any good with a sword.

He was. He stalked Fasal around the circle with the catlike stride of a swordsman. His blade flirted with Fasal's, the ringing taps barely audible over the murmur of voices.

Then Garren saw an opening—Soraya never knew what it was—and leaped forward, his sword flashing in. Fasal's sword clashed against it; then he disengaged in a slithering rasp of steel on steel. He sprang back, balanced and ready, and Garren stalked after him once more. Soraya found she'd pressed one hand over her breast— a girlish, poetical gesture she had always considered ridiculous, until her heart tried to beat its way out of her chest.

The massed voice of the crowd took on a tinge of disappointment—why did Sorahb keep backing away? Was he afraid to exchange blows with the governor?

But Soraya, growing up in her father's household, had seen many practice combats—fights very like the duel she watched now, except that they used wooden practice swords. Her father's voice, coaching countless young swordsmen, echoed in her memory.

If your opponent is older than you, he's probably more experienced—so forget about heroics! He's better than you are! Don't rush in swinging like a fool. Let him spend his strength attacking while you just parry. Use some of that cursed energy of yours to outlast him. Then, when he's exhausted, you might stand a chance.

For a moment it was as if her father stood beside the circle, prompting his young protégé. Soraya's throat tightened and her vision blurred. And in that moment, thick, cold drops began to fall. She was influencing the storm, curse it! She hadn't time for this!

She wiped her eyes impatiently, but another scatter of raindrops pelted down. Her tears might have prompted the rain to start, but once started it wasn't going to stop. And a Hrum strategus, who must have fought in many campaigns, would have far more experience fighting on foot in the mud than Fasal would.

Garren leaped forward again, and swords clashed. It looked as if Fasal barely disengaged his blade in time, but when he stepped back he was still poised, still on guard.

Never taking her eyes from the fight—no full trance today—Soraya let her shilshadu drift into the storm until she sensed the swirling movements of the high clouds as clearly as she felt the cold wind in her hair. Lightning cracked nearby—too

571

near, and Soraya flinched, but the fighters didn't. She drew courage from that, easing her will into the currents of the wind, twisting them aside, creating an open space in the tumult of the storm.

With the part of her spirit that was the storm, she felt the great release of rain pouring over the rest of the city, darkening the stones in the empty streets. But here, over the flags-and-lances field, only a few drops fell.

Garren must have understood Fasal's strategy, for he pressed the youth harder, their swords ringing and ringing again. Once his attack pushed Fasal out of the circle, and the guards descended on both of them, knocking up their blades, pulling them apart.

So one of the rules was that the fight wasn't allowed to leave the circle. When it did, Soraya saw now, the guards escorted both combatants to the opposite sides of the ring and allowed them to begin again. That was to Garren's advantage, for it let him catch his breath as they returned to their places—and although it was hard to tell at this distance, he seemed to be tiring. Even the audience had realized that despite the fury of Garren's attack, he had yet to break through Fasal's guard.

This surprised them, for watching them both it was clear that Garren was the better swordsman.

Of course they didn't know, as Soraya did, that Fasal had spent most of the last year teaching men to fight with swords. He might not have gained much skill on the attack, but he could clearly parry with the best of them, and his stamina had to be phenomenal.

Garren had spent the last year sitting in meetings and behind a desk.

For the first time, hope that Fasal might win surged in Soraya's heart—and as it did, the lightning crashed. It struck in the palace gardens, just the other side of the stands, and people in the nearby sections jumped to their feet and hurried down, seeking lower seats or standing behind the guarded barrier.

Lightning blazed through Soraya's nerves—not the fire she'd expected, but as if the burning light of the sun had been made solid.

The old terror, the desire to release the storm, to hide from the lightning, seized her—but if she let go, the ruin would fall here, too, and Fasal was beginning to maneuver against his experienced opponent.

He too realized that Garren had left the circle deliberately, to gain a chance to breathe. Now Fasal danced around the Hrum officer, still defending, but keeping both of them inside the circle, giving Garren no chance to break out and gain another respite. This was trickier than parrying as Garren pushed him, and the audience cheered.

Soraya could almost hear her father's steady voice: *Wait. Wait for it.* She wondered if Fasal could hear it too, but that hardly mattered. What mattered was the arc of her will, holding the pouring rain off the field, refusing Garren that advantage.

He was tiring now, his stride not as graceful, as cat-certain, as before. But when he came to his decision, he showed no sign of it, suddenly leaping to a full attack, his sword surging forward again and again.

Fasal met the attack with parry after parry. His face gleamed with sweat, but it wore an odd, exalted peace, as if he too felt his commander's presence.

This, Soraya realized, was the duel that should have been fought at the Sendar Wall—only this time Farsala would win!

Another lightning bolt was born of her triumph, and this time it crashed within the flags-and-lances ground. People fled the nearby stands, but Soraya didn't care. The clouds pressed in on her will, trying to complete the part of their pattern that her will denied them—and Fasal was launching his attack.

He wasn't as good a swordsman, but he was young, and Garren was visibly tiring. Now it was Garren who pulled back, parrying Fasal's strokes. He tried to break out of the circle, but Fasal kept turning him back toward the center. Then Garren shouted something and lowered his sword.

Soraya couldn't hear what he said, but Fasal stepped back, his blade still lifted—his gaze flying to the platform where Kavi no longer stood but crouched on his hands and knees. One of Garren's guards had placed a foot on the rope that bound his ankles, and Soraya saw another step forward onto the rope between his wrists, pinning him down. Yet another guard drew his sword.

"No!" Soraya's cry was lost in the great shout that rose from the stands. Lightning crashed in half a dozen places at once.

The thunder swallowed all sound, almost drowning thought as well. But in that instant, when the storm's violence held everyone frozen, Soraya suddenly realized that Kavi didn't deserve a traitor's death, not from anyone. Yes, he'd betrayed the deghans, and the Hrum in turn, but he'd been true to Farsala from beginning to end. Garren was cheat—

Her gaze flew back to the governor just in time. Everyone else was watching the threatened execution, the ruse, up on the dais. Soraya thought she was the only one who saw Garren reach down, grab a handful of sand, and cast it into Fasal's face.

Fasal had started toward the dais, shouting a protest, even as the senators and the Hrum officers surged to their feet.

He jerked back when the sand struck him, brushing frantically at his eyes, blocking wildly with his sword. It was sheer luck his blade met Garren's.

The clash of steel drew all eyes back to the circle, and those on the dais—including, Soraya was relieved to see, the executioner—turned to watch the fight once more.

She had lost all control of the storm. Rain was falling, faster and faster, but the storm had already spent most of its strength, and the rain wasn't thick enough to conceal the two fighters as Fasal leaped back again, still wiping furiously at his eyes.

Garren's sword swung in, under his guard, slicing through the flesh above one knee, and Fasal cried out and fell.

Soraya watched in numb horror as Garren stepped forward and raised his sword, sweeping it down in a killing strike. But this was no subtle thrust that blurred, streaming eyes might miss. Fasal's sword swung up to block the stroke—and Garren's blade shattered.

Somehow, even through the roar of the crowd, she heard the peddler's shout of triumph. This was the first time a Hrum sword had broken, as so many Farsalan blades had broken at the Sendar Wall, where her father . . .

Garren will cheat, Jiaan's voice whispered in her mind.

Fasal staggered to his feet. Some fragment of Garren's blade must have nicked him as it flew past; blood streamed from a cut on his jaw, and still more blood darkened the knee of his britches and ran down his boot. Soraya was amazed he could stand, that he could walk at all, as he limped forward.

Garren didn't back away. He stood, head high, the image of a governor, an officer.

"He's going to die well," a woman murmured.

Then Garren lifted one hand and brought it slashing down, and a dozen arrows leaped from the bows of his guards and buried themselves in Fasal's body.

Garren will cheat. Just as he cheated the last time.

The rest of the crowd screamed. Soraya stood frozen, as Fasal stumbled to his knees, then fell and died. As her father had died.

It wasn't the Hrum who killed my father.

Some of the townsfolk ran, fleeing the stadium, fleeing the deaths. But after the first moment of shock, most of the crowd surged down from the stands, tumbling onto the field like a human avalanche. Garren had murdered their champion— they would make him pay. They rushed forward, pushing over the barriers, overwhelming the shocked Hrum guards—who in truth weren't fighting very hard. A flight of arrows arced from the stands, riding the wind, but the storm was all but spent, and they fell short.

It wasn't Kavi's betrayal that killed my father.

The senators, the Hrum officers, had drawn

their weapons. Some of the senators' guards were fighting with the governor's, trying to break into the circle where Garren stood, sword raised, beside Fasal's body. But most of them, seeing the mob streaming toward the dais, were already forming a perimeter around the senators. Soon all of them would be swept up in that defense, and Garren would escape. Garren . . .

That bastard killed my father!

Soraya opened her shilshadu and launched her spirit into the storm. Most of its power was spent, its rain fallen, its twisting winds unraveled, but she found one spinning knot of energy and seized it with her mind and will. It wasn't strong enough on its own, so she fed it her anger, her hatred, her grief—not only for her father, but for Fasal, for all the damage this Arzhang-possessed man had done. And in the spinning vortex of her fury, lightning was born.

She felt it, distantly, streaming through the nerves of her body, but Soraya was now almost wholly the storm, and she no longer cared if it destroyed her, as long as it destroyed her enemy, as well. She hurtled power earthward, straight at the man whose actions had given so much strength to the energy that formed it. She felt it strike the earth, the blow ringing through her body. When the lightning dissipated, it took her consciousness with it.

SORAYA WAS LYING on the ground, wet sand and grass under her face and hands, rain striking her body. When she opened her eyes, still not thinking, she saw nothing but a pair of muddy boots, and more boots beyond them, running.

"You all right, lass?" a man's voice asked. A warm hand tightened on her shoulder. "I saw you go down, and that's no good thing in a mob like this."

Soraya lifted her head. She was no longer in the stands, but lying on the flags-and-lances field, almost halfway to the dais. She had no idea how she'd gotten there.

"I don't . . . I . . ."

Her whole body tingled and throbbed, as if it held an echo of the lightning. She also felt bruised, as if she'd been stepped on. She couldn't see the dais from where she lay.

"What's happening? Is Garren . . . ? the governor . . . ?"

"Oh, he's dead." The savage satisfaction in the man's voice contrasted with the gentle hands that helped her sit upright. "That lightning bolt near blew him apart. Some are saying Azura himself did it, but some say it was Sorahb Storm-bringer's last act on his way to greet the god. Either way, we've just seen a true miracle—not like the ones the temple used to fake. More than half the crowd took off like rabbits. Can't say I blame them—it's a terrifying thing, lightning. Still, that's no excuse to be knocking a girl down and trampling on her. You want me to take you out of this, lass?"

"No," said Soraya, pulling herself to her feet. "Get me closer."

The man looked askance at her, but he wanted to get closer too. At first he almost had to carry her along, but by the time they reached the edge of the crowd around the dais she was walking on her own, strongly enough that he released her shoulder and made no protest when she left him and squirmed into the seething mass of bodies.

Garren's guards had seized Kavi. He was no longer on the platform but down in the circle, pinned once more on his hands and knees. He was talking to the guards around him, intense, persuasive. But they were looking at the mob that surrounded them, surrounded both the circle and the platform where the Hrum officers stood with swords drawn to protect the senate committee.

Not that swords would do much good against the bows that were now visible scattered throughout the crowd. The lightning strike had thinned the mob considerably, and the people who remained were the ones who meant to fight. All of Jiaan's archers were now within range. If the Hrum made one wrong move, Fasal's death would be avenged in the blood of every Hrum present today. But that thought, which once would have pleased her, only made Soraya shudder. She wiggled between two stocky men and caught a glimpse of Garren's charred, ruptured body. *Revenge enough.*

Her searching gaze found Jiaan's hard, white face, and she understood why he'd withheld the order to fire. But what now? The attitude of the Hrum guards and officers made it clear that if Hrum blood washed away Sorahb's, plenty of Farsalan blood would join it—but the crowd, equally clearly, wanted revenge on everyone involved in Garren's treachery.

One of Garren's guardsmen looked at the

mob's determined faces and reached the same conclusion she had. "The governor's last orders!" he cried defiantly. The words would have been meaningless if he hadn't stepped toward Kavi and drawn his sword.

Kavi stopped arguing and struggled to pull the ropes that held him from under the boots of the Hrum guards, but he wasn't going to succeed, and everyone could see it. The guard's sword rose above Kavi's bare neck. The unarmed crowd surged forward and then back, driven off by Hrum swords. If Kavi fell, they would probably overwhelm the guard. But Kavi would be dead, others would die too, and Soraya didn't want more blood, not today. But she had used up all her will and all her weapons—she felt a flash of pure despair.

"Stop!" The voice ringing over the field spoke Faran with an accent, just as it spoke Hrum, but it was a voice trained to command armies in the deafening chaos of battle, and for a moment everyone stopped.

That was all Substrategus Barmael needed to jump from the dais and push his way into the circle, over to Kavi—where he grabbed the would-be executioner's wrist and took the sword away from him. "Just stop, everyone, and let us think for a moment."

Kavi's whole body sagged with relief, almost falling to the ground. The crowd eased back, but only a bit. Barmael turned, not to them, but to the dais, to the senators who perched there.

"This is futile and you know it," he said. "We cannot win."

"Almost a centri of Hrum soldiers against a mob? I beg to differ, sir," said one of the senators.

The mob growled. It should have sounded silly, but it made the hair on the back of Soraya's neck stir.

"If you think that," said Barmael, "it proves you've never fought them. But even if we win this fight, in this field, right now, what after that? For we have already lost the war."

Half a dozen Hrum voices cried out in protest, but Barmael ignored them. "Yes, the strategus defeated this land's army—although one city still holds against him, and I don't think it will fall within the month we have left. But even if Mazad does fall, I ask again, what after that? Strategus Garren has ruled so wrongly that half this land seethes with rebellion. And the rest will join them once this day's tale is told! How many troops will it take to subdue Farsala now?"

Silence fell as the crowd awaited the committee's answer. The senators said nothing. The soft creak of pulled bows relaxing lent emphasis to Barmael's next words.

"We probably couldn't win free of this field with our lives, but even if we could, there is no point in it."

"No mob dictates to the Iron Empire!" said one senator. But several faces on the platform had become thoughtful, and Soraya remembered that the committee had its own agenda.

"This isn't a mob," said Barmael. "This is the Farsalan army. The new Farsalan army that's been fighting us, and mostly winning, since the battle at the Sendar Wall. We will not subdue this land in a month—I don't care how many troops we bring in. It would take years to conquer Farsala, and by the time we finished . . . even if we won, our victory would cost far more than we'd gain."

The Hrum's own law, that conquest must take place within one year, was designed to prevent just that kind of war. The senators were silent.

"Farsala has won this war," Barmael told them flatly. "It's not a matter of us granting their independence—they've *taken* it. We can acknowledge that truth and survive this day. Or we can die, knowing that whoever follows us will be forced to acknowledge it in the future."

The mob rumbled agreement, as fierce as the thunder of the storm now passing into the distance. Even the most arrogant Hrum officers weren't completely immune to the lure of survival, Soraya noted gratefully.

"But with whom would we negotiate?" another senator asked. "If their commander is dead . . . Was that boy really Sorahb? He seemed very young."

Barmael shrugged. "I don't know, but Tactimian Patrius might. Sorahb's army held him prisoner for a time. Patrius"—he gestured to Fasal's limp body—"is this Sorahb?"

Tactimian Patrius came slowly toward the front of the dais. His eyes weren't on Fasal but searching the crowd. Only someone who knew what the tactimian was looking for could have seen the swift, negative shake of Jiaan's head.

Jiaan's gaze went to Kavi, who was still on his

knees, for his guards had just stepped back. The peddler was already shaking his head, emphatically. Kavi turned to Soraya, the question in his eyes: *Do you want it?*

To be Sorahb herself? Surely she had the least right to that title . . . or did she? She too had spied and fought and risked herself. But then, so had many Farsalans. Some of them . . . She looked at Fasal's body, crumpled in the grass. Some of them had died for it.

There was a time when she'd have thought that as a deghass she had not only the right, but a duty to take that job—that deghan blood must rule. She had learned better, Azura be praised— there was nothing in the world she wanted less. She looked at Patrius and shook her head.

He made no sign of acknowledgment, jumping down from the platform and making his way to where Barmael stood, not far from the place Fasal had fallen.

"I only saw Sorahb a few times," he told Barmael. "And only at a distance, for his identity was kept secret."

It seemed to Soraya that the whole crowd held their breath as he looked down into Fasal's still

587

face. "Yes, this is Sorahb. And I believe your prisoner here, who worked closely with him, can confirm that."

"Yes," said Kavi instantly. "He was."

A sigh of awe and grief whispered around Soraya. In Kavi's voice she heard an echo of that grief—as well as considerable relief at having ducked the title himself. Odd that when the time had come to name Sorahb, Jiaan had looked to him.

"With whom can we negotiate?" the senator asked again. "The old ruler's heir is a child, and most of the lords of this land are dead."

"Ah . . . I have a suggestion about that." Kavi struggled, still bound, to his feet. "You could have every city, every town, even the small villages that want to, each send a representative to speak for them. Like the old gahn's Council of Twelve Houses, only bigger. I know that's what Sorahb intended."

Soraya suppressed a hysterical desire to laugh. Fasal would have been appalled at that idea. But even though he'd go to his pyre under Sorahb's name—a few of the bolder townswomen had already pushed through the circle of guards to tidy his body, reverently straightening the bent limbs — he had only given the legend flesh. Everyone who had fought for Farsala had given it heart.

Some of the senators grumbled when the majority appointed Barmael to lead the army. It seemed that Substrategus Barmael was the one who had written to the emperor about Garren's misrule, and even though the committee had been sent to check that rule, they were mostly ex-strategi themselves, and they didn't like promoting a man who had informed against his own commander. But Soraya had little doubt how it would end, especially when Barmael said that it didn't matter to him who was appointed interim governor, as long as the land was handed over to Farsala's new rulers as soon as possible. It wasn't so much that the speech clearly marked Barmael as the best man for the job, it was the cheer that burst from the crowd when he made it.

Now that politics had suppressed their martial spirit, the idea of dying at the hands of the Farsalan mob clearly didn't appeal to the senators. Somehow, in all the chaos, as the townsfolk of Setesafon carried off Fasal's body and Garren's guardsmen took his away as well, Farsala's freedom declared itself, without anyone making a fancy speech or even a decision. That was appropriate, Soraya thought, staring after the men who carried Garren's shattered body. Farsala's freedom had been decided by every Farsalan who had fought for it.

She grieved for Fasal's death. She hadn't known him well, but she recognized a deghan's heart—once, she had shared it.

She didn't grieve for Garren at all, though she was sorry she'd used magic to kill him. The rain had stopped, but it was still cold enough to make her shiver in her damp clothes, for the sun hadn't yet returned. Yes, she was sorry she'd used magic— magic should be given to life, not death. Yet it had been the only weapon, the only tool within her grasp. Maok had once told her that magic was only a tool; it was the use that made it good or bad. Soraya understood that now.

However she had done it, she'd accomplished what Fasal set out to do—Kavi would live, Garren was dead, and Farsala was free. And, Soraya suddenly realized, she too was free, for the first time in her life, to choose a future that she wanted.

CHAPTER TWENTY-ONE

JIAAN

HAVE YOU HEARD what they're wanting now?" Kavi demanded, bursting through the flap of Jiaan's tent, where the lady Soraya had already found him.

The peddler's face was flushed with indignation. His bruises had long since faded, but the memory of how he'd come by them still had the power to make Jiaan flinch.

After Fasal's death, after Kavi had been freed and the attention of the Hrum had turned elsewhere, he'd walked stiffly up to Jiaan. "Today, salute, mile, serve, deep. And I am *never* doing that again."

Sometimes treason was easier than it should b̶
The sudden realization of his own betrayal had
stricken Jiaan speechless, and his newfound
sense of guilt had enabled him to work with the
peddler over the past weeks, as the new Farsalan
government took shape. He hadn't forgiven the
man, at least not as completely as Soraya seemed
to have done, but he knew that the peddler . . .
that Kavi had paid a high price for his actions. As
Jiaan watched him speaking out in support of
this town or that village, he also saw that Kavi
had earned the loyalty of the people who'd spied
for him. So even if Jiaan couldn't completely forgive, he'd abandoned revenge. In truth he was
glad to see it go.

It was still unusual for the peddler to burst
into his tent.

Shortly after the members of Farsala's new
governing council started arriving, they'd decided
to move their gathering out of the city, for the
country folk claimed that meeting in the city—any
city—gave the townsfolk an unfair advantage.

The Hrum senators, as a gesture of goodwill,
had provided them with Hrum army tents. Jiaan,
who was representing the armed Farsalan rebels,

had been living in one for some time. He was beginning to get used to it.

"What who wants now?" Soraya asked calmly. Somewhat to Jiaan's surprise, she had come to tell him good-bye. But the peddler . . . Kavi was so excited, he didn't even notice the pack at her feet.

"The Ruling Council, or the Governing Council, or whatever the idiots finally decide to call themselves. They can't even agree on a name! But they're agreeing that they want me to run them. Every last one of them voted in favor! I think it's the first time they've agreed on anything unanimously since they first met. Even Governor Siddas agreed, and he's a man I can usually count on for sense!"

Mazad's council had appointed Siddas as the city's temporary governor. The title might change, but Jiaan had no doubt that Siddas would keep the job. Unless, of course, Mazad's townsmen learned about his taste in drinking companions. Working together on the council, Siddas and Barmael had become friends. When they settled in a tavern in the evening to discuss the siege from their different perspectives and share tales of battles long past, half Setesafon seemed to gather to watch them drink. And the other half gossiped about it the next day. To Jiaan their friendship wasn't surprising. Not since he'd come to know them both.

"The council wants you to run them?" Soraya asked.

"To organize them," said Kavi, pacing across the small floor. A decimaster's tent was barely bigger than those of his men, even though he was expected to meet with all of them there. "To run things whenever they hold a session, and make emergency decisions in times between. 'Council headman,' they're calling it. I think 'council herdsman' would be a better term. Or better yet, 'council goatherd,' for they're being as stubborn as goats. No, they're worse—they make goats look like sensible folk!"

"But where else," asked Jiaan reasonably, "are they going to find someone who knows the needs of the small villages, and the midsized towns, and the mining camps, and the craft houses—and grew up in a large city? You're the only one I know who could understand their different problems and not favor one group above the others."

It was all true—as Jiaan had pointed out to

quite a number of representatives over the last few weeks. Maybe Jiaan hadn't abandoned the idea of revenge after all—this was a good one too. He hoped Kavi never found out about it.

"But all they're wanting me to do is organize—and stand between them when they start butting heads. I won't have a scrap of real power. Trying to get even a third of them moving in the same direction . . . it'll drive me mad within a year!"

Jiaan tried not to smirk.

"Stop whimpering," said Soraya impatiently. "You love the idea."

"Council goatherd," Kavi muttered gloomily. But his eyes were very bright. He seemed to actually notice Soraya's presence for the first time.

"I'm glad you're here," he told her. "I was going to look for you next. You know how the Hrum have already started returning the slaves, since we're letting them launch their fight against Kadesh from here?"

"Of course," said Soraya. "Though it may take some time before those who were sold far away can be returned. I've arranged for someone from the village near our manor to come for me when my mother and brother arrive."

"Well," said the peddler, missing the implications in his excitement, "letters are traveling faster. I've one here addressed to the head of the House of the Leopard, so I figure it's for you." He handed the girl a small roll of parchment.

Jiaan's nerves tightened, fearing bad news, but joy lit Soraya's face. "It's Pari's writing! She must have survived!"

Jiaan remembered Pari, vaguely, from the commander's family gatherings. She was a plain girl, a bit younger than he was, who'd been polite to the servants. That was more than he could say for Soraya in those days!

She broke the seal and unrolled the scroll, her eyes sweeping over the neat, black letters. "She says she's fine," Soraya reported, relief brightening her expression. "She says she's . . . she's . . ."

"What?" Jiaan asked.

Soraya's voice was thin with astonishment. "She's gotten *married*. She says she was sold into the household of a prosperous merchant. One of his younger sons fell in love with her—she with him, too, it seems. She raves about his virtues for several paragraphs. He talked his father into buying her freedom, and they were married two months ago.

She's not coming back, not yet, though she says she will someday. With her husband. For a visit, or perhaps to trade."

She rolled up the letter, her face a study in bemusement. "I didn't know a Hrum slave could do that. Marry Gain her freedom that way."

"I told you all along, the Hrum aren't that bad," said Kavi softly. The words were addressed to Soraya, but he was looking at Jiaan.

Jiaan took a deep breath. "You're right," he admitted. "They're not that bad."

Under the circumstances, he could hardly deny it.

Soraya snorted at his grudging tone. Kavi looked at her, and finally noticed the pack. "You're leaving?"

"We both are," Soraya told him. "Though Jiaan won't be going for a few more weeks." She grinned at the peddler. "Ask him where he's going."

Kavi turned obediently to Jiaan. "Where are you going?"

Jiaan sighed. "It's no secret. You know that when the Hrum conquer a country, they enslave most of the people who resist them. But sometimes, if they think they can trust them, they ask

597

the best of the officers they fought against to join their own army."

"I didn't know that," said Kavi. "But it sounds like them."

Heat rose in Jiaan's cheeks. "It doesn't happen a lot, because mostly they can't trust them. But they say that other armies, even armies they've beaten, usually have something to teach them. And they . . . Patrius says that's even more true of armies that have beaten them. So he asked me to join them, and I agreed."

He knew his face was scarlet. He'd once vowed to kill this man for allowing himself to be recruited by Patrius.

Kavi's grin held little sympathy, but all he said was, "With the Kadeshi forces gathering on the border, Barmael will need good men."

"Yes," said Jiaan gratefully. "Siatt's still got that mob of peasants—though in a straight battle, they'll probably get in his way more than they'll help him. Strategus Barmael is already holding meetings, trying to think of ways to spare them as much as we can."

"Meetings," said the peddler with distaste. "I hope Barmael's accomplish more than the council's

ave—those poor Kadeshi need someone rescuing
hem."

"They are," said Jiaan. "Accomplishing things, I mean." The Kadeshi did need rescue, and not only the peasants Siatt had blackmailed to fight. All Kadesh would benefit from Hrum rule—unlike Farsala, they needed the Hrum. Or had Farsala needed them too? What Kavi and the council were building now . . . It wasn't as black and white as Jiaan had thought.

"What matters now is peace," he said aloud. "The council's plans sound promising, but it's going to take time for Farsala to grow into them, time to put down roots. Until then, we won't be able to defend ourselves from the Kadeshi or anyone else. If Farsala lies inside the empire's border, no one will be able to attack it. If we have some space to grow, it could be very good here, for a very long time. But for that we need peace, so I'm going to go with the Hrum and be a part of their wall."

There were other reasons for his decision, of course. The knowledge, bone-deep now and from both sides, of how commanders with conscience—or without it—could influence a war. And the knowledge . . .

"It's a good choice," said the lady Soray firmly. "You're an excellent commander, not just for making men obey you, but for tactics and strategy and things. My father would have wanted you to use that."

He'd been Jiaan's father too, though he'd never acknowledged it aloud. Nor had Jiaan, come to think of it. Had his father been waiting for him to speak first—to say the word "father" as Jiaan had waited for his commander to call him "son"? It was a painful thought, and Jiaan pushed it aside as the peddler spoke.

"From the looks of your tent, they're starting you as a decimaster. Quite a comedown from running your own army. They still don't know you're Sorahb?"

"They know I led the army," said Jiaan. "Some of them, at least. But I'm not Sorahb, no more than you are, or the Lord of Lightning here."

Jiaan still found it unnerving that Soraya could work the Suud's magic; she seemed no different from before, sitting on his cot, wrinkling her nose at Sorahb's latest title. New and even more wonderful bits of Sorahb's legend were sprouting like mushrooms. Thank Azura, Jiaan had had the presence of mind to refuse the name when Patrius turned to him.

"Unless you want to claim it," he continued, looking at the peddler. "We could still change our minds." He took malicious satisfaction in the alarm that flashed over Kavi's face.

"Don't you dare!" the peddler exclaimed. "Besides, that poor lad deserves to get something out of it."

The fact that Kavi would refer to any deghan, even a dead one, as "poor lad" told Jiaan something about how far he'd come—though Fasal himself would have found his sympathy insulting. Jiaan felt a deep regret for Fasal's death, and an even deeper regret for having failed him as a commander. Thinking about the changes that were sweeping over Farsala in the deghans' absence—even aside from what the council was doing—Jiaan felt as if all the deghans, both the good and the bad of them, had died with Fasal. He was glad Fasal could be Sorahb—that much, at least, Fasal would have approved of.

In many ways the new Farsala that Kavi and his council were building would be better than the old one, and in some ways it would probably be worse. But that was true of all rulers, of all lands, and Maok had been right—when the world gets kicked, making it come out a little better than before is the best you can hope to do. And if it should come out worse . . . someday the Creator Spirit would kick the world again.

"In fact," Soraya said now, "that Lord of Lightning business is the only thing that worries me. Almost everyone is attributing it to Sorahb, or to Azura, but I've heard a few people talking about the storm at Mazad, and they finally remembered that there were 'Suud demons' in the city at the time."

"What's the problem with that?" Jiaan asked. "There weren't any Suud, or anyone who could work their . . . their magic, in Setesafon except for you."

It chilled him to say it aloud—and he knew the Suud. Perhaps she was right to worry. "Besides," he went on, trying to reassure himself as much as them, "it's only a few rumors, and the other versions are more popular. Any talk of Suud sorcerers will die soon enough."

"Maok didn't want it getting about that the Suud could work magic," said the peddler,

oking almost as concerned as the girl. "And I
think she's . . . wait, I've got it!"

"Got what?" Soraya asked warily.

"The answer," said Kavi. "Since they're so
busy making me high official goatherd and all, I
might as well take advantage of it. Most folk think
I worked for Sorahb, so no one will disbelieve me
if I start telling his story. The true story of what
really happened."

"The true story?" Jiaan asked, alarmed.

"No, but it will be by the time I'm done with
it," said Kavi confidently. "A good lie beats the
truth any day."

Soraya snorted, though she also looked
thoughtful. "How will you explain the lightning?
Not even Rostam could throw light—"

A warbling whistle interrupted her. It wasn't
loud—Jiaan would have dismissed it as a birdcall—
but Soraya smiled and rose to her feet. "That's for
me." She picked up her pack. "And it's not farewell,
not really. I'll come back to Farsala from time to
time. I'll probably see both of you again."

Jiaan wasn't as certain as she seemed to be,
and the peddler was frowning. "Back to Farsala?
Where are you going?"

"You can't guess? Herd your councilors we[?] Kavi. And you," she turned to Jiaan. "You remember . . . what you're about."

It wasn't what she'd started to say, but the whistle sounded again. She shook her head sharply, cutting off further speeches, and marched out of the tent.

Kavi and Jiaan followed her out and stood, watching her walk through the untidy sprawl of the Farsalan camp toward the low, rolling hills. Jiaan would have sworn there was no cover—the robed and hooded figures seemed to appear out of nowhere, out of the earth and rocks. Jiaan wondered if he was seeing magic, and shivered.

"I should have guessed," said the peddler.

"It still surprises me," Jiaan admitted. "I mean . . . she's a *deghass*. I know there's not much here for deghans, not anymore. But will she be happy living in exile?"

Kavi snorted. "You've not seen her with the Suud, have you?"

"No, but what's that got to do with it?"

"If you'd seen her there, you'd know."

"Know what?" Jiaan asked, trying to keep his rising impatience out of his voice.

He must have failed, for the peddler grinned. "She's not going into exile," he said. "She's going home."

Watching Soraya, Jiaan realized that Kavi was right. She was walking up the first hill now, eagerly, not looking back. *How very like her.*

Only the ache in Jiaan's heart proclaimed that she was his sister—in truth now, as well as in blood. Like his father, she would never say the word. Curse her for it, and curse him, too! It was time Jiaan stopped waiting for his family to claim him. A man who hoped to command shouldn't be a coward.

Heart pounding, Jiaan cupped his hands around his mouth and bellowed, "Farewell, SISTER! I'll see you again when I come back to Farsala!"

People two hundred yards away were staring at him. Soraya jerked like a hooked fish and stiffened. She turned, slowly, and lifted a hand in acknowledgment. Then the Suud reached her, and she was swept off among them.

The peddler stood beside him, shaking with suppressed laughter. "Well, that took long enough," he said. "I don't envy you."

Jiaan wasn't entirely sure where this sudden acceptance would lead either. The next time he saw her, she'd probably have young Merdas with her, and perhaps the lady Sudaba as well. He took a deep breath and straightened his shoulders. "I'll manage. It may be harder than fighting the Kadeshi, but it'll probably be easier than managing the council."

That wiped the grin from Kavi's face. "You're right about that. In fact, I'd better get back to it." He turned to go.

"Don't forget about the legend," said Jiaan. "And make it . . . make it . . ."

"I'll make it a good one," the peddler promised, serious for once. "I owe him that, at the least." Then the familiar glint of mischief lit his eyes. "Don't worry. I can take care of Sorahb."

SO SORAHB DIED ONCE *more, in all the power and beauty of his youth. And if the god promised him another return to this world, no living man knows of it.*

In the centuries that have passed since that fateful day, councilherd after councilherd has followed Sorahb's great plan, guiding Farsala to the peace and prosperity it now enjoys.

Despite time's passage, men still remember the tale of how the treacherous Hrum strategus killed Sorahb, and how the god Azura slew the strategus in turn with a bolt of his own lightning. But until now the events before that tragic day have never been revealed—for it is only in the newly discovered papers of my own distant ancestor, Kavi, the first councilherd of Farsala, that their truths were written down by a man who lived at that time and knew of them.

And who could know better? For as all men know, the first councilherd was himself the clumsy soldier whom Sorahb so nobly saved at the cost of his own life.

Modern scholars have speculated that Sorahb might have been more than one man, for how could one man—no more than a youth!—have been all that he was, accomplished all that he did?

But the final proof that the boy the Hrum strategus killed was indeed Sorahb lies not in these papers, but in the years that followed. Years in which Kavi the Honest guided the council, shaping Farsala into the land it has become. Years in which, ironically, many men from the army Sorahb had led joined forces with the Hrum and liberated the downtrodden Kadeshi. Years in which the desert tribesmen that Sorahb had recruited traded with Farsala, learned to irrigate their desert, and grew into the powerful ally they are today. In all these years, no one ever came forward to claim Sorahb's identity and his deeds. By this fact alone we may be assured that he slept, as he still sleeps, in peace.

The End

ABOUT THE AUTHOR

Hilari Bell is a librarian in Denver, Colorado, where she lives with her family.

Her favorite books are fantasy, science fiction, and mystery—all the ingredients for a great novel! Hilari is also the author of *Fall of a Kingdom*, *Rise of a Hero*, *Songs of Power*, *A Matter of Profit*, and *The Goblin Wood*.

PULSEit

Did you **love** this book?

Want to get the
hottest books **free**?

Log on to
www.SimonSaysTEEN.com
to find out how you can get
free books from **Simon Pulse**
and become part of our **IT Board**,
where you can tell **US**, what **you** think!

SIMON
PULSE

APR 0 8 2014